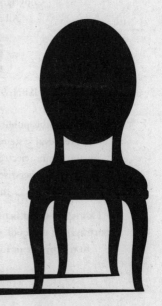

An Abaddon Books™ Publication
www.abaddonbooks.com
abaddon@rebellion.co.uk

Published in 2019 by Abaddon Books™,
Rebellion Intellectual Property Limited,
Riverside House, Osney Mead, Oxford,
OX2 0ES, UK.

10 9 8 7 6 5 4 3 2 1

Creative Director and CEO: Jason Kingsley
Chief Technical Officer: Chris Kingsley
Head of Books and Comics Publishing: Ben Smith
Editors: David Thomas Moore,
Michael Rowley and Kate Coe
Marketing and PR: Remy Njambi
Design: Sam Gretton, Oz Osborne
and Gemma Sheldrake
Cover: Sam Gretton

ISBN: 978-1-78108-647-6

Printed in Denmark

THE HANGING ARTIST

JON STEINHAGEN

ABADDON
BOOKS

WWW.ABADDONBOOKS.COM

Dedicated to my godmother,
Judith Coolbaugh Peters,
the best there is or ever was—
my eternal gratitude for continuing to
gift me all the detective stories,
and all the love.

"...you have been entrusted with a given task, you have the strength to carry it out (neither too much nor too little, you have to make sure you don't waste it, but without undue concern), you have the necessary free time and you are not lacking the desire to work. So what is the obstacle that stands between you and the completion of this extraordinary undertaking? We should not waste time looking for obstacles, perhaps there are none."

—Excerpt from Franz Kafka's diary,
16 January 1922

CHAPTER ONE
AN UNEXPECTED WEDNESDAY

FRANZ KAFKA AWOKE one morning from unpleasant dreams, to find himself face to face with an enormous insect that was attempting to take his temperature; the insect, however—either confused as into which end the thermometer was to go or set upon giving Franz an abrupt and rude awakening—had the thermometer nowhere near Franz's mouth.

Franz recoiled, and was surprised to find he had the strength to recoil. When last he checked—the night before?—he had been too weak to do anything except close his eyes in what he thought would be his final slumber, but here he was, awake and recoiling from the insect with the thermometer.

Insect.

"I didn't mean to awaken you," it said. "I do hope you'll forgive me."

Franz took in the insect's domed brown belly, divided into stiff arched segments; and its numerous legs, pitifully thin compared to the rest of its bulk, which moved in various unsettling directions all at once. At the moment, one leg wielded the dreaded baton-sized thermometer while two others poured water from a battered ewer into a glass tumbler.

"I'll forgive you so long as you change the destination of that thermometer," Franz said.

Said. He hadn't *croaked*, he'd *said*. His clear voice surprised him more than the fact that the giant insect tending to him also possessed the power of speech.

Franz assumed he was deep in a dream, although it was unlike any of the dreams he'd endured his forty years of life: bright, sunny, calm, and courteous. He ruled out 'dream' and tried to adjust his thinking to reality.

The room, a regular human room, only rather too small, sat in stillness between four antiseptic walls. Beyond the bed was a spindly chair meant for visitors and a shabby wardrobe missing its knobs. Next to Franz was the bedside table, to the surface of which a small electric lamp had been screwed. The lamp and the table stood in front of the room's sole window, its shadeless panes clear and giving onto a view of—where?

"You're still in the sanitarium," the insect said, offering Franz the water. Franz, reacting from instinct, grimaced and turned away before it could touch his lips. "You must be thirsty," the insect said. "Drink."

The insect's voice was soft and unrefined, crude but not unpleasant, like velvet gravel running down a sluice. Its head was a brown sphere of exaggerations: shiny black eyes the size of dinner plates and a mouth resembling a complicated gardening tool, which made scissoring motions when it spoke.

"You can manage this now," the insect said, pressing the water upon on him. "Trust me."

Franz nearly trusted the thing, but aggressive memories of pain kept him from taking the water. His throat was raw and dry, a convulsive hell useful only for producing spasms of red hot knives followed by blood, neither of which could be considered joyful.

"Trust me," the insect repeated.

Franz did not.

The insect either rattled or sighed, or perhaps its rattle was a sigh. "You need fluids, Herr K," it said.

Franz bristled at the informality of the address. "Kafka," he said. "Herr *Kafka*."

"I apologize for the liberty," the insect said.

"Forgiven," Franz said. And swallowed.

Nothing.

No fiery pain, no convulsion, no cough.

And no blood.

Which was encouraging.

And suspicious.

He swallowed again.

Nothing. A pleasure, actually.

And he was thirsty as hell.

He snatched the tumbler from the insect and drank as he'd never drunk before. The water was gone in an instant. "More," he said.

The insect handed him the ewer. "Might as well cut out the middle man," it said.

Franz put the ewer to his lips, the pewter delicious to his formerly swollen tongue, and gulped the water down without taking a breath.

Finished, he belched.

The insect took the ewer from him. "You shouldn't try to run when you've just learned to crawl," it said, "but I'm sure allowances can be made in your situation." It placed one of its stick-like legs on Franz's forehead, and Franz shuddered at its touch. "I apologize if my touch is a bit brusque, I have a tendency to be a bit heavy-legged," it said, discarding the thermometer with another leg. "You are as a cool as a cucumber," it said, "assuming cucumbers are cool, that is; I haven't felt one. But it seems a nice enough saying."

The mention of a cucumber sent pangs of hunger bouncing around Franz's freshly-watered but otherwise empty stomach, which gurgled like a drained sink. Franz excused himself.

"I've heard worse," the insect said, "and usually coming out of myself."

Franz settled back into the pillow. Whatever was happening to him was happening too fast, and it was catching up to him. He looked at the solid white walls and ceiling, the crisp white counterpane on his bed, the dark blue piping on his cheap, store-bought yellow pajamas. The linens felt like linen, the pillow felt like pillow, the air smelled like air (with just a hint of carbolic), and the June sunlight that lazed through the window was definitely sun-like.

But was it June?

Yesterday had been June, but Franz wasn't sure today was June. He seemed to have a vague understanding that he had been cured of his disease, but—if that were true—could such a thing have happened overnight?

"Today is the fourth day of June," the insect said, again anticipating Franz's questions. "Unless you only wanted to know what day of the week this is, in which case it's Wednesday."

"And the year?" Franz asked.

"It's still 1924," the insect said. "You don't look a day older. Actually, you *do* look a day older than you did yesterday, because you *are* a day older. I'm just trying to put you at—"

"Overnight," Franz said.

He was no longer a clenched fist of raw, bloody tissue. He could stretch his arms and legs without his entire body constricting into a resistant mass of dry agony. He could speak. He could drink. He could breathe.

He could not, however, explain the enormous talking insect at his bedside.

"And yet I know I'm not dreaming this," he said.

The insect drew the chair to the bedside and did its best to arrange its awkward shape upon it, but its great round back made it impossible. It cursed and turned the chair around, sitting as best it could astride it.

"Tell me how you know you're not dreaming this," the insect said.

Franz weighed his thoughts carefully and found them on the light side. "When something is real," he said, "it gives you the strong impression that it couldn't be anything else."

As the insect seemed disinclined to comment on this, Franz said, "Which is not to say that I don't have questions."

The insect nodded. "Fire away."

"Yesterday I was done for," Franz said. "There was no doubt about it. The tuberculosis I've been battling forever had won; I knew it, the doctors knew it, the disease knew it. I had ceded the battle. I had closed my eyes for the last time, or so it felt when I did."

And so he had. He had not known who, if anyone, had remained in the room. He had assumed he had been completely alone, abandoned. Not even Dora at his bedside. Or had she been there? In the oily, indistinct swim of his labored last moments, he hadn't been conscious of anyone or anything except himself, adrift on a hard sanatorium bed, air dwindling until the tiniest wisp was a gift and a farewell. He recalled finally lowering his eyelids—like ringing down a curtain—with a feeling of relief and surrender.

"And now," Franz said, "I'm awake, thirsty, hungry, drawing great pails of air into my pink, fresh lungs—at any rate, they feel pink and fresh—as if I've never had a sick day in my life. I can smell the faint tang of carbolic in the air, and I think I heard a wretched soul being sick down the hall. I'm well. I'm better than well: I'm nothing like I *ever* was. I'm robust, acute, conversant, and I haven't seen a doctor or nurse the ten minutes or so I've been awake."

"As you say, it's only been ten minutes," the insect said. "Perhaps someone will show up soon."

"I have a strange feeling that no one will. And if they do, they'll get a shock of a lifetime."

"And how do you account for me?" the insect said, leaning closer.

"Easily," Franz said, and smiled his first genuine smile in what must have been ages. "You are my compromise."

"Your compromise?"

"My exchange."

"Explain."

"Something inexplicable happened to me overnight," Franz said, and noticed, for the first time, that the white paint at the corners of the ceiling was flaking away, revealing a mucous green color beneath. "Something incomprehensible and—wonderful?—yes, perhaps wonderful, but as miracles don't come without a price, I understand I may have had to give up something in exchange for my health. And what did I give up? My sanity, apparently. And that is how I explain your manifestation."

"I'm glad you didn't say 'infestation,'" the insect said. "I'm a trifle touchy about hurtful remarks."

"Well, there's only one of you, so it's hardly an infestation."

"True."

"And I haven't found your presence completely offensive."

"The slightly dung-y smell that accompanies me is, I'm afraid, unavoidable, although I borrowed your eau de cologne in the hope that it would take the edge off."

"Ah."

"The cheap stuff your sister bought you for your last birthday."

"Ah."

"I ended up using all of it."

"Ah."

"Didn't do much good, did it?"

"I'm getting used to it," Franz said. Which was a lie.

The insect stood and moved the chair back to its corner, staying a respectable distance from the foot of the bed, its antennae swaying this way and that.

Franz propped himself up. "I'm starving," he said.

"What would you like?" asked the insect.

"Everything," Franz said, and his stomach emitted another vulgar plea for food. "Ring for somebody, will you?"

"It's probably for the best if I fetch whatever you require," the insect said. "What would you like? Stewed prunes? Some fruit? Perhaps a salad. Oatmeal? Gruel?"

Franz felt his stomach do an indignant turn. "God, no," Franz said. "I want meat. A beefsteak the size of that table, for starters. A selection of wurst. Schnitzel, every kind they have. All drowning in gravy. 'Fruit and salad'—to hell with that rabbit food. Come to think of it, I'll have a nice saddle of rabbit, too…"

He stopped, as he realized what he was saying.

"Then I take it your vegetarian days are over," the insect said.

Yes, Franz thought, those days were over, and he wondered at the sudden, reawakened craving for flesh. What else had changed about him; or, more to the point, how many of his past convictions had sloughed off and been forgotten in the space of a night? He didn't pursue an inventory, as he felt his head and eyelids becoming heavy again, as if the buffet of heavy, rich dishes revolving in his mind was already putting him into a postprandial slumber.

"Days… over…" he said.

He would try to understand everything when next he awoke, but one all-important question remained to be answered.

"Why?" he asked.

"Why what?" the insect asked.

"Why didn't I die?"

Somewhere, a clock ticked, although Franz knew a clock had never been placed in his room in the nearly two months he had languished there.

"Why didn't I die?" he asked again.

He heard the giant insect sit.

"Who knows?" it said. "Maybe someone, somewhere, needs you."

Franz laughed; it was his first laugh in an age that didn't cause him pain. It felt good.

"No one needs me, my friend," he said.

"That, too, is possible. Oh well. Have a pleasant nap, Herr Kafka."

"How long are you to be with me?" Franz asked.

"It's anyone's guess," the insect said. "For now; for tomorrow; until the week is out; for the rest of my life."

"You might as well call me Franz," Franz said. He was preparing to dive into a massive bowl of hunter's stew, using a huge spoon as his diving board. He'd swim to the nearest dumpling and nap. "What should I call you?"

"You know my name," the insect said, something of a smile in its coarse, low voice.

Did he? Yes, he did.

"It's too coincidental, too neat," Franz said, opening his eyes to see the room fast fading from white to yellow to amber as the sun set with unseemly speed. "I can't believe you."

"Why not?"

"Because my creation can't have become a reality."

The insect waited a moment before responding. The shadows grew longer.

"Perhaps you are a better writer than you think," it said.

"Don't be fatuous," Franz said.

"Perhaps you didn't create me at all," the insect said. "Perhaps I created you."

Franz listened to the emptiness of the sanitarium; every shred of noise had ceased, leaving the oppressive weight of dead silence surrounding his narrow bed.

He closed his eyes again. He swam through the warm, fragrant stew, already thinking of dessert.

"You say 'perhaps' too often," Franz said. "'Perhaps' is a convenient linguistic escape."

"Escape from what?"

"Everything."

"Perhaps you're right," the insect said. "Good night, Franz."

"Good night," Franz said, "Gregor."

CHAPTER TWO
AN EVENING OF ENTERTAINMENT

THEY WERE, AT first, dubious, although 'dubious' was not the word they would have used, as they were basically simple people, not uneducated, but not blessed with extensive vocabularies, either. The word they would have used was... well, they wouldn't have used a word, because they said things like, "What the hell is a hanging artist?" and, "What's he hang? Wallpaper?" and, "Let me guess—he's an artist who just hangs around," and—this from Prinsky, who came off as more sensitive than the others, possibly because he was trying to impress the girl who lived on Wunderstrasse and stuffed anise drops three at time into her mouth—"Perhaps he brings meaning to his art."

The girl who lived on Wunderstrasse wasn't impressed. Mainly because she was trying to get the attention of the handsome cashier whose name was so unlike its possessor that no one could remember it.

His name was Hermann Herbort, and an uglier name one couldn't imagine for such a beautiful man. He lived with it, however, because he didn't have any creative resource when it came to making things up, and besides, it would look funny if a bank cashier went by an assumed name and was later discovered. It would take a lot of explaining. Herbort didn't like to do any explaining.

Which is why he loved to go out and be entertained: he could sit in his seat, slightly dozy from beer and knackwurst, and let another human being feed him thoughts, ideas, music, jokes, beauty, excitement, color, dance, delights, wonders...

Herbort was one of the best audience members in Vienna.

His salary, however, did not allow him to indulge in particularly majestic art; he was never to be seen at the opera, for instance, not even as a guest, as his friends and cohorts all belonged to his own class (which is to say, one pay packet away from selling something to survive). It had been suggested to him, more often than he was comfortable admitting that he ought to let his achingly good looks provide him a grander manner of living by attracting a wealthy middle-aged or elderly widow dripping in disposable income—by becoming, so to speak, a gigolo—but the thought filled him with loathing. He'd only choose that route if he found himself not much better off ten or fifteen years down the road, assuming his looks held out.

In the meanwhile, Herbort joined his friends for an evening at the Traumhalle, one of the more modest yet bright and reasonably modern venues of Vienna. Of the many music halls of the city, the Traumhalle lived up to its name: it *was* a dream, and not just one dream but a dream of such magnitude that it answered to everyone's idea of a dream.

It was Herbort who had heard of the Hanging Artist, and had encouraged his friends to remain in their seats for the entirety of the bill. "He's all I've heard about these past few weeks," Herbort told them. "Not just from the others at the bank, but from customers, too."

"What do they say?" one of them asked.

"That he has to be seen to be believed."

"What does that mean?" another asked.

"I don't know," Herbort said, and it was true. "I take it to mean that what he does is—well—beyond description."

"He hangs himself," one of them said. This was the tall blonde girl from Die Verliebte Stockente, where she was noted for her ability to serve eight drunkards nine full steins of beer at once without spilling a drop. "That's all he does," she said. "Hangs himself. It's no secret."

"With a rope?" someone asked.

"I assume," she said. "If he used a string of sausages, we'd hear about it. Now *that* would be fun!"

Prinsky wrested his steady, disconcerting gaze away from the girl who lived on Wunderstrasse and said, "He doesn't, really. He can't."

They humored Prinsky as best they could.

"He can't what?" they asked.

"Hang himself," Prinsky said. "If he really hanged himself, well, he'd be a one-performance phenomenon. He's been here three weeks now." He glanced at the girl who lived on Wunderstrasse to see if she'd marked his practical wisdom. She popped exactly three anise drops into her mouth and sidled up against Herbort, who had smelled her coming and had moved away.

"I don't think it's as simple as that," Herbort said. "I'm led to believe this man is... well, his act... it's... more than a gimmick, it's..."

He looked away from them. These people are so basic, he thought, so dull. To them, whatever they didn't understand was a joke; nothing was worth saying if not to elicit a laugh.

"...it's nearly show time," someone said, and they went in.

Herbort did not join them immediately. He waited on the curb, looking up at rather than into the blazing lobby of the Traumhalle. The girl who lived on Wunderstrasse stopped.

"Something wrong, Hermann?" she asked.

"Not a thing in the world," he said, using the answer he always provided when exactly the opposite was true. "Remind me of your name," he said, "because it's tiring to keep thinking of you as the Girl Who Lives on Wunderstrasse or the Girl Who Smells of Licorice."

"Is that how you think of me?" she asked. "I didn't know you thought of me at all."

"I also think of you as Prinsky's inamorata."

"What's an inamorata?"

"It means lover, girlfriend," he said, "sweetheart."

"I'm none of those things," she said, "to him—or anyone else."

"Tell that to Prinsky."

"I shouldn't have to. I don't pay him the least mind. Why he doesn't get the hint…"

He slid his arm through hers and said, "Let's go in. If you'd be so kind as to sit next to me, I'll have a better chance at learning your name."

"It's Hannah," she said, warmed by his attention, "and I don't live on Wunderstrasse anymore. If you promise to walk me home after the show, I'll show you my new address."

"And make Prinsky jealous?"

"Don't tease me. He's such a pain. I wish he wouldn't come around."

"But then I wouldn't have a rival," he said.

"Now I know you're teasing," Hannah said, but smiled a hot, flushed smile anyway.

Was he teasing her? Herbort wondered. Perhaps he was, and he felt a little shame at doing so. They went in, found their seats—at the end of the row, furthest from Prinsky, whose face changed to thunderclouds when he saw them together—and settled into the warm excitement of the promise of entertainment.

From the moment the modest orchestra of the Traumhalle struck its first notes, Herbort sensed a heaviness in the air, despite the gaiety of the music and shabby elegance of his surroundings; as if a sheer, sober, amber curtain had lowered on the working class Wednesday-evening revelers of Vienna. He couldn't account for the feeling—was it that he knew he would ultimately see a man hang himself?

He reasoned that if his internal darkening grew intolerable, he could always excuse himself before the final act.

After the orchestral selection, the crowd was treated to acts trying desperately to put new twists or variations on their tried-and-true tropes: the Italian tenor (who was about as Italian as a sacher torte) sang songs from Spain; the popular comedienne (popular since before the Great War) had bobbed her hair and offered a slightly amusing, nearly ribald playlet of four scenes, backed by a company of artists who seemed to have been only allowed five lines of dialogue apiece; the Three Dierkop Sisters proved to actually be Four, leaving one to wonder if they'd lost count at some point or merely knew someone needing the work, as the quartet sang tight harmonies and sounded like hornets; the featured comedians tried for laughs in a frenzied, desperate fashion, and looked as if they were grateful for the few titters they were granted, despite their mildly clever use of cream pies ("What a waste of good food," Hannah whispered to him); the Flying Hurricanes made Herculean efforts to overcome their encroaching tubbiness as they bounced, tumbled, and flew about the stage.

What, Herbort wondered, was driving them to perform with such frenzy? As if their lives and not their livelihoods depended on it?

Finally, it was time for the last act on the bill, the one that everyone had shown up to see, although none had admitted it.

The orchestra sat in silence; the music director set his baton on his podium. The musicians doused their lights.

The Traumhalle became total darkness, as if it were about to be dumped into an abyss. Herbort realized it was too late for him to leave, and besides, even if he tried, he couldn't see where he was going.

A blast of cold air filled the theater and chilled everyone, even though the summer heat had made the typically cool building uncomfortably close and warm all evening.

No one moved. No one spoke. It was quite possible that no one breathed.

The curtain ascended on a wall of light.

Once everyone's eyes had adjusted to the sudden rush of brightness, they were presented with a simple stage setting painted in a riot of merry colors: yellows and pinks, robin's egg blue and frog belly green.

To the left, a Parlophone gramophone, outdated by some ten years, sat on an oak table, its brass horn a big, dazzling flower in the intense stage lights.

To the right, taking up most of the stage, was the tallest, starkest object of unease anyone had ever seen: an enormous gallows, nearly as high as the stage would allow, and at its foot a simple cane-backed chair.

The gallows loomed black, austere, and ropeless.

A man appeared.

He was tall and robust, and sported a healthy, well-fed face.

He wore a suit of tan linen, a sport summer suit that fit his sturdy figure well.

On his big hands were delicate, tan calfskin gloves.

He smiled at the audience.

His hazel eyes sparkled.

He began to speak.

CHAPTER THREE
AN AFFIRMATION

FRANZ KAFKA AWOKE from a dream and assumed that what had felt to be real had also been a dream, but he was mistaken, and he didn't know how to feel about that.

For there was Gregor, sitting by the window, reading a pile of papers by the light of the moon.

"So I didn't imagine you," Franz said.

"Huh?" asked Gregor.

"I mean," Franz said, "you are probably still imaginary, but it appears I'm to go on imagining you consistently."

"Whatever you say."

Franz yawned. "Well," he said, "it's a nice change, at any rate, to have something stay the same from one waking moment to the next. If it's to be you, all the better, because after you, there can be no more surprises. What time is it?"

"Wednesday will soon be surrendering to Thursday."

Franz listened to the stillness for a moment or two.

"I don't—"

"Just wait a second," Gregor said.

The clock on the town hall down in Kierling began to strike midnight.

"Has anyone been in to see me?" Franz asked when the

tolling had subsided.

"Beats me," Gregor said. "I haven't been here the entire time you've been asleep."

"And here I thought you were sent to watch over me."

"Hell, no. I just came back because I was bored. And the outside world is… well, I don't have to tell you."

"A terrifying place?"

"Among other things. A dung heap, basically."

"I thought you'd be…" Franz censored himself. Gregor sighed.

"…comfortable with dung heaps?" he said. "You're always quick on the draw with snide remarks about my being, aren't you?"

"I apologize."

"It's all right," Gregor said, setting aside the stack of paper.

"What are you reading?" Franz asked.

"This story of yours."

"A story of mine?"

"It was over on the table."

"Oh. I'd forgotten I was writing something. I'd been pretty much focused on dying the past week or so. Which one is it?"

"About this guy who starves for a living. Weird stuff."

"Do you like it?"

"It passes the time."

Franz thought about his dear friend Max. Had things gone as planned, Max would have been here by now to scoop up the story and burn it along with every other scrap of writing Franz had struggled with and left behind, as Max was the sort of friend who would do anything he'd ask; and Franz had asked that of him, before it had become impossible to speak. Now, in his new circumstances, Franz wondered if he could get Max to burn all of his writing anyway.

"Not a sign of a doctor, I suppose," Franz said. "Nobody has come by to give me a clean bill of health?"

"Not even to give you the bill," Gregor said. "Go back to

sleep and tomorrow—well, today, now—you can worry about what's to come."

"What do you mean by that?"

"By what?"

"What's to come. It sounds ominous."

"Don't be so paranoid. Go back to your dream."

"How do you know I was dreaming?"

"Lucky guess. What were you dreaming about?"

Franz tried to retrieve his dream; fragments floated up. "Music," he said.

"What was the tune?"

And Franz could hear it again, played by a jazz band that sounded as if it was at the end of a long hallway and covered with a wet, woolen blanket. "The most ridiculous thing— 'Ev'rybody Shimmies Now.' Have you heard it?"

"Sure," Gregor said.

"You have?"

"I get around."

Franz closed his eyes and said, "Of all the tunes to come to me. And sounding like it's trying to escape. I don't like it. Not just because it's cheap, but because... I don't know... there's a desperation to it..."

"Maybe if you go back to sleep, the tune will change."

"Maybe if I stay awake, there won't be any more music to deal with."

"Well, then, stay awake," Gregor said.

But Franz was already snoring.

CHAPTER FOUR
A NOCTURNE

WE SEE AN assortment of people on their way to wherever it is they're going. It is late at night, and the Viennese streets and alleys are still loud with music and humanity, the former jazzy, the latter somewhat dazed and silent, as many of them have just left a music hall and seen something they shouldn't have seen.

WE SEE A boy of twelve clutch his mother's hand, a hand he hasn't clutched since he was nine years old, because he had taken great pains to erase the label of Mama's Boy. We see his mother jolted from what can only be described as a troubled reverie by his touch. The boy's nose is running; he is unaware of this. The boy's mother takes a handkerchief from her pocketbook and wipes his nose. Their eyes do not meet.

WE SEE A young man lingering outside the music hall, his hands behind his back, looking slowly up and down the street. People swarm around him. The look on his face could either be that of one who has had all of his concepts of Life and Art and Ambition scrambled at one violent stroke, or that of someone deciding whether to walk or hail a taxi. He has forgotten his portfolio and cap.

WE SEE AN old woman walking along. She looks at the street, but doesn't appear to be studying it for any particular reason. She drops her souvenir program. She stops walking. She begins to sob. She brings her hands to her face and continues to sob, silently, while others walk around her.

WE SEE A rather plain young man, hands shoved into his pockets, stomping homeward. His progress is halted by a blast of laughter from a tavern, and he studies the warm, bright yellow open doorway. He ought to drink. He needs to drink. Because damn all of them who are taller and better looking and thinner and have manners like silk ribbons. No, damn all of the others who make fools of themselves over those golden people. No, damn everyone. Her. Him. Them.

WE SEE A young couple, arm in arm, strolling in tandem, she bewitched by he, he gallant but removed. They stop in front of a respectable but shabby building, every front window open to the summer night air; the young woman says to the young man: "The Wunderstrasse was nicer, but this is all I can afford now. If nothing else, it's clean."

WE SEE A tall, stocky man in a tan suit exit the stage door. He is out of breath, as if he'd been hurrying or lifting an enormous object. He smiles at the five black-haired men waiting for him.

"Thanks for waiting. Anybody hungry?" he asks.

The five men exchange glances. "You buying, Henker?" one asks.

Henker laughs. "If you like," he says.

The shortest of the men says, "I could do with a drink."

The rest of his brothers, as it turns out, could also do with a drink.

"Come on, then," Henker says, and leads them out of the alley and into the next street. "First round's on me, but you're on your own after that. By the way, you boys were truly remarkable tonight. Have you put in extra rehearsals?"

The men grunt.

The tallest of them takes a close look at Henker.

The next tallest elbows him, makes a face: *Don't look.*

The tallest looks away.

A wide figure in a black coat and hat appears from a doorway and barrels into Henker, who is knocked to the ground. The newcomer mutters what sounds like an apology and helps Henker to his feet. He wipes muck from Henker, who brushes him away.

"I'm fine," Henker says. "Only watch where you're going."

The black figure touches his hat by way of leave and hurries down the street.

"…and try not to be so obvious," Henker says. Only one of the five brothers hears him, but declines to ask what he means.

WE SEE TWO women hurrying down a residential street.

One stops and supports herself on the other.

"Pinching something awful," she says, loosening the laces of her boot.

They are under a streetlamp.

The other woman doesn't like the lateness of the hour or the emptiness of the street.

She wishes her friend would hurry.

She wishes her friend would buy better boots.

She looks down and sees their lumpy shadows.

She sees the spear-like shadow of the streetlamp.

She follows the shadow as it stretches across the street.

She sees another streetlamp.

She sees a man standing leaning up against it, his cap over his eyes.

He is looking at the ground.

She leaves her friend lacing her boot, and crosses the street to the man.

"Warm night," she says to him. "I know a cool place, if you're game."

He doesn't look up. Or flinch.

"You don't have to be shy with me," she says.

She touches his arm.

He collapses at her feet.

His cap falls off.

She sees his starting eyes, his darkened face, and his protruding tongue.

She screams.

CHAPTER FIVE
A REVIVIFICATION

THE CARNAGE WAS complete. The whole process had been swift and remorseless.

There was nothing left.

The coffee had been hot and welcoming, and the sugar and cream had held out until he'd drained the last drop from the pot.

The fruit juice—orange or grapefruit; he had slurped it down too fast to know for sure—had been fresh and free of pulp.

The cheeses had been godsends—the sweet, buttery Obatzda and the salty, pungent Weisslacker. How had Gregor found such delicacies?

The fried egg and the boiled egg had been cooked to perfection; the Müsli (two bowls!) hadn't been too much like sawdust, and the yogurt he had mixed into it hadn't been too sour or runny.

The breads—the breads!—had been warm and fragrant, Vollkornbrot, Hörnchen, Laugenstangen, a cornucopia of the staff of life, served with sweet butter, yellow honey, and two kinds of jelly, raspberry-mint and quince.

And he would never forget the exquisite meats: Schlackwurst and fresh farm ham sliced thick, with a generous heel of Leberwurst pâté on the side.

The only evidence there had been a meal was the empty dishes still on the table, all practically licked clean.

Franz was a new man.

And immediately upon finishing, worried that he had ruined his delicate digestive system for good. He would pay for his gluttony, for his gourmandizing, he who, by rights, should be a rigid corpse somewhere in the bowels of the sanatorium, waiting to be claimed by his family.

"As if they would come," Franz said, and felt shame at saying it. His sisters would come; if not both, then at least one of them, perhaps by drawing straws...

No, he wasn't going to think ill of his sisters, he had no right.

His father, on the other hand...

No use wasting a thought on him.

Franz didn't want to ruin the pleasant aftereffects of such a momentous meal.

Gregor had woken him with the breakfast (enough for three breakfasts!), with its heady aroma and his polite, rasping cough, and had said, "I'll take my breakfast elsewhere. My... eating habits are best left unwitnessed. You'll thank me later," and had disappeared. Franz wasn't sure if Gregor had simply vanished, or if he (it?) had skittered out of the room, as Franz had attacked his repast with such gusto that a stampede of extremely disconcerted elephants could have plowed through the room and he wouldn't have been able to swear to which direction they went.

Stuffed to his teeth with rich food and without any visible companionship (human or otherwise), Franz faced his first true dilemma since discovering he wasn't dead.

What was he supposed to do now?

He couldn't remember the last time he had been out of the bed, and he certainly didn't feel like returning to it despite his postprandial drowsiness. What, then?

The corridor. A peek outside his room. A sighting, perhaps, of another patient or a member of the medical staff. He'd chance it.

He went to the wardrobe for his robe, and as he put it on he got a good look at himself in the mirror that hung inside the door.

He looked like a corpse.

A recently well-fed corpse, but a corpse nonetheless.

He was normally (although when was the last time he was truly 'normal'?) on the tall side and lean, with high cheekbones, somewhat prominent ears, strong chin, and pouty mouth, but his emaciation these past seven weeks...

'Pouty' mouth.

Dora had called his mouth 'pouty.'

"I don't have a potty mouth," he recalled saying to her when she had said that to him.

She had clarified the adjective, and even then he had argued with her, claiming that he had no such thing.

And pouted.

Dora.

Franz felt the next worst pang after the hunger: longing.

The longing he now felt for Dora gave him ample purpose as he cinched his robe sash around his broom-like waist. He needed to find a telephone. He put his hand on the doorknob.

"Be circumspect," said a dry voice behind him.

Franz turned. Gregor had reappeared and was clearing the table.

"Be circumspect about what?" Franz asked.

"About everything," Gregor said, piling the breakfast things onto the tray, "but especially about making yourself known." He draped the serviette over the tray and slid it under the bed.

"Don't leave those under the bed," Franz said. "Do you want this place crawling with..." He stopped. Gregor let up the shades.

"Vermin?" Gregor asked. "Too late."

"I have to get in touch with Dora," Franz said.

"Perhaps she'll come of her own accord."

"How is she to know I'm alive?"

"Why would she know otherwise? You were never dead."

"I was on the brink of death."

"All of us are on the brink of death."

"You know what I mean," Franz said. He wrinkled his nose. "Is that you or me?" he asked.

"Both, no doubt," Gregor said. "When was the last time you had a bath?"

Franz couldn't remember.

"Then all the more reason to get out of this room," he said. He turned the knob and nearly wrenched his arm out of its socket.

Locked.

"It's locked," he said.

"I know," Gregor said, humming as he made up the bed.

"Why?" Franz asked. "Why have they locked me in here?"

"For all you know, they didn't lock you in, you locked them out."

"Why would I do something like that?"

"Beats me."

"I just might," Franz said, with a few useless tugs at the doorknob. "You're being much more of an opaque annoyance today." He pounded on the door. It was like hammering on a brick wall, and he hurt his hand. He retreated to the chair and sat.

"Where's the key?" he asked.

Gregor plumped a pillow. "Don't look at me, I haven't got it."

"How have you been getting in and out?"

"Let an insect have his secrets."

Franz suppressed the urge to kick over the table, and checked himself. He wondered from where these sudden waves of violent emotion and appetite were coming. The way he had inhaled the huge breakfast was understandable as he hadn't eaten more than a morsel of solid food in several months, but he couldn't understand the primal lust he'd felt when recalling Dora or the bestial need, now, to squash Gregor like the bug he was.

It wasn't like him.

Not at all.

"You'll get used to it," Gregor said.

"I don't like it," Franz said.

"I didn't say you'll come to like it, I said you'd get used to it."

Franz got up and began to pace.

"Then I'm in Hell, right?" he asked. "Is that what this is? I'm consumption-free and well-fed, but I'm to be trapped in a room with a giant... what exactly *are* you, anyway? Cockroach? Beetle? And don't tell me I should know because I created you..."

"I used to be a salesman," Gregor said, "if that helps, but... well, you told me I shouldn't tell you things you already know..."

Someone was knocking at the door.

"One thing you really need to know right this very minute," Gregor said. "Other people may or may not be able to see me."

"You mean you don't know?"

The knocking continued.

"I'd rather you erred on the side of me being invisible to others," Gregor said, lowering his voice. "I mean, I could leave if it's more convenient, but I don't necessarily control my appearances and disappearances, so it's best that if you can still see me while someone else is with you, don't talk to me like I can be seen by others, because if they can't they'll think you're insane."

"But I am," Franz said. "I am definitely insane."

The knocking increased.

"At any rate," Gregor said, "there's no need for pointless comedy. Just don't address me, even if I say something to you."

"Why are we whispering?"

"I don't know."

Franz turned to the door and shouted. "I'm terribly sorry, but the door's locked, and I don't have the key."

The knocking ceased, the knob turned, and the door opened.

The person who entered smiled at Franz and said, "Just the man I've been waiting for."

CHAPTER SIX
A VISITOR

THE FIGURE THAT now bustled in wouldn't stop talking.

"You're looking extremely well," it said, "for someone who's been in a place like this as long as you, which is to say not as long as others, but certainly not as short as some, if you know what I mean, and if you don't, I mean the hopeless cases, the ones that go out in a box, if I may be indelicate about such things, and I often am. You're not dressed; am I too early? I'm sometimes too early. I try to be on time, but because I take such great pains to ensure I'm somewhere on time I often show up earlier than is socially acceptable, but then again this isn't a social call, although I try to be a sociable—social?—person. If you're in the midst of dressing, don't mind me, I'll turn away, although I've seen everything, not of yours specifically, of course, but you know what I mean, nothing embarrasses me, nor should you be embarrassed by my presence, because we've so much to discuss, so many details to sort out. This is a very pleasant room, very pleasant, and on the top floor, too, I've never been here myself, either as visitor or patient, knock wood, is this wood? It's wood. Very nice, too. If you've a summer suit, I'd recommend that, it's hotter than blazes out there, but I'm getting ahead of myself, you don't know me from

Adam, and why should you? Here's my card."

The figure produced an embossed card and handed it to Franz. In embossed black letters on a smooth cream background were the words:

BEIDE
Inspektor

"You're reading the reverse," Beide said.

Franz turned it over. The obverse, in embossed cream letters on a glossy black background were the words:

Inspektor
BEIDE

Franz took a moment to take in the card's owner.

He was a bright, lithe young man with a boyish softness to his features. The deep blue eyes were merry, the lashes long. He was dressed in a uniform of some sort that Franz did not recognize, its blackness set off by deep red piping along the tunic's clerical collar and narrow lapels. The outfit was dominated by a long black cape pinned to the red-piped epaulets, matched with a smart black cap on his head, set at a jaunty angle.

"Inspector of what?" Franz asked.

"All sorts of things," Beide said, "but mostly crimes—you may keep the card—because that's what the world's come to, although if you ask me the world has always come to crime, and after all it keeps me busy, keeps me busy…"

"Are you local law enforcement, or…?"

"I get around, to be sure," Beide said as he opened the wardrobe, "here and there and everywhere, because there's crime everywhere, or should I say evil? Well, evil is a rather lazy term for all that's bad in the world, wouldn't you agree, as is the word *bad,* I suppose, but our vocabularies are so limited, we have to make do as best as we can with the words we know… I see you have a summer suit, excellent, and you have... oh, I see all of the shirts are plain white, well, that's makes it so easy to dress, I mean, white shirts go with anything, I think this necktie would go smartly with this suit, now, what about shoes? Or do you have boots?"

The effect was not unlike listening to an amateur musician warming up on a flute, yet it was a forceful, urgent flute, and a great contrast to Gregor's.

He turned to look for Gregor, assuming he'd disappeared, but there he was, standing in the far corner. Gregor waved a limb.

"Remember, don't say anything to me," Gregor said. "And I don't know what this is all about, anyway."

Franz turned back to Beide, who was standing in front of him, holding out the suit and shirt.

"Something the matter?" Beide asked.

"I think you might have the wrong room," Franz said, handing back the card.

Beide put the clothes on the bed and took back the card. "Kafka, Franz, of Prague. Age forty," he said. "Although I'd put you at thirty, thirty-five at the oldest."

"Yes, I'm Kafka."

"I know; those weren't questions. Are you sure you won't keep the card? It might come in handy someday. As a bookmark, perhaps, when you're reading something and just have to put it down in order to answer the door, or as a beer coaster, or maybe to get you into a locked room?"

"What do you want?" Franz asked.

"A million things," Beide said, continuing his sweep of the room, "but, please, won't you dress? Not that your current apparel isn't presentable, it's just... well, do as you please, I really want you to be comfortable, as what I'm about to tell you will possibly make you uncomfortable, in a roundabout way, although it might affect you in a more profound way, shake you to the core, if you will, and by that I mean you may find what I have to tell you so chilling that... but I have to hurry, there are so many facts, and by facts I mean features of the situation, or *situations*, actually, because there are now so many, but I hope you'll see they are all linked, and that connection, Herr Kafka, that link, will, I'm hoping, allow you to see there is, if possible, hope of tying everything together into a neat little package upon which we can act."

Franz, dizzy, sat down. He had only been able to follow a little of what Beide had said, but felt that some sort of force was about to compel him to give this curious little man his attention, despite the feeling of dread that now crept up on him.

"All right," Franz said.

"Trousers first, or socks and shoes first?" Beide asked.

"I beg your pardon?"

"Your habits," Beide said. "Some fellows put on their socks and shoes first, and then pull their trousers over."

"Why would someone do that?"

"In case there's a fire."

"Shirt first, actually," Franz said, shaking himself out of stupefaction. Beide handed him his shirt.

"Interesting," Beide said, "very interesting. Most original. I'll leave the rest to you. Now: to begin. It's always a conundrum, isn't it, as to how to begin, don't you think?"

"Begin at the beginning," Franz suggested as he began to dress. If nothing else, he'd humor the man, and perhaps derive some entertainment from whatever tale awaited him.

"Excellent," Beide said, eyes alight. "This is why I knew I'd come to the best person. All right. The beginning. The actual beginning, I'm sure, actually precedes the beginning I'm about to relate, as I've no doubt this whole affair has its roots well-grounded in histories and situations beyond our comprehension or acquisition, but for the purposes of why I'm here, now, with you, having such a delightful one-sided conversation, the beginning begins nearly two months ago, with the murders of several people."

Beide paused for effect, and for air.

CHAPTER SEVEN
A LITANY OF DEATH

"Murders?" Franz prompted.

"Yes. As of the tenth of April."

The date itched Franz's memory for some reason. "Go on," he said.

"On April the tenth," Beide said, "the body of Ulla Stach, age twenty-one, was discovered, in her flat in Rannersdorf, dead. Fraulein Stach was discovered by her mother in the morning; the time of death was placed at somewhere between midnight and one in the morning. Do you know Rannersdorf?"

"I can't say I do."

"It's in Schwechat. Are you familiar with Schwechat?"

Franz hesitated.

"Why do you ask?"

Beide smiled. "I'm trying to gauge if you are oriented. The location is, I think, important."

Franz pulled on his stockings. "Yes," he said, "I know Schwechat. It's south of Vienna, I think. The river runs through it. I went on an excursion, once. On the water. We—the people I was with and I—stopped at an inn for supper. I don't know much more about it. It seemed a pleasant place."

"So it is," Beide said, "and thank you for supplying more

information than I needed, you make an excellent suspect."

Franz, shoe in hand, stopped. "Is that what this is about?" he asked. "You suspect me of murdering this young lady?"

"There's no shame in being a suspect. Now, please, you're getting ahead of yourself," Beide said, and laughed. "Wait. Be patient. I've barely begun."

"You're making me nervous."

"I don't mean to. I rather think my countenance and demeanor have been most congenial."

"That's what's making me nervous."

"To continue: Ulla Stach, dead. Medical report showed she had been strangled. And not just strangled, mind you, but strangled with a heavy rope. A hangman's noose, in fact, an opinion offered by the medical examiner who, I understand, had some experience with such things arising from his early years assigned to a prison."

"The girl hanged herself. A suicide. Did she leave a note recounting why she would have done such an awful thing?"

"Oh, I knew you would be like this. You ask excellent questions," Beide said, barely suppressing glee.

"I only asked the one," Franz said, lacing his shoes.

"So you did. Ah. Well, then. Suicide. If that were the case, she would have been found dangling from the rope."

"I take it she wasn't."

"You are correct. And yet there were signs indicating that a rope had been used, not merely on her neck but also on the broad beam in her room, under which she was discovered. And, to answer your question, no. She did not leave a note."

"Go on. I believe you said *murders* earlier, plural."

"I did indeed. Ulla Stach, as far as we can tell, was the first suicide that wasn't a suicide."

"Who was the second?"

"Walter Furst."

Franz paused in the buttoning of his waistcoat. "So," he said, "Furst was... the second."

He heard Gregor suppress a chuckle and looked to see him hastily put a leg in front of where his mouth might be, if what he had could truly be called a mouth. "Sorry," he whispered, and Franz wondered why he needed to whisper if Franz was the only person who could hear him.

"Yes," Beide said, "Furst was the second. Very clever. And now I suspect you're thinking this is all too ridiculous."

"I'm past that," Franz said. "Go on. Walter Furst. In Rannersdorf, as well?"

"No, in Mannswörth, also in Schwechat."

"I see."

"Herr Furst was a reasonably prosperous merchant of fifty-five years—that is, his age was fifty-five at the time his body was discovered, he wasn't in business that long. Regardless, members of his family discovered his corpse on the floor of his study one morning, five days after the death of Ulla Stach. Everything about his death echoed that of Fraulein Stach: time of death placed at between midnight and one in the morning, signs of strangulation assigned to a thick, heavy rope of a type that would be used in an execution, and no sign of said rope. And no note confessing suicide."

"Were either Fraulein Stach or Herr Furst known to suffer from melancholy?" Franz asked. Beide beamed at him.

"You are too good to be true," Beide said. "You know just what to ask. No, Herr Kafka, neither of them were given to melancholia, nor had they at any time to anyone expressed a desire to take their lives."

Franz considered this. "I suppose not every suicide is required to blab about it before it happens," he said. "The less said, the better, right? I mean, if you've really got your heart set on taking your own life, you don't want people on alert, watching you, worried about you. Or am I just making things up?"

"Three days after Walter Furst... Emmanuel Buchner," Beide said.

"How old?"

"Thirty-two."

"Occupation?"

"Custodian."

"Schwechat again?"

"Yes."

"And the same…"

Beide nodded. "Every circumstance the same as Stach and Furst."

Franz went to his wash basin and looked for the hair pomade he hadn't used in well over six weeks. Had it been thrown away? In answer to his search, Gregor slid the jar to him. I hope Beide didn't see that, Franz thought.

"Three murders staged to look like suicides in less than a fortnight," Franz said.

"Five."

Franz paused in his grooming. "Come again?"

"Five," Beide said. "The fourth two days after Buchner, and the fifth the day after that."

Franz put down his brush and turned away from the mirror to face Beide.

"That's monstrous," he said.

"Yes," said Beide.

"By then, the whole of Schwechat must have been in an uproar."

"A very nervous uproar."

"I don't doubt it. There was a madman on the loose."

"That was the impression."

"Was?"

"It still is, but it's only one of the speculations at present, and more are posited as the body count climbs."

"Climbs? Inspector, how many people have been killed in this manner?"

Beide stopped smiling.

"As of this morning, Herr Kafka," Beide said, "twenty-three."

Franz was not given to whistling in astonishment, but on this occasion, he whistled.

"Yes, Herr Kafka," Beide said, and repeated the whistle.

It was then that April tenth flipped a switch in Franz's memory.

"I didn't do it," Franz said, feeling his breakfast begin to rise in his gorge. He stood, trembling. "I didn't do any of them," he said, his voice rising in fear. "Dear God, man, how can you suspect... how did you come to think I had anything to do with one death, let alone twenty-three? Why, I've been here, in this sanatorium..."

"Since April tenth," Beide finished, quietly. "Yes, I know, Herr Kafka. You checked in on Thursday, April tenth, 1924, at a little past noon. You were taken directly to this room."

"I've been tremendously—"

"—ill. Yes, we know."

"Would you let me finish a—"

"—sentence? Please calm yourself, Herr Kafka—I do wish you'd let me call you Franz—you are not believed to be the author of these crimes."

"I'm not a suspect?"

"No."

"Then who—"

"—do we suspect?"

"—sent you to me? I asked you to let me finish my sentences."

"That's a difficult question to answer. May I answer it later?"

"This is maddening. Twenty-three murders in Schwechat and you're here, in Kierling, giving a man who has just survived—although heavens knows how—a fatal disease the runaround."

"Only five of the murders occurred in Schwechat," Beide said. With a swirl of his cape, he sat gracefully on the chair.

"Where did the others occur?" Franz asked. Please don't say within one mile of the sanatorium, he thought.

"I think," Beide said, "that now would be a good time to introduce The Hanging Artist. Please, relax. Have a seat."

Franz couldn't. "The Hanging Artist?" he asked.

"Yes," Beide said. "The Hanging Artist."

CHAPTER EIGHT
A HANGING ARTIST

"YES?" HENKER ASKS.

The door to his sitting room opens. An impressive woman, her dyed hair done up in a towering, cobweb fashion popular some fifteen years ago, enters.

"A gentleman to see you, Herr Henker," she says. Henker notes that she seems genuinely pleased to announce this caller. Still, he must ask.

"Another policeman?" he asks.

"No," the woman says, her stays stiffening along with her posture. "Herr Spindler."

Ah. Henker thinks, *It's about time*, but he plays with the woman.

"Spindler, Spindler..." he says, feigning a deep search of his memory.

The woman can't hold to decorum any longer.

"*Max* Spindler," she says.

"Of course," Henker says. "By all means, Frau Alt, show him in."

Frau Alts departs.

Henker adopts an informal attitude on the shabby settee. He picks up yesterday's newspaper and pretends to read.

Frau Alt ushers in a prosperous-looking gentleman. She gives a slight curtsey, casts a glance at Henker, and leaves the room, shutting the door behind her.

Max Spindler doffs his hat.

"Good afternoon, Herr Henker," Spindler says.

Henker returns the cordial greeting.

Spindler indicates the stump of a cigar in his mouth.

"This bother you?" he asks.

"Not if you've another and are a fellow given to sharing," Henker says, tossing the newspaper aside.

Spindler produces a cigar from his breast pocket.

Henker approves of the cigar.

Spindler offers Henker the use of his cutter.

Henker cuts the cigar.

Spindler lights Henker's cigar.

Henker admires the lighter.

"Gold," he says.

"Gold leaf," Spindler corrects. "The good things in life, Herr Henker, not the ostentatious and impractical. Yes?"

Henker nods, puffs away.

"You know who I am?" Spindler asks.

"Of course. You were announced."

"I mean... you know *who* I am."

Henker nods again, smiles. "Who in the theatrical profession doesn't know who Max Spindler is? Won't you take a chair? I've been expecting you."

Spindler raises his eyebrows as far up on his bald head as he can manage. "Have you?" he asks, sitting.

"Merely the natural course of events," says Henker, "which is to say, natural for my own particular course: a sensation in a backwater like Schwechat is one thing; an unheard of move to the Traumhalle—the largest music hall in Vienna—in a fortnight is another; and it's only the first week of June. I feel safe saying that, because I've also been expecting that contract in your right inner coat pocket, Herr Spindler."

Spindler adopts a sly look, reaches into his right inner coat pocket and extracts a folded contract.

"I was told you'd be a mystifying fellow," Spindler says, and hands the contract to Henker. "A cool customer, too."

Henker reads the contract, unmoved. The atmosphere in the small room begins to cloud with cigar smoke.

Spindler notices two cups on the table. "Is Frau Henker at home?" he asks.

Henker follows his gaze to the cups, smiles, and returns to his perusal of the contract. "There is no Frau Henker, only a Fraulein Henker. My sister."

"Ah. It will be a pleasure to meet her."

"I'm sure it will, one day. She's resting at the moment. And before you probe any further, she's unwell. Not ill, unwell. She is often unwell. And therefore she rests, often. This says I'll receive a bonus if I begin next week. How much of a bonus?"

"In my personal opinion," Spindler says, "that's a princely sum of money for any artist, established or otherwise. But your act—if you can call it an act—"

"Call it anything you wish," Henker says.

"—will be worth it."

"No questions asked?"

"About?"

"My act."

"You mean the police business."

"Yes."

Spindler gives the slightest of pauses and says, "No."

Henker crosses his legs and fans himself with the contract. "I'm glad to hear it," he says. "It's all an unfortunate coincidence, anyway. So you have no hesitations?"

"I don't understand the question."

"About the nature of my Art," Henker says, making sure Spindler recognizes the capital A in his inflection.

"I know three things, Herr Henker," Spindler says. "One: whatever it is you do fills seats, and I have nine hundred seats to fill—nine hundred and three, to be exact. Two: you have the potential to become an international sensation, and I'd like to be a part of that."

"And the third thing you know?"

"Nothing can stop you from realizing that potential."

Henker smiles. "That may be true," he says.

"Only one caveat," Spindler says.

"Yes?"

"Two a day."

Henker scans the contract, finds the clause.

"Yes, I see it here," he says. "You want me to die twice a day."

"So to speak. Will that be a problem?"

"Your left inner coat pocket, Herr Spindler," Henker says, reaching out a hand.

"My what?"

"Your fountain pen, sir."

Spindler hands him the pen. Henker signs the contract.

"You didn't answer my question," Spindler says. "Will twice a day be a problem?"

Henker hands him the pen and contract.

"I wouldn't have signed if I thought it would be a problem," Henker says. "No, Max—and I will call you Max—this is exactly what I was hoping for."

CHAPTER NINE
A PLEA

"AND PEOPLE PAY to see that?" Franz asked after he had paid close attention to Beide's description of The Hanging Artist's performance.

"Night after night," Beide said. "Packed houses."

"Standing room only, eh?"

"Henker won't allow standees."

Franz chanced a glance at Gregor, who was now prone on the floor, resting his unwieldy bulk.

"I'd pay to see it," Gregor said.

"Let me get this straight," Franz said to Beide. "This man, this nobody who goes by the name of Hans Henker, comes out on stage, plays a phonograph record, and gives a little speech about the history of killing—"

"No; the history of execution," Beide said.

"Then produces a noose—"

"Of silk."

"Yes, all right, a silken noose, puts it around his neck, sends the end of the rope flying—you did say flying, correct?"

"Flying, yes. It's quite graceful, actually."

Franz continued to try to picture the scene. "The rope coils itself around the gallows," Franz said, "Henker climbs atop a chair, fastens the noose around his neck, kicks the chair away, and snap goes his neck, the record plays out, all is silence, and he's just hanging there, dead."

"And then the curtain comes down," Beide said.

"To thunderous applause."

"To no applause whatsoever, actually. The audience can't believe what they've seen."

"They must know it's a trick."

"One would assume. Still, it does something to them," Beide said, rubbing his smooth chin, as he searched somewhere above Franz's head for exact words. "It unsettles them. You'd have to be there to experience the effect this performance—if you can call it that—has on every man, woman, and child who sees it."

"Good grief," Franz said, "children see this as well?"

"They're not supposed to, but they get in, somehow. They dress like adults. The management can usually spot the youngsters, but a few slip through."

Gregor, from the floor, said, "Don't forget the volunteers."

"That's right," said Franz.

"That's right, what?" Beide asked.

Franz reminded himself to be careful about Gregor. "The volunteers," he said. "One per show."

Beide nodded. "And not shills, either. He asks if someone wants to come up on stage to inspect the rope and noose, pat him down to see if he's wearing hooks or braces or who knows what all; he comports himself not unlike your typical third-rate magician."

"And he always gets a volunteer?"

"You should see the hands shoot up when he asks," Beide said. "I don't know if it's morbid curiosity, or fascination with the macabre, or the tone of Henker's voice, or the music, or a combination of all those things, but everyone wants to get their hands on the rope, on *him*. Even I, when I saw the show after the sixth victim was found, found myself fairly leaping out of my seat in an effort to get Henker to pick me."

Beide shook the memory of his actions out of his face; Franz sensed at once that his babyish features were, in fact, edged with a certain hardness, and thought for a moment that Beide was changing, somehow, from the inside out. He lost this observation in an instant when Beide leapt from his chair and resumed his bouncy, sunny perambulation about the room.

"So that's it," Beide said. "The parallel phenomena. Bodies begin piling up at the exact same time this Hanging Artist begins performing his grotesque act, first in Schwechat, then in Vienna…"

"There's a music hall in Schwechat?" Franz asked.

"Tiny place," Beide said, "not much more than a hallway with a stage on one end, can't seat more than seventy at a time. Now, at the Traumhalle, which can seat three hundred, he's now reaching more people."

"And you think he's the killer," Franz said.

This put a stop to Beide's energy. He turned to Franz, looked him full in the eye, and said, "It would be wonderful it was as easy as that.

"Everyone thought the same: The Hanging Artist arrives, people are found hanged. Makes sense. Henker was brought in for questioning. Insisted he had nothing to do with any of the deaths, didn't know any of the people, and had no reason to murder his public, as he put it. He's quite the fellow, let me tell you: cheerful, cooperative, bland… rather like one's Cousin Karl—and everybody has a Cousin Karl—that one unremarkable relative who goes through life affable, friendly, and totally forgettable. There's nothing memorable about the man at all.

"That aside, there's no proof that he had anything to do with these murders. Not a shred. He's been followed. He's been searched, subtly, by some of the best pickpockets in our employ."

Beide enumerated the facts on his fingers. "All of his actions are accounted for. He is always accompanied to the theater by at least one person. He always returns to his lodgings in the company of others. He doesn't even live alone, but with his sister, Mathilde, who is an invalid. He dines in beer halls or at the communal dinner table at his boarding house, which caters to artists and performers. And he never has the rope on his person. He doesn't take it to the theater; he doesn't take it home. As far as anyone can tell—and we've done our best to ascertain this—the only time Henker comes in contact with the rope itself is when he is on stage with it!"

Franz coughed. At first, he thought nothing of it; then he remembered that one little cough, years ago, had led to...

...what?

He had nearly thought "his death," but his death hadn't happened.

And this one little cough, now, after Beide's litany of measures against this ludicrous grotesque Henker, signified... what?

Perhaps it was just a cough.

He looked at Beide, who seemed to be expecting him to say something.

"I understand why you think I might have killed these people," Franz said. "I know I cut an... unusual figure in society, so to speak, and my few published works"—he raised an eyebrow at Gregor, who was attempting to clean away the dirt he had collected on his shell—"are not of the normal strain of fiction and could be considered to come from a mind of a troubled person... and I admit that my admission to this place of healing on the exact same day as the discovery of the first victim is too coincidental to overlook... well...

"I can't account for my actions thereafter. Yes, I was here, confined to this room, or sometimes on the open-air gallery in a vain effort to afford my taxed, infected lungs some chance at healing or respite from pain... But most of the time, I was languishing. Too weak to take food. Starving, in the end...

"But the end didn't come. I'm here, now, talking to you, thinking, feeling, eating, miraculously cured..."

It then occurred to Franz that he had perhaps better shut his big fat mouth.

He didn't. He looked sharply at Beide, and a new panic filled his body.

"Of course!" Franz said. "I'm perfectly fine! These past months—you think it was all an act! Of course you do! After all, I wasn't supervised the entire time, no one watched over me twenty-four hours a day, there were great dark patches of time when I received no visitors, no immediate care, not even so much as someone barging in only to find it was the wrong room. In the dead of any night, I could have slipped from this place, travelled to any of the places you've mentioned, carried out my nefarious work, and returned to this room before dawn, and no one would be the wiser!

"And here you are, you ingenious person, paying me a friendly visit for no comprehensible reason despite my continuous questions, toying with me. Get to the point, man! You're here to arrest me for these crimes! Do it, already!"

Beide didn't smile, nor did he express any emotion other than what could be interpreted as a mild pang of sympathy.

Beide said, "You make a strong case for yourself as mad killer, Herr Kafka. In fact, I'd venture to say that you would find some relief in learning you are the prime suspect, despite what I've told you about The Hanging Artist. But as I've already said, you are not. I'm sorry that I can't offer you that relief."

He paused. He approached Franz, his kind smile returned.

"What I can offer you," he said, "is a job."

"A job?" Franz asked.

"A very important job. In fact, it's almost a plea."

"A plea?"

"I beg you," Beide said, "to solve these crimes."

CHAPTER TEN
A TRANSFORMATION

FRANZ ASKED BEIDE to repeat the last sentence, and he obliged.

"It's my fault for not demanding you reveal who put you up to this," Franz said.

"I beg your pardon?" Beide asked.

"It's an enormous joke," Franz said. "I sensed it from the start, from your entrance. Who's the author of this prank? Lowy? Brod? Weltsch? It can't be Werfel; I don't think he *has* a sense of humor."

"This isn't a prank, Franz," Beide said.

"I haven't given you leave to be familiar with me," Franz said.

"Herr Kafka, no one is pulling your leg," Beide said, the sparkle in his eyes fading. There was a cloud there, and Franz found the change disturbing. "I'm deadly serious," the inspector said. "If my manner has led to believe otherwise, I apologize."

"All right," Franz said. "Then by whose authority do you deputize me?"

"I beg your pardon?"

"I've taken you at your word, thus far, that you are an inspector, but in whose employ? The Viennese police?"

Beide became sheepish and fumbled with the ends of his cape.

"We're not as straightforward as that," he said, in such a fashion as to indicate he hoped the subject was closed, but Franz persisted.

"I'm not saying another word until you tell me under whose agency you conduct your investigations."

Beide raised his head. "The ICPC," he said.

"I've never heard of it," Franz said.

"We're new," Beide said. "Formed just last year. The International Criminal Police Commission."

Franz squinted hard at Beide. He had no reason to believe this man, this boy. He strung a lot of impressive words together, but they were just words, not realities.

"And these crimes," Franz said, "are considered international crimes?"

"They have the potential," Beide said.

Franz snorted. "A facile answer," he said.

"Yes," Beide said, "and vague, I know, but that's how it must be at present."

Franz rose and went to the window. He glanced at Gregor, whose expression was, as ever, inscrutable. In fairness, the creature truly couldn't be said to have a face. Franz could make nothing of the empty onyx orbs he assumed were Gregor's eyes. He considered speaking to him, if for no other reason to have Beide think him a madman.

Gregor, however, wasn't going to play along. He shrugged, and moved to the further corner of the room, behind Beide, where he busied himself with an inspection of the floorboards.

Franz turned his gaze out the window, looked up and down the street—a young man on a bicycle, two girls carrying bread, an old woman poking around in a trash barrel—and envied anyone living a nice, quite, rational life that morning.

"What about the victims?" Franz asked. "Are any of them connected to Henker?"

Beide shook his head. "Not a one," he said.

"And none of them knew Henker, or he them?"

"Again," Beide said, "no."

"Then what you are saying is that aside from this man Henker playing around with a rope—in public!—during the period when these murders occurred, you have absolutely no reason to be hounding him, let alone suspecting him of the murders. Had any of the victims even *seen* Henker's act, either at the Traumhalle or back in Schwechat?"

"None—"

"See?"

"—until last night."

Gregor stirred in the corner. Franz faced Beide.

"Last night?" he asked.

"The twenty-third victim, here in Vienna," Beide said. "Hermann Herbort. A bank cashier. Twenty-seven years old. Found in the street, under a streetlamp. He had been to the Traumhalle last night, in the company of friends. He had stayed for the entire show. He had seen The Hanging Artist."

Franz thought about this. Twenty-three strangers, and none of them theatregoers, apparently. Until last night.

Franz said, "I've never been a detective."

"That's not true. Your duties at the Worker's Accident Insurance Institute—"

"—had nothing to do with crime. I investigated and assessed compensation for personal injury to industrial workers—"

"You see? You *were* an investigator!"

"Inspector…"

"True, not the sort of investigator trained to deal with homicides and such, but an investigator nonetheless."

"Stop."

Franz wanted to face him, but it would only encourage the conversation to continue. Franz thought it all ridiculous, joke or not, and wanted it to end.

There was silence for a moment, then the sound of Beide rising from his chair. "May I have some of this water?" Beide asked. "All this talking…"

Franz heard Beide pour himself a glass of water and drink.

"When you've finished, you may go, Inspector," Franz said. "As you've admitted you have no official business with me—that is, you don't wish to arrest me, or question me—you may go. I'm very sorry to have heard about the atrocities that have been visited upon these poor people, and I thank you for making me aware of them, but... well, we've nothing more to say to each other. Good day."

"Please have the kindness to hear me out," Beide said, in a fresh tone that made Franz think there was a new person in the room. "Don't turn around just yet, please," Beide continued, sensing Franz's change in attitude. "Let me say what I have to say, and then you may face me.

"Is it so difficult to see yourself as an instrument of justice, Herr Kafka? I know that's a grandiose way of putting it, but let's start with *grandiose* and work our way to *practical*. Is it so difficult to learn of someone or something completely dedicated to evil and still insist you've no interest whatsoever of stopping it? Because that's what solving a crime means; to me, at least, and possibly to others... possibly to you, too, if it weren't for fear.

"Fear of coming face to face with evil and not being able to stop it—that's one fear. There's also the fear of assuming someone else's pain, certainly the victim's, but mainly the survivors', those who are innocent and desperately searching for answers themselves. It's an awful thing to ask of anyone, that they shoulder the burden of finding the answers.

"And there mayn't be any answers, you'll say. But there are. They mayn't be the answers we want to find, and they mayn't be answers we can understand, or *want* to understand. But there are always answers. A man, a woman—perhaps even a child, if we can't plunge in and do everything we can to stop this—a human being is strung up, hanged by the neck until dead. Someone did that. And someone took away the rope, or ropes. Those ropes may be gone, destroyed, burned... but the executioner is still at large. The executioner is meting out some sort of twisted justice, or simply killing for the pleasure of killing; either way, too many people have died, and I see no justification for that. These crimes must be stopped. The executioner must be caught.

"And someone has asked for your help to do it. It doesn't matter if that person was me or a whole fleet of police officers, or the Emperor, or one of the victim's sweethearts or spouses or children. Someone has reached out to you and asked you to step in, to look, to listen, to think, to see what we cannot.

"Because you, Franz—and forgive me for being familiar, but I mean it in kinship—you, Franz, can see things differently from other people and, in that manner, understand them, and empathize. It's all a matter of how you look at life; and you have tried many ways, over and over, to look at life in such a way that it offers you comfort, not misery."

A pause. In a softer voice: "Because you are a miracle, Franz Kafka. You have succeeded in doing, in real life, what this Hanging Artist, through illusion, does at every performance. You have cheated Death. You have been resurrected. You are Lazarus."

Franz heard the door open.

"You may face me now," Beide said.

Franz turned.

There was no doubt about it. Inspector Beide had definitely become a woman.

Franz couldn't think of anything to say.

It wasn't that Beide had made a drastic change in appearance: the clothes were the same, the manner, the face, the eyes...

...but Inspector Beide was now a woman.

She smiled. "There's an answer for this, too," she said, indicating herself. "I, personally, don't know the answer, but I've come to live with it, and maybe someday I will have the answer, although I'm not actively pursuing it. I am who I am, whatever I am, whichever I am."

"I don't know what to say," Franz said.

"About my request?" Beide asked.

"About any of it," Franz said. He slowly sat in the chair Beide had vacated.

"I'm going to give you until this evening to think about it," Beide said, putting on her hat and gloves. "I'd love to give you more time, but there's always a shortage of time, isn't there? Too much has passed already, and for all we know there's another unsuspecting person being hauled up to a makeshift gallows as we speak."

Franz grimaced.

"I'm sorry I had to put it that way," Beide said.

"It's all right, I understand," Franz said. "What will happen if I decide to remain uninvolved, Inspector?"

"Any number of things," Beide said. "I can't say I know for certain what, exactly, will happen—to you or me or any number of people."

"What would happen to *me?*"

"I just said I don't know."

"But something *could* happen to me. That's the intimation. What *could* happen to me?"

"Please, don't press me, I said that knowledge is beyond my scope of certainty."

"Then what is within your so-called scope?"

"The killings will continue, of course. And you'll have to live with the knowledge that you could have helped, when asked, but decided against it, and that might cause you to think that those future lives were in your hands...that you could have done something if it hadn't been for your fear."

"My fear?"

"Of being that instrument of justice to which I referred. It's an awfully big responsibility."

"And if I agree to investigate this for you?"

"Not for me, Franz, not personally."

"You know what I mean. What happens if I agree to make a

go of it, to try to make sense of all of it?"

Beide smiled. It was an authentic, winning smile. "I'll tell you when you do," she said, and left the room, shutting the door behind her.

Franz let out his breath, closed his eyes, and bowed his head.

"Gregor," he said.

"Yes?"

"I need a drink."

CHAPTER ELEVEN
THE REAL WORLD

FRANZ REGRETTED THE beer as soon as he tasted it; regardless, he swallowed the mouthful.

"Something wrong?" the innkeeper asked. He was a large, florid man who parted his remaining twenty strands of hair in the middle of his shiny head. Franz forced a smile. "Just what the doctor ordered," he said. Lying, lying, lying, thought Franz. My doctor wouldn't have ordered any such thing.

And where, exactly, had Dr. Hoffmann been this entire time? Never once in the past forty-eight hours had the man made an appearance to check on Franz's condition, not even to register displeasure at being robbed of the opportunity to pull the sheet over his lifeless face, had it come to that.

In fact, Franz and Gregor had experienced no difficulties whatsoever in leaving the sanatorium in quest of refreshment. The door of his room—previously unfriendly to Franz, before Beide's appearance—had opened with ease, and the third floor corridor had been absent of traffic. Empty, too, had been the electric lift, no sign of the pimply youth who acted as its attendant. Franz and Gregor had spent a moment or two trying to figure out the mechanics of the thing before opting to travel by stairway. They felt for certain they would eventually meet another living soul, and they did, two: an elderly gentleman in a bath chair, being piloted by a severe woman wearing pince nez. "Good afternoon," Franz had said to them, Gregor close at his heels. The elderly man had not replied, vacant stare fixed at the other end of the reception hall. The woman, however, had given Franz a severe look and said, "If you insist," without breaking stride.

Gregor had directed him to the nearest inn, and together they had rehashed Beide's visit and subsequent plea.

"Not so much as a word about how I'm to proceed," Franz had said, no longer conscious of whether or not the citizens of Kierling would or would not see Gregor, who managed to keep pace with him in an ungainly seesawing fashion.

"Haven't you ever read any detective novels?" Gregor had asked.

"Certainly not."

"Well, you needn't say it in that tone. I've not asked you if you've ever eaten a turd sandwich. Detective stories are splendid entertainment. I used to read them on long train journeys when I was a salesman. Of course, I can't remember the plots of any of them, but I remember being entertained at the time I was reading them."

"Even if I had read any, I imagine there's a big difference between the detection done in books and inquiries made in real life."

"Ah! Then you concede this is real life!"

"I haven't decided one way or the other on that score," Franz said, enjoying the heat of the day and the strength of the air, and then enjoying his newfound enjoyment of such things. "All I've decided is that whatever kind of life this is, I'm stuck with it, and I'm living it. Am I crowding you?" It had been the third time Gregor had bumped into him.

"Sorry, it isn't the easiest thing in the world for me to walk along like a normal person, since I'm not. So you've decided to accept the case?"

"I haven't decided any such thing!" Franz said, but they had arrived at the inn, and Gregor had disappeared.

The innkeeper watched Franz drain his glass. "Another?" he asked.

"A glass of water, please."

The innkeeper gave him a glass of water, and then drew another glass of beer. He took a raw egg from the bowl on the bar, cracked it, emptied its contents into the beer, and shoved it at Franz. "You look like you could use beefing up," he said. "Get you a sandwich?"

Franz turned down the offer and looked at the other men at the bar, all of whom were busy talking to one another without any regard as to what the other was saying.

Franz sipped his eggy beer and chanced a conversation with the innkeeper.

"Dreadful about the people in Vienna," he said.

"Which ones?" the innkeeper asked, wiping a spot that didn't need wiping.

"The murders," Franz said.

"Which ones?"

Franz felt he was already failing at being a detective.

"The hangings," he said. "I mean the stranglings. The stranglings that look like hangings."

"Oh," the innkeeper said, "those. Serves them right, is what I say." He began filling three steins while a bored-looking barmaid waited.

"Why do you say that?" Franz asked.

"All of them killed like that, well, it stands to reason."

"Explain."

The innkeeper eyed him. He slid the steins to the barmaid, who collected them with one hand and trundled off to a table. The innkeeper leaned into Franz.

"Those people were either somewhere they shouldn't have been," he said, "or messing around with people they shouldn't have been messing around. That's an unhealthy way to die, is what I'm saying, and if someone's got to go to such lengths to get these people killed, well then, they had it coming."

Franz tried to understand him. "Are you saying," Franz said, "that those poor people brought this on themselves?"

"In a manner of speaking," the innkeeper said.

"So they all deserved to die."

"How do I know?"

"You just said."

"I didn't say any such thing. Maybe they did, maybe they didn't. I don't know. I didn't know them."

"But don't you think it strange that they all died in the same manner?"

"Not really. Look how many people are killed by streetcars."

"Yes, but…" Franz really didn't know what to say to that. He wished Gregor hadn't chosen this moment to make himself invisible. Unless he'd simply not come in.

"It's people being careless," the innkeeper said, "plain and simple."

"It's not the same thing," Franz said. "A streetcar is a machine, it's operated by a human being, and a streetcar accident—"

"Same with a rope," said the innkeeper.

"But it's more likely a person will walk in front of a streetcar than get a noose around their neck."

"You know that for a fact?"

"Actually, yes, I used to work for an insurance company—"

"You a detective?"

Franz didn't know what to say, although he almost answered that he was. This surprised him, and so he said, "In a way. I, er, look into things."

"You looking into these hangings?"

"I just mentioned them because they happened to be on my mind."

"Why?"

"Why what?"

"Why were they on your mind?"

"I'm sorry I brought them up," Franz said, exasperated. The innkeeper was doing a better job at getting information out of Franz than Franz was at getting even the simplest opinion out of the innkeeper. "What do I owe you?" he asked.

"Sure you don't want a sandwich?"

Franz said he was sure, paid what he owed, and left.

Gregor was nowhere to be found.

It irritated him unreasonably. What good was an imaginary companion if it didn't show up when he actually needed to talk to someone, anything?

Particularly when he hadn't been able to speak for some time: thanks to his condition, thanks to the gradual starvation of air, food, communication. He had learned to live with it, he thought, learned to live with being cut off completely from the world, physically, as he had long felt to be cut off from the world on so many levels...

But wasn't he *still* cut off from his world? He'd been living his miracle for twenty-four hours without so much as a word from his friends and family... from Dora. How was it possible that he had been unable to share his good news? Was he unable? Unwilling? How had a day passed with his only contacts being a giant, disgusting insect and a fast-talking...?

What *was* Beide? Man? Woman? Both?

He reviewed his activities since arising to find himself healed: a conversation with Gregor, another long, deep sleep, an enormous breakfast, and the long visit from Inspector Beide, a visit which had crammed his head with incredible facts regarding an equally incredible situation, in which he was now expected to play an incredible role.

Incredible.

Would he accept that role? How could he, in good conscience? Yes, Franz had an inquisitive nature, but never before had he turned that curiosity to the solution of mysteries, unless those mysteries originated from within his own tortured self.

Now, why did he just describe himself as 'tortured'?

If anything, Franz had always considered himself...

Nothing.

Insignificant.

In fact, Franz thought, he was no better than a bug. If he was alive now thanks to some sort of cosmic regeneration—a reincarnation or second chance at life—then by rights he should have returned as Gregor. An enormous, vile insect reeking of cheap cologne.

But he hadn't. Gregor was Gregor, and Beide was... disconcerting... and Franz was—what? Beide had called him Lazarus. Franz knew the reference, of course, but his field of interest and his studies had been exclusively of the Kabbalah and...

He really needed to talk to Rabbi Guttman.

He also needed something to eat; that beer wasn't sitting too well.

He stopped and gained his bearings. He was far from the sanatorium, somewhere in the heart of town. He had broken into a sweat, not because he had been barreling along, lost in his thoughts, but because the early June weather felt like mid-July.

Was the sun hotter?

The sun.

Franz looked down.

Yes, he still had a shadow.

"Well, I'm still real," he said.

"Assuming you were real in the first place," a voice said.

It wasn't Gregor's voice; the hallucinatory sidekick had yet to materialize.

The voice came from a bored-looking little bald-headed man whose impressive mustache had been brushed to suggest a pair of wings, an effect repeated in the tufts of hair on either side of his head.

The man stood in a dark doorway, and Franz looked from him to the sign on the large window beside him:

BOOKS AND IDEAS
E. Murek, Prop.
Est. 1899

"Are you E. Murek, Prop.?" Franz asked.

The little man nodded.

"Your sign is redundant," Franz said.

"One of the smartasses, are you?" Murek asked.

"Books *are* ideas, aren't they?"

"Books are merchandise," Murek said. "And evidently you've not read enough of them to know that *not* all books are ideas, although I can name many books that were *bad* ideas."

"Then you sell ideas as well?"

"No," Murek said. "The sign was of my brother's devising. This was his shop. He's dead, I took over. I'm not the smart one of the family."

"But you just told me you are E. Murek."

"I am. My brother and I happened to share an initial. He was Emil; I'm Emmanuel."

"So that's why you didn't have the sign changed."

"No, I didn't change it because that costs money. Are you going to come in and buy something, or stand there all afternoon confirming you're real?"

A new thought struck Franz. "No," he said, "because it's occurred to me that I can ascertain the reality of this world with one simple test."

Franz strode into the bookstore; it fit comfortably in his conception of a bookstore: tables and cases piled high and crammed with books of all sizes and colors and smells, the lighting just dim enough to suggest a great scholar who didn't have anyone in to clean, ever.

"Something you're looking for?" Murek asked, following Franz.

"Oh, yes," Franz said. "Do you have *Contemplation*? It's a collection of stories."

"No."

"What about *A County Doctor*?"

"I'm sure I must have something in stock with such a banal title as that. Is it a romance?"

"No."

"Oh. Who's the author?"

"Kafka."

"Who?"

"Kafka. Franz Kafka."

"Never heard of him."

It was then that Franz knew for certain that he was in the real world.

CHAPTER TWELVE
THE THEATREGOER

LEO KROLOP GIVES the stationer a few coins, pockets the notebook, and leaves the shop.

It is a beautiful afternoon.

Leo hasn't thought any afternoon has been beautiful for some time.

He shifts his parcels from his right hand to his left—the box of silk handkerchiefs from the haberdasher's, each bearing his monogram; the ominous brown bottle from the chemist—and turns the corner.

He uses his free right hand to tip his hand to each lady that passes. His smiles are returned. He feels very smart in his checkered suit. White and black, white and black, white and black. A somewhat garish red necktie fastened by a pearl stickpin. Too warm for the season and a riot of patterns, but it was his only suit, and he kept it clean and pressed, while it kept him feeling like a dandy.

He hasn't smiled for some time.

It feels good to smile, although he does notice some tightness around his mouth, which he attributes to being out of practice in the smiling department.

He raps on the window of the Traumhalle box office. A

young man appears. Leo smiles to him, tips his hat.

"The man at my hotel telephoned this morning," he says. "One for tonight. Krolop."

"The show doesn't start for another six hours."

"I was in the neighborhood and thought I'd collect my ticket now."

The young man takes a bored bite from the apple he's been eating. "What's the name again?" he asks, shuffling out of view.

"Krolop," Leo says, louder. The clerk does not appear. "KROLOP!" Leo shouts, but the clerk has returned, a ticket in his hand.

"Heard you," the clerk says, and quotes him the price.

"It's already paid for," Krolop says.

The clerk gives him a dubious look, takes another bite of apple, and shuffles off again, out of sight.

Krolop reminds himself that he must remain happy, hopeful, and grateful for the beautiful afternoon.

The clerk reappears.

"So it is," he says, and shoves the ticket through the aperture.

"May I trouble you for an envelope for that?" Krolop asks.

Another look from the clerk.

"I'll see," the clerk says, finishing the apple and shuffling away.

"Never mind," Leo says, and pockets the ticket.

It is a beautiful day.

He hopes it will be the first of many.

Especially if everything he wants will come to him tonight.

CHAPTER THIRTEEN
THE JOURNEY

FRANZ HAD A million things to do.

Perhaps not exactly a million, but close to it, and he wanted to do all of them at once, as all but one seemed extremely important. He had to get in touch with Dora, first and foremost, then certainly Max and Jacob, then his sisters—his father could wait, as Franz was certain the man didn't care one way or another if Franz was alive or dead, and that was fine with him. And he had to find some way of getting in touch with Inspector Beide: the card he had been given offered no help in this matter, listing as it did only Beide's name on both sides. That vexed him, as he had several questions and many more points to go over with the inspector before he made a decision about his proposed participation in the case, and he didn't wish to wait until evening, when Beide had said he or she would return. It was then that Franz cursed Gregor's absence, because if nothing else he could set the great bug onto some menial tasks and, perhaps, get him to rustle up another astounding meal. Franz was, once again, starving.

But what if Gregor's hallucinatory presence had only meant to sustain him through his first twenty-fours of astonishment at recovery? What if Gregor was never to return?

Perhaps that would be a good thing, after all. It would be a bad sign to become dependent on an incredible apparition.

Franz bounded up the steps of the sanatorium, marveling that he was bounding, as he hadn't been able to bound in longer than he could remember.

The reception hall was teeming with people, orderlies and inmates and sickly people dressed in clothing that no longer fit them, some clutching walking sticks, some already in bath chairs. Franz skirted past the electric lift and took the stairs to the third floor, again bounding, and relishing it.

He opened the door of Room 301.

He was greeted with the sight of a middle-aged gentleman receiving an emetic from a nurse. The nurse and the gentleman started at his energetic intrusion, and the gentleman promptly vomited into a basin in his lap, presumably held there for just that purpose.

Franz shut the door.

There was a man vomiting in his room. He could still hear the poor soul retching.

Franz took a moment to sort through his confusion, checked to see if he'd mistaken the room—he hadn't—and reasoning that not everything of late had appeared to be as it should, he waited for silence and opened the door again.

The nurse and the gentleman again started at the intrusion. The nurse strode to the door, but Franz shut it just in time, catching a glimpse of the gentleman embarking upon a second round of vomiting as the basin slid from his lap to the floor.

Franz retreated to the ground floor as fast as he could.

Don't tell me I was never here, he thought as he made his way to the reception desk. As he approached, a young, smartly dressed man dispatched an infirm guest to the care of a white-coated attendant, made an entry in a large leather-bound book, and appraised Franz as he approached.

"Where are my things?" Franz asked.

"I beg your pardon?" the young man asked, adjusting his spectacles.

"I was in 301," Franz said. He put the parcel he had been carrying on the desk.

"Herr Kafka?" the young man asked. "I was under the impression you'd gone."

Franz was relieved to be recognized. "No, I haven't died," he said.

"Of course not," the young man said. "I mean I was under the impression that you'd left the sanatorium."

"I had, for a few hours," Franz said, "but... remind me of your name?"

"Tomas, sir."

"Yes. Tomas. I remember you. Anyway. I went out for a few hours, but only for a stroll. I'm better, you see."

"Yes, sir. Congratulations. We're very pleased."

"But I had meant to return. And I did. Just now. And there's someone in my room."

"Of course there is, sir. You've been discharged."

"By whom?"

Tomas consulted the great book and followed his finger down the column on the page.

"It just says 'discharged,'" Tomas said, and showed Franz the entry which, sure enough, read DISCHARGED. "I hope your stay with us was completely restorative."

"Yes, yes," Franz said, "you've no idea. But the thing is, I didn't—I mean, I haven't packed my things, I haven't settled up." He caught himself, then, because he realized he might not have the means to pay for his stay; after all, he'd been languishing in the sanatorium for eight weeks, and he had no illusions that his medical and physical upkeep had been anything other than expensive. Had he enough money to pay his bill? He had only a few marks in his wallet. He had concluded, weeks ago, that his condition was irreversible, and that needn't concern himself as to how or by whom his expenses were to be paid once he had succumbed.

Franz's old friend, panic, revisited him.

Tomas busied himself with the book.

"It says 'paid,'" Tomas said, and before he could turn the book for Franz's inspection, Franz said, "All right, yes, fine, that's correct, wonderful, but my things..." He fell backwards over a pile of objects.

Which turned out to be his luggage.

A passing orderly helped Franz to his feet, and Tomas, after confirming that Franz was unharmed, reached under the counter and produced a large envelope, upon which the single letter *K* was written in black ink.

"I'm glad you returned, however, sir," Tomas said, handing Franz the envelope. "This was left for you."

Franz took the envelope. "By whom?" he asked.

"I've no idea, sir," Tomas said.

Franz didn't want to press the point, because something told him that there would be no answer of any satisfactory nature.

A thin man with a black mustache like a boot brush approached Franz and removed his cap. "Hey," he said, "taxi's waiting. Meter's running."

"Taxi?" Franz asked.

"You know what a taxi is, don't you?" the man asked.

"Yes, but..." Franz stammered.

Tomas stepped forward. "Your taxi," he said. "Everything is ready and waiting for you, Herr Kafka. Have a pleasant trip."

Franz began to resign himself to Fate. "Thank you," he said, "I will. Where am I going?"

"The train station, naturally," Tomas said, giving the impression that humoring morons was the least favorite part of his job.

"Of course," Franz said, "because that is where one goes if one is to catch a train. Now then, if I could get some assistance with my—"

But his luggage was gone.

*   *   *

THE ENVELOPE CONTAINED a letter and three smaller envelopes. The letter read:

Herr Kafka,

I, personally, think you have made the right decision, and you should remember this whenever anyone tells you different, especially yourself, as I know you will sooner or later. That said, I will be in touch with you at some point to discuss anything you wish to discuss, as I'm sure you have many things you wish to discuss, because who wouldn't? I say this knowing full well that I also wish to leave you to your own devices, whatever they may be. You might not have any devices, and that's perfectly acceptable, even encouraged, because I want you to feel like you have a free hand in regards to your investigation, and I am so excited to be writing those two words, YOUR INVESTIGATION, because that's how I want you to see it, as an investigation that is entirely yours, to make what you will of the facts and the circumstances and the people and all sorts of other things that are going to be involved, and are already involved, if you know what I mean, and I think you do.

I've taken the liberty of making some arrangements for you: you will find three envelopes with this brief (ha ha) note; the contents of each are specific to the corresponding directions written on the front of each. Enjoy. Is 'enjoy' the proper entreaty? Possibly not, although I do hope you find some enjoyment in the investigation, grave though its implications might be, because I, personally, feel that any journey lacking joy, at some point or another, is not a journey at all but a burden, and...

There I go again. My apologies and my best wishes for a speedy conclusion.

> *Although I don't mean to imply that I want you to hurry. 'Hurried' is the progenitor of 'slipshod.'*
>
> *But, of course, time is also of the essence, because the faster an end is put to these grisly killings, the better.*
>
> *Either way, I have complete faith in you and your abilities, whether those abilities exist or not. I'm sure they do. And even if they don't, I believe in you.*
>
> *Your servant,*
>
> *Beide.*

FRANZ INSPECTED THE three envelopes.

The first read: *TRAIN TICKET (VIENNA) AND A LITTLE MONEY FOR A SNACK OR A MAGAZINE OR BOTH OR NEITHER.* So he was to go straight to Vienna, no chance to return to his home in Prague. He had feared as much; he didn't want to plunge right in—but on the other hand, he hadn't exactly decided he was going to do this yet, had he? Had he been leaning towards acceptance? He eyed the parcel next to him on the taxi seat: yes, he had been leaning. But leaning was not plunging.

He read the second envelope: *YOUR LODGING (MONEY): FRAU ALT'S EXCLUSIVE THEATRICAL BOARDING HOUSE. DON'T USE YOUR OWN NAME UNLESS YOU TRULY CAN'T THINK OF A PHONY NAME FOR YOURSELF. ADDRESS INSIDE.* He opened the envelope and found a card clipped to the wad of cash. The address was in central Vienna. A theatrical boarding house, and an exclusive one at that? And why shouldn't he use his own name?

He was about to read the third envelope when the taxicab slammed to a halt and the driver opened the door for him. Franz fumbled for the fare.

"All taken care of," the driver said. "If you don't hurry, you'll miss your train. Although if you want to give me a little extra something for the highly professional and discreet way in which I allowed you to ride in peace and quiet, I—"

Franz gave him what little change he had left and ran into the depot.

FRANZ PLOPPED ONTO the plush cushions of the first class carriage as the train lurched into motion, not because he wanted to plop, but because of the suddenness of the train's departure.

He was winded and not at all pleased at being hustled around as he had, as if by some invisible hand. He felt lucky to have kept all of his things intact, from parcel to envelopes to coat and…

"Your hat," said Gregor.

Gregor was, in fact, wearing the hat.

He sat opposite Gregor as best he could. Franz snatched the hat from his head.

"Where the hell have you been?" he asked.

"That's a new way of saying 'thank you,'" Gregor said. He reached over and pulled up the window shade. The train built up steam and slid out of the depot with a spine-shattering whistle. "First class," Gregor said. "Wow."

"Where were you when I needed you?"

"When did you need me?"

"I…" Franz began, but didn't finish, because he couldn't think of a moment where he had actually needed the disgusting beast.

"It would have been nice to have had someone to talk to these past few hours," Franz said. "I thought that was your purpose."

"Did you." It wasn't a question.

"Well, as your purpose has never been fully explained to me…"

"What's in the parcel?" Gregor asked, picking it up from where it sat at Franz's side. "Box of chocolates?"

"No," Franz said. "Give me that."

Gregor shook the parcel. "A brick?"

"Now, why would I have purchased a brick?" Franz asked. He grabbed the parcel and began to unwrap it. Gregor shifted in his seat.

"First class is no more comfortable than any other class," he said. "But I suppose it wasn't designed with the comfort of three-foot-tall vermin in mind, was it? Do you mind if I..." He sprang to the wall of the carriage.

"Don't do that," Franz said, swatting at him. "It's unsettling."

Gregor sprang to the window.

"And for the love of all that's good, get off the window," Franz said.

Gregor sprang to the ceiling.

"Much better," he said. "So what's in the parcel? Ah, it's a book!"

"Brilliant deduction," Franz said, "particularly coming after I unwrapped it."

"Smutty?"

"I beg your pardon?"

"Is it a smutty book?"

"No," Franz said, ready to throw the book at Gregor and knock him down.

"What's it called?"

The door of the compartment slid open and two nuns entered, one carrying a newspaper, the other a bag of walnuts. They sat opposite each other; the nun with the newspaper opened it and used it as a wall while the other went about cracking a walnut by placing it in the hollow of her elbow, making a fist, and bringing her forearm sharply back. She nodded to Franz.

"Walnut?" she asked.

"No thank you," Franz said. The nun glanced at his book.

"Lovely red cover," she said. "*How Not to Be a Successful Detective*, by Irena Baumhover," she read. "Is it a murder mystery?"

The wall of newspaper came to a snapping collapse, and the

other nun glared at Franz. "Murder is a sin," she said.

The first nun cracked another walnut. "No one's saying it isn't, Sister Agata," she said. "I was just reading the title of this young man's book."

"Did I hear you right?" Gregor asked from the ceiling. "It's called *How* Not *to*..."

"You've had enough walnuts, Sister Jana," Sister Agata said.

"They're good for you."

"They're noisy." Sister Agata turned her steely gaze to Franz again. "As I was saying, young man," she said, "murder is a sin."

"This is true," Franz said.

"Don't say it in such a patronizing tone," she said. "It's a fact."

"A horrible fact," Franz said, and tried a smile on her, to no effect.

"A fact can be neither horrible nor beautiful," she said. "A fact is a fact."

"Oh, brother," said Gregor.

"That murder is a sin is a fact," Sister Agata said, "and even thinking about murder is a sin."

"You mean contemplating murder."

"I mean what I say."

"But not every person who considers murdering another actually... murders anyone at all."

"Are you the expert?" She rattled her newspaper at Franz. "These murders in Vienna. Sin, sin, sin. On every side."

Sister Jana cracked another walnut.

"On every side?" Franz asked.

"Don't engage her," Gregor said.

"Yes," Sister Agata said. "All around. The murderer, the victims, the detectives, the public itself... an overload of sin."

Sister Jana giggled, and Sister Agata slapped her across the face with the newspaper.

"The world is obsessed with Death," Sister Agata said, straightening her habit and fixing an acid gaze on Franz. "Death in and of itself, naturally, but Death by nefarious means, even Death as an anodyne to Justice. While it is important to be familiar with Death as the natural end to our corporeal Life, that's about as far as its contemplation should go. What is the fascination, sir? I ask you! What is the fascination?"

Franz had an answer for that, but was prevented from giving it, as Sister Agata barreled on. "It's a sickness, a global sickness," she said. "And it stems from mockery. We mock the thing we are to be, and since we are all going to be dead one day, we mock Death and being dead. I say 'we,' but what I really mean is the rest of you. Everyone else. I don't mock Death, I daren't. But all of you? Mock, mock, mock. And this"—here she brandished the crushed newspaper locked in her grip—"is daily evidence of the result of that mockery."

Crack.

Sister Jana chewed her walnut and said, "What Sister Agata means—"

"I'll thank you to not interpret what I say," Sister Agata said. "I speak plainly enough."

"—is that no one is taking any of it seriously," Sister Jana finished. A soft pattering on the paneling drew Franz's attention to Gregor, who was now above Sister Jana, intent on the walnuts.

"But I don't think that is entirely true," Franz said, ignoring Gregor as best as he could. "The police are taking it seriously. The citizens of Vienna. Myself."

"Yourself? In what way?" Sister Jana asked.

Franz wanted to tell her that the mere fact of his presence on that very train, that very day, was evidence enough of his seriousness of purpose. But would she understand the circumstances that had brought him there, when he himself didn't know if his purpose was of his own volition or the product of some unseen, mysterious manipulation that included in its package the sudden eradication of a fatal disease and the companionship of a conspicuously large scavenging insect?

"Are you a detective?" Sister Jana asked.

"He's no Christian, I'll tell you that," Sister Agata said.

Franz looked at her.

"What does one have to do with the other?" Franz asked.

Sister Agata squinted at him. "Everything," she said, "has to do with everything, young man."

Gregor scrambled back to the ceiling.

"Christ," he said, "it always comes back to religion, doesn't it?"

Franz felt a prickly, indignant warmth on the back of his neck. He had an answer for Sister Agata, but was again prevented from giving it, as the train, at that moment, roared into a tunnel with a prolonged shriek, and all was blackness.

CHAPTER FOURTEEN
THE HOT COMPARTMENT

"How much money did you waste on that book?" asked a soft, lilting voice.

Franz strained his hearing as best as he could over the amplified clattering of the train as it pressed on through the darkness of the tunnel. How had he heard the voice at all?

"I know the author," the voice said. "She means well, but I have to tell you, she wrote it to capitalize on a trend. That said, you might find it amusing."

The train burst out of the tunnel, and Franz found himself sitting opposite Inspector Beide. Gregor and the nuns were nowhere to be found.

"What am I imagining and what is actually happening?" Franz asked. "And don't answer me with another question."

"Everything is actually happening," Beide said.

"Horseshit."

"You wanted an answer; I gave it to you."

"Did you give me the actual answer, or just the one you thought I might like to hear?"

"Now, how would I know which answer you'd like to hear?"

"I told you not to answer me with a question."

"That was for your first question."

Franz threw the book at Beide. She caught it, opened it, and scanned its first few pages.

"Do you really think you'll need this?" she asked.

"It's all he had," he said.

"Who?"

"The bookseller. E. Murek."

"Oh." She turned a page. "We'll skip the introduction," she said. "Here we are—'Chapter One. A Mystery. You will not be a great detective if you cannot recognize a mystery or differentiate it from something that is clearly not a mystery...' Really, Herr Kafka."

"He sold it to me at the 'get acquainted' price," Franz said. "It was in a wire bin with a bunch of other books."

"You didn't open your third envelope," Beide said.

Franz looked at it. Unlike the first two, there was nothing written on it.

"What's inside?" he asked.

"Beats me," she said.

"But isn't it from you?"

"No."

"But you left me three envelopes."

"Yes. But just because I left you three envelopes doesn't mean that all of the envelopes were from me. Do you understand?"

Franz nodded.

"Then who gave you the third envelope to give to me?" he asked.

"One way to find out is for you to open it," Beide said.

"And another way for me to find out is for you to tell me," Franz said.

"Perhaps I don't know."

"You know *something* about it."

"Perhaps I don't want you to know."

"Well, that's different. Why don't you want me to know?"

"Why do you think I don't want you to know?"

Franz felt the heat on his neck again. Was he to go through

this every time with the Inspector?

"What's so important about this envelope?" he asked.

"How should I know? Open it," Beide said.

"No," Franz said.

"Now you're just being stubborn."

"Can you blame me?" Franz asked. "I'm being treated like a cat's paw. It feels like every move I've made today has been made for me, invisibly, in advance; that something or someone has decided what I should be doing and has been nudging me into doing it. Things have not been as they ought to be. Things and people appear and disappear. My own existence isn't as it ought to be, either. And you know it!"

Beide crossed her legs and looked out the window. "It's lovely this time of day," she said. "The way the sun works its way over the hills as it sets. I've always loved the hills. The Kahlenberg, the Leopoldsberg... and, of course, the sheer majesty and mystery of the woods. I love making this journey, love it going either way, I haven't a preference. I love the journey north, and I love this, the journey south. Any time of day. I don't know why.

"People live there, in the woods, on the hills; people I'll never meet, never know. I'll never pass them on the street, as I might do in the city, our destination. But even seeing people on the street, well—I won't know them, either, even though I've seen them and witnessed their existence.

"Are they like me, like you? On some level? I'm sure they are, even if there's no way I could ever prove it. I assume all of them, country folk and city folk alike, are stuffed with the same essential clockwork as I: they hunger, they envy, they desire, they need, they love, they hate...

"And this train races us along, past the hidden strangers to the unhidden strangers; this train, this railway that wasn't here fifty years ago. We've found a way to cut right through it all, to connect one place to another, to get us from one group of people to another group of people, faster and faster still. It's stupendous. And frightening. Why should that be, Herr Kafka?"

"It's a mystery to me," Franz said. The heat in the compartment was stifling.

"Good," Beide said, tossing the book back to Franz. "According to the first chapter of Fraulein Baumhover's book, you're on the way to being a great detective."

For some reason, this angered Franz.

"Your face is so red," Beide said.

"Like a furnace in here," Franz said. He pulled the strap that lowered the window, but he gained no relief, as he caught a blast of soot square in the face. He moved aside and struggled to raise the window again.

"Would you like some help?" Beide asked.

"I'd like some square answers," Franz said, shoving at the window, which would not budge.

"Square answers? As opposed to ovoid answers?"

"Honest answers, no tricks."

"Perhaps if you didn't slam it like that…"

"What am I to do for money while I'm investigating your case?" Franz asked, slamming at the window frame.

"You've been given money," Beide said.

"Will there be more? I have to live, you know. Will you arrange to have my pension forwarded to me? And even then, it's not the most luxurious sum…"

"Your needs will be met."

"And what of my friends, family? Dora? Every time I want to get in touch with any of them, something happens and I'm prevented from doing so."

"That might be for the best."

"What do you mean by that?"

"Herr Kafka, quit fooling with the window and listen to me."

Franz sat down, out of the blast from the window. Beide had changed while he had been busy at the window, had returned to being male. Franz blinked, just to assure himself, but he had not been mistaken: Beide was a man.

"Your involvement in this case," Beide said without a trace

of a smile, "could be dangerous." He waited to see if his statement made any impact on Franz. "I thought we had been through this. Murder is a dangerous business, especially when you, as yet, do not know what you are dealing with. Would you place your friends in harm's way? Willingly? Or your sisters, your mother? Never mind your father, I know your feelings for him. But think: would you want Dora to be in the path of danger?"

Franz dropped his gaze to the unopened envelope on the seat. A gust caught it, and it fluttered up; he caught it.

"One last question," he said, looking at Beide. "You... how do I put this? You *change*. Physically. And in other subtle ways. I have never met anyone like you, someone who is one thing and then the other."

"Yes you have," Beide said, sitting back.

"No. No, I haven't. Not in this way."

"Maybe you have and just didn't recognize it. What is your last question?"

"How," Franz said, measuring his words, "am I to treat you?"

Beide smiled. "Like anyone else."

Franz looked again at the unmarked envelope, which flapped in his hand like a captured bird.

"Open it," Beide said. "For all you know, it could be the solution to the crimes."

"I hardly think that's possible. Otherwise I wouldn't be here, alive, healthy, famished, on this train, here with you, heading straight at danger."

"But how do you know?"

Franz frowned and let go of the envelope. It zipped out the window.

Beide merely looked at him.

"I know this game," Franz said, standing. "Or I should say I'm learning your little game."

"What game? There's no game."

Franz smiled.

"The tunnel trick," he said.

"Tunnel trick?"

"And there's one coming, I saw a glimpse of it when I was at the window."

"What tunnel trick?"

"Oh, I'm way ahead of you. Goodbye, Inspector."

The train entered a tunnel, and the compartment was plunged into darkness.

Seconds later, the train emerged, and the compartment was flooded with the light of the afternoon sun.

"Was something supposed to happen?" Beide asked.

Franz sat down.

"Never mind," he said.

The train passed through a grove of tall trees, flitting past the western sun and causing a startling strobe effect in the compartment. Franz felt for a dizzy moment as if he were looking at a zoetrope of Beide, and shut his eyes. It was only for a second, but when he opened his eyes again he was alone in the compartment, the window closed. He stood up, tried the window and, when it didn't budge, crossed the compartment to the door and found that it, too, was locked.

What was left of his rational mind did its best to convince him that he had been asleep the entire time, that he had been lulled to sleep by the rocking of the train, and Inspector Beide, Gregor—even the nuns—had been a dream. He went to sit.

And stepped on a walnut shell.

CHAPTER FIFTEEN
A STROLL

JULIA DIERKOP STOOD on the landing and saw The Hanging Artist at the foot of the stairs. What was the appropriate greeting? *Was* there one? There was a chance he wouldn't see her, and anyway, why should she *want* him to see her? She wasn't afraid of him, not here, not now.

"Good evening," Hans Henker said to her.

Julia smiled and descended the staircase. The smell of Frau Alt's overboiled dinner lingered in the hallway.

"Good evening," Julia said. "You're late leaving for the theatre, Herr Henker."

"As are you, Fraulein Dierkop," Henker said.

"I'm afraid the dinner disagreed with me," she said. "But you've spared yourself the indignity of these communal meals. I envy you and your sister, taking your meals in your rooms."

"We learned early that Frau Alt's cooking is a measure of last resort." He smiled, looked away. "At any rate, I'm sorry to hear you were taken for a turn, but you seem fresh as a rose now." He tugged at his gloves, smoothed them. "Your sisters didn't wait for you? Or are they... indisposed as well?"

"Oh no, they're quite well. They can shovel in any old muck and be ready for the races, so to speak. And I'll let you in on a little secret: they're not my sisters."

"Ah. You are a poseur."

"Worse: I'm a cousin."

"And therefore technically a Dierkop."

"Technically, authentically."

"How charming. I understand now why they bill themselves as The Three Dierkop Sisters, but I would think they'd want to acknowledge you in some way."

"The Three Dierkop Sisters and Cousin? It might be accurate, but it doesn't read as well on the bill."

He wasn't moving. They heard the parlor clock strike the hour. They both looked in the direction of the sound.

"I'd better hurry along," Julia said, stepping past him.

"I say," he said, turning to her, "my companions seem to have forgotten they were to walk with me tonight."

"The Flying Hurricanes?"

"Yes. No doubt they've been drinking all afternoon, or are perhaps overindulging at table once again."

"The Italians show as much relish for their food as we Austrians."

"I'll let you in on a little secret, too. They pretend to be Italians, but they're from Stuttgart. And they've become too tubby for their costumes. You may have noticed."

"I can't say I've bothered to watch them."

"At any rate, I thought… well… seeing as we are headed in the same direction, I was wondering if you might care to walk along with me?"

"My dear Herr Henker—can't you go *anywhere* unaccompanied?"

He lost his smile then. "I'll just wait, then. Frau Alt typically takes a perambulation at this hour, I'll ask her if she'd come along."

"I didn't mean to offend you," Julia said. "I was merely

remarking on the fact that you... well, I *never* see you alone, outside of this house."

"I like company. I'm an amiable sort."

"Well, it would be a pleasure. And an honor—to be seen with a celebrity."

He blushed at that. "I doubt anyone would even notice me, in the company of such a charming girl."

They set out for the Traumhalle. Julia liked that: *girl*. Of course the man was a flatterer; she hadn't been mistaken for a girl in years, even when she *was* a girl she hadn't been mistaken for a girl. He was such a pleasant fellow, with an affable demeanor that made her think of a sheepish dry goods clerk who had seen very few customers that day. It made her quite forget the nature of his act.

"Your sister is well, I hope?" she asked, as they detoured down a boulevard, past the shops and restaurants.

"She, I am happy to report, has enjoyed uncommonly improved health since we've come to Vienna," he said.

"How cheering. To what do you attribute that?"

"Hmmm?"

"Her improved health, I mean."

"Oh. Any number of things. I'm no physician. And I don't question life when it takes a turn for the better. I don't need to know a reason."

"But if you knew the reason, you'd be able to reproduce it when she took a downturn again... hoping that she doesn't, of course."

"That new number you've added," he said, changing the subject. "It's very... 'jazzy,' I think is the word for it."

Julia wasn't fooled; he knew perfectly well *jazzy* was the word for it. He had the pulse of the times; his phonograph records were of the latest and jazziest dance bands in Germany and Austria.

"Thank you," she said. "I didn't know you listened to us. After all, we're on in the first half, and you... well, you have the star spot."

"If it gets much hotter," he said, "I'm wary of what July will be like. We'll all be baked like gingerbread."

They walked in silence then, for the length of three streets, where Julia pulled up short.

"How odd," she said. Henker turned and waited for her.

"Everything all right?" he asked.

Julia shook her head, smiled, and resumed walking.

"That gentleman," she said. "Outside the Schweigerhaus. At one of the tables. No; don't look."

"What's the matter with him?"

"Have you ever seen someone you know only in one particular context... somewhere completely out of context? Oh, dear, I said not to look."

"Which man? The one in the extraordinarily loud checkered suit?"

"Yes."

"And the necktie that looks like a stable fire?"

"That's the man."

"Do you know him?"

"Only by sight," Julia said. "Oh, I think we should hurry along, don't you?"

"If you like," said Henker, mild and obliging as always. "Where have you seen him?"

"Why, the theatre, of course," she said, the color rising in her cheeks. "I'm surprised you haven't seen him before. He's hard to miss."

"So many people come to the theatre."

"Oh, but he's come more than once. So many times. At least, I think it's the same man."

Henker stole a last look at the man in the checkered suit, who sat at his table with his dinner untouched in front of him. He was writing in a journal or notebook of some sort.

"Perhaps he's a critic," Henker said, but Julia hadn't noticed the journal, so she missed the joke.

"Well, he's certainly fond of the theatre," she said. She

pressed her handkerchief to her damp upper lip.

"It could be that he's fond of you," Henker said.

Julia laughed. "I doubt it," she said. "I'm one of four, remember."

"Ah, but you are the Dierkop that isn't a sore for sight eyes," he said.

"You mean a sight for sore eyes."

"No, I meant what I said. I thought it would be funnier, but I suppose it didn't make much sense when it came out of my mouth. In my defense, I'm not billed as a comedian."

Julia's expression darkened. "No," she said, "you aren't. Definitely not."

They had reached the stage door of the Traumhalle, and were gratified to find the dark interior backstage considerably cooler than the June evening they had left behind.

"Thank you," Julia said, "for such a pleasant walk."

He bowed to her, and began to ascend the stairs to the better dressing rooms.

Something compelled Julia to stop him. "Aren't you going to, er... check your props?"

He stopped and looked down at her.

"Everything will be ready when I'm ready to go on," he said.

"I see. How comforting. You must be on excellent terms with the stagehands. Do you bribe them?"

He laughed. "I don't rely on help from anyone. That is to say, I don't need anyone's help."

"You're very fortunate."

"Would you like to... see my dressing room?"

"I've never seen a star's dressing room before. Dare I? Will it put ideas into my head?"

He said nothing, but continued up the stairs. She followed.

When he opened his door, there was nothing.

No trunk, no costumes; only the dressing table, the mirror, and a simple chair before it. Nothing littered the table: it was absent of greasepaint, brushes, towels, and anything of a personal nature; no telegrams or notices, no framed photographs.

Julia gaped at the emptiness.

"It's a very simple act," Henker said.

"I see," Julia said. "That is, I *don't* see. Anything. Not even—"

"The rope?" he asked. "Oh, it will be there when I need it, don't you worry. And so, too, might your young man in the checked suit."

"He's not my young man," she said, but he was already closing the door.

"Have a good show," Henker said.

CHAPTER SIXTEEN
MONSIEUR CHOUCAS

Everything Franz deduced about Frau Alt was wrong, and thus began his life as a detective.

The moment he met her, he saw in the imposing woman a long-forgotten soubrette considered a great beauty some forty years previously, a woman who clucked over her theatrical lodgers with a mix of out-of-date high morals and envy of those still treading the boards. He saw in her a gassy windbag crammed with career advice and impossible-to-verify scandals from the days of the carriage and bustle. He saw her holding 'informal salons' every Monday evening in the parlor in which she would modestly warble one number and commit seven encores, mostly in a bosomy contralto straining in a soprano key, chiefly from *The Merry Widow*, in which she would claim she would have been cast as the lead had it not been for her unflagging adherence to her virtue and strict avoidance of managerial offices furnished with anything longer than a chair. He saw in Frau Alt a gossipy, prying martyr to the memory of a late husband, a doleful mite of a man whose photograph, edged in black, loomed prominently over the mantelpiece.

Frau Alt had, in fact, nothing whatsoever to do with the

theater in her entire life, except for a brief stint in her late teens as an apprentice confectioner in a sweet shop two doors down from the Musikverein.

As for widowhood, Franz discovered she was anything but widowed, as Herr Alt—who was every bit as big and solid as his wife—could still be seen in the boarding house, barging from room to room, carrying a tool bag.

Despite his miscalculations about the landlady, Franz soon discovered he was not wrong about the room he was given.

He had imagined little more than a cupboard with a sliver of dirty window overlooking the cesspool out back. He was only wrong in that the tiny window was clean. That the room was generally considered the cupboard was verified by Frau Alt shoving the pail, mop, and broom out onto the landing when she showed him in.

Franz had introduced himself as Monsieur Francois Choucas, the closest French approximation of his real name that he could muster, and thought to himself that it sounded rather dashing and artistic. Gregor had suggested 'Johann Schmidt,' but Franz had told him he could do a little better than that.

"It's the coziest nook in the house," Frau Alt said, and sneezed at the dust her opening the door had stirred. "Perfect for a solitary gentleman in search of repose and quietude."

"It's perfect," Franz said, lying. He spoke in his own voice, as his attempt at a slight French accent had prompted Gregor to accuse him of sounding like his teeth were slipping out.

"Meals in the dining room at seven, twelve, and five," Frau Alt said. "We take supper at an earlier hour, naturally, as all of the lodgers are, I am proud to say, engaged at one theater or another. That said, you're on your own for Pausenbrot and coffee and cake; this is a home, not a restaurant. No cooking is allowed in the rooms, except, of course, in the deluxe suite, which is already taken." Here she gestured out the door and to the next landing. Franz looked up the stairs and saw a set of elegant doors, now closed, framed by pots of flowers on small tables. "The deluxe suite also has its own private... well. I'm sure you know what I mean."

Franz did, and asked where the 'you know what I mean' for everyone else was. Frau Alt made a vague gesture down the flight of steps they had ascended. "Next floor down at the end of the hallway, just turn left at the foot of the stairs. Coming from this direction, that is," she said. "Coming from downstairs, of course, you..."

"Turn right," Franz said, pleased that he had made at least one correct deduction that day.

Frau Alt smiled one of those meant-to-be-indulgent smiles one sees schoolteachers reserve for moronic parents of vexing children.

Franz watched as Gregor scuttled under the sad-looking bed. "Thank you, Frau Alt," he said, taking his envelope of money from his coat pocket.

She stayed his hand. "On Sunday evenings," she said. "Naturally, I never refuse money, but it's nice to establish a routine, and you know what they say about routines."

Franz did not, and admitted as much. Frau Alt, however, did not enlighten him, as she had been fixated at the wad of cash he had produced.

"If, monsieur, you are looking for more *spacious* accommodations," she said, "there is a distinct possibility that I might have a vacancy soon that would suit your purposes."

"Oh?" Franz asked, a little less brilliantly than he would have wished.

Frau Alt nodded again at the double doors on the landing above. "The deluxe suite, in fact," she said. "But nothing is confirmed yet. I don't want to get your hopes up."

"Someone is thinking of leaving?" Franz asked.

Gregor, coated in dust, emerged from beneath the bed. "Jesus," he said, "the questions you ask! Do you want her to think you a nitwit?"

Frau Alt lowered her voice and closed the door, making the

tiny room all the more claustrophobic. She smelled of lavender and pickling spices. Franz took a step away from her and banged his head on a shelf.

"Herr Henker," she said. "You've heard of him, no doubt."

Gregor said, "Remember, you're pretending to be French."

"The name is not familiar to me," Franz said.

"The Hanging Artist," Frau Alt said.

"What does he hang?"

"He hangs himself!"

"Incredible! Night after night? His neck must be unusually resilient."

Gregor groaned and crawled back under the bed.

Frau Alt laughed. "Yes, it must," she said. "I won't spoil it for you."

"It?"

"His act."

"Ah."

"You simply must see it. It's the rage of Vienna."

"Why is Vienna so upset?"

"Overdoing it!" Gregor called out from beneath the bed.

Frau Alt was clearly charmed by her supposedly foreign lodger. She opened the door and glanced onto the landing. "Monsieur misunderstands," she said. "When I say he's the rage, I mean he is *la mode*."

"Ah. Well, then I certainly must see his performance, if for no other reason than to be *a la mode*... and as a gesture of respect from one artist to another."

"Then I'd advise you to do so quickly, if you wish to see him at a reasonable price."

"What do you mean?"

"Well, I'm not one to gossip, but I can tell you he received a visit today from Max Spindler, who is the king of impresarios in Vienna, as he owns Die Feier, the biggest variety theater in Austria, and, well..."

"Yes?"

Frau Alt said, "Well, Max Spindler must *really* want to engage Herr Henker, as Spindler leaving his offices for anyone is a nearly unheard of occasion. And if Herr Henker will be playing Die Feier, he and his sister will be moving to a… well, let's just say my humble little home can't compare with the finest hotels. So you should see him while he's at the Traumhalle, which only charges half of what a cheap seat at Die Feier costs."

"You mentioned a sister," Franz said. "Is she part of the act?"

"Heavens, no," Frau Alt said. "She's an invalid, poor dear. Never leaves the suite."

"What ails her?"

"I've no idea."

Herr Alt clomped up the stairs, glanced in at Franz, then grumbled something that sounded like a prolonged belch while brandishing a rubber mallet at the upper floor, to which she responded, "Well, be quick about it."

Alt went upstairs. Frau Alt handed Franz the key to his room.

"I know you'll be comfortable, monsieur," she said.

"Is there a performance tonight?" Franz asked.

"A performance?"

"The Hanging Artist. You've piqued my interest."

"Oh, yes, but you'd have to hurry, you've less than a half an hour before the curtain goes up, although Herr Henker performs at the end of the program."

"Is it far?"

She gave him directions to the Traumhalle, and he thanked her. At the top of the stairs, she turned back with an exclamation.

"Oh! How rude of me, monsieur!"

"Madame?"

"I didn't have the courtesy to ask the nature of *your* act."

Gregor crawled out from under the bed, munching a rotten apple core.

"Forgot about that," Gregor said.

"My act, madame?" Franz asked.

"Your talent," she said.

Franz tried to keep his eyes from bugging out as his brain raced for an answer. "Ah," he said, "my talent, yes, well, how can I describe it? I'm, that is, you could call me a, you see, the thing is, I'm…"

"A verrilionist," Gregor said.

"A verrilionist," Franz said.

"How charming!" Frau Alt said. "Well, we'll have to be very careful with your glasses, won't we?"

"No need, Madame, my eyesight is perfect," Franz said.

Frau Alt had a good laugh at that as she descended the stairs, repeating, "'My eyesight is perfect!' Brilliant!" all the way to the main floor.

Franz shut the door behind him and took off his coat.

"What the hell is a verrilionist?" he asked.

"I don't know," Gregor said.

"You don't know? Then why the hell did you tell me to tell her that?"

"It's the first thing that came to mind."

"A word like that? What kind of mind do you have?"

"Don't get upset, it's—"

"Now I have to find out what a verrilionist is and pray that I can pass as one!" He unbuttoned his vest.

"What are you doing?" Gregor asked.

"What's it look like I'm doing? I'm undressing!"

"Now?"

"I need a bath, and it's smarter to use the bathroom now while the other lodgers are out doing their theatrical things than tonight or tomorrow morning, when there will no doubt be a line."

"But didn't you hear what that woman said?"

"I heard everything she said. Why do you ask?"

Gregor rubbed himself up against the curtains to clean the grime off his shell. "Henker's going to move on," he said. "Now's the night to see him in action."

"I'm sure tonight is not his last performance," Franz said,

removing his collar and undoing his necktie. "I'll go tomorrow night."

Gregor, somewhat presentable, snatched up the vest and coat and held them out. "Now!" he said. "Go!"

"What's the rush?"

Gregor fixed what Franz assumed was a steady, sober gaze at him. "When," said the insect, "are you going to do some real detecting?"

Franz returned the vermin's gaze for several moments before he retrieved his collar and hooked it in to place.

"All right," he said, dressing himself. "I'll go. But don't think I haven't learned anything, my disgusting friend. I have."

"About the murders?"

"Well, no, not about the murders, per se, but…"

Gregor handed him his hat.

"You'd better run along," he said. "May I come with you?"

Franz put on his hat and checked his appearance as best he could in the saucer-sized mirror that swung from a peg above the battered bureau. "I didn't think I had any control over your comings and goings," he said. He regarded his reflection and said, "I look like I'm starving. And you know why that is? Because I am. It feels like it's been a week since that breakfast this morning."

"We'll get you a nice hot pretzel with mustard on the way," Gregor said, watching as Franz opened the door and the doorknob came off in his hand.

"The hell with it," Franz said, throwing the knob on the hall carpet.

Pretzel. Mustard.

There was work to be done.

CHAPTER SEVENTEEN
THE PERFORMANCE

HANS HENKER SAT in his empty dressing room, eyes closed, and began the process of escorting every trace of himself away from his mind.

This was never easy.

He had always encountered difficulties putting up the gray wall that would separate Hans Henker from The Hanging Artist. It took time, and it took dedication.

Most of all, it took cunning, which didn't come naturally to him; and practice, he had learned, did not always make perfect. Still, it had to be done, and he continued to conjure up a mental Pied Piper to lead his reality away to a secret chamber in the dark depths of his soul.

Soul?

He led that thought away.

The show had begun. The voices of the performers, the hum of the audience, even the clatter of the machinery used to raise the curtain and olio reached his ears.

One by one, he lured the sounds away.

He heard the Dierkop Sisters begin to chirrup their first song. He listened, trying to separate Julia's voice from her cousins. There it was: the alto. Her voice alone didn't sound like a confused hornet: it was mellow, a warm thread underneath the—

No. He led her away to the other side of the gray wall, down into the darkness.

He resorted to his words.

He knew his words, and would probably know his words until his dying day, perhaps even longer. He knew his words but said them anyway, because they were of The Hanging Artist. There would never be any variation to his words, because variation indicated contemplation—a constant fiddling about, making things better or worse—and Hans did not require variation or improvement. What he needed were the words, and…

The smell of Spindler's cigar, the crispness of the contract… of quality paper…

It had been another step for him, more of a leap, and—

No. Out. Away, down, in, shut, locked.

Good evening, my friends, my dear new friends.

THE HANGING ARTIST leaves his dressing room and closes the door behind him.

He walks down the spiral staircase, one hand on the railing.

He hears the audience laugh, but he hears the strain in their laughter, because they are waiting, waiting for The Hanging Artist. They've been waiting all week, all day, all night. Any other reaction is automatic: surprise, appreciation, laughter.

He does not step aside as a clutch of barely-clothed dancers rush to get to the stage. They flow around him, southbound geese parting and rejoining around an unexpected weathervane.

He waits where he always waits, next to the harp case, which may or may not contain a harp.

He knows the dancers are doing their brightest routine. The music is wicked, the stamping insistent, defiant.

He hears the applause for their efforts, plentiful but meaningless.

The dancers swarm backstage, all tearing off their beaded headdresses at the same time, file up the stairs, their shoes making sounds like cannonball raindrops falling into tin pails.

The Hanging Artist hears his music.

It is the music of sunshine and romance.

The violin has never sounded sweeter, the muted trumpet more coy.

A young man in a cap and shirtsleeves, his powerful arms prepared to haul up the curtain, nods to The Hanging Artist, who smiles, but does not return the nod.

The curtain and the olio rise.

The orchestra stops. The conductor nods to the musicians. They douse their lights.

The Hanging Artist walks onstage. He stops center stage and gives the audience a moment to take in his smart linen suit the color of fresh caramel, his pomaded hair, his spring green necktie, his polished fudge-brown shoes, his butter-colored calfskin gloves.

He assumes a casual but authoritative stance: legs together but feet turn slightly outward, one foot an inch forward of the other, the left hand in the pocket, the right hand, unconcerned, at his side.

He speaks.

"Good evening, my friends, my dear new friends—and, I hope, new friends who have become old friends who have returned. You are welcome, and I thank you. Thank you for finding me."

He turns to his right and crosses to the gramophone perched on its delicate table. He winds the machine until the spring has no more give. He pushes the turntable brake, and the record spins. He lifts the reproducer and lowers it onto the spinning disc; the needle slides into the groove.

He crosses back to center as the elegant, spry music— "Gigolette," performed by Marek Weber & His Famous Orchestra—flows from the gramophone's flowered horn, sounding as if smothered beneath a wet woolen blanket.

He smiles.

"I propose to hang myself," The Hanging Artist says.

He waits for the reaction to abate. It is much the same as it always is: the low, rolling expressions of alarm and disbelief, one or two nervous laughs.

He continues.

"Because justice must be done. And who am I, you might ask, to judge myself and pass sentence? Who am I to take my own life? Why, I am myself, and who else would know better than I for what sins I must answer?

"The sins of living, my friends. The sins that live in my thoughts, my desires, my regrets, my hurts, my slights, my envies. Are these sins or are they demons? They are both.

"But are all of our internal demons just that—internal? Perhaps they are real: external, and gnawing at us. Perhaps those demons are your friends, your neighbors, your lovers, your spouses, your children...

"The list, my friends, goes on and on.

"And so, the rope, fashioned into a noose and slipped around the neck. The noose that cuts off air, cuts off consciousness, cuts off your relationship to this place of suffering and offers—what? Peace? Perhaps. An escape? Definitely.

"Am I taking my own life? No. Do I do this to encourage you to take yours, to pass your own harsh judgments on yourselves? I would never do that. I would never encourage anyone to do something that I myself have not done.

"Lastly, who am I to ask you to sit there and watch me do it?

"I am The Hanging Artist, my friends.

"It is expected of me."

He sketches a military bow to his audience and returns to the gramophone, as "Gigolette" is over. He replaces the record with another, winds the gramophone, and drops the needle on the new record. Everyone recognizes the tune: "Ausgerechnet Bananen," although most of Europe has been singing the nonsensical American song in its English iteration: "Yes! We

Have No Bananas!" The audience loves this record—loves the popular band, Efim Schachmeister Dance Band—and toes start tapping.

While the audience adjusts and is soothed by the music, The Hanging Artist walks upstage to the chair. He takes up the rope coiled on the seat and returns to the audience.

He shows them the rope, spooling it out as he speaks, until the noose is revealed.

"This," The Hanging Artist says, "is the artist's instrument, the finest there is, delicate silken strands braided together into a larger and stronger form. And why shouldn't this rope be made of excellent silk and not ordinary Manila hemp, or jute, or common straw? One could argue that the sinner deserves nothing more than the roughest fibers, that the demons must be routed by the coarsest means possible.

"But this is the theater!"

He raises the noose so all can see.

"Does the sight of this strike fear in your heart? Terror? Be calm. Be sensible. Be joyous! There is no need to fear anything— for, as you know, whoever turns his mind to true goodness will be met with fortune and honor, and forever be free of sinful shame! Observe."

He gently shakes the rope, and the noose becomes undone.

The audience responds in awe, because they think it's impossible to undo a hangman's knot so quickly. The Hanging Artist nods, holds up a hand.

"Please, it is no miracle. I'm just showing you there is nothing to fear. This is just a rope. And to prove it to you—to prove *myself* to you—I will need a volunteer, someone to come up here, with me, to inspect this fine silken rope and my own person, to demonstrate that, after all, there is no trick. Now— who will do it?"

A hundred hands, two hundred, three hundred.

One arm rises from the front row, slowly but with confidence. Its owner signals as if hailing a taxi: index and forefinger.

He points to the front row, to the calm, confident arm and its owner.

"You, sir," says The Hanging Artist, "the gentleman in the checkered coat. Please."

The Hanging Artist returns to the gramophone, just in time to lift the needle from the record as its last calamitous sounds play out. When he turns, he will have a new friend. He selects the next record, but a fresh needle in the reproducer, cranks the machine, and plays the new selection: "Tutankhamen." Exotic, lively, mysterious.

The Hanging Artist returns to center stage to meet the young man in the checkered suit, who does not appear to be at all nervous or awkward in front of an audience.

"Thank you," The Hanging Artist says. "And what is your name, sir?"

"Leo," says the man in the checkered suit.

He does not take his eyes off The Hanging Artist for one second.

The Hanging Artist places the beautiful, smooth rope in Leo's hand.

"Take your time inspecting it," he says, removing his own coat.

But Leo does not inspect the rope. He holds it, waiting for The Hanging Artist to complete his undress.

"You trust me implicitly?" The Hanging Artist says, and laughs.

"I trust the rope," Leo says.

A smattering of laughter from the audience.

The Hanging Artist removes his necktie, then reaches behind his neck and unfastens his collar. He tosses his coat, waistcoat, necktie, and collar offstage, then extends his arms.

"You may search me," he says.

Holding the rope in one hand, Leo pats The Hanging Artist's shoulders and arms.

"That's all?" The Hanging Artist asks. He winks at the audience.

Leo hands him the rope. "That is all," he says, "and thank you."

Leo leaves the stage.

The Hanging Artist hesitates again, but recovers to ask the audience to show their appreciation for Leo. They applaud.

"And with that," The Hanging Artist says, "we begin!"

As the pseudo-Egyptian fox-trot thumps from the gramophone's shining horn, The Hanging Artist twirls the rope once, twice, thrice, and restores it to the hangman's knot.

The audience is astounded.

"There is no trick, my friends, my witnesses," The Hanging Artist says. "Mere dexterity. And because I know how superstitious we all can be, I only use twelve coils, not the traditional thirteen. Because why not? No one needs *invite* bad luck, when bad luck is often sitting right there, or there, or there..."

He stops, as he notices the man in the checkered coat—Leo—has not returned to his seat.

The Hanging Artist concentrates.

"The gallows!" he says, and he tosses the noose into the air.

To everyone's astonishment, the rope does not fall, but continues to sail up, winding itself around the stark gallows. It comes to rest, the noose hanging perfectly above the chair.

Wild applause.

The Hanging Artist accepts the applause with a gracious bow, one gloved hand resting on his breast.

"And now," he says, "we begin... the end."

He crosses to the gramophone, removes "Tutankhamen," and places the final record on the turntable. The music is delightful. There's not a member of the audience doesn't recognize the tune. Is that Eric Borchard's jazz band? It is.

The Hanging Artist climbs onto the chair.

It wobbles. He regains his balance, smiles. He always smiles.

"No worries," he says, and fastens the noose around his neck.

Collectively, the audience makes low noises of protests. A few stand from their seats. Will this happen? Is it a trick?

"What, after all, *is* a trick?" The Hanging Artists asks from his rickety perch. "By definition, a trick is a cunning or skillful act or scheme intended to deceive or outwit someone.

"But I have no intention of deceiving or outwitting you. I am here to do what I proposed to do. I intend to pass judgment on myself and live.

"Do I deserve to live?

"I leave that to you."

The song shouts from the gramophone:

"Ev'rybody shimmies now.
Ev'rybody's learning how.
Brother Bill, Sister Kate
Shiver like jelly on a plate.
Shimmy dancing can't be beat,
Moves ev'rything except your feet.
Feeble folks, mighty old,
Shake the shimmy and they shake it bold.
Oh! Honey, won't you show me how?
'Cause ev'rybody shimmies now!"

The Hanging Artist kicks the chair out from under him. It clatters into the dark behind him.

He drops.

His fall—and neck, from the sound of it—is broken by the rope.

The audience cries out.

The Hanging Artist swings at the end of the rope, back and forth, as the lively music plays on. The audience cannot move.

The record ends.

The needle remains in its final groove, tracing an endless, ghostly ribbon of dull noise as the record wears down the needle and the needle wears down the record.

The Hanging Artist's body ceases to sway.
Stillness for ten seconds.
And the curtain comes down.

CHAPTER EIGHTEEN
A NOCTURNE

WE SEE THEM leave the theater, their steps mechanical, their eyes unfocused.

"Of course he lives," one says, after strolling along in heavy silence.

"Then he should have taken a bow," says another.

"He's always back the next night," says another.

"But he mightn't be back tomorrow night," says another.

"Well, if something went wrong tonight, I suppose we'll read about it in the papers tomorrow," says another.

We see them continue to their homes, wrapped in thought.

"What was the purpose, then?" asks one.

"What was his reason?" asks another.

"Why were we subjected to that?" asks another.

"I suppose we could have just left," says another.

We see them in their shadowy bedrooms. Some of them, who would kneel in prayer any other night, wonder if they should bother.

Some of them, who have never knelt in prayer, do so.

* * *

WE SEE FOUR women in a dressing room.

"You're not walking home with him tonight, Julia," one says.

"Why not?" Julia asks.

"You shouldn't have walked here with him in the first place," another says.

"He's very nice," Julia says.

"All of them are very nice," the third says, "and by that I mean all of them *seem* to be very nice."

"They can be very nice by daylight," says the first, "and something else entirely at night."

"He's a fellow artist," says Julia.

"It's hardly the same thing," the second one says. "We don't blow our brains out after the last song."

"*He* doesn't blow his brains out."

"You know what I mean."

We see them hesitate at the foot of the stairs. The evening's performance is being packed away, the stage cleaned. An old man in shirtsleeves carries a ghost light to the empty stage. We see three of the four women glance at the stage exit.

"He'll be waiting for you, I presume," one says.

"I don't know," Julia says. "After all, I didn't offer to walk home with him…"

"We'll go out the front," says another. "Come along."

WE SEE A man in a checkered suit flag the attention of the night clerk at his hotel.

We see him ask the clerk to prepare his bill, as he will be leaving in the morning.

We see the clerk nod.

We see the man in the checkered suit ask that the bill be brought to him no earlier than eight in the morning.

We see the clerk nod again and ask the man if he enjoyed his stay.

We see the man in the checkered suit saunter to the lift.

"I'll let you know in the morning," he says over his shoulder. "After I'm gone."

We see the night clerk think nothing of the curious answer.

WE SEE A woman and a man linger at the back door of a smart, three-story house. The house is in the center of a row of smart, three-story houses that look exactly alike.

"The garden door leads to the alley, and from there it's your choice," the woman says.

"Choice of what?" the man asks.

"Which way you wish to go," she says.

"Oh," says the man. "You keep the gate unlocked?"

"I'll lock it behind you," she says.

We see them cross the dark yard where nothing grows. She opens the wooden door in the rear wall of the garden. We see him pause.

"A good-night kiss?" he asks. "Or is that extra?"

She kisses him.

"That's extra," she says.

"You could've told me that before you kissed me," he says.

"You can settle up with me next time," she says.

We hear a dog barking in one of the unseen yards; from the sound of it, it is a small dog, and highly excitable.

"If there *is* a next time," the man says, and we imagine he is smiling, although it is too dark to tell.

"There's always a next time," the woman says.

We see the man leave.

The woman shuts the door, locks it.

She crosses the yard.

"SHADDUP!" she yells.

We hear nothing more from the excitable small dog.

We see the woman go into the house. She locks the door behind her.

She goes through the dark kitchen, into the hallway, up the

stairs, and into her boudoir.

We see her reach for the one light still burning: the one nearest her mirror.

She regards herself in this close, harsh light.

She thinks she has a haggard, starving look.

She aches.

She turns off the light.

Her head turns sharply to her left, as if she has heard something.

"Sneaking up on me?" she asks. "Anything more is extra, you know."

She reaches for the light.

"How did you get in?" she asks.

The light does not come on.

WE SEE A tall, thin man, his hands in his pockets, walk away from the theater.

He looks this way and that.

We hear him singing softly to himself: "Honey, won't you show me how…"

We see his silhouette as he turns down an alley.

He is accompanied by the silhouette of a remarkably large insect.

Who is also singing.

CHAPTER NINETEEN
TWO ROOMS AT MIDNIGHT

"IN OTHER WORDS, you were of no use to me at all," Franz said as he undressed.

"I was of great use. You're just not looking at it properly." The voice came from underneath the bed.

"Gregor," Franz said, picking at a severely knotted shoelace, "not seeing anything out of the ordinary... is no help."

"But isn't the fact that I saw nothing out of the ordinary... extraordinary?"

"What are you eating?"

"Nothing you'd like."

Franz gave up on the shoe. His body was tired, his mind was overloaded; he felt as if he were far too many guests crammed onto a rickety yacht that had recently run aground.

"I wish Yitzchak were here," he said, falling back on the bed. The bed didn't appreciate this, and one or two springs gave in protest.

"Ouch," Gregor said from below. "Who's Yitzchak?"

"Yitzchak Lowy. A good friend of mine. And one of the finest actors in Prague."

"Never heard of him."

"How often do you attend Yiddish theatre?"

"Never."

"Then it's no wonder you've never heard of him."

"Tonight was my first visit to any theatre at all. Plenty of rubbish—actual rubbish, I mean. I was in heaven. Why do you wish he was here?"

"He could tell me how Henker pulls off his illusion."

"He's a hanging artist, too?"

"No. But he's a man of the theatre. I'm not."

"I'm still wondering why you're fixated on this Henker fellow anyway. Isn't there some sort of general consensus that there is no way he could be performing the actual murders? Is that the correct verb: performing? Or is it enacting? Perpetrating? Doing?"

Franz sat up and removed the other, cooperative shoe.

"Regardless of the verb, it's vexing," Franz said. "And if these murders aren't connected to Henker, then they're certainly connected to the act itself, or the act's emotional impact on the audience."

"Do you feel like strangling someone?"

A moment's silence. "No," Franz said.

"What a liar," Gregor said. "I've fixed your shoelace."

Franz looked at his foot; the shoelace was unknotted.

"Thank you," he said. "And don't call me a liar."

"Then don't lie."

"Come out from under there!"

"There isn't enough room in this closet for both of us to be knocking about."

Franz wriggled out of his pants, bed springs creaking all the while.

"I wasn't lying when I said I didn't feel like strangling someone," he said. "Don't put words into my mouth."

"Your father," Gregor said, and the munching sounds continued.

"You don't know what you're talking about."

Gregor crawled from beneath the bed, snorting dust.

"It's possible I don't," Gregor said, "but then again, I'm not the one who wrote the letter."

The letter. Franz closed his eyes and hung his head. The creature had mentioned the letter. He wouldn't ask how it had known; it knew things it shouldn't know, and claimed ignorance of things it should. As for the letter—where was it now?

"I was about to ask you the same thing," Gregor said. "Did you destroy it?"

"It's somewhere."

"Are you ever going to give it to him?"

"I tried, once."

"I hate to correct you, but you didn't try to give it to him. You gave it to your mother to give to him."

"And she didn't."

"She gave it back to you. Where's it been the last five years?"

Franz removed his shirt, eager to be asleep, eager for anything that wasn't talking about the letter or his father.

"It hasn't been five years," Franz said. "It's been four years, seven months, and two days." He smiled. "But who's counting?" He stretched out on the bed as best as he could and covered his eyes with his arm. It was too hot for pajamas. He had tried to open the pathetic aperture that passed for a window, but he had not been able. He concluded it was not a window at all, just a smeared portrait of an exterior covered by a window frame. "It was a stupid thing to do, anyway," he said. "As if I could make him understand… oh, let's forget about my father and try to figure out what we're to do next," he said.

Gregor slid under the bed. "'We'?" he asked.

"You're the only one who comes around. I've not seen the inspector since the train, and who knows when—or if—he or she will come again? As far as I know, I've been cut adrift. All I've got is a list of dead people and the weirdest magician I've ever seen."

"Magician?"

"The Hanging Artist. Wouldn't you call him a magician?"

"I don't know if 'magician' does him justice."

Franz rubbed his eyes. "Just because you told me you saw nothing?" he asked.

"You dismissed my eyewitness report."

"Which, at your behest, I am now considering in a new light. You saw the act from high above the stage."

"Correct."

"What were you doing up there?"

"What difference does it make?"

"Fine, fine," Franz said, shifting on the mattress in an effort to find comfort. "You told me none of the crew or other performers watched his act."

"Not a soul. The curtain went up and the backstage area emptied in the blink of an eye."

"And no one returned during the act."

"Correct."

"And there was no one up in the—what did you call it?"

"Flies."

"Which is a nickname for the space above the stage where the big set pieces are flown and stored, and where the various ropes and cables…"

"Yes, although I went up there because I actually thought I'd find flies."

Franz opened his eyes and began checking off points on his fingers.

"So," he said, "first, no one watches his performance from backstage; two, no one is manipulating the rope, which would have explained its completely disconcerting ascent to the gallows and fixation on said object; three, Henker remains hanging from the hope until the very second the final curtain hits the floor, at which time the backstage area is plunged into darkness; four, said darkness lasts a mere five seconds, and when the work lights come on, Henker and the rope are gone, and the stagehands have returned. Have I got that right?"

Snoring from below.

Franz bounced on the mattress.

"Wake up!"

He felt Gregor move around beneath him.

"What is your conclusion?" Gregor asked.

"That I really, really wish Yitzchak was here," Franz said. "He could put my mind at rest."

"How?"

"By assuring me that The Hanging Artist's performance is exactly that—a performance. And nothing else."

"What else could it be?"

"I don't know. But I will tell you one thing I *do* know: it's a highly evocative and disturbing performance. It could appeal to anyone seeking to... well, anyone who might be a trifle unhinged. Or completely unhinged."

"You think that someone is copying Henker's performance? In a homicidal way?"

"It would explain how the killer gets around, particularly as Beide assured me that Henker's been shadowed for several weeks, and his movements are always accounted for."

"That doesn't necessarily mean Henker couldn't go about unnoticed," Gregor said. "After all, if he's engineered this inexplicable illusion on the stage, why couldn't he engineer an equally inexplicable illusion to fool the police?

"And if it is some maniac copying the basic effects of Henker's act, how do you propose to identify them? To date, there's only been one victim who was known to have been in Henker's audience—the young man from last night. How do you account for the others?" Franz wanted to scream. What had he gotten himself into?

"I can't account for anything," he said. "I'm going to go mad if I think of it any longer—as if I haven't gone mad already! If it is someone other than Henker, then there must indeed be some link between all of the victims, some relationship we're not seeing, or—good God."

"What?"

"…Or there isn't any connection to anything or anyone, and it will be impossible to find the killer."

"Good luck sleeping tonight," Gregor said.

"Where's my book?"

"What book?"

"The book on how not to be a great detective."

Gregor sent one of his arms up from beneath the bed, holding the book in question, slightly nibbled.

"Don't tell me you've been eating this," Franz said.

"I was getting around to it. I thought you didn't want it anymore."

"I'm desperate."

He opened and read. "Here we are—'Chapter Two. Questions. You will not be a great detective if you cannot ask questions, particularly questions that will give you the answers you need to solve the crime.' Oh, for the love of—"

He closed the book and tossed it under the bed.

"Bon appétit," he said.

"YOU'RE LATER THAN usual tonight," Mathilde said, closing her book. "Everything all right?"

"I'm sorry I kept you up waiting for me," Henker said, closing the door.

"When have I *ever* been asleep when you've returned?"

"Ah."

He stood in the parlor, staring vacantly at an empty armchair.

"I'll get you some coffee," Mathilde said.

"You know that I don't like you to wait on me," he said.

She held out her hands to him.

"Up," she said.

He reached for her.

"No," she said.

She looked at his hands.

He looked at his hands.

"Oh," he said.

He slowly removed the calfskin gloves, then placed them on the side table and held out his hands to her. She grasped his hands, and he pulled her to her feet. She freed a hand and grasped a cane, and then another. She made her way into the dining room on her two canes, inch by inch, breathing heavily with the effort.

"Who brought you home tonight?" she asked.

"No one," Henker said.

"You came home alone?"

"I had no choice," Henker said as he sat. "None of my so-called fellow artists were left when I was ready to go."

"Were you late in leaving?"

"No."

"Then how did you come home?"

He heard her in the kitchenette lighting the tiny stove, the clinking of china cups.

"I had to follow groups of people," Henker said. "I stayed close to as many as I could find who were headed this way."

"That can't have looked good."

"What else could I do?"

"You could defy them, Hans—the police, whoever's following you. You could just walk anywhere you like, whenever you like. You've nothing to be afraid of. They must certainly know that by now. As for that, they might not be following you anymore."

"Oh, they are. Just last night one of their henchmen knocked me down in the street, pretended it was an accident. It was no accident. I was being searched. Oh, they won't let me alone."

"Except for your fellow artists."

"I wish you wouldn't call them that."

"They're jealous, that's all."

"Why?"

"Well, I'm quite sure none of them has received a visit from Herr Max Spindler, Hansel. When will you quit the Traumhalle?"

Henker rose and removed his coat. It was cooler at the top of the house, and Mathilde kept all of the windows open; the light breeze eased his discomfort.

"Tomorrow night will be my final performance," he said.

"And then on to bigger things," came the voice from the kitchen.

"Yes," Henker said. He absently gazed at the detritus they'd collected over the years and placed around their rooms: ancient volumes, gramophone records, elephants carved from jade, his war medals.

"Your coffee will be ready soon," Mathilde said, returning from the kitchenette. "Get some rest."

"Yes."

"It went well tonight, otherwise?"

"Full house."

"Splendid."

"Except..." he said, and stopped.

"Yes?"

He shook his head. "The fellow who volunteered," he said.

"What about him?"

"I don't know."

"What don't you know? What did he do?"

"Nothing," Henker said. "That is, he... well, he seemed to trust me, Tillie."

"Trust you?"

"Perhaps *trust* isn't the word. He... Tillie, he seemed to *know*."

Mathilde gazed at him for a moment. It was a hard look.

"Impossible," she said. She turned and made her slow, painful way to her room. "Good night, Hansel."

"I've been thinking of taking rooms at the Hotel Das Gottesanbeterin," Henker said. "A suite. I can afford it now. Would that make you happy?"

"Happiness," Mathilde said as she struggled into the void of her room, "happiness..."

CHAPTER TWENTY
THE GIRL WHO SMELLED OF LICORICE

FRANZ WAS AWAKENED by an eerie hum that seemed to change pitch in a syrupy way. At first, he assumed he had been dreaming of the legendary Sirens, who sang to sailors passing their rocks and lured them to their watery deaths. Franz was not a sailor, but a ship, and as he dreamed he sailed on with determination, all the while trying to warn those aboard him that they needed to stop their ears, to resist; yet one by one they jumped into the sea, succumbing to the waves as the Sirens sang on, while he, without anyone at his helm, faced his eventual destruction and sinking.

When he opened his eyes, however, he beheld Inspector Beide—in full female mode—standing behind a tray of wine glasses, each filled with various quantities of colored liquid, circling this rim, then that with her hands.

Franz recognized the tune: "Vienna, City of My Dreams."

Beide stopped when she saw Franz was awake.

"Get dressed. You have five minutes," she said, wiping her wet hands on the miserable strip of curtain. "Things are happening, faster than I had anticipated."

"Leave the room," Franz said, drawing the bedsheet to his chin.

"There's nothing you've got I haven't seen," Beide said, "or am not personally well acquainted with, if you know what I mean. Hurry up. I have a car waiting for us outside."

"Well, I'd hardly expect it to be waiting *inside*."

"Oh, you're one of *those* people. I suppose I deserve that. At any rate, hurry."

"If you're in such a hurry, why did you waste time playing those wine glasses you brought in?"

"I didn't bring them in. They were here, set up and ready to go. I assumed you'd been practicing. Aren't they yours?"

"They are not."

"You're passing yourself off as a verrilionist," Beide said. "They must be yours."

Franz swung himself out of bed and reached for his socks and underthings. "Oh, that's just terrific," he said, dressing. "A verrilionist..."

"Plays the glass harp," Beide said. "Is there no room to pace in this room?"

"You don't need to pace when you're impatient. Did you say glass harp? It's just a bunch of wine glasses filled with... dare I ask what's in them?"

"Wine, of course," Beide said. Franz reached for one and drank, and promptly spit the mouthful into the washbasin.

"That wasn't wine," he said.

"You shouldn't be drinking this early in the morning," Beide said. She sat on the bed, watching Franz with fascination as he put on his shoes.

"You put on your shoes before your put on your trousers?" Beide asked.

"Stop looking at me. If you need to busy yourself until I'm ready, begin by removing that..."

"Glass harp."

"...from my room."

"I told you, it's yours. You told that woman you were a verrilionist; suppose she comes in one day and finds there's nothing here but your clothes and piles of manuscripts? With your real name right under the titles?"

"But I can't play the thing," Franz said.

"Then you shouldn't have told her you could."

Franz was about to place the blame on Gregor, but caught himself just in time. He wondered where the vexing creature had gone. Nothing but silence came from beneath the bed. Franz took his trousers from the foot of the bed and carefully pulled them on.

"Incredible," Beide said. "I ask again: why put your shoes on before you put on your trousers?"

"In case there's a fire," Franz said, turning away to button his fly.

"So it's better to be fully shod as you escape from a burning building than trouserless?"

"Look," Franz said, putting on the rest of his clothes, "why don't you forget about me, my habits, and my lack of musical ability and tell me what's happened? Has there been another murder?"

"Indeed there has," Beide said.

"Good grief," Franz said. "That's the second night in a row, isn't it? There was one on Wednesday night, now last night. Who was it this time?"

"She was what some Victorian novelists referred to as a 'woman of easy virtue.'"

"A prostitute."

"Well, not exactly."

"Explain."

"She didn't walk the streets."

Franz buttoned his vest as fast as he could, discovered he'd misbuttoned, and started over again. "I don't understand," he said.

"Talk of sex making you nervous?"

"No. And we're not talking of sex, we're talking about a... a whatever-you-want-to-call-her. She was known to you?"

"Let's just say she was a familiar figure to the local constabulary."

"'To' or 'with'?"

"That's another line of inquiry altogether. Regardless, they identified her right away. She is—was—Immerplatz Inge."

"Because she lived on Immerplatz, no doubt. What a creative nickname."

"Well, she began her career on Immerplatz, but she's been operating out of a rather elegant address on the Flumstrasse these last few years."

"Who found her?"

"Not a *who*, a *what*."

Franz had a feeling he did not want to know what Beide meant by that, but asked anyway.

"A cat," Beide said.

"And this cat reported it to the police?"

"Inge Hersch employed a charwoman. You know what a charwoman is?"

"Of course I do. There's one plays a prominent role in one of my stories, the one—"

"Oh, yes, the one about the poor fool who turns into a big bug. Anyway—"

"That hardly does the story justice, Inspector; in fact, it—"

"At six o'clock this morning, the charwoman arrived by way of the rear entrance to the property and house by unlocking the wooden door into a small yard behind the house. She found several cats gathered at the back door all agitated. She assumed they were her mistress's pets—"

"Why did she assume that? Didn't she *know* whether Fraulein Hersch had pets?"

"She told the police that the deceased was a whimsical woman whose purchasing habits emphasized impulse over necessity, and *anything* could have been purchased since she had last seen her the morning before."

Franz shuddered. "May I guess the rest, even though the thought disgusts me?"

"You may."

"The charwoman opened the door, the cats ran in, the charwoman busied herself with the fires and the preparation of a morning meal and, after an unusually long interval, went to look for the lady of the house... I take it the cats were *not* Fraulein Hersch's pets?"

"As far as we can ascertain, they were not domesticated creatures."

"And thus hungry."

"And not picky about what they ate," Beide concluded. "Perhaps it's a good thing you've missed breakfast."

Franz grabbed his pocket watch. Ten minutes past eight; Frau Alt had told him breakfast was at seven.

"Why did you let me sleep so late?" Franz asked.

"Because you were asleep," Beide said.

"That's not a rational answer."

"It is, and besides, you can't go visiting people at an indecent hour."

"People? Me? Visiting? What people?" Franz poured water into the basin and stooped to wash his face.

Beide smiled. "I'll bet you regret throwing away that third envelope now, don't you?"

"You and that envelope. Who are we visiting?"

"You said you needed to talk to people, and I agreed. I thought we'd begin with Hannah Bickel, as she's the freshest link we have to this case."

"Did she know this Immerplatz Inge?"

"No, no," Beide said. "Fraulein Bickel was at the theater with Herr Herbort on Wednesday night. She has nothing to do with Immerplatz Inge."

"And did Fraulein Bickel find Herr Herbort in his, um, posthumous state?"

"Oh, God, no. He was found by a couple of whores."

Franz bumped his head on an unexpected shelf, cursed, then realized he didn't know if there was a washcloth in the room or, if there was, where it was. Blinded, he groped for the curtain, walked into something, and heard the smashing of two dozen wine glasses as the delicate table hit the floor.

"Bravo," said Beide.

BEIDE'S AUTOMOBILE WAS everything Franz expected: sleek, black, and driven by an unseen driver.

Franz asked if he could roll down the opaque window that separated them from the front seat.

"You can't," said Beide, "and you shouldn't bother the driver while he's driving. What did you think of The Hanging Artist?"

"I didn't meet him."

"You saw his act."

Franz considered his response before he gave it. "And I never want to see it again," he said.

"Why not?"

"He displayed a certain disrespect for death," Franz said. "I suppose I expected someone more morose. Someone closer to my concept of a death's figure. And yet Henker was a very pleasant fellow. Nothing sallow or gaunt about him, as if he'd just enjoyed a good meal and was ready for parlor games. And then there was that infernal music from the gramophone. 'Ev'rybody shimmies now,' and all that."

"Did you volunteer when he solicited the audience?"

"I wasn't going to," Franz said, "but the vexing thing is that I found my hand in the air, just like everyone else. I can't account for it."

Beide became animated. "Oh, please tell me he chose you!" she said.

"He did not," Franz said. "That would have been a little too convenient, wouldn't you say?"

"How do you mean?"

"Then I would have known for certain this has all been staged for my benefit."

"All this?"

"Every last minute of it, from the time I awoke fit and able on Wednesday morning until now. Had I been picked from the crowd on my first visit to The Hanging Artist, well… then I'd have no doubt I was in some other hellish realm instead of the hellish realm I'm used to living in."

"Be that as it may—who was the volunteer?"

"Some fellow in a loud suit."

"Loud?"

"Checkered. A broad check, too, like the store-bought suits you see bumpkins purchase when they decide to make a big splash in the city."

Beide laughed. "You certainly are a snob," she said. "But go on. You were criticizing Henker's performance."

"No, I wasn't. As far as I could tell, it was flawless. I was explaining why I have no desire to sit through it again. There was the unsettling show of that rope flying up and entwining itself around the gallows, and him smiling all the while, talking about justice and judgment and… and it was all rather confusing."

"And that ghastly finale. Henker, just hanging there."

"And the crowd?"

"No one moved. No one said a word. How could we? The curtain came down, we just sat there. We knew it was an act, that it *had* to be an act, but I'll be damned if it didn't seem all too real. And no comfort of rectitude; no parting of the curtains to reveal Henker unsullied and smiling.

"It was awful."

"Yes," Beide said, her voice growing coarse, "awful is the word for it."

"I DON'T KNOW anyone who didn't adore Hermann," Hannah Bickel said to the Inspector and Franz. "I've said that so many times since Wednesday night and, truly, I've given it much thought, too. I simply can't think of anyone who wanted to do him the least bit of harm, let alone…" She put her hand to her throat.

Beide had changed to his masculine self during the ride across town to the notions shop at which Hannah Bickel was employed, much to Beide's own chagrin, as "…women are more comfortable around me when I'm… well, let's just say I wish I had some control over this." Franz hadn't known what to say.

Fraulein Bickel had shown them nothing but cordiality, however, and had seemed to be especially taken with the handsome, boyish Inspector. "It's the uniform," Beide remarked later when Franz pointed it out to him.

Franz had been relieved to learn he wouldn't have to continue his masquerade as Monsieur Choucas while speaking with the—what, exactly? Witnesses? Suspects? He could be plain old Herr Kafka, an insurance investigator.

"All I need to know, Fraulein Bickel," Kafka said to her, "is what went on Wednesday evening, particularly at the Traumhalle."

"Why particularly there?" Hannah asked.

Franz caught Beide looking at him as if to caution him not to tip his hat to The Hanging Artist; it was unnecessary: Franz had no intention of leading the girl down that path. He felt, for some reason, that too much emphasis was being placed on Henker and his novel, albeit disturbing, act.

"The music hall is a public place," Franz said, "and, as such, a hub of humanity. Someone could have seen Herr Herbort at the theater, or followed him there, or followed him afterwards."

"You mean like a thief, or…?"

"I don't know what I mean until I hear your account of the evening; that is, up until the time he left you."

"He didn't leave me; I left him," Hannah said.

Franz forgot what he was going to say when he heard this, and tore off in another direction.

"I was told he escorted you to your home," Franz said.

"He did."

"And yet you say you left him, not the other way 'round?"

"What's the difference?"

Franz thought a moment, and decided to correct himself. He had been thinking of her as a girl, when in fact she was a woman, and now he wondered what it was had made him think of her as a girl; possibly the sharp aroma of licorice she exuded.

Or the mixture of eagerness, fear, and sadness she displayed whenever she spoke of the late Hermann Herbort. It was the way she put things: "adore," and "I left him," even "Hermann," when "Herr Herbort" would have been appropriate in this semi-official interview.

"You fancied him," Franz said. "I understand."

Hannah waited before she spoke. "All of us did," she said. "But Adeline and Frieda—my other friends who I was out with that night—were only interested in his looks."

"You didn't care about his looks," Franz said. "You felt something deeper. Less superficial. And you didn't realize that until you got him to kiss you, and it frightened you, a little. I understand."

"How can you understand?" Hannah asked.

"Because you said you left him," Franz said, "when, in fact, if you were already home, it would have meant that he would have left you. But you kissed him, and you had that troubling realization, and you fled from a feeling you'd never encountered before—you felt that if you lingered with him any longer, you couldn't be responsible for your actions…"

"I've never done anything—"

"Of course you haven't," Franz said. "You've told me as much without actually saying it. I'm not scolding you or anything; as I say, I understand. You left him because you felt that anything further that night would have caused you to compromise yourself, or at least give him the idea that you could be compromised."

Hannah studied her lap. She looked up, her eyes wet.

"And what does any of that have to do with insurance?" she asked.

Beide interrupted. "You'd be surprised. Herr Kafka is very... *modern*, and, um, well, the details of the evening are what we are after. For Herr Kafka's benefit."

Hannah sighed, shrugged, and repeated the events for Franz: how the seven of them had decided to go to the Traumhalle to see The Hanging Artist—

"Seven?" asked Franz.

"Yes, seven of us," Hannah said. "Us girls and the Bank Boys."

"The Bank Boys?"

"They work at Citizens Bank. We call them the Bank Boys, which I suppose means we're not too original when it comes to... well, anyway, that night it was myself, Hermann, Adeline, Frieda, Peter Schussler, Georg Jaeger, and—oh, yes—Prinsky. Robert Prinsky."

"Was someone unable to join you?"

"How do you mean?"

"It sounds to me," Franz said, "as if your little theatre party was meant to be an octet, not a septet."

"Why do you think there was supposed be eight of us?"

"The division of sexes," Franz said, ignoring Beide's inquisitive stare. "Three women, four men. A couples' evening out. Which leads me to believe that there was another woman who couldn't make it, or..."

"...Or?" Beide asked.

Franz sat back, blushing. "I'm sorry," he said to Hannah. "Perhaps it's better if you told the story, not me."

"You're suggesting there was some sort of matching up going on," Hannah said. "I suppose, in a way, there was. But, then again, there wasn't."

Beide cleared his throat and said, "So you all went to the theater, bought your tickets, sat down..."

But Franz wouldn't let go of the thread.

"I don't mean to be personal about this," he said, startling Hannah as he leaned forward again, "but this is a very personal business, you understand, I mean it should be *considered* a very personal business, what happened to Hermann. If there was no intentional matching up going on, then it was unintentional. And if there wasn't a fourth girl—and I see now that there wasn't, since you so charmingly intimated that the evening was simply meant to be a group of young people out to have a good time and, underneath, to see if things naturally sorted themselves out amongst you by evening's end."

"I don't know how to answer that," said Hannah.

"It wasn't a question," Franz said, "I'm just piecing the picture together, in my mind, based on the odd way you've put things."

"Odd?"

"Not odd, that's the wrong word, forgive me. Unique. Not just unique to you, but unique to the situation. And judging by the look on your face, I'm making this worse that it already is. I'll stop there."

Hannah blinked and looked to Beide for help, but Beide only shrugged and asked her to continue recounting the evening's events. She backtracked to how everyone had taken supper together and walked to the theater, had chatted out front before going in—

"How did you go in?" Franz said. Beide sighed at the new interruption.

"By the front door, of course," Hannah said.

"I mean, did all seven of you go in together? At the same time? As a group?"

"Oh. No, as a matter of fact, we didn't."

"Ah. How, then?"

"Is it important?"

"I don't know."

"Adeline and Frieda and Georg and Peter went in, but

Hermann didn't. I started to go in, but I saw that Hermann hadn't joined us, so I turned back, and there he was."

"Why hadn't he gone in?"

"He just hadn't. He seemed lost in thought."

"About what?"

"He didn't say, and I didn't ask."

Franz sat back and scratched his chin. What was he trying to achieve with these questions? What, in fact, difference did it make how these young people had taken their seats that night? These half dozen people, these…

No, he was wrong. Seven, not six. Why had he forgotten the seventh already?

"Because you didn't mention him," he said aloud.

"Who didn't I mention?" Hannah asked, startled.

"The seventh fellow. What was his name? Pinksy or something like that?"

"Oh," Hannah said. "Prinsky. Yes, I'd forgotten. He may have gone in with the others, he may have hung back or gone to the gentleman's lounge or done any number of things, I didn't notice."

"Prinsky," Beide said to Franz, "was chosen as Henker's volunteer at that night's performance."

"Yes," Franz said. "Tell me about that."

"There's nothing much to tell," Hannah said. "When the time came for The Hanging Artist to request a volunteer to come to the stage and inspect the… rope… and his person, we all raised our hands; that is, all of us except myself and Hermann, and…"

"Why didn't you raise your hands?" asked Beide. Franz smiled at him.

"Oh, Inspector, don't embarrass the girl," he said. "It's obvious."

"It is?"

"Their hands were otherwise occupied."

"Herr Kafka!" Hannah said.

"I mean you were holding hands, ma'am," Kafka said as she turned the color of a beet. "Am I right?"

"You don't have to answer that," Beide said. "Herr Kafka isn't trying to rattle you, he knows that would be disrespectful, not to say counterproductive. Now, then. How did The Hanging Artist come to choose Herr Prinsky?"

"He just did," Hannah said.

"How many in the audience had raised their hands?" Franz asked.

"Most."

"And it was a full house that night?"

"Oh, yes. Packed. Awful hot, too."

"And where were your seats?"

"Our seats?"

"Were they close to the stage?"

"Oh, no, we were about three-quarters back. It was the only section we could find six together."

"Seven," Franz said. "See? You've forgotten Herr Prinsky again."

"I just don't have a habit of thinking that much about him."

"You don't like him."

"I didn't say that."

"You didn't have to. Every time you refer to him, you call him 'Prinsky.' Not 'Robert,' nor even 'Herr Prinsky,' which would at least be polite, if coldly formal."

"I never said I disliked him."

"But there's something about him that causes you to dismiss him," Franz said. "And I think the others do, too. 'Prinsky'— maybe you picked up that way of referring to him from the other men?"

Hannah thought about that. "Perhaps you're right, sir," she said.

"Did you find it odd that Henker picked Prinsky, considering he was sitting so far back?" Beide asked.

"I don't think she was considering anything other than Herr

Herbort," Franz said. "But you paid attention to Prinsky when he went on stage?"

"Well, yes, of course; there he was, fiddling around with the rope and looking like a baboon."

"How did he handle the rope?" Beide asked.

"He took it from The Hanging Artist," Hannah said slowly, intent on recollection, "and held it with both hands, turned it this way and that... and then The Hanging Artist coiled the rope and put it on the chair... and he turned back and asked Prinsky to search him. Oh—he took off his coat before he asked."

"And Herr Prinsky searched him."

"I suppose," she said. "He fumbled a bit, but I guess he got a bit more comfortable and made a thorough job of it. The record was playing, you see, and that made things a bit more cheery. And The Hanging Artist laughed once or twice, said Prinsky was tickling him. It was all very light and silly, you see. We didn't see what all the fuss was about—I mean about The Hanging Artist."

"And then?"

"He asked Prinsky if he was satisfied. Prinsky said yes. And he returned to his seat."

"And then?"

Hannah's expression darkened.

"Have you seen the act, sir?" she asked Beide.

Beide nodded sympathetically.

Hannah concluded her account of the evening by reporting that after the show they all went their several ways, everyone much quieter and more sober than when they had gone in. As for her, she had walked home with Hermann Herbort, although both of them were silent for much of the time.

"We didn't really know what to make of what we'd seen, sir," she said.

She affirmed that when she and Herr Herbort had arrived at the door, the scene was just as Franz had described. It was the last she saw of Hermann.

She began to cry.

"It was an awful night in every way, wasn't it?" she asked, as Beide gave her his handkerchief. "I'll never forget it as long as I live." She blew her nose and said, "Although God knows I'll keep trying."

"THAT WAS QUITE an original line of… questioning," Beide said to Franz as they rode away from the shop.

"Are you being critical?" asked Franz.

"No," Beide said as carefully as possible.

"I told you I'm no detective," Franz said. "But you insisted—begged—I get involved in this."

"I know."

"And now you're having second thoughts. I don't blame you."

"About your involvement? Not at all. If I'm having second thoughts about anything, it's about this Prinsky person. You seemed to keep circling back to him."

"Only because she kept circling away from him."

"Do you suspect him? The man has an airtight alibi for the time of Herbort's death."

"You're sure about that?"

Beide attempted to not bristle at the suggestion. "A tavern full of people can swear to it," he said.

"All strangers to him? I find it hard to believe that so many people, at that time of night, and in varied stages of inebriation, could recall a person who, from the impression I've been getting, is one of the most overlooked and unmemorable people on this planet, let alone in Vienna."

"Herr Prinsky became quite drunk and spent the bulk of his evening singing bawdy songs at the top of his lungs."

"I see."

"But you still think he somehow managed to kill Herbort."

"I don't know what I think."

"Yes, you do."

Franz braced himself as the car lurched around a corner.

"I'm thinking of Prinsky—of what it must be like to be him," Franz said. "And I'm hesitant to admit that I don't find it too much of a stretch to know what it must be like."

"A nothing, a nobody… as you described yourself yesterday, as I recall."

"Yes," Franz said, turning his head and gazing out the window. "Something like that."

"But why would Prinsky want to kill Herbort?"

"Why would such an unremarkable, unprepossessing person, who is clearly viewed as an annoyance by the people he thinks are his friends, who is probably always the odd man out on the few social occasions where he finds himself in the company of women and seen in comparison with a Hermann Herbort, who is—was—tall, handsome, aloof, and the object of all feminine attention? Why would he kill someone like that? The question, Inspector," Franz said, "is why *wouldn't* he kill someone like that?"

"We'll talk to him again, if you like."

"I think we should."

Beide, as brightly as possible, asked, "Shall we go see a corpse?"

CHAPTER TWENTY-ONE
A CONVERSATION OVER A CORPSE

FRANZ'S FIRST TWO thoughts were that Inge Hersch did not look peaceful and that he was glad that he had not eaten breakfast.

Franz had been met by two medical attendants in the morgue, the more senior attendant much younger than the junior, which ought to have surprised Franz, but life was fresh out of surprises for him. The senior—and younger—attendant noticed Franz's greenish complexion and drew the sheet over the corpse.

"Perhaps you'd like some water, Inspector Kafka," he said. "Enzel, get the inspector some water."

"I'm fine," Franz said, looking around. There were three more sheeted figures in the morgue. He braced himself on the slab and took a deep breath. "Coming in from the heat like that," Franz said, "I suppose I haven't adjusted as well as I ought."

Enzel had gone for the water anyway, and returned now with a glass for Franz.

"Inspector," he said, glancing at his superior.

"You don't listen," the young man said. "The inspector said he didn't want any. Or maybe it's that you don't hear. Eh?"

Enzel didn't answer. The younger man shook his head and shrugged to Franz. "These new recruits, they're all alike. What can you do?"

Beide had left Franz at the entrance, citing an urgent telephone call, which Franz had suspected was a lie. Beide had practically pushed him through the door, saying, "I've already seen her, and I want you to do your thing without me breathing over your shoulder."

"My thing?" Franz had asked.

"Go," Beide had said.

As for the two attendants, they had accepted Kafka as the insurance investigator he said he was, and had shown him the cold remains of Immerplatz Inge without batting an eye.

Franz collected himself, and thought of the best questions to ask.

"You put the time of death as just after midnight?" he asked the young man.

The young man consulted his wristwatch. "It's my opinion that, as of this moment, this woman has been dead for not more than twelve hours and not less than ten, which means the time of death what just before midnight or just after midnight."

"But not *at* midnight," Franz said.

The young man gave Franz a dry look, but managed to say, "It could be exactly at midnight, yes, of course. But we'll never know, for certain. That's how it is. Unless the murderer tells us."

"Then she was definitely murdered?"

The young man motioned to Enzel and the old man drew back the sheet again.

"She sure as hell didn't do that to herself," the young man said, referring to the twisted, bruised neck.

"I beg your pardon, Dr. Wolberg," Enzel said, "but you said yourself earlier that she *could* do that to herself."

Wolberg gave his assistant a withering look.

"Did I say those exact words, Enzel?" he asked. "Or did I speculate?"

Enzel looked down. "You speculated, sir," he said.

Wolberg turned to Franz. "You must understand," he said,

"they bring these bodies in here, I take a look, I say 'Oh, suicide!' because of the marks, you know, and then they tell me they didn't commit suicide, and I say it's not possible, and they say 'Oh, really?' and I say if it's not suicide then someone made it look like suicide, and then everybody gets very officious and starts harrumphing and I'm told to keep my mouth shut and told to do an autopsy anyway."

"Autopsy?" Franz asked. He looked down at the Y-shaped stitching across the corpse's chest. He braced himself on the slab again.

"I'm sure you've requested thousands yourself," Wolberg said, "in your line of work, that is. Even when the corpse in question hasn't been hanged... or *chewed,* as it turns out."

Franz remembered the cats and blanched. "Yes, of course, so many," he said, piling on another lie to the many he'd told that day. "May I ask what, if anything, you found?"

"You mean like stomach contents?" Wolberg asked.

"Only," Franz said, closing his eyes, "if there was anything unusual."

"Oh, there's something unusual all right," Wolberg said. "Perhaps not particularly unusual for a woman in her—ahem—profession, that is, but... Well, she was riddled with syphilis."

"Syphilis?"

"You know what syphilis is, right?"

"Yes, but..."

Wolberg looked down at the remains of Inge Hersch as if appraising a ruined beefsteak dinner. "How old would you say this woman was, Inspector? Even if you already know, take a glance and give me your first impression."

Franz looked. Gray and washed, denuded of paint and powder, he guessed fifty-five.

"Thirty-one," Wolberg said. "And it is my opinion that she wouldn't have lasted the rest of the year, not in her condition. Wouldn't you agree, Enzel?"

"I, er..."

"I forgot, you don't have an opinion yet," Wolberg said, winking at Franz.

"And she knew of her condition?" Franz asked.

"I don't see how it could have escaped her notice. Not with *that* face."

Inge Hersch's face looked hammered, sunken. There was practically nothing left of her nose.

"And am I to understand that this woman, um… earned her living by…"

"Entertaining gentleman?" Wolberg asked, grinning.

"That's a much more delicate way of putting it, yes."

"Give him the nose," Wolberg said to Enzel, who nodded and went to a side table, returning with a triangular hunk of white material which he handed to Franz.

"Keep it as a souvenir," Wolberg said.

"What is this?" Franz asked.

"What's it look like?"

"A nose."

"You'd make a fine anatomist," Wolberg said, chuckling, and allowing his elder assistant what must have been a rare communal laugh. "It is indeed a nose. Carved ivory. A beautiful job, too, I might add. You see," he said, drawing Franz's attention to Inge's sunken face, "tertiary syphilis causes superficial and deep ulcerations, along with destruction of the bony framework of the nose and shrinking of the fibroid tissues. Sufferers have been using false noses for centuries. If she kept her lights low and her cosmetics thick and balanced, she could still receive her illicit lovers without much fear of detection. Although there'd be quite an uproar if she ever sneezed."

Wolberg and Enzel laughed heartily at that. Franz didn't much care for the men's flippancy.

He returned the false nose to Enzel. "Then she had every reason to commit suicide."

"Yes."

"And yet you say that she couldn't have done that to herself," Franz said, gesturing at the dead woman's twisted neck.

"You insurance people," Wolberg said, "are all alike. You always want it to be suicide. Never want to pay up, do you? Listen, I stand by what I said. She couldn't have done that to herself and then disposed of the rope."

"How many of these ropeless suicides…"

"…murders…"

"…have come through your morgue, sir?"

Wolberg looked at Enzel and raised an eyebrow. Enzel was slow to get the hint, then said, "Oh," and walked over to a corner desk, where he flipped through pages of a thick ledger for a few moments. "Eleven," he said eventually.

"Eleven," Wolberg answered.

Something occurred to Franz, and for a full second he thought that he was about to be brilliant.

"Tell me," he said, "about the murderer."

"The murderer?"

"In your opinion, could the murderer have come up behind her, slipped the rope or noose around her neck, and choked her from behind?"

Wolberg appeared stupefied.

"I've no idea," he said.

"No," Enzel said, approaching the slab. "This woman was clearly hanged." He pointed an arthritic finger at the impressions on the neck. "The rope always leaves a trace of its path of execution. Notice how the marks are here, tight across her throat, up under the chin and behind the ears. Asphyxiation from behind, well, you get the entire neck, like a collar, it's generally uniform. But here—and with the others—they were hanged from above. Yanked off their feet, by the looks of it."

Wolberg blinked at Enzel. "And how," he asked, "do you know this, Enzel?"

"I used to work at the prison," Enzel said. "I had to cut them down after they swung."

Wolberg smiled at Franz. "Well," he said, "*that* certainly kills the conversation, doesn't it?"

"Thirty-one," Franz said thoughtfully, gazing at Inge Hersch. "I, myself, am only forty."

"Beg pardon?"

"I used to think that was old," Franz continued, "that it was ten years more than I should have been allowed. May I?" He took the sheet and drew it over the corpse. "Had things gone as I expected them to go, I'd be staring down at myself, and you'd be pulling the sheet over me."

"Inspector?" Enzel asked.

Franz looked at them. "Musings of a Lazarus," he said. "I apologize. You see hundreds of dead bodies, you never get used to it." And he would strive to never see one ever again, let alone hundreds.

"Oh, you get used to it," Wolberg said. "Somewhere around the sixth or seventh, I'd say. At any rate—is there anything else we can do for you, Inspector?"

"I can't think of anything. You've been very helpful."

"Did she carry a great deal of insurance, Inspector?" Enzel asked.

"How's that?"

"On her life."

Franz glanced for the last time at the impersonal sheet drawn over the wasted figure. "Let me put it to you this way," he said. "No matter how much, it's never enough, is it?"

His words echoed in the cold chamber.

CHAPTER TWENTY-TWO
AN IMPROVISED INTERVIEW

FRANZ KAFKA STOOD in front of the morgue, thankful for the heat, and cursing Inspector Beide. The inspector was nowhere to be found—in either form—nor the sleek black automobile.

He wished he was more familiar with Vienna, but he also wished he knew what he was supposed to do next. He knew what was expected of him—to put an end to the murders, or at least lead the authorities to the culprit so they could.

But Franz could think of no way he could do that.

First off, there were too many murders that were too disconnected and too far apart. Aside from bearing the markings of having been hanged, there was nothing to link the two dozen currently known together.

Currently known. Were there unknown murders, too?

Franz shuddered at the thought.

Second, the connection to The Hanging Artist was tenuous at best. Yes, the man's act was many things, including tasteless, sensational, macabre, and disturbing, but the man himself appeared to be above suspicion given the known facts. Why this focus on Henker? Franz felt it was a waste of time.

Third, he was getting nowhere.

He paced in front of the morgue, hands in his pockets, and

waited for Beide to appear.

And what of Beide? As far as Franz could tell, Beide seemed to be the only person working on the cases. Wasn't the entirety of Vienna's police force committed to solving these crimes? If so, why had he not seen any other official? True, Beide had claimed to be a member of the mysterious "ICPC," but why would Beide operate alone? The scope of the murders was too great for one person.

Two people, Franz thought. I'm mixed up in this, too.

Franz went over what little he knew about some of the victims. According to Hannah Bickel, Hermann Herbort was nothing more than a handsome young man, and no one would profit by his death. As for Inge Hersch, her reputation as some sort of professional mistress might not have won her any awards for good conduct or pristine morals, but who would have wanted to kill her, especially if her health would have put a stop to her in a few months anyway?

Some nearby clock struck the hour of eleven. A church? The town hall? A bank?

A bank...

Franz startled a young woman pushing a perambulator by asking her in a highly excited manner for directions to the Citizens Bank. The young woman obliged, and Franz was off and running down the street.

ROBERT PRINSKY COULDN'T decide if the gentleman from Zurich was an utter moron or an inveterate ass. From the looks of him, anyone might think him a schoolteacher or even a Lutheran minister, with his high cheekbones, gaunt features, and severe demeanor. But to hear him talk...

"Herr Herbort had no business telling you that, sir," Prinsky said. "Not that it would have done you the least bit of harm, of course, you would have been directed to the correct person, which would be me, but... well, that's as it may be."

"God rest his soul," the gentleman said, crossing himself.

Not Lutheran, Prinsky observed.

"Yes," Prinsky said. "Indeed."

"If only I'd returned to Vienna sooner," the man continued, "I could have seen him before his unfortunate accident."

"It wasn't an accident," Prinsky said. "Now then, let's see what we can…"

"I just assumed it was an accident," the gentleman said. He looked around the big, cheerless bank, shafts of weak sunshine dropping in from high windows. "You know, it's funny: I walked in and saw all of the employees wearing black armbands, and I thought, 'What an unusual dress requirement for a bank!' and then I thought, 'That's nonsense, I must have entered a mortuary by mistake!' and then I thought, 'No, I see a vault,' and then I reasoned that someone very important must have died." He beamed at Prinsky, as if proud of his chain of thought.

"No, no one important," Prinsky said. "Herr Herbort was hardly important." He glanced at a framed photo on his tiny desk.

"He must have been quite popular," said the other man, surveying the employees. "All of you are in mourning; that is to say, it's a very somber picture, everyone in armbands, and—oh. Well, everyone but you."

Prinsky cast a glance at the unadorned sleeve of his gray suit and shifted his gaze back to the gentleman from Zurich.

"I… yes," he said. "I had to remove it, you see, because… it was too tight, my arm kept falling asleep."

"How inconvenient for you. I don't recall Herr Herbort being ill."

"Beg pardon?"

"Well, if he didn't have an accident, I assume it was some illness?"

Prinsky cleared his throat and lowered his voice. "He was killed," he said.

"You mean he was *murdered?*" the stranger asked, with such force that everyone in the bank turned around.

"Yes," Prinsky said, "and if would be so good as to lower your voice…"

"But who would want to kill such a nice man as Herr Herbort?" the gentleman asked, even louder.

"I'm sure I don't know. Now, then, as to the sorts of accounts we have available…"

"So full of life," the stranger said. "So young, so much potential, and such a good-looking man. I quite envied him in that regard. I know it's a sign of vanity to admit it, but… well, *you* understand."

Prinsky glanced at the photo on his desk. "Yes, yes," he said, "a tragedy. We were all aghast."

"Naturally. You saw him day after day, right here… and socially?"

"As a matter of fact, he went to the theater with us the night he met his unfortunate end."

The gentleman from Zurich smiled. "Ah, yes. He was a great patron of the theater."

"How well did you say you knew him, Herr…?"

"My dear Herr Prinsky, one doesn't have to know someone their entire life to know a great deal about someone."

"I suppose that's true," Prinsky said. "Now, as to the transfer of foreign accounts to our…"

"I hope he enjoyed his final outing," the stranger said.

"I have no idea. He seemed to be having a good time."

"Oh! You were with him?"

"In a manner of speaking. There was a group of us, and he…"

"Had you gone to the Musikverein? I adore that place."

"No, Traumhalle."

The stranger gave the dyspeptic-looking little man a look of kinship mixed with surprise.

"What a small and completely bewildering world we live in," he said. "I was there last evening!" He leaned closer to Prinsky and, with a knowing looked, whispered, "The Hanging Artist."

Prinsky paled. "Yes, indeed," he said.

"A performance I'll never forget."

"No," Prinsky said.

"I see you were affected by it the same way as I."

"It was singular."

"And I tried so hard to be chosen to join him on the stage," the gentleman said, sitting back. "The man's a genius. Imagine what a privilege it would be to be near him! To assure myself that he isn't a… a… a phantom!"

Prinsky tugged at his sleeves. "As a matter of fact, sir," he said, betraying the hint of a smile, "I shared the stage with him for a moment."

The gentleman from Zurich's eyes widened. "Go on," he said.

"It was… unique."

"You searched him thoroughly?"

"Short of asking him to strip, yes."

"And you found…?"

"Nothing. Nothing but the man himself, that is."

"And the rope?"

"It was just a rope," Prinsky said.

"Surely it was more than that."

"Well, a rope of silk, to be sure."

"To be sure."

"Warm to the touch."

"Interesting!"

"I credited that to the stage lights. It was hot as blazes up on that stage."

The man regarded him for a moment or two while Prinsky wiped his hands on a handkerchief.

"Your wife must have been so proud of you," the gentleman said.

"My wife?" Prinsky asked.

"I sense that you are the most devoted of husbands," the other said, "and you are to be congratulated."

"And how do you sense that?" Prinsky asked.

"Pardon me for noticing, sir," the man said, "but you have been stealing glances at the photograph on your desk. No doubt it's of your wife. She is a lucky woman."

Prinsky hesitated, then reached for the photograph as his brow cleared.

"It's kind of you to say so," he said, handing it to the stranger. "I consider myself equally as lucky."

The gentleman looked at the photograph: a snapshot of Hannah Bickel. He returned it to Prinsky.

"The picture of youth and beauty," he said.

"Now, then," Prinsky said, restoring Hannah's photo to its hallowed spot on the desk, "how much were you thinking of depositing today?"

The man looked at him, began to say something, and then searched his coat pockets.

"Ah, yes," he said, "money. Money. Naturally. The reason I'm here. Now where did I put my billfold? I must have…"

Two men entered the bank just then, each in black uniforms, caps, and capes. One looked straight at the gentleman and Prinsky and nudged his companion, and the two strode to Prinsky's desk. They stood on either side of the gentleman, each placing a hand on his shoulders.

"You're wanted," one said.

"By whom?" the gentleman from Zurich asked.

They hoisted him from the chair and propelled him across the lobby.

"Immediately," said the other, "if not sooner."

"Now just a moment—!" were the last words Prinsky heard from the gentleman from Zurich. He watched as the trio banged out of the bank.

He dabbed at his straggly moustache with his handkerchief, glanced at the photo of Hannah, and wiped the perspiration from his hands for the forty-eighth time that day.

CHAPTER TWENTY-THREE
THE UNSETTLED GUEST

FRANZ HAD NO time to recall that a mere hour-and-a-half previously he had vowed to never see another corpse, as the sight of the second prompted him to faint.

Later, he would attribute this to missing breakfast.

At the moment, however, he attributed it to the corpse itself, hanging from the ceiling, its face black, its tongue protruding, its eyes nearly out of its sockets, indecorously presented without clothing.

MANY SAY THAT the only way to appreciate the Old World grandeur of the Hotel Das Gottesanbeterin is to approach it as royalty of a century past once had: sedately, by horse-drawn carriage, past the glorious Palais Windisch-Graetz, and then onto Tiefer Graben, where the hotel's eponymous mantis was displayed in terra cotta bas relief above the gleaming brass and polished wood of its grand entrance.

Franz, however, was denied such an atmospheric approach. The automobile into which he was forced by the two men raced down Taborstrasse and over the canal—the wrong way down Laurenzerberg, the wrong way along Fleischmarkt, and then up Wipplingerstrasse, where it screeched to a halt in front of the hotel. This was the only screech the automobile had produced; all of the other screeching had come from the many people nearly flattened by it during its record-breaking journey.

The two men had fairly carried Franz into the hotel; trapped between them and held by the elbows, he had been working up the language to deliver a livid remonstration when he was bundled into the elevator and whisked to the top floor. Once there, the doors slid open with such speed that one would assume they had been greased, and Franz had been propelled into a grand suite where the first thing he saw was…

ACRID SAL VOLATILE sent swift arrows into his brain, and his eyes opened.

To the naked corpse hanging above him.

He had not been mistaken.

"Very good, Herr Kafka," said a soothing feminine voice. "That's it. Come back to us. Gentlemen, some assistance."

Franz was conscious of hands hauling him to his feet, dragging him to a chair, and dumping him into it. Again, the lilting voice: "That's a brave boy."

Inspector Beide came into view, smiling.

"You've had quite the morning, haven't you?" she asked.

Franz gurgled a response.

"Water," Beide said, and a hand appeared with a full tumbler. Franz drank, looked up, winced, and sputtered.

"What," he asked, "is going on?"

"A great many things, as you've no doubt noticed," Beide said.

He took in his surroundings. Beide was accompanied by the two men who had rushed him to the hotel, and by two more men, similarly uniformed, lurking in a corner. One was setting up a camera on a tripod.

The suite itself was possibly the most elegant accommodation

Franz had ever been inside: the walls were papered in a shimmering pale yellow, the silver-gray drapery framed wide French windows, the white carpeting was as soft as fresh butter, and the furniture looked as if it had been transferred from the court of Louis XVI. A wide bed, big enough for a small family and draped with a satiny maroon-and-silver coverlet, dominated the room. It was unmade, and upon it a checkered suit had been meticulously laid out.

Franz recognized the garish suit at once.

He stole a look at the body hanging in the center of the room, one of the delicate chairs on its side beneath it. Disfigured as the face now was, he knew where he'd seen the man: the night before, on the stage at the Traumhalle.

He looked away.

"Must he stay up there?" he asked.

"All right, cut him down," Beide said to one of the men. "And don't be savages: care over expedience. And I want as much of that rope left intact as possible."

One of the men removed a pair of shears from a leather case while another moved an exquisitely carved chaise near the body.

Beide said, "Wait." Then, "Step aside."

The men stepped away from the body and the man with the camera took a photograph.

"One more, this side," Beide said.

The photographer crossed to Beide, reset the tripod, focused, and took a second photograph of the body from a new angle.

"Another in repose, when ready," Beide said to the photographer, who nodded. "And images of the room from each corner, as many as you like, but remember film is expensive."

She turned to the fourth man: "Inventory." He nodded as well.

The man with the shears climbed on top of the chaise while his partner stabilized it, and began to saw at the rope.

Beide turned to Franz.

"We don't have to sit and watch this," she said.

She led him to the anteroom, but kept the door to the bed chamber open in order to check on progress.

"Have you sufficiently collected yourself?" she asked.

"I'll be fine," Franz said. "Would you object if I loosened my necktie and collar?" he asked.

"Not in the least," Beide said. "Where have you been?"

"You know exactly where I've been," Franz said, "or you wouldn't have known where to send your goons. The question is, where have *you* been?"

"I apologize for leaving you with the late Inge Hersch; it couldn't be helped."

"You didn't answer my question."

Beide's attention drifted to the officers moving about the bed chamber. The shearsman was still working away at the rope.

"Leo Kropold," Beide said and, reaching into her tunic, withdrew a slim cigarette case and a lighter. "Cigarette?" she asked.

"I don't smoke," Franz said.

"It will cloud the smell of death." She lit a cigarette.

Franz discovered that he did indeed smoke.

"What was that name again—?"

Beide waited for his coughing to subside. "Better?"

Franz massaged his throat. "An all-too-familiar tightening," he said. "For different reasons, now, but still... go on, I'm fine."

"The gentleman hanging from the ceiling was Leo Kropold," Beide said. "At least, that is the name under which he was registered. He checked in three weeks ago—to the day. Gave his address as 'Bern,' which may or may not be the truth. We'll be checking on that, naturally.

"Regardless of his origin, Herr Kropold returned to the hotel last night at fifteen minutes past eleven. He asked the clerk to prepare his bill and to have it ready for him in the morning, as he had decided to leave."

"Is that what he said to the clerk? That he had decided to leave?"

"According to the clerk, yes. Why?"

"It would seem obvious that he was intending to leave if he asked for his bill. Why would he bother to point out the obvious?"

"I don't know," Beide said, blowing smoke. "Perhaps to make a point? After all, he had booked the suite for the month."

"I see. Notification of early departure."

"In more ways than one," Beide said, and put out her cigarette in a compact ashtray that she then covered and tucked into her tunic. "You're not satisfied."

"It doesn't make sense, that's all," Franz said. "A man returns to his hotel, asks for his bill to be prepared, goes to his room… and sometime during the night, hangs himself. Why ask for a bill if one has no intention of paying it?"

"Perhaps he hadn't decided to hang himself until much later," Beide said. "We might get a better idea of that once the medical examiner takes a look at him."

"He returns to his hotel with every intention of departing the next day," Franz said, "and no intention of hanging himself, but somewhere in the night he gets the notion to do away with himself. Is that what you're saying?"

"It's one possibility," Beide said.

One of the officers stood in the doorway. They had finished cutting Kropold down and had placed the body on the floor. The officer gestured to Beide.

"Are you willing to take a closer look?" Beide asked as she rose.

"Before I continue with this," Franz said, "I'd like to know why I'm here."

Beide nodded to the officer to leave them.

"You're part of this investigation," Beide said. "And I've been very happy with your participation thus far. Why do you ask?"

Franz shook his head. "That's not what I wanted to know," he said. "I meant why are we *here*, investigating this man's death?"

"Why shouldn't we?"

"Inspector," Franz said, "it's nothing like the others."

"Superficially, perhaps," Beide said.

"No," Franz said. "In every way. For one thing, we can prove this man has been in contact with The Hanging Artist, which I'm sure will make you happy, as you are keen on assigning these crimes to Herr Henker."

"How can we prove that?" Beide asked.

Franz led Beide into the bed chamber and pointed to the checked suit spread out on the bed.

"Herr Kropold was at the Traumhalle last evening," Franz said. "Furthermore, he was Herr Henker's 'volunteer.' So that's one difference from the other cases—Herr Kropold was actually on stage with the man."

"What's the other difference?"

Franz crossed to the corpse and pointed to the noose around its neck. "This is the first time," Franz said, "that you have an actual murder weapon to examine."

CHAPTER TWENTY-FOUR
TOO MANY CLUES

FRANZ'S FIRST IMPRESSION of the late Leo Kropold was that he looked like a young man grown suddenly old, and not merely because the trauma of his hanging had twisted his features into a mask of torment.

"This man was struggling with something," Franz said. "Look at how care and worry have etched themselves into his skin—at the corners of his eyes, at the turning of his mouth. I've seen faces like his before."

"Live faces?" Beide asked. The voice now had a boyishness to it. Franz looked up to confirm that Beide had become male.

"I wish I could get accustomed to that," Franz said.

"Accustomed to what?" Beide asked.

"Never mind."

Beide looked at himself in the dressing mirror opposite the bed. "Oh," he said, "that. If it makes you feel any better, I wish I could get accustomed to it, too." He turned to the four silent officers. "If this is everything," he said, as they came to attention, "you may leave us. One remains stationed outside the room. You others know what happens next."

The men saluted and left the room.

Beide went to the two items his minions had placed on the vanity.

"Interesting," he said.

The first item was a small, leather-bound journal or notebook. The second was a brown bottle with a paper label affixed to it. Beide ruffled the pages of the journal and handed it to Franz. "Words," he said. "Your department."

Franz opened the journal. Page after page had been filled, in a sturdy, plain hand, that of someone unused to writing and only marginally schooled in the art. He selected a page and drew Beide's attention away from the bottle.

"Listen," he said, "to this: 'Who am I to judge myself and pass sentence? Who am I to take my own life? Why, I am myself, and who else would know better than I for what sins I must answer?' Does that sound familiar to you?"

Beide nodded. "The Hanging Artist," he said.

"Yes. The performance."

Franz ruffled through the pages. Over and over again, the words of The Hanging Artist were written in block letters, not always in order, but often repeated.

"And again," Franz said, "the very words of Hans Henker: 'But are all of our internal demons just that—internal?' And here: 'Do I deserve to live? I leave that to you.' And so on. Every word of the performance, Inspector, taken down several times over, as if Kropold were taking dictation."

"Assuming that's his handwriting," Beide said.

"Can you find out?"

"We can try."

"May we assume, for the meanwhile, that Kropold is the author of these notes?"

"That's an interesting way of looking at it, Kafka."

"What is?"

"Kropold being the author of the notes. On the one hand, as we understand it, he *isn't* the author of the notes, because these are the words of Hans Henker..."

"...but on the other hand, who's to say Kropold *isn't* truly the author of the words?" Franz said. "Do you mean to suggest...?"

"That Kropold wrote the act for Henker? It's a thought."

"It doesn't make sense."

"It will if we tug at it long enough."

Franz placed the notebook on the vanity. "And what of the bottle?" he asked.

Beide showed him the label. "Bichloride of mercury," he said.

"The man was ill," Franz said, stealing a glance at Kropold's corpse.

"Syphilis," Beide said. "A fresh bottle, too—dated yesterday, by a chemist's hand. This is easily traced."

"Why would Kropold obtain a new bottle of mercury bichloride on the same day he hangs himself?"

"Excellent question."

"I know it's an excellent question, Inspector," Franz said, "but what we need right now is an excellent answer."

"What's your opinion?"

Franz rolled his eyes. "Must you always do that?" he asked. "Don't you have any opinions of your own?"

"We do," Beide said. "But I'd like to hear yours first."

Franz thought. "I'm not a doctor," he said, "but from the looks of him, you wouldn't think he was ravaged by the disease. It might have been his first time with the drug and, upon taking a dose, he decided he couldn't abide ingesting poison for the rest of his life, no matter how foreshortened it was."

"So he decided to hang himself."

Franz nodded. "Or..."

"Or?"

"Or he's been taking the stuff for some time now, and only bought a new bottle because..."

"Yes?"

"He knew it would be found."

"By whom?"

"Us."

"Us particularly?"

"Us as in people who are trying to piece things together." Franz put his hand to his head and closed his eyes. "My head is throbbing. This is all giving me a migraine, Inspector."

"Indeed."

"And now it's your turn. What are you thinking?"

Beide put the bottle next to the notebook.

"I'm very interested in how everything seems to point to The Hanging Artist, as I suspected," Beide said, "and yet—at the same time—points away from him, too."

"God help us," Franz said.

"Yes, that would be nice, if such a being existed, but for our own good, let's take a look at that noose."

Beide knelt next to the body.

"May we remove it from his neck?" Franz asked.

Beide drew on his gloves and nodded. Gingerly, slowly, as if handling a venomous snake, he eased the rope from Kropold's neck.

Franz regarded the ceiling. "Are all the rooms in this hotel the same?" he asked.

"I don't know. Why?"

Franz studied the room's construction. "How tall would you say the late Herr Kropold was?" he asked.

"I'd place him at just under six feet tall," Beide said, concentrating on the removal of the rope. "Certainly no taller."

"And how high is this ceiling?"

Beide spared a glance. "Twelve feet," he said. "It's an old building, Herr Kafka, it's—"

"You may call me Franz by now, surely," Kafka said, his gaze wandering about the room. "Or simply 'Kafka,' if you like."

Beide stopped what he was doing, opened his mouth as if to reply, then thought better of it and returned to his work. "Why are you interested in the room's dimensions, Kafka?" he asked.

"I don't know why I'm interested in anything," Franz said,

"only that I'm finding everything I encounter these past couple days to be of enormous interest, even when they may not be interesting at all. Why is that?"

"It's the nature of the murders," Beide said, finally slipping the noose off the dead man's head. "They've had the same effect on me. Now, please, go on. The ceiling?"

"Perhaps it's not so much the ceiling as the beam," Franz said, standing. "A massive oaken beam runs the length of the room, and we're on the top floor of a hotel with a pointed roof. This wasn't always a hotel, was it?"

"I don't know. I can summon the manager if you like; perhaps he can answer your questions."

"It's an idea," Franz said. "I'll do it."

He went to the telephone, tapped the receiver for the desk, and asked the answering voice to send the manager to the room. He returned to Beide and the corpse.

"Perhaps we should put a sheet over Herr Kropold," Franz said.

"The manager's already seen him in this, um, state," Beide said.

"Doesn't mean he has to continue doing so," Franz said, looking around the room. "And perhaps the manager will be a little freer with his answers if he isn't distracted by a dead naked body. I'd rather not disturb the bedding; let's see if there are sheets in the wardrobe."

He opened the wardrobe. Gregor, eating something foul, waved at him.

Franz started. "Damn you," he said. "Get out of there!" He slammed the door.

"Say that again?" Beide asked from the foot of the bed.

"Nothing, just a minor observation," Franz said, and opened the wardrobe door again.

Gregor handed him a bedsheet. "Smashed one of my antennae," he said. "Be a little more careful when you're slamming—"

Franz took the sheet and slammed the door again.

After he and Beide covered the corpse, they took the severed noose to the window and pulled back one of the drapes. Beide held the noose up for inspection.

"Silk," he said.

"I'm not going to touch it," Franz said.

"There's nothing to fear."

"I'm not afraid of it, Inspector. It's just that it's an instrument of death."

"Yes. But it's also central to these murders."

"No, it's central to Herr Kropold's suicide."

"Are you correcting me?"

"Simply observing that the only death in which this object has been complicit is Herr Kropold's, no one else's. I'd go so far as to say we're not even certain of that."

"A moment ago," Beide said, "I was about to tell you how glad I was to at last be able to consider you a cooperative companion, and one who, now, appears to be readily, even eagerly, involved. But I refrained, because I thought you might either deny the observation or become emboldened and adopt a rather high-handed attitude towards me."

"For the past two days," Franz said, "nothing has been as it should be, and you, more than most, have been symptomatic of that fact, so—no, I'm not being high-handed, I'm just telling you that we can't take anything for granted. This room, this body, this hotel, that suit, this noose…"

He grabbed the noose, then exclaimed.

It had come apart in his hand.

It appeared to writhe at his touch, like a mass of thick worms escaping from each other, but was shortly revealed to be nothing more than a mass of twisted cloth. Most fell to the floor; Beide stooped and retrieved one. Franz examined the cloth that remained in his hand.

"See what I mean?" he asked, fluttering the twisted cloth. It unfurled just enough to suggest its original form.

"A handkerchief," Beide said, counting as he retrieved the rest from the floor. "Two dozen, Kafka," he said. "Exactly two dozen silk handkerchiefs."

Franz caught sight of something from his vantage point at the window: an awkward, bumbling movement in the alley below. Gregor, crawling among the rubbish bins.

"What do you see?" Beide asked, but Franz was saved from answering by the approach of Herr Fautz, the manager of the Hotel Das Gottesanbeterin.

Beide said, "It just occurred to me that this man has only seen me in my 'other' state, and we've no time to go about explaining things or making up excuses. I'll return when you've finished questioning the man," and hid behind the door as the visitor entered, ducking out unseen once the man was in the room.

Herr Fautz was a handsome man of middle age with only a few flecks of white in his black beard. He bore himself with unconditional dignity; Franz thought at one time he must have been with the military. His striped trousers had been crisply pressed, and his forest green morning coat bore an embroidered mantis on one lapel. If he had lost any composure at all at the discovery of Leo Kropold's body, he showed no sign of it, and even now paid the sheeted corpse on the floor little attention. He accepted Franz's introduction of himself as a special consultant to the police with a peremptory nod.

"Then I assume the Inspector and her men are out making the necessary arrangements to remove this gentleman from the premises?" Fautz asked.

"Exactly," Franz said, hoping that was the case. "In the meantime, Herr Fautz, I'm wondering if you could spare me a few moments to clear up one or two points that may or may not have any bearing on the present situation?"

"I'm at your service," Fautz said, straightening cuffs that needed no straightening.

"Thank you. How old is the hotel?"

"One hundred and eighty-nine years old," came the answer. "It was built in 1735. I think you'll find my math correct."

"Was it always a hotel?"

"It was not. It began life as the private residence of the Marschallin Klischat, who inhabited it from its completion until 1777, at which time it passed along to her nephew and his family. It remained in the Klischat family until the death of the wife of the youngest son in 1843. The following year, the property was sold to my grandfather, who converted it to its present state as the finest luxury hotel in Vienna."

"You've every reason to be proud of it, Herr Fautz."

Fautz clicked his heels and inclined his head slightly in acknowledgement of the compliment.

"Brahms once stayed with us," he said. "A fortnight. A small portion of his ninetieth opus was extensively revised here during that visit. Several measures of the *poco allegretto*. Not in this room; on the floor below. I was a boy at the time, but I remember him vividly. Particularly the penny candy he would bring for me."

"What a sweet recollection," Franz said, at a loss as to the identity of Brahms's Opus 90 but not wishing to appear ignorant. Fautz did not laugh at Franz's joke, but remained stoic, shoulders back, chin high. "Now then," Franz said, "about the floors of this building, since you so adroitly referred to them, saving me much preamble... are the rooms here the only ones with angled ceilings?"

"To the roof peak, yes," Fautz answered. "When it was a residence, this floor was kept for the servants with storerooms above it. When my grandfather bought it, he removed the floors of the attic so that the rooms would have loftier ceilings."

"Ergo the strong beams that run the length of the floor."

"Yes, sir."

"An unusual feature."

"Unique to the Hotel Das Gottesanbeterin. They are very well-known, sir."

"By whom? Guests who have stayed here?"

"Naturally."

"How many suites of this kind are on this floor?"

"There are two suites and two apartments."

"Apartments?"

"The suites may be reserved for guests who are here for a luxurious but brief visit—say a fortnight—while the apartments are reserved for guests who are looking for more of an extended stay."

"Not unlike a tenant, eh?"

"Precisely. An apartment may be leased monthly, biannually, or annually."

"Why was Herr Krolop given a suite instead of an apartment?"

Fautz's starchy demeanor creased a little. "Sir?"

"Did he request this suite when you offered him an apartment?"

"I don't recall."

"Do you recall his registry?"

"No. One of the under-managers handled it."

"Did you ask your under-manager why he put a guest seeking an extended stay in a suite rather than an apartment?"

"Why would I do that?"

"Because you're an excellent businessman, Herr Fautz, and you care about this building as much as you care about your family's legacy of hospitality. That said, if the price tag on an apartment is higher than that of a suite, if you'd discovered your under-manager had booked Herr Krolop into the cheaper accommodation, I suspect that under-manager is no longer in your employ. What's his name? I'd like to get in touch with him."

Fautz stiffened. "There is no need, Herr Kafka," he said. "Since you press the point, I admit to handling Herr Krolop myself. Yes, he did tell me he wanted rooms for a month or longer…"

"But you didn't like the looks of him," Franz said. "Not that he seemed—what? Unsavory? Disreputable? No, I'm guessing he seemed…"

"Coarse," Fautz said.

"Yes," Franz said, "but he had money—which he probably made sure you saw—so what could you do? Tell him you were full up, when you weren't? And things being what they are, in the post-war economy…"

"Herr Krolop's death is most unfortunate," Fautz said. "And, as such deaths are… unfortunate… I trust nothing need be said publicly about the location?"

Franz smiled. "That's not for me to say," he said. "One man rewrites a few measures of a symphony, another hangs himself. Does it really matter where?"

"I'm glad to see you take my view of it, sir."

"Did you look into Herr Krolop's livelihood once he took up residence?"

"I would never do something like that, sir. I took him at his word."

"That he was from Bern."

"Yes. Anyone could come from Bern. Or anywhere else, for that matter."

"And his attitude?"

"Attitude, sir?"

"His demeanor. When you saw him. Morose? Cryptic? A perpetual look of doom in his haunted eyes?"

"You're suggesting I have the ability to predict a man's suicide based on how he behaved to me and my staff?" Fautz asked.

"I just wanted to know what his attitude was like."

"He was happy with his accommodation," Fautz said, "and pleasant to everyone. He was generous to the waiters, the chambermaids; everyone. He was a model guest."

"Until this morning."

"I ask you, Herr Kafka," Fautz said, turning to the loud suit on the bed, "would you think a man capable of suicide who wore a garment such as this in public?" He picked up the coat as if it were somehow woven out of excrement. "Someone with taste as wretched as this wouldn't have the *brains* to kill himself, although he might cause others to wish he would."

A folded sheet of paper fluttered from the coat to the floor.

Franz picked it up, unfolded it, and read it.

In the same clear, blocky handwriting found in the notebook, the following words were written:

Thank You

Hanging Artist

"What is it, Herr Kafka?" Fautz asked.

"Another piece of a pictureless puzzle," Franz said.

"Come again?"

Franz pocketed the note. "You've helped me beyond words," he said, "so I'll not bother to try to come up with any. Thank you, Herr Fautz. I'll do my best to see that all of this is cleared up."

"Please do," Herr Fautz said as Franz escorted him to the door. "I don't wish to seem unfeeling, but... well, an unoccupied room is..."

"Yes, yes," Franz said, closing the door on him, "money waiting to happen."

Fautz gone, Franz faced the silent, empty suite; empty, save for the sheeted corpse at the foot of the bed.

He sat in the chair that Leo Kropold had used as his makeshift scaffold. So many things were bumping around in his brain, things that were doing their best to be noisy and elusive at the same time. He had the dizzying impression that everything he was experiencing was adding up and subtracting simultaneously; one fact led to a possible answer, while another led away from it.

What did he have?

A rope of handkerchiefs.

A note directly referencing The Hanging Artist.

A notebook filled with the words of another man.

A bottle of mercury bichloride.

And the stiffening corpse of Leo Kropold.

"And don't forget the boots," said a raspy voice.

Gregor was there, brandishing a pair of dirty boots.

Franz sighed.

"Boots?" he asked. "What boots? And what have boots got to do with anything?"

"You tell me, Herr Detective," Gregor said.

"Where'd you find them?"

"In the alley. Chucked out."

"Whose are they?"

"Smart money says they belonged to the dead body."

"And what makes you think that?"

"The way they were chucked out."

"All right," Franz said. "Explain."

"I'll do better than that," Gregor said, lifting the bottom of the sheet over Leo Kropold. He began to force the boots onto the feet, and when Franz protested, he hushed him. "I'm being useful," he said. "And... hold on a minute... he's not as flexible as I'd hoped... there... I'll just have to force him a little to get the foot... damn..."

"Gregor," Franz said, "leave it alone."

"They're his," Gregor said, continuing his work with the other boot.

"You don't know that. And he has a pair of boots." Franz pointed to a pair of polished black leather boots resting neatly at the foot of the wardrobe.

"He had the boots he came with," Gregor said, grunting, "and bought the other pair when he bought the new clothes. Makes perfect sense."

"He'd been here three weeks," Franz said. "Wouldn't he have pitched out the old boots when he bought the new?"

"Who says he didn't?"

Crack.

"I think I broke him," Gregor said, holding a limp foot.

Franz groaned. "Listen, just because you find dirty old boots in the alley—"

"Among the dustbins, which are regularly cleaned, from the taste of them—"

"Gregor!"

"—but not actually *in* any of the bins. And the bins are directly beneath that window. He's been keeping these old boots, for some reason, and then last night, as he prepared to off himself, he opened the window and tossed them out."

"Why would he do something like that?"

"That's your department," Gregor said, his task complete. "There. Look. Boots. They fit. They're his. Tell me I'm wrong."

The boots did indeed seem to fit.

"Just because they fit doesn't mean they're his," Franz said.

"You are exasperating," Gregor said. "I apologize for saying that, but somebody has to tell you. Can't you just accept the fact that these were his boots and that he got rid of them much later than anyone else might have done?"

"A pair of dirty boots only means that the boots were dirty!"

Gregor yanked the boots off the corpse. "For Heaven's sake," he said, lifting one of the boots to what Franz assumed was his mouth. "I'll settle this once and for all," he said.

"What are you doing?" Franz asked, aghast, but it was too late.

Gregor had taken a good long taste of the filth. He sat there making smacking noises for a moment or two.

"Dung," he said.

"I'm going to vomit," Franz said.

"Then look the other way," Gregor said, then took another taste of the dried muck on the boot. "Yep," he said, "cow dung, and enriched soil. Field soil. Herr Kropold was a farmer. A remote farm, I'd say, if there's cow dung involved. He grew his own food, from beets to beefsteak."

"Gregor, how in the world can I—"

"Just a moment," Gregor said, and tasted a sample from the other boot. Franz watched as the great insect made savory noises as it took its time with the filth. "I'd say—and this is just my opinion based on ten years as an insect at large, mind you—that Kropold's farm can be found south of Vienna—no, southwest—in the... yes, I'd place it as west of Schwechat."

"Schwechat?"

"West of it. Yes, definitely west of Schwechat."

"Gregor," Franz said, "I can't go to Inspector Beide—or anyone, actually—and tell them that I know where Kropold comes from based on the taste of the cow shit on his old boots!"

"Sure you can," Gregor said.

"How? 'Oh, by the way, a decidedly outsized vermin that's been following me around the past few days was rummaging about in the trash and happened to find...' Oh, yes, that'll go over well."

"You're a writer," Gregor said. "Come up with something."

"I'm not a writer," Franz said, wishing he could throw something at the beast.

"You've written stories, yes?"

"Yes, but..."

"Then you're a writer."

"This is not the sort of thing I usually..."

"Well, no kidding."

Franz gave up. He wanted someone to come in and tell him his services were no longer needed. He wanted to return to Prague, to Dora, to his friends, to certain members of his family. He wanted to never again sit alone in a room with a corpse. He wanted lunch.

"All right," he said, "here's what we'll do. Take those boots and put them back where you found them. I'll tell Beide that a search should be made of... well, I don't know, they've already searched the room. I'll suggest the trash bins should be searched, to see if Kropold disposed of anything before he hanged himself."

"But this dried mud is important," Gregor said.

"No doubt," Franz said, "but what am I to do about it? Tell them to have the mud analyzed, once they find the boots? Even if they have the science for that, I doubt it will go so far as to pinpoint its source, as you've done."

"I keep telling you…"

"I know, I know," Franz said, "but you have to understand the limits of my participation in this godawful mess. Right now, I only have your word that Kropold comes from a farm west of Schwechat, where the unexplained murders began in conjunction with Henker's first appearance as The Hanging Artist, and while I am happy to *take* you at your word, no one else is likely to do so, because *you are a damned insect!*"

He rose, went to the corpse, yanked the boots from its feet, went to the window, and pitched the boots down into the alleyway.

"Well, if that's the way you feel about it," Gregor said, adopting the best hurt tone he could—but he didn't finish, because he had gone.

Which was just as well, as at that moment the door to the suite opened.

CHAPTER TWENTY-FIVE
TOO MANY THEORIES

"YOU LOOK LIKE death warmed over," Beide said. The four silent officers, who had returned with him, set about removing Kropold and anything related to Kropold from the room.

"That's because I probably *am* death warmed over," Franz said.

"Do you say that in resentment or in fun?" Beide asked.

"I'm too tired for resentment."

"Good. Was your interview with Fautz successful?"

"In a roundabout way."

"What do you mean by that?"

The officers were executing their duties swiftly, which caused Franz to say, "Before we go any further, may I make a request?"

"Of course?"

"I'd like your men to do a thorough search."

It happened so fleetingly that it was hard to tell if the men paused in their labors, but they paused.

"I can assure you," Beide said, "that they've performed the most thorough search imaginable of this room; however, if you suspect they've missed something…"

"Of *this* room, perhaps, although I've found something they didn't—"

"Oh?"

"—but I meant of the premises. Anywhere Kropold could have gone around the hotel itself. Inside, outside; specifically, the bins."

"The trash?"

"While he seems to have left plenty in the room for us to consider," Franz said, "there's always what he did *not* that should be considered, too."

"What are you looking for?"

"Anything," Franz said. If he could only direct them to the boots without tipping his hat to the infuriating-yet-useful Gregor.

Beide shrugged, turned, snapped his fingers, and one of the men clicked his heels, saluted, and left the room.

"Now, then," Beide said. "What did you find that my men had not?"

Franz took the folded note from his pocket and showed it to Beide.

Thank You

Hanging Artist

Beide studied the note for several moments, turned it over several times, and held it up to the light.

"And how did this come into your possession?" Beide asked.

"It fluttered to the floor," Franz said.

"From where?"

"Kropold's coat."

"What made you examine the suit in the first place?"

"I didn't. It was Fautz who handled the coat. Does it matter?"

Beide glanced at the men, whose increased activity barely masked their keen interest in the note. Beide took Franz by the arm and steered him from the room.

"There's a communal guest parlor across the corridor," Beide said. "We'll talk there."

The inspector led him out of the room, taking care to leave the door to the suite wide open. They stepped across the hall to a paneled room littered with overstuffed furniture gathered around a fireplace. The room was lined with floor-to-ceiling bookcases.

Franz sat on a settee. Beide sat next to him, so close that Franz noted, for the first time, that he smelled of orange blossoms.

Beide unfolded the note again.

"How do you interpret it?" he asked.

Franz, somewhat intoxicated by the fragrance, said, "I don't."

"You don't? Of course you do. You can't look at a thing like this and not go leaping to all sorts of conclusions. Kafka? Stay with me, man."

Franz closed his eyes and tried to clear his head. "I'm going to faint again," he said.

"No, you're not. You're not a fainter. Well, yes, you fainted earlier, but…"

They watched as two of the officers carried the corpse from the suite.

"Are you better?" Beide asked, looking into Franz's eyes.

"I'm fine," Franz said. "The note. I don't know what to make of it."

"What you mean is, you don't want to commit yourself to a supposition."

"Whatever you say. Look, I'm having difficulty processing all of this."

"This note fluttered to the floor, you said," Beide said, "when Fautz held up Kropold's coat. So it wasn't in a pocket, as that would have required a search—and remind me to rake those idiots over the coals for not doing so earlier—or shaking out the coat. No, it just fell out. That's interesting."

"It's *all* interesting, Inspector," Franz said, "and it's all confusing, too. My question—"

"Yes?"

"—is why a note like this was left in a way it could be *eventually* found rather than where it could be *immediately* found."

"You mean why didn't Kropold leave the note out in the open?"

"Or better hidden."

"Assuming he wrote it."

Franz sighed. "Yes, I suppose there's always that concern," he said. "I imagine his rather basic handwriting would be easy to imitate... but if someone else wrote this note, why not leave it in a prominent place, like pinned to the body?"

"Kropold wasn't wearing any clothes," the inspector pointed out. "No place to pin it."

Franz laughed. "So you think we have a delicate, sensitive killer on our hands? One that doesn't mind hanging his or her victims, but draws the line at harming freshly murdered flesh?"

Beide was staring at him.

"What did I say?" Franz asked.

"Do you really think Kropold was murdered?"

Franz had to think about that for a moment. What had he said? He hadn't been aware of it when he was saying it, but that was exactly what had slipped out. He shook his head.

"No," he said, "I don't think the man was murdered. I don't really know what I'm saying or why I'm saying it. No, I think this is a genuine suicide. As for this note, we have to consider the way it was written."

Franz took the note and showed Beide its curious construction:

Thank You
Hanging Artist

"There isn't any punctuation," Franz said.

"Should there be?" Beide asked.

"Yes and no. It depends on what it's trying to say. Was he, Kropold, thanking Henker, the performer? If so, there should be a comma after 'you.'"

"Why would Kropold thank Henker?"

"I don't know. Another possibility is that it's a signature. That Kropold is the one you've been after all this time, and this is his way of saying farewell."

"What?"

"Bear with me a moment while I talk this out," Franz said with renewed energy. He stood and began pacing back and forth in front of Beide. "You've admitted yourself that despite thorough investigation of and a constant vigil on Henker, you've no way to pin any of these killings on him. Well, who *haven't* you been suspecting or tailing, all that time? Everyone else in the world—including Kropold, while he was still among the living.

"It's clear that Kropold has been studying Henker—those obsessive notebook entries are evidence of that. And he's certainly been in contact with Henker at the theater, as I saw him last night, and not just by chance—the man was onstage as a volunteer!

"We know from Fautz and the clerks that Kropold has been in residence at the hotel for three weeks, which means he was in town and within walking distance of the Traumhalle for at least that long, if not longer."

"But that would only explain—"

"Just a moment," Franz said. "If you will only give me a chance to follow my line of thought, we might get somewhere. Kropold was the killer. Last night was the last of his killings. He knew this; he had planned this. And when he had finished, he planned to put an end to himself, as well. He was ill and couldn't bear the idea of suffering from that dreaded disease for however long it would take to finally kill him off.

"I'm saying he was a murderous soul from the very beginning; that he discovered Henker, either by observation or reading about him in the newspapers, and conceived of a plan that would throw suspicion onto The Hanging Artist, as a public, sensational figure.

"It explains the notes, transcribed from Henker's act. It explains his residence at this hotel and the pleasant, affable demeanor that Herr Fautz claims he always displayed. It explains the absence of a noose every time a body is discovered—Kropold fashioned his own from handkerchiefs, used it on every victim, took it away when he was finished, and, ultimately, used it on himself.

"And think—the sheer symbolism of the thing!"

Beide, stunned, managed to muster a quick, "The what?" before Franz barreled on.

"Kropold's noose!" Franz said. "He made it of twenty-four silk handkerchiefs, didn't he? Twenty-four! One handkerchief for each murder!"

They were interrupted by an officer at the doorway; this one, at last, evidently had a name, which Beide now used.

"Well, Gründlich? What did you find? Anything unusual?"

"These, sir," Gründlich said, and handed Beide two square blue boxes.

"Is that all?" Franz asked. Where were the boots?

"They were the only items of note, Herr Kafka," Gründlich said. "All else was refuse from the kitchen."

Judging from his smell and appearance of his uniform, Gründlich had been thorough.

Beide had opened the boxes and was studying a bit of paper he had found in one of them. He passed it to Franz.

"Another note?" Franz asked, taking it. It was a sales slip.

"From a reputable haberdasher nearby," Beide said. "For two dozen silk handkerchiefs."

Franz studied the slip. "Purchased when?" He almost hated to look.

"Yesterday," Beide said.

"Yesterday?" Franz asked, shaking the sales slip as if to force it to confess a lie.

"As in the day before today," Beide said. He put a comforting hand on Franz's shoulder. "You're doing a splendid job, Franz," he said, smiling, "and your passionate line of reasoning was inspiring to observe. But I'm afraid we must dig deeper."

Franz returned the sales slip to Beide.

"Yesterday," he said.

"I think you're tired," Beide said, signaling for Gründlich to depart. "You've had a busy day, and you haven't had a decent meal. In fact, you haven't had any meal at all, and it's my fault for not looking out for your well-being."

He studied Franz's vacant expression. "You seem disappointed. Was there something you expected to find but didn't?"

Franz opened his mouth to speak, but thought better of it.

Beide conducted him to the electric lift and rang the bell for the operator. The machine whirred to life beneath them and began its rattling journey up the shaft.

"I'm sending you back to Frau Alt's," Beide said. "You'll have plenty of time before dinner, and I understand she makes an excellent goulash on Friday nights. I'll be in touch with you later. I think we're on the right track, or at least we're on a track that could be parallel to the right track. At any rate, we're on *a* track, and we've learned so much. If it's any consolation, I don't think we would have come so far so quickly without your invaluable help. Now, what do you say to that?"

"Shit," said Franz.

CHAPTER TWENTY-SIX
AMONG THE GARBAGE

KROPOLD'S BOOTS WERE nowhere to be found.

Of course they weren't. Nothing was easy.

And there's nothing so fragrant as alley garbage on a hot June afternoon.

Franz knew he had thrown the boots out the window.

He gave up. Things would be found when and if they wanted to be found.

That was Franz's newest outlook on life.

Unless...

Unless Gregor, in a snit after Franz had shouted at him, had crabbed down to the alley and taken the boots.

Just to spite Franz.

Or spur Franz on to dealing with the evidence of the boots, because something about their discovery and what they told of their dead owner still gnawed at the soft cheese of Franz's brain.

Mmm, cheese.

Stomach a-growl, despite the wet, fetid odor of his surroundings, Franz reentered the hotel and made his way to the lobby and from there out onto the street like any respectable, sane person.

If only.

* * *

"As a matter of fact, sir, Brahms once stayed with us. A fortnight. A small portion of his ninetieth opus was extensively revised here during that visit. Several measures of the *poco allegretto*. I was a boy at the time, but I remember him vividly. Particularly the penny candy he would bring for me."

"You don't say."

Franz turned at the reply.

He knew that powerful baritone.

"Although the Brahms Room is just that," Fautz said, "merely one room. You were thinking along the lines of…?"

"A suite," said Hans Henker. Dressed in his light summer suit, wearing his summer gloves, he sauntered shoulder to shoulder with Fautz as they headed towards the lift.

"Ah, a suite," Fautz said, trying to mask his discomfort. "Yes, well, all of the suites are booked up at present, although I'm sure one could be made ready soon."

"How many rooms to a suite?" Henker asked.

"Two. A bedchamber and an anteroom."

"I see. Then what I'm looking for is an apartment."

"Very good, sir. One is available. I'll show it to you at once."

"Excellent."

"How long were you planning to stay with us, sir?"

Henker smiled his benevolent smile.

"Indefinitely, perhaps," Henker said. "I open at Die Feier on Monday; tonight's my farewell performance at the Traumhalle."

"Ah! Die Feier! Well, it's but a five-minute walk from here."

"I know. Tell me, Herr Fautz—this hotel. Why is it named after the mantis?"

"Ah! I'm afraid the legend is unknown to me, lost over time. The mantis is to be admired, of course. A most useful creature."

"Yes," Henker said. "And very efficient, too, and not choosy at all. It devours whatever it can catch."

Franz didn't hear Fautz's toadying response, as the

conversation was whisked up into the hotel along with the lift.

Franz left the hotel. He was sick of symbolism.

And insects.

CHAPTER TWENTY-SEVEN
A GIFT

FRANZ RETURNED TO Frau Alt's in a condition he would have embraced three days ago, when he was lying on his deathbed: hot, tired, frustrated, and singularly aromatic after his romp through the Hotel Das Gottesbeterin's garbage. As he was no longer on his deathbed, he did not embrace his condition. He had missed the lunch, and his thoughts and hopes were focused on the prospect of the goulash dinner.

He had yet to meet any of his fellow boarders, and perhaps that was a blessing. He had barely been a guest for twenty-four hours, had yet to share a meal with them, or chance upon any of them in the parlor or anywhere else. He was sure the arrival of 'Monsieur Choucas' had been announced to them by his landlady, but what would that mean to them? As it was, it meant little enough to *him*.

He climbed the endless stairs to the third landing and his snug quarters, overwhelmed with despair. He reviewed all he had seen and heard that day, and his gross mismanagement of all of it: he was fairly certain that Beide had summarily dismissed him from the case without saying as much, and why would he not? Kafka had thus far proved to be as capable a detective as he was a... what?

What was he? A pensioned insurance investigator? A writer? A lover?

He was none of those things, although he had, at various points in time, been all of those things. His failure at all of them—and at so much more, if he had the energy to enumerate the entire list—had culminated in his final failure to even *die* properly.

Leo Kropold, he reflected, had died properly, at least.

What did he mean by 'properly'?

Well, Leo Kropold wasn't about to come back to life. Nor was 'Immerplatz Inge,' or Hermann Herbort, or any of the so-called victims stretching back to Ulla Salich. Had Kropold been responsible for all their deaths? Beide had thought it possible, but Beide had also been convinced that Hans Henker, The Hanging Artist, had been responsible, too, with even less to go on—other than a gut feeling.

Franz's *current* gut feeling was hunger. And a little nausea: the sight of two dead bodies in less than six hours was more than any self-respecting stomach could handle, even without grotesque additions of Kropold's twisted, blackened, strangulated face, and Inge's practically noseless, disease-ravaged face...

Her face.

There was the link.

Leo Kropold and Inge Hersch.

She had shown the advanced stages of syphilis.

He had been taking bichloride of mercury.

Both had died on the same night.

Had Kropold contracted the disease from Inge?

Had he killed Inge, and then killed himself?

Timing.

What had been the timing of Kropold's visit to the Traumhalle, his return to the Hotel Das Gottesbeterin, Inge's death, Kropold's suicide?

These were the questions he should have been asking Beide and the grim officers, or the mismatched duo at the morgue.

It was now that he wished that people's penchant for appearing out of thin air could be relied upon. He wanted Beide, male or female or both, to be sitting on the top landing, waiting for him. He'd have been happy enough even to find Gregor chewing on a spoiled bratwurst or expired rodent.

What he *did* find when he opened his door was a sparkling set of wine goblets neatly arranged on a glittering tray on his bed.

MATHILDE HENKER LAY the Morocco-bound edition of Goethe's *The Tragedy of Young Werther* she hadn't truly been reading on her lap and attempted to straighten herself in her seat, although she didn't know why, since she hadn't been able to straighten herself for years. What was the long-forgotten thrill that had so nearly penetrated her useless spine? Breathless anticipation? Hope?

A visitor?

Of course it was a visitor. She had planned this, and whatever she planned always played out to her satisfaction.

"You may enter," she called.

The door opened, and Monsieur Choucas entered.

He was every bit as handsome and earnest as Frau Alt had said. Too severe and stiff to be Parisian, but as Mathilde hadn't been to France since the war, she no longer had a reliable frame of reference. Perhaps everyone the world over had become severe and stiff since the war. She could believe that.

He was stammering something.

"—too great a—a gesture—gift—to a stranger—"

Could she smile? She tried. Her face nearly cracked off.

And yet he did not recoil at her hideousness.

He could be blind.

But then how could he have read her note?

"I apologize for receiving you so informally, monsieur," she said when he had run out of phrases. She gestured to her misshapen body. "The spring has long gone from my step, and even with the aid of those"—she nodded to the two canes within reach—"it would take me the rest of the afternoon to get across the room to open the door."

What was going through the man's mind as he stood before her, long and lean and flushed to his eyebrows? She could not tell, but she noted, with surprise, that he did not avert his eyes from her.

"It took me a moment to comprehend what you meant when you referred to my 'little accident' this morning," he said. "And then I remembered."

"To have your livelihood reduced to a pile of broken, useless glass at a stroke must have been heart-rending, monsieur," she said. "I do beg your pardon; would you be more comfortable if we conversed in French?"

The monsieur assured her that not one word of French need be spoken. "Only one, perhaps," he added, "and that, of course, is *merci*."

While his manner was as casual as a flagpole, his shy charm, at least, was evident.

As for her own manners, she had forgotten them; but then, she had forgotten nearly everything warm and human over the years. She invited him to sit. He protested that he did not wish to prolong his intrusion, and she told him his intrusion was not an intrusion at all, but a welcome ray of sunshine on…

…on an already sunny afternoon?

He then did something no man had done in her presence for such a long time. He laughed.

Had she been *funny*?

She had become an expert at sarcasm, yes, and irony, but *humor*?

No, it was no mistake. He had found humor in the way she had awkwardly backtracked on the miserable cliché she had embarked upon.

"Oh, please do sit," she said. "Unless I'm keeping you from something? Like those beautiful goblets?"

"Oh, no," he said, taking a chair. She noted how he perched on it rather than sat on it, not unlike a hungry but patient bird. Perhaps that was how he came by his surname: Choucas. Jackdaw.

"I do hope they're suited to your purpose," she said, closing the book in her lap.

"They surpass it," he said. "I'm almost afraid to touch them, they're so delicate, so beautiful."

"Perhaps they will make your music all the more sweeter," she said, but quickly added, "I don't mean to imply that your music isn't already as sweet as it can be."

He had been angling for a glimpse at the title of the book in her lap. "*Young Werther*," he said. "You admire Goethe?"

She passed a gnarled hand over the volume. "I often wonder," she said, "if I admire the author, or if I admire the author's work."

He showed interest in the remark. "Are you not of the opinion that a writer and their work are one and the same?"

She admired his use of pronouns. "I am not," she said. "When I read Werther, I don't for one moment think that Herr Goethe is he. Werther exists as words on a page. Goethe existed. Existed as you or I are existing right this moment. Goethe was merely responsible for dipping his pen into his ink and putting Werther on the paper. They cannot be one and the same, because one created the other."

"And yet it is said that God and Man are the same, even though one created the other."

Oh. That was *warmth* she felt. A brief flare of warmth, or at least something resembling her memory of warmth.

"Ours is too short an acquaintance to voyage into a discussion of God and Man," she said. "As for Goethe, I can't say I admire him because I didn't know him personally. He was a bit before my time, no matter how old I look."

He cocked his head at her again, and said, "I would put you at thirty-one."

Mathilde thought only the French could be so brazen and yet so winning at the same time. "Thirty-two," she said, "although it's just as impolitic for a young woman to confess her true age as it is for a young man to guess it."

It was the first time he looked away from her. "I beg your pardon," he said, "I didn't mean to... that is, I'm not always... that is to say, when it comes to social graces..."

"I'm teasing you," she said, and he returned her gaze.

The conversation lapsed. Then, suddenly:

"I'll be forty-one next month," he said.

"Ah," she said. "I would have guessed younger."

"Ah," he said.

More uncomfortable silence.

"That's a very fine copy you have," he said.

"It's an early edition," she said.

"It must be rare."

"Rare enough."

"Passed down from generation to generation?"

"Oh, no," she said. She held the book out to him, and he took it. "It's a part of our collection," she said. "We have a passion for rare and beautiful things."

"When you say 'our,' to whom do you refer?" he asked.

"My brother and me, of course," she said. "Forgive me, I thought everyone knew him by now. But you've only just arrived, haven't you? My brother's name is Hans. I call him Hansel. Makes him sound like a little boy, doesn't it? It keeps him in line. He's certainly not a little boy. He and I are the same age."

"The same age?" he asked. "But... are you, then...?"

"I wonder how you're going to finish that sentence."

Franz blushed. "I don't know why my first thought was that you were born so close together. Month-wise. Oh, I don't know what I mean. You're twins."

"Yes. Although it would be possible to be, say, ten months apart."

Eager to steer clear of any further misinterpretation of the senior Henkers' reproductive history, Franz said, "You call him Hansel… does he call you Gretel?"

"He tried, once. I corrected his error. He won't again. I prefer Tillie as a nickname, if one must go around giving people nicknames."

"Tillie."

"For Mathilde."

"A very pleasant, comforting name."

"Which? Tillie? Or Mathilde?"

"Both."

She looked at him. She raised her eyebrows. He was slow to get the hint.

"Oh," he said. "Mine is…"

"Yes?"

"Francois."

"I thought you'd forgotten it, the way you paused."

"I had."

She laughed.

"No, truly," he said. "I'd forgotten it."

"How can anyone forget their name?"

"I don't think of myself that often."

She didn't know what to say to that. She also didn't know what to make of his physical attitude; he seemed both desirous to stay and eager to leave at the same time.

"May I offer you some refreshment?" she asked.

"Oh, I didn't mean to overstay my welcome," he said. "And as it's near the dinner hour…"

"Then it's the perfect time for an aperitif," she said.

"Well…"

"You wouldn't insult me by refusing my hospitality, would you, monsieur?"

"No, no, of course not, but—"

"Good."

"—you've already given me so much. Too much."

"I have?"

"The goblets."

"Well, I could have hardly given you the entire set one goblet at a time. Unless you perform one-note songs. Now, let's not be so deferential to each other and have a drink. You'll find a decanter of Schwabach Goldwasser and some glasses on the sideboard in the next room. I'm a gracious hostess, but not a terribly mobile one; if I served you myself, dinner would be long over by the time I made it to the sideboard and back, and as these canes occupy my hands, carrying any sort of liquid is a challenge."

"It would be my pleasure," he said, and went into the next room.

She heard the delicate clink of the crystal stopper as he poured the drinks. Should she ask him for music, too? The late Caruso on the gramophone? Would that be making too much of the Frenchman's visit?

A sharp pain prevented her from any further pleasantries. She struggled to alleviate it by shifting her weight, stifling a cry as she attempted to haul herself into a sitting position. Sadly, her desperate, awkward movements caused the cushion supporting to dislodge itself and slide to the floor along with the book from her lap. Without support, the pain in her back became excruciating, and she drew in her breath sharply before emitting a wholly unladylike gasp.

Monsieur Choucas returned with the liqueur at that moment, saw her discomfort, and immediately set down the glasses.

"What may I do for you?" he asked.

She could not speak, but nodded at the cushion. He returned it to its place. She made a twirling gesture with her hand, and he puts his arms around her.

"A thousand pardons," he whispered.

She clutched his arms as he rotated her until she was seated upright. He released her and stepped away, as if repulsed by her frail, corkscrew body.

"Thank you," she said, regaining her breath and waiting for the throbbing in her back and hips to subside.

At last she smiled.

"We pay for our sins," she said. "Let's have that drink now. I could certainly use it."

He gave her a glass, and he raised his to her. "Your good health," he said, and drank.

"Merci," she said, raising her glass as well, "although I haven't known good health for quite some time."

She drank. He took another sip from his glass.

"It's delicious," he said. "It doesn't taste metallic at all."

"The gold flakes make no difference whatsoever."

"And they don't affect the... er...?"

"No," she said. "All they do is make it pretty. Have you never had Goldwasser before?"

"I confess that I always thought that, because of the gold flakes, one glass would be obscenely expensive."

"That's charming," she said. "Your naiveté is arrestingly winning."

"You called it something else, though."

"Did I? Oh, yes. Schwabach Goldwasser."

"What does Schwabach mean? Is it a flavoring?"

She lowered her eyes then, feeling as though a shadow had crept upon her. She studied her empty glass.

"It was my home," she said. "In Germany, near Nuremberg. This particular Goldwasser is made there. Schwabach is tiny, but it's there. Are you at least familiar with Nuremberg?"

"I am."

She looked at him.

"You are?"

His attitude changed at that, similar to the way it had when he had forgotten his name. "By name, I mean," he said. "I... well, of course, I must have passed through it on the journey to Vienna. Wouldn't I?"

"It would depend on where you were coming from, of course," she said.

"Of course." He took her glass. "Another?"

"As the first was offered to my health," she said, "it's only fair the second be offered to yours."

While he poured, she tried to retrieve the book from the floor. Seeing her difficulty, he picked it up and handed it to her. She thanked him.

They toasted his health and drank.

"I happened to notice the military paraphernalia. Are they collectibles as well?" he asked.

"The what?"

"In the dining room, on the little table next to the sideboard. Are those old things as well?"

"Oh," she said, handing her unfinished drink to him. "I've taken too much, would you mind? That extra sip... thank you. You were saying?"

"Asking. About the medals."

"Yes, the medals." She smoothed her dress. "Those are my brother's."

"He served in the war."

"He did his duty."

"Admirable. And so many medals."

"Yes."

"Light cavalry?"

"Engineers."

"He must have plenty of hair-raising stories."

"Yes, he must."

"You must have been worried sick while he was away."

She attempted to straighten herself and give her visitor her full gaze. "I served, too," she said, a hint of steel in her voice. "Nurse. Red Cross. I wasn't about to let him go off on his own, even if our country required..." Her voice trailed away. "I wasn't always like this, monsieur, the way you see me now." She clutched the book as she spoke. "My current state isn't the result of childhood disease or a birth defect. I wish it was. I could accept that. No, my ruined body is... was... the cost of helping humanity."

"I don't understand."

"Which? My disfigurement, or helping humanity?"

"Both, perhaps. I didn't mean to pry. If you'd rather not discuss it…"

"You weren't prying," she said, and sighed. "To make a long story short… and vague… Let's just say that my brother survived the war without as much as a scratch. Well, perhaps he was *scratched* once or twice, but you know what I mean. I, however, stuck my neck out just once, and… Well, I was nearly killed."

He finished his drink and collected the glasses.

"May I wash these for you?" he asked.

"Leave them," she said. She heard the harshness in her tone, and tried to correct it. She smiled at him.

"I beg your pardon," she said. "You're very kind, and attentive. I appreciate that very much. You also listen extraordinarily well, although I don't know if that's just your nature or if you're only being gracious because I gave you those old goblets.

"Don't answer, please. I'll choose the reason that pleases me. Our family has always done that, you know. Chosen things that please us—fine things, elegant things, old things, things that have history. Do you know what I mean by that? Perhaps you don't."

"Things that have passed from person to person over the decades?" Monsieur Choucas asked, sitting. She nodded.

"That's partly it," she said. "Not just decades, centuries. Those goblets I gave you supposedly date to the early nineteenth century."

"I could never use them, Fraulein! I'd be too self-conscious that, clumsy mess I am, I would destroy them—just as I ruined my own set this morning."

"I don't think you're clumsy at all," she said. "At least, not from what I've seen. You've been unnervingly delicate and careful around me and my things during your brief visit, and your manner is so gentle that... well, if your glasses were broken this morning, it's because of a rare and unfortunate accident, not because of clumsiness. Else you wouldn't do what you do.

"What I mean by 'history,' monsieur, is a palpable connection. I don't know if I can describe it to you, but perhaps you'll understand. Take, for instance, those wine goblets I gifted to you. Whenever I would touch one, I would immediately get a sense of those who had used them before me. I see lords and ladies at sumptuous banquets. The walls are hung with beautiful tapestries, a generous fire blazes in an enormous hearth. There are lovers' secrets, whispers, compromises, dark dealings, celebrations..."

"I *do* understand," Monsieur Choucas said. "We imbue our belongings with our personalities."

She blinked at him.

"Yes," she said. "I believe that."

"And perhaps one day whomever gets the goblets you have given me will sense... oh, I don't know..."

"The music that was once played upon them."

"Yes."

She gathered her canes. "And if someone, someday, should get hold of *these*," she said, "perhaps they will sense... oh, I know not what."

"They are quite beautiful."

She regarded the pair as if for the first time. "That is the first time a stranger has ever said that. I suppose they must be, to anyone who doesn't have to rely on them."

"Were they made especially for you, if you don't mind my asking?"

Her eyes clouded over somewhat as she drew one of the canes to her cheek and absently caressed it. "My dear father," she said. "He was a magician."

"A conjurer?"

She shook her head. "Not in that sense," she said. "He was

one of the finest craftsmen in Europe, monsieur. These canes are fashioned from South American snakewood, which is one of the hardest, strongest woods in the world. It takes a wizard to work with snakewood, and my father... well, my father could work with anything, and he wanted... at any rate, they've saved my life." She looked sharply at her visitor and returned the canes to her side. "I'm being melancholy now. Do forgive me."

"There's nothing to forgive."

"I very much doubt anyone will sense anything if they hold my canes some distant century from now."

"They will sense your determination."

"My determination?" she asked.

"Your strength."

"'Strength,' the man says!"

"That's what *I* see, at any rate."

"Based on what? This brief meeting?"

"It doesn't take long to get a feel about people," he said.

"And what else do you see in me, monsieur?"

"Well, now I'm embarrassed," he said. "However, aside from the determination, I feel that you..."

"Oh, Hansel! You startled me!"

Her brother stood at the door.

"I didn't know you had a visitor," he said. "How delightful."

Mathilde introduced the Frenchman.

"Pardon the gloves," Henker said as they shook hands. "Psoriasis."

"Say that again?" Choucas asked.

"I suffer from psoriasis vulgaris," Henker said. "Are you familiar with it?"

"No, sir."

"And don't describe it to him, Hansel," Mathilde said. "Not before dinner."

"Let's just say that it's far more pleasant for everyone if I leave these gloves on," Henker said. "To what do we owe the pleasure of your visit, monsieur? No, wait—my mind is elsewhere. The goblets. Of course. I hope you enjoy them."

"I'm sure they will make exquisite music," Choucas said.

Henker went and stood by his sister. "We can't wait to hear it," he said. "I'm sorry I wasn't here to greet you. I had some new business to see to."

"And?" Mathilde asked, now entirely focused on her brother.

"They will have an apartment ready for us by Monday noon," Henker said, kissing one of her misshapen hands. He looked at Choucas. "We will be moving to the Hotel Das Gottesanbeterin," he said. "I do hope you'll visit us."

"It would be my pleasure and privilege," Choucas said.

They heard a bell being struck three times somewhere in the depths of the old house.

"Frau Alt summons one and all to the dining table," Henker said. "Don't let us keep you from your dinner."

"You won't be joining us?" Choucas asked.

"It isn't convenient for Tillie," Henker said. "I'd ask you to share ours, but our repast is typically frugal, and…"

Choucas made a polite bow. "I wouldn't dream of intruding," he said. "I've already enjoyed a surplus of your generosity for one day, and while it would be an honor to dine in the presence of such a great artist…"

"Oh," Henker said, "you've heard of me?"

"And seen you, sir."

"You have?" Mathilde asked. "You hadn't mentioned that you'd seen Hansel's performance."

"Last night," Choucas said.

"Oh?" Henker asked. "And what was your impression, monsieur?"

The Frenchman, unsmiling, said, "It affected me greatly, sir. In fact, so profound was its effect upon me that I still remain unsure as to what it all truly means."

"Must it have meaning?" Henker asked.

Choucas nodded to the book on Mathilde's lap. "One never

knows what will have an effect on anyone," he said. "Take Goethe and his *Young Werther*," he continued. "What effect had he hoped for when he wrote that book? Who can say?"

Henker smiled. "He made suicide fashionable," he said, "for a little while, at any rate."

"And you might do the same," Choucas said, and, bidding his hostess a pleasant evening, left the room.

"What news is there?" Mathilde asked. Henker sat next to her.

"Two dead," he said, his smile gone.

"Two?" she asked. "How?"

Henker shook his head. "I don't know. How was your visit with this Monsieur Choucas?"

She hesitated. "Lovely," she said.

"Oh? What did you learn?"

"Nothing, oddly," she said. "Only that if he's a Frenchman, I'm an Olympic athlete."

CHAPTER TWENTY-EIGHT
THE LANDING

FRANZ PAUSED OUTSIDE The Hanging Artist's rooms and wondered if he had botched everything. He felt as if he'd managed to somehow gain entrance to a secret tomb, yet not make any discoveries whatsoever, and to depart without so much as a trinket. He shook off the sense that he had been 'caught' when Henker had suddenly appeared, and descended the stairs to his tiny room off the upper landing.

He hadn't gone four stairs when the door above him opened and Henker called down to him.

"I don't know your plans for the evening," Henker said, "but as you expressed such fascination with my performance and I always make a habit of walking to the Traumhalle in the company of one person or another, would it be too bold to suggest you accompany me this evening?"

Franz didn't know what to say. On the one hand, he was a bit at a crossroads as to how to proceed with his investigation, as he didn't know for certain if his services—such as they were— were still required. On the other hand, if he chose to satisfy his own curiosity and travel to Schwechat, he wouldn't be able to catch a train until well after the dinner hour, and even then, a nighttime investigation was not likely to yield much in the way of anything useful.

"I'd be delighted," Franz said.

"Excellent," Henker said. "I'll meet you at the front door at seven. It will be such a pleasure to have intelligent, cultivated company for a change." He waved a hand and entered his rooms, shutting the door behind him.

Franz noticed a woman standing on the landing below him. She, too, had been looking up at The Hanging Artist. Franz recognized her as one of the four singing sisters who only billed themselves as a trio. How long had she been standing there?

It took her a moment to notice Franz, and when she did, she bid him a good evening.

The bell below sounded once.

"We'd better hurry," she said. "She's very strict."

She turned and trotted down the stairs, her blue chiffon evening dress trailing after her like a delicate parade of banners.

Franz decided not to risk taking the time to change his shirt. The gorgeous aroma of the waiting goulash was too much for him. He hurried to the landing and down another flight of stairs.

He was about to enter the dining room when a deep, rich voice said, "Kafka, you old son of a bitch!"

CHAPTER TWENTY-NINE
AN ACTOR ARRIVES

BY NOW, FRANZ had lost count of the times he couldn't believe his eyes.

And yet Yitzchak Lowy stood in the hall, every bit as impressive and grand as when his revered figure still graced the stages of Europe.

"Lowy?" Franz said, not because he doubted his friend's identity, but because he wanted to rule out a hallucination brought on by acute hunger.

Lowy approached Franz in two strides and took him firmly by the shoulders.

"By God, man, you look like shit!" he said, and embraced Franz with such force that Franz knew he'd find bruises on his arms later.

"What are you doing here?" Franz asked.

Lowy laughed one of his glorious laughs, famous for ringing in the upper balcony.

"It's just like you to say something innocuous like that," he said.

"No, seriously. What *are* you doing here?"

"Waiting for you to tell me," Lowy said.

"To tell you what?"

"What I'm doing here."

"That's what I asked you."

"Feydeau dialogue," Lowy said, removing his hat, "is best left to Feydeau. Now, come on, Franzel, I came as fast as I could, just as you instructed, and now I'm here, I'm at your service, I'm surprised you're still alive, we've all been worried sick about you—well, not literally sick, you're the one who's supposed to be sick—now what's this matter of life and death?"

"Matter of life and death?" Franz asked.

"That's what you wrote in your radiogram. And precious little else."

"I never sent you a radiogram," Franz said.

Lowy began a search of his pockets.

"It's to be a joke, then, eh?" he asked. "Well, God knows we've played plenty on you over the years, so... no, that's not it. This morning, Kafka. Radiogram. It said 'Come at once. Life and Death. Will explain.' And it gave this address. I'd've been here sooner, but those wretched trains, and it's four hours from Prague, and..."

He came up empty-handed.

"Well," he said, shrugging, "I've misplaced the damn thing. But what difference does it make? Did you or did you not send for me?"

"I don't know," Franz said. "And the reason I don't know is because while I know for certain I never sent you a radiogram this morning, I also know that I had been wishing you were here, because I needed your expertise on something, but... Oh, Lowy, it's all so confusing. Everything's been at sixes and sevens since I left Hoffmann's."

"Yes, that's one of my first questions for you," Lowy said, grasping Franz by the arm. "But first... what is that ambrosial smell? Goulash? I'm ravenous!"

"So am I," Franz said, "but this is a... I'm ashamed to say it... a *theatrical* boarding house."

Lowy nodded vigorously. "The establishment of the estimable

Frau Alt!" he said. "Know it well. Roomed here in '13 when I was touring with *Broken Sabbath*. She's a wonderful cook. Well, then, let us stuff ourselves and I'll get reacquainted with that fine lady."

Franz pulled away and grabbed Lowy by the lapels, steering him away from the dining room. "Listen, Yitzy," he said, "I've so much to tell you now you're here, but this isn't the best place for it; in fact, it's the worst place in the world, not at a dinner table in front of who-knows-how-many people, and... listen, let's find ourselves a restaurant and I'll tell you all about it."

"I'm not dining at one of those vegetarian places you favor," Lowy said, pushing Franz away. "I don't begrudge you swilling down that muck, but I need meat, man, great slabs of—"

"Fine by me," Franz said, opening the front door. "There's a promising beer hall just around the corner, I passed it earlier and noticed they had schweinshaxan on the bill of fare—"

"Just a moment," Lowy said, his manner changing to that of a grand inquisitor or some equally stern, forbidding character. "Before this goes any further."

"Yes?"

"Who's paying?"

BARELY AN HOUR later, it took three people to clear away the carnage. Only the bones were left of the pork knuckles, which had been done to perfection, from the crispy skin to the succulent meat. Of the fried potatoes, red cabbage, and beer there was not a trace.

"I don't know what was more remarkable," Lowy said, "the tale you've just told me or that meal."

Franz, unable to move or think, belched. He had unburdened himself of everything that had happened to him since awakening on Wednesday morning to just before Lowy arrived, editing out one or two items he thought the actor wouldn't readily grasp, such as Inspector Beide's shifting gender and the entire existence of Gregor.

"So many questions," Lowy said, casting a wary eye on the liqueur and coffee the waiter set before him. "I don't know if I can handle much more."

"I completely understand," Franz said, "but there it is. It's incredible, and I'm right in the middle of it."

"I meant the coffee and kirsch," Lowy said. "Maybe if I just take a sip of each every five minutes…"

Franz couldn't even look at his after-dinner drinks. He pushed them away. "Perhaps if we just sat here and said nothing," he said. "Just… think. Reflect. Digest."

"Yes," Lowy said. He lit a cigarette, watched the smoke laze its way to the ceiling. "If I didn't know you are always so deadly earnest about everything," he said, "I'd say you had just told me the premise of one of your amusing fictions."

"I wish it *was* fiction," Franz said, "then I could do with it as I pleased."

"Have you finished that story you were working on, the one about the man who finds himself arrested for a crime, only no one will tell him the nature of the crime?"

"I hadn't finished it, no."

"Or the one about the—"

"No."

"Why?"

Franz shrugged. "I don't know."

"You should finish them."

"When I've the time."

"Don't wait for time, Franzel. God knows time won't wait for you."

"Do you always churn out such trite aphorisms?"

"You can't insult me with your big words you think I don't know. As an aphorism is a pithy observation containing a kernel of truth, the answer is yes, I do. Now, what I don't understand—"

"Only the one thing?"

"—is where I come in."

"It was clear to me this morning," Franz said. "Now, not so much. I'm sorry. If I had any control over this whole mess, I wouldn't have sent that radiogram, which I didn't send in the first place, and yet…"

Lowy waved it away. "Inexplicable or not," he said, "it didn't put me out. Just last night I was considering coming to Vienna anyway, so it all worked out."

"You thinking of coming here? Why?"

Lowy gave an anguished groan worthy of a dying monarch, which caused a few nearby diners to look towards their table with concern. He flicked ashes. "The bane of my existence, of course," he said. "Christian Werdehausen. And that's the last time I wish to hear his name."

"Werdehausen? The actor?"

"I told you I didn't want to hear his name!"

"Sorry. What's he done to you?"

"What he's always done to me," Lowy said, forgetting his prior objections and gulping down his kirsch. "Usurp me."

"From what?"

"From everything."

"Yitzy, I don't understand…"

Lowy ground his cigarette into the ashtray. "Proxauf has a new play. It's magnificent, so I'm told. Well, of course it is; it's Proxauf, for God's sake. The man couldn't write shit if you paid him. You recall the enormous success I had with his *Tarsinian* a few seasons ago?"

"I do indeed, it was a—"

"Well, he's got this new one, *The Scapegrace*, and everyone who's read it says I'm the only man for it, only Lowy deserves it, it was written for the great Lowy… and I haven't been able to so much as get my hands on a copy…"

"Did you ask Proxauf?"

"One doesn't solicit a playwright for a peek at a script when one is... well, *me*. And besides, he should have had sense enough to send it to me straight away. And now there's a rumor that... oh, damn, I suppose I'll have to say his name... they say he wants that fat hack Werdehausen for the production..."

"I don't recall Werdehausen being fat—"

"He's a barrel of lard!" Lowy said. "My God, if they wanted to produce *The Comedy of Errors*, they could engage him as *both* sets of twins!"

"So... *The Scapegoat*—"

"*Scapegrace.*"

"—is being produced here?"

"That's the rumor. And they say that if it's to premiere in Vienna, then Two-Ton Werdehausen is the natural choice. Natural choice, my incisors! As if an actor can't travel! I've crisscrossed Europe in my time, Franzel, you know that, and had successes anywhere you point your finger on a map. Werdehausen, the only choice for Vienna! Horseshit! I can be in Vienna in four hours. I just proved that! Travel aside, and given its subject matter, Vienna is definitely not the best place for its premiere. It belongs in Prague. 'Let it play Prague!' is what I say, and after I've made a brilliant success with it and wrung out two years of packed houses, then it can come to Vienna and that slob Werdehausen, and good luck to him once they compare him to me! Are you going to drink that?"

"My coffee?"

"Your Benedictine."

"No."

Lowy drank the Benedictine.

"I wouldn't stoop to confronting Proxauf or Werdehausen," he said. "I want to see Ernst Lothar. He's to produce it."

"I've never known you to grub for work," Franz said. "Are you sure that's wise?"

Lowy looked as though he had been stabbed in the heart. "Grub for work? *I?*" he asked. "How dare you, Kafka? I have no intention of grubbing for work. Lothar and I go way back...

No, I was considering just dropping in for a pleasant word. The I-happened-to-be-in-the-neighborhood sort of thing, swap some stories, have a few laughs, ask him how business is, naturally he asks me to lunch, I say 'Just for a quick bite,' emphasize how trim I am, unlike that elephant Werdehausen…"

"My dear Lowy," Franz said, passing him his untouched coffee, "it's no use obsessing over it. Don't let it consume you. No good can come of it."

"No good can come of *Werdehausen*. He's a disgrace to the profession."

"You're the king of Yiddish theater."

"And you can bet Lothar will hold that against me!" Lowy said, rather too loudly for the other patrons. The waiter, who had been approaching with the dessert cart, rolled it away without a word.

"Calm down."

"Don't think I don't know the prejudices people have," Lowy said. "You're kind to call me the king of Yiddish theater, Franzel, and there's no shame in being known as such, but still… Just because Werdehausen and his herd are gentiles… Oh, the hell with it."

He drank Franz's coffee.

"Why do you want me to see this Hanging Artist?" he asked, his mood completely changed. "You know it's all tomfoolery, don't you?"

"Well, that's just the thing," Franz said, adjusting to the sudden change of tack. "It's a hodgepodge of this and that, and I'd love to know just how much of it is magic and how much of it is authentic."

Lowy shook his head. "It has to be one thing or the other, not a mix of both," he said. "You're not so much a stranger to the theater as to not know that."

"Then I've expressed myself poorly," Franz said. "I want to know if it's *authentic* magic."

"None of it, then," Lowy said, lighting another cigarette.

"There's no such thing as authentic magic, because magic doesn't exist outside of the theatrical realm."

"Is that so?"

"Stagecraft, Franzel. I don't care how real it looks to you, it's fake."

"You haven't seen him."

"I don't have to. A man can't hang himself and then take a curtain call."

"He doesn't take a curtain call."

"But he shows up for the next performance, doesn't he? He rents rooms at rooming houses, he wears gloves and tan suits, he eats food (we presume), he has a sister, he served in the war, he asks you take a stroll with him... He does everything, in fact, except be anywhere near these people who have been killed when they were killed."

"Explain, then, how he does it."

"I'm not a magician."

"But you've had experience with—"

"Well, I've known plenty, seen plenty, yes. And God knows I've seen how our stage managers arrange certain effects for my productions—rainstorms, thunder, lightning, the sound of horses, howling wind, wolves, ghosts, knifings, gunshots—and my God, the buckets of stage blood I've dealt with over the years."

"That's what I mean."

"You want me to assure you that the Big Bad Man doesn't really hang himself."

"Don't say it like that. I'm not a child; I know he doesn't. However..."

"What you truly want to know is how The Hanging Artist is able to convince you that he's truly hanged himself."

Franz toyed with the salt cellar, avoiding Lowy's gaze. "It's not that, either," he said. "Or maybe it is, partly. Am I so gullible? I didn't think I was. It's a combination of things, actually, that has me worried."

"Worried?"

"Yes. Not just for me, but for everyone who watches his act. Give me a cigarette, will you?"

His cigarette lit, Franz drew deeply, exhaled, coughed, said, "I can't get used to this," then took another drag and blew smoke.

"We see a sign that advertises a Hanging Artist, and we're intrigued," Franz said. "We wonder what it means, why someone is claiming to be an artist in a method of execution. We buy our ticket, we take our seat. There's light, there's music. There's a pleasant man, even friendly; not at all what we expected. He talks about judging oneself, about sins, about redemption, about justice. He talks about demons, imagined and real. He asks a stranger to test the noose, search his person. The stranger is convinced there is nothing out of the ordinary, and our Hanging Artist thanks and dismisses the stranger. He then intimates that his survival relies on us, his audience. He has already claimed he can hang himself and live, so why, exactly, does he need us? Why does he involve us?

"In the end, he hangs himself. And he does not survive, or so we think. The music ends, and there he swings, lifeless. We are faced with awkward moments of silence, as if no one knows what to do. Who decides to bring down the curtain, douse the lights, cut the poor man down? We don't know.

"But the curtain comes down, finally. And he does not reappear. The band doesn't strike up a triumphant chord as The Hanging Artist parts the curtain with a flourish, unharmed. No, we will have no reassurance until the next night. He leaves the theater by means of an obscure doorway off an alley to steal away into the night, while we walk like automatons to our beds, uncertain as to the meaning of death itself.

"It's a trick, we say. We can understand trickery. Fine. But why has this man decided we need to see this *particular* trick? And why are we rushing to see him?

"And why," Lowy concluded, "are people being murdered?"

"Not only murdered," Franz said, "but in this fashion."

"And why," Lowy countered, "involve you?"

"It's certainly an interesting if troubling way to spend my new lease on life."

"That's just it, Kafka," Lowy said. "You, yourself, are a magic act."

"How do you mean?"

"You know exactly what I mean."

"I do not."

Lowy closed his eyes and conjured up his best, most rounded tones, as if he were reciting a Shakespearean prologue.

"You see before you, fellow revelers," he said, "a man hitherto condemned to death by no other authority than life itself. The disease that once afflicted him tightened its suffocating grip on him until he and everyone he knew despaired of his recovery. Thus felled by the inevitability of judgment, our hero consigned himself to a retreat that segregates the well from the unwell, the convalescent from the terminal. There he faced his final moments wondering, we have no doubt, what he had done to deserve such an end."

"Please, Lowy," Franz said. "That's not funny."

"You see before you, fellow revelers," Lowy continued, "a real, live, bona fide miracle, as that same condemned man is not condemned after all, but upright, vigorous, free of any trace of the dreaded disease which until recently had claimed him as its own. How are we to understand his magical restoration? Has he merely recovered from his illness, or is he Lazarus, returned from death and sent to us to restore our faith in something or other? What is the lie: his disease, or his recovery?"

Several of the other diners had turned to watch Lowy's oration, and a few now broke into applause, which he acknowledged by rising from his seat and making a few quick bows in all direction.

"I'm sorry I wanted you here," Franz said, once his friend had returned to his seat.

"Am I wrong?"

"Is that how you see me, see my situation?"

"It's one way to see it, my friend."

"And did anyone try to see me after Tuesday? After Hoffmann said there wasn't a scrap of hope left for me?"

Lowy stirred his coffee, only to discover there wasn't any coffee left. Franz leaned into him, his voice measured, calm, simmering with suppressed anger.

"No one," he said. "Is that it? I was left to die alone in that room. What were you waiting for, a call from Hoffmann to come claim the corpse? And when that didn't happen on Wednesday, everyone reconciled themselves to waiting for Thursday. And when yesterday came and went, well... why not wait until Friday? Surely that bag of bones can't last the weekend."

Franz sat back and fought a wave of nausea.

"I apologize," he said.

"It isn't the easiest proposition in the world to see a treasured friend have the life sucked out of him," Lowy said without a shred of histrionics. "I apologize, too. For myself, yes, but also for everyone who loved you too much to wait out your fate at your side."

"Everyone except my father," Franz said.

"The less said about your father, the better," Lowy said.

"Do you know that monster actually saw my disease as the culmination of my lifetime of uselessness? He said, time and again, that the only reason I contracted the tuberculosis was because I was weak—morally, physically—and was looking for any excuse to escape the responsibility of living. Can you believe that?"

Lowy nodded. "Knowing your father as I do," he said, "I can believe it."

"I'm most surprised," Franz said, "by Dora's absence."

"Perhaps she found the prospect of your mortality unbearable."

"Don't make a mockery of our... of our..."

"Yes?"

"Never mind. It's the way you put things. You've had so many words put into your mouth in your profession that I often wonder which are original to you and which are from the third scene of the second act of something you're rehearsing."

"It if sounds good, it's my own. Do you still intend to take that girl to Palestine?"

"Yes. Why do you ask in that tone?"

"And open a... what was it? A vegetarian restaurant?"

"It was an excellent idea, Lowy, I don't see why—"

"And spend the rest of your life as a waiter?"

"I'll not have you make sport of my plans."

"Good luck trying to sell a vegetarian regime in the Holy Land after the way you put away that schweinshaxan."

"I can't account for my sudden reversion to being a carnivore."

"And a decidedly non-kosher carnivore, at that."

"Dora fully endorsed the idea, Lowy."

"Did you give her a choice?"

Franz squinted at him. "What do you mean by that?" he asked.

"Nothing, said the actor, sensing the ice along the dialogue and taking his cue to drop the subject of the absent *amour* altogether."

Franz checked the time; it was nearly half past six. He needed to return to Frau Alt's to meet Henker for the promised stroll to the theater.

"Yes," Lowy said, "action. That's what's needed. Now then, here's what I propose: I'll not only watch this Henker's performance with the hawk-like eye of a malicious critic, but I'll also contrive to be the volunteer."

"How are you going to do that?" Franz asked. "The place holds some three hundred people."

"I know how to draw attention to myself," Lowy said,

straightening his necktie and placing his hat at a rakish angle. "Any blemishes upon my person of which I should be aware, before we sally forth unto battle?"

"None, surprisingly."

"Excellent. Then hie thee to yon Hanging Artist, O Lazarus, and make the most of your private time in his company. I shall meet thee after the performance and tell you all I know and, I trust, allay your fears that this man is more than a cheap illusion."

"Thank you, Yitzy," Franz said.

The waiter brought the bill to the table, hesitated, put it in front of Lowy, bowed, and walked away. Lowy looked at the bill, then looked at Franz.

Franz reached for his wallet.

CHAPTER THIRTY
THE SUDDEN ENTREPRENEUR

"AND WHAT BROUGHT you to Vienna, monsieur?" Henker asked. "The pastries?"

Henker and Franz were strolling along Fleischmarkt en route to the theater, and had made no momentous comment to one another except to remark on the coolness of the evening and the possibility that at some point over the next few days Vienna might see a little rain.

"The music, of course," Franz said. "The home of Mozart, Beethoven, Brahms, Strauss..."

"I was making a little joke," Henker said. "Although the pastries *are* remarkable."

"No question."

"But they're nothing compared to French pastries. Am I right?"

"You are, if you'll forgive my national pride."

"Forgiven."

"That's the fifth time."

"Monsieur?"

"I was merely remarking to myself that that's the fifth time people approaching us have chosen to cross the street."

Henker laughed. "You are paranoid, monsieur."

"Perhaps."

"They could have crossed the street for any other reason. Perhaps their destination is to be found on that side of the street."

"Perhaps."

They continued their walk, Henker fascinated by the evening breeze rustling the leaves of the new trees along the street, Franz confounded for a way to steer away from the superficiality of their conversation.

"Is tonight to be your final performance, Herr Henker?" Franz asked.

"Oh, no," Henker said, "I'll be performing for quite some time yet, I hope."

"I meant at the Traumhalle."

"Ah. No, tonight is my penultimate performance. I have had the great fortune to be transferring to Die Feier on Sunday."

"It is magnificent, this new theater?"

"Opulent, monsieur. Seats three times as many as Traumhalle. Better class of people, too." He cast a glance at Franz. "Not that I am class-conscious, you understand," he said. "I'm merely stating it as a fact. It costs more for a seat at Die Feier, and pays more."

"To the customer?"

"To the artist."

"Ah."

"That's not to say that its *artistic* dividends are not to the audience's benefit, too."

"Of course. Then perhaps I should buy an advance ticket now to celebrate your premiere on Sunday evening."

"Monday evening, monsieur."

"But you said—"

"My equipment will be installed on Sunday, but as for me, I never perform on the Sabbath day."

Franz nodded as if he were in the presence of a great religious sage. "Truly admirable, sir," he said. "So many of our profession disregard the Sabbath."

"I'm cheered to see you are of a similar mind."

"Indeed."

"Perhaps we'll see *you* on the stage of Die Feier one of these days, eh?"

"It is too much to hope."

"Do you currently have an engagement?"

"Alas, I am currently 'at liberty,' as the Americans say."

"I haven't seen a verrilionist in years," Henker said. "I had thought the art had died out."

"There are one or two of us left."

"How fortunate. Would you like me to drop a word to the Traumhalle people? After all, with my departure there will be a spot on the bill in need of filling. Would you like that?"

"You humble me with your ongoing generosity," Franz said. "Perhaps I shouldn't have been so bold as to begin my search for stardom in Vienna. I might have done better to have begun somewhere in the provinces."

"It would seem silly to backtrack now that you're here."

"It wouldn't be too much of a backtrack. I understand there are a few places near the city that might be more amenable to a poor Frenchman who wishes to make music on a rack of wine glasses."

"More amenable, possibly, but certainly less profitable."

"Schwechat, for instance."

Henker glanced at him. "Odd that a foreigner should know of Schwechat," he said.

"Only by name. I may have misheard."

"Oh, there's a fine little theater in Schwechat, all right. Know it well. If you're truly interested in starting small, maestro, I can put in a good word for you."

"I would be ashamed."

"Nonsense," Henker said. "It's one artist helping another."

"But you haven't seen my act, Herr Henker."

"How could it be other than delightful?"

"You're too kind."

"Whereas you," Henker said, "have seen mine."

"Yours?"

"My act."

"Yes. I did."

"Does its effect on you remain as profound as you admitted to me this afternoon?"

"It does."

"I must say, it's the first time I've heard anyone admit that."

"I find that hard to believe."

"It's true."

Franz sensed that Henker was watching him closely, although his attention appeared to be focused on the path ahead.

"Would it be gauche of me to inquire as to the *nature* of this profundity you experienced?" Henker asked, as casually as if he were asking Franz what he liked about café au lait.

"It wouldn't be gauche at all," Franz said, choosing his words with care. "Not between artists. I suppose it's many things about your thoroughly impressive performance that intrigue me, and give me much to ruminate upon."

"For instance?"

"How much of it you actually believe."

Henker stopped and faced Franz. His smile was gone.

"My dear sir," Henker said. "All of it."

"Then you believe that the only form of justice that can be visited upon oneself is justice from… within?"

"*True* justice."

"With no regard for the law?"

"The law is just that, monsieur. The law. It's called the law because it is laws upon which it relies, and from which it metes its definition of justice."

"And therefore it's biased."

"Exactly."

"But aren't we, as human beings, biased as well?"

"Are we?"

"Of course. We favor ourselves."

"Do we?"

Franz did not want to be standing there, lingering outside a confectionary. Not because he had anything against sweets, but because the Friday evening parade of Viennese enjoying their leisure seemed out of step with the serious business at hand.

"You like to answer me with questions," Franz said. "You force me to answer your questions with questions of my own. I observed that we, as people, favor ourselves, and you asked if that were true. I ask you, then: *don't* we?"

Henker put up his chin, as if wishing to look down on his companion, but realized that he was exactly the same height as Franz. He looked him straight in the eye.

"Not if we're honest with ourselves," he said.

"I take it, then, that you do not favor yourself," Franz said.

"I treat myself honestly. I know my shortcomings, my deficiencies, my history of sins..."

"Ah, your sins. Which you believe are not truly sins ,but demons."

Henker shrugged and continued on his way with a faster step, Franz trailing after him.

"You French are quite the philosophers," he said, and laughed.

"It's the concept of demons that frightens me," Franz said.

"But as you'll no doubt recall, I said the sins of living are both sins and demons."

"I understand that, but what struck me especially is that you said you think demons actually do exist."

"They do."

Franz tried to catch up with him.

"Metaphorically speaking," he said.

When Henker stopped, Franz nearly ran into him.

"No," Henker said, his affable demeanor replaced by a gray sobriety. "They exist."

Two young women, laughing together, looked up and saw Henker and Franz. Their expressions exchanged immediately, and as one grabbed the other by the elbow to steer her across the street, the latter made a hex sign at them.

Henker watched them go.

"It seems you were correct, monsieur," he said. "People have indeed been going out of their way, but not because of you. It seems I'm now recognized."

"What do they fear?" Franz asked.

"Everything, if you want the honest truth," Henker said, and resumed his walk, slower this time, so Franz could keep up with him. "These people are basic, superstitious. Just because they live in a great city like this doesn't mean they're any better than bumpkins."

"I don't understand."

"They think I'm the Devil."

It was Franz's turn to laugh. "Even now, in the twentieth century? And wasn't the so-called Devil expelled on the bloody fields of—"

"Let's not talk about the war, if you please," Henker said.

"As you wish."

"And who's to say I'm not a devil, eh? Let them take to the other side of the street. It won't make any difference." A nearby clock tolled the half hour. "We're nearly there," he said. "I like to be calm and composed in my dressing room before the show begins, even if it's some time before I go on."

He grabbed Franz by the arm and jerked him backward, nearly off his feet.

"Careful, monsieur!" he shouted as a streetcar ground its way past them, its bell clanging furiously.

Franz had not been watching where he was going. He thanked The Hanging Artist.

"Death by streetcar is an embarrassing way to go," Henker said. "It's messy, public, completely impersonal, and entirely avoidable. You deserve a dignified death, my friend. And here we are."

As they approached the Traumhalle, they were accosted by

a short fellow in a long yellow coat with a makeshift wooden tray slung around his neck. His underfed face had not seen a razor in days, and his bowler was at least one size too small and ten years out of date.

"Protection!" he bellowed to the crowd waiting to get into the theater. "The very latest in protection against the rampaging evil! Of my own construction, so I can vouch for its authenticity and efficiency! Wearing one myself; and, as you can see, I'm still alive!"

He caught sight of Franz and Henker and came over to them.

"For gentlemen as well as ladies, er... gentlemen," he said, thrusting the tray at them. "Only five marks. A bargain, considering."

The tray was filled with little more than scraps of bent tin of various sizes.

"What are they?" Henker asked.

"Anti-hanging devices, sir," the man said, with a hint of conspiracy. "People are dropping like flies, none of 'em see it coming. It's the rope, sir, the rope that comes in the night to anyone and everyone, the Devil's rope that does its business and disappears. Only way to combat it is by having one of these around your throat at all times."

He took a tin collar from the tray and handed it to Franz.

"This'd do you nicely, sir," the man said. "Made it myself. Fashioned each and every one by hand. That's the sign of quality. Try it, sir. No, the other way, sir; the open end at the back of your neck, so the throat's one-hundred-percent protected. Like a priest, sir."

"Go on, monsieur, try it," Henker said. He was holding back laughter.

"I've one for you, too, sir," the man said, rummaging in his tray. "Something a little larger for you, sir, given your size." He produced one for Henker. "Only five marks. All the same price, no matter the size."

"Have you sold many, my man?" Henker asked.

"They're quite popular, sir," the man said, "and you can understand why. All these killings, people getting hung up like beef, it's enough to scare the bejeezus out of anybody." He nodded to the Traumhalle. "It's that Hanging Artist, sir. Stirred up something, he did, stirred up something terrible. Listen, I'll tell you what—if you buy the pair, I'll make it nine marks altogether, as an introductory discount."

"Have you seen this Hanging Artist?" Henker asked.

"Bless you, no," the man said. "I haven't the stomach for show folk."

Henker paid the man ten marks, insisting he accept the full amount.

"Thank you, sir," the man said, cheered and possibly amazed by the sale. "And may God watch out for you... not that you'll need his help, what with one of those around your neck!"

"A word of advice," Henker said. "Your peak market for your product will be *after* the performance, so don't go off to the beer halls once the show starts. Stick around."

The man smiled and pocketed his money. "Money thanks, sir," he said, tipping his hat. "I mean, 'Many thanks,' sir!" He jingled off to the queue, his sales pitch reinvigorated by the money in his pocket.

"*Manus manum lavat*," Henker said. "Words to live by. Come along, monsieur. I'll get them to give you the run of the theater while I prepare for my performance."

Franz discovered the tin collar was too large for his coat pocket, and felt a fool for having accepted it.

Even if he hadn't accepted the thing, he still would have felt a fool.

CHAPTER THIRTY-ONE
BEHIND THE SCENES

BY THE INTERVAL, Franz had been pushed out of the way no less than fourteen times.

Henker had abandoned him after introducing him to the dour stage manager, a humorless man with a walrus moustache and a physique to match. "Anything you say, Herr Henker," the man—Schmeide—had said before turning to unleash a string of profanities to three younger, trimmer men who were fooling about with a bank of ropes.

"I leave you now," Henker had said, "to concentrate on my art. I know that sounds awfully pretentious, monsieur, but it's the truth. I use my early arrival to clear my head of the clangor of the world."

"How can you concentrate and clear your head at the same time?" Franz had asked, immediately regretting it.

"I concentrate on clearing my head," the answer had come. "Now, if you'll excuse me, I'll leave you to your own devices. May I be so bold as to request your company back to the rooming house? We'll wear our tin collars." He had laughed.

Franz had agreed, and Henker instructed him to meet him at the stage entrance fifteen minutes after the final curtain.

It was his fourteenth shoving aside that introduced him to Julia Dierkop.

"You shouldn't stand there," she said, as her three cousins preceded her off the stage and into the dimly-lit backstage area, where they clanked up the spiral stairs to their dressing room. "Oh," she said, "you're the new lodger, the Frenchman Frau Alt was telling us about."

The olio was whisked into the flies and another was dropped into place. The Traumhalle orchestra launched into its intermission music.

"Will you be appearing here?" Julia continued.

"Have we met?" Franz asked.

"Not formally," Julia said, introducing herself. Franz introduced himself as Choucas and hoped the woman wouldn't start speaking French to him.

"You're a friend of Herr Henker?" she asked.

"A recent acquaintance," Franz said.

"You've been to his rooms," she said.

"I paid a visit this afternoon, yes."

She was clearly sizing him up. "You're one of the lucky ones," she said.

"*Comment*?" Franz asked, hoping that was the correct word.

"I mean, to make such an influential friend so quickly."

"He and his sister have been exceptionally gracious to me."

"You've met the sister?"

"Yes, I have. A most congenial woman."

"You don't say. Then she really exists."

"Was there doubt of this?"

"*Julia!*" came a sharp voice from above. They both looked up; one of the sisters was at the top of the stairs.

"In a minute," Julia said, and the woman went away. "One of my cousins," she said.

"The soprano, yes?" Franz said.

"Theoretically."

"I don't wish to detain you."

"You're not. They want to leave."

"So soon after your performance?"

"They're terrified of this place."

Two men carrying a large flat—representing someone's artistic idea of a barn exterior—said something rude to them as they stepped aside to let them pass.

"Let's get out of the way," Julia said, leading Franz to the stage door. "A breath of fresh air, monsieur?"

Franz followed, because he had nothing better to do than wait around to be bumped again. Once outside in the narrow alley that ran between the Traumhalle and the café next door, Franz noted that the darkness of Vienna matched the darkness backstage.

"I hate this place," Julia said.

"Vienna?" Franz asked.

"Vienna's all right, I suppose. I was referring to the theater."

"The theater as a profession, or this one in particular?"

"I suppose both. But at the moment, I'm referring to this place."

"Ah. And why the hatred, Madame?"

"Mademoiselle."

"*Pardonnez-moi*," he said, thereby exhausting his knowledge of French.

"It's dreadful," Julia said, and Franz wondered whether she shivered from the cool night air or her mood. "It's not that it's filthy, or cramped, or old... Most every theater we've played in is like that, and one gets used to it, even expects it. No, it's the aggressive shadows, monsieur."

"I don't understand."

"They've come alive, this past month. Sounds insane, doesn't it?"

"How have they come alive?"

"Something—or some *things*—are watching us. From every dark corner, from above, from below. They're staring at us from the orchestra pit, waiting for us up among the bags of ballast."

"What things, mademoiselle?"

"I don't know. I've not seen anything, but of course one *wouldn't* be able to see them, only feel them. The feeling is strongest during the closing act. That's why we leave after the interval."

"The closing act. Yes. Monsieur Henker."

"Yes."

"And you feel he is somehow responsible for these… How did you put it? Aggressive shadows?"

"Responsible?"

"You imply that Monsieur Henker is the cause for this evil you feel."

Julia clutched his arm. "Good heavens, not at all," she said. "Herr Henker is a kind and good man. A genuine artist."

Franz glanced at the white hand on his arm. She released him.

"I beg your pardon," she said. "I apologize. My…concern for Herr Henker got the better of me."

"Your concern?"

"If I'm not imagining things—and I don't think I am, *everyone* clears out before he goes on: my cousins, the other performers, even the stagehands and the manager—then it's clear that this malevolence is here for *him*."

Franz could not tell if the woman was mad, infatuated, simple, or a combination of all three. He debated how to get her to keep talking, but feared that if he did she would devolve completely into gibberish.

"Malevolence," he repeated, slowly. "Yes, I understand. If that's so, mademoiselle, why do they wait?"

"I can't fathom their ultimate goal," she said. "The more I talk about this, the crazier I sound. Listen to me, speaking of evil manifestations as if they could be assigned human qualities. Or *any* comprehensible qualities."

A thought struck Franz, and he asked, "You say everyone leaves as soon as Monsieur Henker takes the stage?"

"That's right?"

"Then who brings up the curtain?"

"The last remaining stagehand."

"And then he leaves?"

"Yes. His name is Jan. A young man, probably only a boy, really."

"But, mademoiselle... if no one is backstage when The Hanging Artist performs... who brings the curtain down?"

The stage door opened with such force that it nearly knocked Franz over the railing. He dropped the tin collar. The Three Dierkop Sisters paid him little regard.

"Come along, Julia," said one of them, handing her a hat and pocketbook. "You forgot your coat."

"It's not that cold tonight," Julia said.

"Or something for your throat," said another. The sisters all wore the ugliest silk scarves Franz had ever seen. "You catch another cold, we're out of business again."

Franz picked up the tin collar and offered it to Julia.

"What is this, monsieur?" she asked.

"Protection," he said.

"From?"

"Ills."

She took it and went off with her sisters.

"THEN WHO OPERATES the curtain, the lights?"

Jan kept his eyes on The Flying Hurricanes onstage, hands on the ropes and muscles tense.

"I think they're *all* drunk tonight," he said. "I hope they fall into the bloody pit."

"For Henker," said Franz, trying to get the youth's attention. "*Someone* must remain."

"We all beat it up front," Jan said, and began a furious hand-over-hand as the audience laughed at the acrobats' sloppy tableau. As Jan hauled, the backdrop of an Italian countryside rose into the flies.

"Then you don't leave the theater," Franz said, trying to be heard above the brassy blare of the orchestra as the inebriated brothers scampered around.

"We'd be sacked," Jan said, spitting on his hands and reaching for another set of ropes to lower a backdrop of what should have been the Coliseum, had the scenic artist had any talent.

Another wave of laughter. "One's of them's run into another," Jan said, with satisfaction. The laughter gave way to jeers. "God, I hope nobody's carrying rotten fruit tonight, who do they think has to clean that up?"

The backdrop camp down with a heavy thump, and Jan wiped his brow.

"Asking an awful lot of questions," he said to Franz. "Who are you again?"

"A representative of Herr Spindler," Franz said, adopting his best authoritative tone. "We wish to ensure all is prepared for Herr Henker when he transfers to Die Feier."

"Well, that's all I can tell you. This act ends—and thank God when it does—Max and me bring down the curtain, and off we go. We head up to the lobby, wait out there until people start coming out, and then it's back we go, to clear the stage for the night."

"If the Traumhalle staff doesn't run Henker's act, who does?"

"He has his own people."

"Ah! You've seen them?"

"No."

"Then how do you know he has his own people?"

"Curtain goes up, doesn't it? And comes down again?"

"Yes, but…"

"It don't do it by itself, I can tell you that."

Schmeide strolled over, walrus moustache twitching.

"Get Number Four ready," he said to Jan, "and hurry it up, there's no way these idiots are going to do the Pyramid Inferno tonight. If they do, I want you and Max and the other riggers to have the sand buckets at the ready."

Jan nodded, then touched his cap to Franz and disappeared into the shadows.

"From Spindler, eh?" Schmeide said to Franz, keeping an eye on the onstage melee. "Thought you were a performer or something."

"I'm just making sure we have the appropriate amount of—"

"Henker's not taking his own to Die Feier?"

"Ah, yes, 'his own.' Just who are they, and when do they arrive?" Franz peered into the shadows of the wings. "Are any of them here now?"

"Only us as work here are here. Listen, the Hanger's got his secrets, he doesn't want anyone to know how he does what he does, I've seen plenty of magicians and tricksters, and I know how they are. Let them have their secrets, is what I says."

"But his so-called people..."

"We had an agreement when he began," Schmeide said, "that we're to clear out when his act begins, that his own people would handle the technical aspects of his performance, and then we can come back."

"You allowed that?"

"There was a little extra in it for us," Schmeide said, rubbing his fingers together. "Something you should know over at Die Feier. How *is* old Spindler? I remember him from his days as prompter over in the old..."

There was a racket as one of the Flying Hurricanes flew into two others at the wrong angle and all three fell into the backdrop, tearing a hole in the canvas. Roars of laughter. Had Schmeide been equipped to emit steam from his ears, he would have. He turned away from the mess.

"That's going to cost them," he said through clenched teeth. "Look," he said to Franz, "if you're so interested in how many people the Hanger's got working for him, stick around. Never agreed that *you'd* be up front when he does his act, did he?"

"No, he didn't, but—"

"Well, there you are. Excuse me."

The Flying Hurricanes were, after all, attempting the Pyramid Inferno. Schmeide started directing the stagehands to get as many sand buckets as they could and be at the ready.

Franz turned and ran up the spiral staircase to the line of dressing rooms. All were empty, including that of The Hanging Artist.

The audience's laughter had now turned into cries of concern as a flash of orange light came from in front of the backdrop. Franz cast a quick look down and then went into Henker's room. There was nothing there, not even a sign of the man himself. The room was as stark as a disused closet. Had Henker already gone down to the stage floor?

An urgent drumroll rose and fell as the acrobats persisted in their folly.

Franz ran to the staircase, caught his foot on something, and fell halfway down the stairs, knocking his head on the steel axis. He clutched his head in agony, hauled himself up, and discovered he had snagged his foot on a thick coil of metal.

A tin collar.

It had worked its way around his ankle in the fall, and he was caught in the grillwork of the top step. Practically upside down and on his back, he reached up to the railings and hoisted himself into something like a sitting position, and then faced the problem of how to uncouple himself from the stairs while both hands were busy elsewhere.

His first cry for help came at the exact moment the orchestra struck its final, deafening chord and The Flying Hurricanes came staggering offstage, cursing at each other.

Franz felt more than saw the curtain come down, and cried out to the acrobats as they headed out the stage door, unaware of anything except their own drunken remonstrations. He pulled himself up again, and saw Jan run from the ropes to the stage door, which banged shut behind him.

Then the entire backstage was plunged into darkness.

He listened as he had never listened before, and heard

movement in the pitch black from every corner. Franz couldn't know if it was real, or thanks to Julia Dierkop's frightened suggestion. He broke out into a sweat and groped for the railing.

Below, he heard the gramophone playing "Gigolette."

The Hanging Artist's voice came to him in fits and starts.

"...I propose to hang myself..."

Franz managed to hook an elbow around a metal support. He stretched for his ankle with his free hand.

And sensed something moving towards him from above.

Please let it be Gregor.

"...the sins that live in my thoughts, my desires, my regrets, my hurts, my slights, my envies... Are these sins or are they demons...? They are both..."

Something was above him, looking down at him. He knew it. He froze, his back aching from the strain of holding the railing and reaching for the tin collar that kept him fixed to the top stair. What was above him? And why did he have the feeling— no, he *knew*—it was watching him?

Then he realized that if he did manage to free his leg, he could very well tumble down the stairs to his death, if not down the spiral then off the side to the hard, dusty floor below.

Whatever was above him was now moving.

The gramophone again: "Yes, We Have No Bananas!"

Franz heard the thing in motion, feeling as if it were a liquid mass, hidden by the inkiness of the upper corridor. Not unlike rapidly rising bread dough, growing larger, rolling on...

It was going to roll down on him, smothering him.

"...does the sight of this strike fear in your heart? Terror? Be calm. Be sensible. Be joyous. Whoever turns his mind to true goodness will be met with fortune and honor, and forever be free of sinful shame..."

Franz closed his eyes and summoned the strength to cry out. He could not. Whatever was above him, expanding, obliterating, had found him, he knew it.

"...you, sir... the gentleman right here, in front of me... please... oh! Ladies and gentlemen, we seem to have a celebrity with us tonight..."

The gramophone: "Tutankhamen."

Franz clung to the railing, his leg going numb. If he had heard right, Yitzchak had done as he had promised, and was now onstage with Henker. If Franz could cry out, he would risk interrupting the performance, and Yitzchak would not be able to—

There was a new danger in the dark. One thing, two things, many things filling the backstage area and the deep, heavy darkness. Things that hurried.

On wings.

Unseen creatures, stealthy and silent but for the nearly imperceptible flutter of their wings, swirled and swooped around him. Bats?

And what of the heavy, looming thing above him?

Franz could no longer sense it. He made a final effort to free himself.

"...take your time inspecting it..."

Franz yanked himself up the stairs, managing to seat himself one step higher.

"...you may search me..."

Franz caught hold of the tin collar around his ankle and tried to work himself free.

The numbness turned to pain.

"...that is all, and thank you..."

The invisible flying beasts around him disappeared, and, as Franz worked the collar around to its open end and align it will the railing support, he encountered a new horror: that of the blackness closing in on him; not just from every corner, but from above and below, and from every angle. A gradual, inevitable pressing.

His shoe. He could free himself if he could just get his shoe off...

"…The gallows!"

Henker's noose would be flying through the air now, up, up, to wrap itself around the gallows…

Franz tore at his shoelaces. Why so goddamned many?

"…do I deserve to live? I leave that to you."

Franz felt the knot that kept his shoe anchored in place.

The theater was pressing down on him, watching him as it moved, relentlessly.

The gramophone screamed.

Ev'rybody shimmies now

Franz ripped the lace apart.

Ev'rybody's learning how

His foot slid from the shoe.

The tin collar gave, and his ankle passed through it.

Franz fell backwards.

'Cause everybody shimmies now

A chair, kicked away, falls to the stage.

A sharp *snap*.

A collective gasp from three hundred people.

Franz reached out for the railing as his legs sailed over his head.

The gramophone: *swish swish swish*, the needle stuck in the record's dead space.

CHAPTER THIRTY-TWO
A NOCTURNE

WE SEE TWO young men, one bareheaded, one in a straw hat, to what we must assume is the latter's home.

"You've not said a word since the theater," says the young man in the straw hat.

"Forgive me," says the hatless man.

"It wasn't very nice, was it?"

"I wasn't expecting it to be *jolly*."

"The acrobats were immensely entertaining."

"They were drunk."

"We mustn't linger here."

"I'll say good-night, then."

"Let's walk on a bit."

"Not for too long."

"No, just around the block."

"Your father gave me the fish-eye when we left."

"He can't understand why I haven't asked the bootmaker's daughter to marry me yet."

"I don't think anybody besides me *can* understand."

"Yes, well… let's not talk about it."

We see the young men walk away from the house and down to the first corner. We see them turn right.

"I know it was ghastly," says the young man in the straw hat, "but don't let it get you down. It was only a trick."

"And all that gibberish about inner demons?" asks the hatless man.

"Oh, I listened, I listened."

"He was looking at us."

"That's just your imagination."

"No, he was looking at *us*, at *me*."

"This is the last time I let you take me to the theater. It's the cinema from now on."

They turn right at the next corner.

"It does seem to be one way to quiet them," the hatless man says.

"The inner demons?"

"Fool. My parents."

"There are other ways," says the man in the straw hat.

"Have you ever considered…?"

"Of course I have. But then I met you."

They walk on a little in silence, and turn right at the next corner.

"Don't you go getting any ideas," says the man in the straw hat.

"I don't own a rope," says his companion.

The young man in the straw hat laughs.

"But what if we're the ones who are wrong?" asks the bareheaded man.

"Has it felt wrong to you?"

"Yes."

"Go to Hell."

"And no."

"It can't be both, you know."

"Yes, it can."

"Let's not talk about it."

"I don't have your confidence."

"I'm not confident at all."

"Then I lack your assuredness."

"Assuredness?"

"About us."

They turn right at the corner. We see them approach the house again.

"It's hopeless," says the hatless youth.

"Come over here, in the shadows," says the man in the straw hat.

"No."

"What's the matter with you?"

"I don't want to risk it. Not tonight."

"Just a kiss, fool."

"No."

The young man in the straw hat climbs the steps and lets himself into the house.

"See you later," he says. He takes off his hat as he enters the house.

The hatless man hears the lock click, sees the light behind the transom go out.

We see him shove his hands in his pockets and walk away.

He walks to his own home and into the building.

We see him pause on the first floor landing, outside his door, behind which his parents are dozing in the parlor, waiting for him to return.

We see him climb the stairs to the second floor.

We see him climb the stairs to the third floor.

To the fourth floor.

The fifth floor.

He climbs five narrow steps to the door to the roof.

He opens the door.

Birds flutter from the roof as he walks across it, his step quicker.

We see him step off the edge.

* * *

WE SEE A hot, bright room full of hot, bright men.

We see beer, billiards, clumsily made sandwiches heavy with meat.

We see cigars, and the bluish haze the cigar smoke has produced for the past two hours.

We see a handsome gentleman take a half dozen exaggerated bows in response to the whooping cheers and thunderous applause of his companions.

"That's him, all right," says one.

"You could be his understudy," says another.

We hear the cruel laughter.

The handsome gentleman affects a wounded expression. "I've never been an *understudy* to anyone!" he says.

There is renewed laughter at that remark.

"And just remember, my friends," he continues, "he might be doing the same to me right this moment!"

"He had some nerve coming in here in the first place," says one.

"He had every right," says the handsome gentleman.

"It's an exclusive club," says another one, draining his beer in one gulp.

"He's a member of the profession," says the handsome gentleman.

"Like it or not," says another one. He breaks wind, to roars of laughter.

"I choose to like it," says the handsome gentleman.

"You actually *defend* him," says an older man, fanning the air.

"The world is big enough for everyone," says the handsome gentleman.

No one says anything to that; the talk has diffused to betting, drinking, eating.

The handsome man regards the bunch with what might be bemusement.

We see him leave the room, and cross the hall in search of the lavatory.

We see him enter a darker, quieter room.

He smirks at the sight of two elderly gentlemen asleep in chairs, empty brandy snifters at their elbows.

We see him turn his head sharply, as he, like we, has heard something unusual.

He is yanked, suddenly, into the air.

We hear his cry.

We see one of the old gentlemen blink awake.

WE SEE A woman of fifty years return to her modest home.

She forgets to lock her door as she enters the dark hall.

We see her absently fumble for the switch before finding it. The light is warm and inviting, shaded as it is by a paper lantern she was once given as a party favor.

We see her go to the telephone alcove and pick up the instrument.

We hear her ask for a number and wait.

We hear her halting words.

"Son?" she asks. "Yes. It's Mother. I know. Son, I... we... please listen to what I have to say... please. I... I've just seen... Please let me finish—no, don't hang up, I... Son, I was wrong. Yes. I have been wrong. And I thought, perhaps..."

We leave her to her conversation.

WE SEE A swarm of them around the little man with the tray around his neck.

He's making change.

We see tin collars exchange hands.

Some of the swarm laugh about them; some put them on immediately.

We see the little man smiling.

CHAPTER THIRTY-THREE
DEPARTURES

"WHY ARE YOU limping?"

Franz finished negotiating the stairs from the stage door and met Yitzchak, who had just rounded the corner.

"I'd be all night explaining," Franz said. "And..."

"Kafka, he's magnificent!" Yitzchak said.

"He's what?"

Franz was taken aback by Yitzchak's display of euphoria. The actor was practically dancing on his toes.

"The illusion is so perfect," Yitzchak said, "as to almost seem genuinely magical! I mean magically genuine! No wonder he's a sensation! I was completely taken in, Franzel. I, jaded by every trick of the theater, taken in! It was spellbinding."

"Calm down," Franz said.

"And how I feel!" Yitzchak said. "Positively elated!"

"By seeing a man hang himself?"

"It's not that at all," Yitzchak said. "At least I hope it's not that. No, it isn't, at that. It's something inexplicable. But I feel... I don't know... years younger? Unburdened? Full of life, full of energy!"

"You seem to be annoyingly vital," Franz said, sitting on the stairs to massage his ankle.

"I studied the man closely, just as you asked," Yitzchak said. "I watched his hands, watched for any signs of misdirection. Every time he went to the gramophone, every gesture while he spoke, every minute movement of his body. I didn't take my eyes off him. I couldn't! In fact, I was so enrapt by every detail that I nearly forgot to raise my hand when he asked for a volunteer."

"He chose you."

"Of course he did."

"I heard him refer to a celebrity…"

"You weren't watching?"

"Go on."

"There's really nothing much to tell," Yitzchak said, removing his hat and wiping his brow. "I don't know why I'm perspiring, it isn't warm at all tonight. This is rain weather."

"What did you see when you took the stage?" Franz said.

"Nothing more than a man and a rope," Yitzchak said. "The purity of everything is exactly why the act was so astounding."

"The rope?"

"It's a rope. Made of silk. It was everything you would expect a rope to be. Not unusually heavy or light. Neither stiff nor supple. A genuine, beautiful, silken rope."

"Beautiful?"

"Beautiful, Kafka. You have to see it up close."

"And Henker?"

"Who?"

"The Hanging Artist," Franz said. He was losing his patience.

"Yes, yes, Henker," Yitzchak said, nodding. "Just a man. A plain, simple man."

"You searched him when he invited you to do so?"

"Thoroughly."

"And?"

"Franz, if there had been anything untoward, I would have said so immediately."

"So: nothing."

"No hooks, no wires. Nothing but flesh and cloth."

"You had your eyes on him at all times?"

"Yes. Even when I returned to my seat, so don't look at me like that. There was one particular play a few years ago in which I was required to keep my eyes on the leading lady as I made my way from her boudoir after she denounced me as a—"

"All right, all right. Then everything's as everyone says. He's a genius."

"Or a wizard!"

Franz rolled his eyes. "Help me up," he said, and Yitzchak helped him to his feet.

"It was one of the cleanest, most miraculous things I've ever seen," Yitzchak said, quieter. "Isn't that what you hoped to hear?"

"I didn't say what I hoped to hear."

"I thought you wanted to ensure his exoneration from all these killings."

"When I was recruited," Franz said, putting his weight on his ankle and breathing a sigh of relief that the pain had abated, "all signs seemed to point to this man, but..."

"Well, I don't know if my opinion exonerates him or not," Yitzchak said, "but in my eyes he's a consummate conjurer. This is no luncheon party magician pulling rabbits out of hats and colored scarves out of his pocket. I don't know how he does what he does, but what he does is sheer artistry."

"Were you even listening to the things he was saying?" Franz asked.

"Of course," Yitzchak said. "Every word! It's given me a great deal to reflect upon, I'll tell you that much."

"Such as?"

"Our demons!"

Franz cast a glance at the imposing, solid, black stage door.

"What do you mean by that?" he asked.

Yitzchak looked at the ground. "I rather embarrassed myself

earlier," he said. "I had gone 'round to the Aktorhalle after dinner..."

"To where?"

Yitzchak looked at Franz. "It's a club for actors and theater folk," he said. "Men only."

"Are you a member?"

"Not this Aktorhalle, no."

"Then why the hell did you...? Never mind, I know why you went. You wanted to see Proxauf about that wretched play of his. Oh, Yitzy, did you make a fool of yourself?"

"Almost immediately."

"What did you say?"

"I'd rather not reenact the scene, if it's all the same to you. I don't give encores."

"Oh, you do, too, I've seen you. Was Werdehausen there?"

"Yes."

"And you made a fool of yourself in front of Werdehausen."

"Not entirely in front of him," Yitzchak said, "but he was at the bar, which is sort of set back from the main part of the—"

"Never mind," Franz said. "When, pray tell, did you make it back to the theater?"

"In time for The Hanging Artist, obviously."

"Oh, Yitzy," Franz said. "You made a fool of yourself."

"Yes, I admit it, I was a first-class horse's ass, but it doesn't matter anymore."

"And why is that?"

Lowy filled his lungs with air and blew out, thumping his chest. He employed the grandest, most sweeping gesture in his repertoire to indicate the world around him.

"Life is beautiful, Franzel!" he said. "Don't you see it? I mean, don't you understand by now? This pettiness between me and Werdehausen means nothing when up against the scope of life's beauty!"

"Don't tell me you're giving up acting."

"Not at all. I'm going to *return* to it, with renewed gusto, my boy! Let Werdehausen do whatever it is he does, and in whichever plays to whatever approbation. Why should it matter to me? I'm Yitzchak Lowy, and nobody can be Yitzchak Lowy better than Yitzchak Lowy!"

Who has gone completely mad, thought Franz.

"And to hell with Proxauf and all the other playwrights and producers."

Franz shook his head. "Perhaps you ought to meet Henker and thank him for your new outlook," he said. "He said he'd meet me here after the performance."

"No time," Lowy said. "I'm returning to Prague."

"Tonight?"

"Sooner, if possible!"

"Well, sooner isn't possible, but tonight? It's a quarter past eleven!"

"There's a 12:05, the last of the night. Or first of the morning, however you wish to look at it."

"I think there's something wrong with you, Lowy."

Lowy hugged Franz. "Thank you for insisting I come here," he said. "It's made all the difference in the world to me. And it's so *splendid* to see you alive and well and thriving. I mean that, I really do."

"Thank you."

"And am I still under a vow of silence?"

"You're not a monk, Itzy. What are you talking about?"

"Am I to continue to keep your whereabouts and condition a secret to one and all?"

Franz shrugged and turned away. "Do what you like," he said.

"Dora will be thrilled."

Franz spun around.

Dora.

Dora would come to Vienna.

He glanced at the stage door again. He thought of the oppressive blackness behind it. The unseen dark masses that watched you. The invisible winged creatures.

The world as it came closing in on you.

He couldn't have Dora here.

Even if he alone in the world had been a witness to the silent, insistent malevolence that had made itself overwhelmingly present during The Hanging Artist's performance, he couldn't share it with anyone, not until he'd done something about it.

But what?

What *could* he do?

His clumsiness had left him trussed up like a hare throughout the performance. He'd seen nothing, only felt a hundred suffocating things, all of which, now, he could rationalize.

The blood had rushed to his head. He had been on the verge of blacking out; only the pain in his leg and ankle and foot had kept him conscious. Ergo the hallucinations.

Of course, he could be wrong. The evil could be real, and otherworldly; and he couldn't do anything about it.

In fact, he'd been completely ineffectual the two days he'd been alive.

Alive?

Had he been *dead*?

Why did he think that?

Regardless, Dora couldn't come here.

He said as much to Yitzchak, but Yitzchak was gone.

"THERE YOU ARE, monsieur," Henker said. He was standing at the top of the stairs, holding open the stage door. He held a tin collar. "Is this yours?"

"What the hell goes on here, Henker?" Franz asked.

"I beg your pardon?"

"Are your people still here?"

"My people?"

Franz bolted up the stairs, his ankle smarting, and pushed past Henker, who followed him in.

"I don't understand, Monsieur Choucas," Henker said.

Franz saw Jan and his fellow riggers tying everything down for the night. He saw Schmeide returning sand buckets to the hallway. The gramophone was gone. The scaffold was gone.

"I'm not Choucas," Franz said, turning to Henker. "I'm Kafka. Franz Kafka."

Henker smiled. "Oh, I know that," he said.

"You do?"

"I just said I did."

"Why didn't you tell me?"

"I assumed you already knew you are Kafka."

"I mean, why did you keep calling me 'monsieur' and all that?"

Henker shrugged. "If you want to go around pretending to be a Frenchman, who am I to spoil your fun?"

"How long have you known?"

"Since this afternoon."

"How? What gave me away?"

"The manuscript in your room."

Franz had to think about that one. What manuscript?

"The Hunger Artist," Henker said.

Of course. He had brought it with him from the sanatorium.

"How did you get my manuscript?" Franz asked. "What were you doing in my room?"

"The Borgia goblets."

"The what?"

"The goblets my sister gave to you as a gift. Who do you think delivered them to you? Tillie? It would have taken her all day, even if she *could* have carried them herself."

"Do you mean the famous Borgia family?"

"We never had them authenticated," Henker said, "but we trusted their source."

"Why would your sister give me such a…"

"…valuable gift?" Henker asked, amused. He lit a cigarette. "You ought to ask her yourself. I certainly have no right to speak for Tillie." He drew deeply on the cigarette. "Mmm," he said, "strangely soothing on the throat at the end of the day."

Franz felt he was being diverted, somehow.

"How do your people manage to come and go without anyone seeing them?" he asked.

"I never ask," Henker said. "Tricks of the trade; professional secrets. I have mine, you have yours…" He shrugged. "They have theirs."

"I don't have any tricks of the trade," Franz said.

"Your little story."

"I began writing that story long before I even knew of your existence, Henker," Franz said. "And as its subject bears no relation whatsoever to your… whatever you want to call what it is you do…"

It was the first time Franz saw Henker without some degree of smile on his face.

"What I do is incomparably important," Henker said.

Schmeide passed them with the last sand bucket. "No smoking on stage," he said to Henker, holding out the bucket. "Rules is rules."

Henker tossed the cigarette into the bucket, and Schmeide tipped his bowler hat and went about his business.

"Closing up, gentlemen," he said as he disappeared into the wings.

"We should go," Henker said. "There's no more show tonight, Herr Kafka." He handed him the tin collar, and smiled again. "Don't forget your souvenir."

"It's yours."

"No it isn't."

"Yes it is."

"I gave mine away the moment I came in," Henker said. "I only bought it off the man to be a sport."

Jan, whistling, passed them on his way out. He was fastening a tin collar to his throat. "G'night," he said as he left the building.

"I mean, how would it look for The Hanging Artist to be

seen with one of those things on his person?" Henker asked. "It must be yours."

"I gave mine away as well," Franz said.

"Then we have a mystery. Perhaps we can discuss it over a drink?"

Franz recalled the look on Julia Dierkop's face when he had given her the collar.

"Herr Henker," he said, stepping closer to the man, "there are people who think you are in grave danger."

Henker laughed. "We're all in danger, Herr Kafka."

"I'm serious."

"You look it. And which people think I'm in danger? Yourself?"

"Perhaps you don't know because you're out there, onstage, performing. But back here, when it all goes black, when your unseen people are supposedly running things..."

"Yes?"

Franz heard a distant door slam, and its echo alerted him to the fact that he and Henker were now all alone in the theater. The only light came from the lone lamp that had been placed on the stage to illuminate the night. The ghost light, they called it, to make the night less lonely for the theater ghosts.

"Herr Henker," Franz said, "I know that I am a highly imaginative person, but the things I imagine are nothing compared to what I experienced tonight."

"And what, exactly, did you experience, sir? My goodness, you're as white as a winding sheet!"

Two figures in black stepped up behind Henker.

"Hans Henker," the shorter of the figures said, "you're to come with us."

Henker, who hadn't flinched at the sudden appearance of the men in coats, turned to greet them. "Am I?" he asked.

"Yes," the taller of the two said.

"Whatever for?"

"You're wanted."

"I am?"

"Yes."

"By whom?"

"Just come along," the shorter of the two said.

"To answer a few questions," the taller said.

"About?" Henker asked.

"The murder of Leo Kropold," the shorter said.

"Whom?" Henker asked.

"Come along," the taller said.

They led the unprotesting Henker out the stage door, which slammed behind them.

Franz blinked.

Now he was entirely alone in that horrid theater.

"Nothing I could do about it," a voice said beside him.

CHAPTER THIRTY-FOUR
THE ILLUSIVE DETECTIVE

BEIDE CRADLED HIS jaw and prodded his teeth with his tongue.

"Nothing loose," he said. "You didn't have to hit me."

Franz nursed his left hand. The blow, he felt, had possibly caused *him* more pain than Beide.

"If you'd behave like a normal, considerate person and not sneak up on me all the time," Franz said, "that wouldn't happen."

"That was quite a punch."

"I've had a very trying evening. Where are you taking Henker?"

"*I'm* not taking him anywhere."

"Quibble, quibble, quibble," Franz said, his fright hardening to anger. "You know exactly what I mean, and I'm sick of you toying with me. Verbally and otherwise."

Beide took his hand away from his face and revealed that she had morphed into her feminine persona. Franz didn't even blink.

"Those aren't my men," Beide said.

"Who are they, then?"

"The police."

"They think Henker murdered Kropold? It's absurd.

Although there is a great deal that is absurd about all of this, so I guess that's not saying much."

"They want to question him," Beide said. "Why not let them?"

"Because it's a waste of time."

"It's their time to waste, Franz."

Franz grunted and walked onstage.

"Where are you going?" Beide called after him.

"To stand where there's light," Franz said, "such as it is. Come out where I can see you clearly."

Beide joined him at the ghost light. Franz took a careful look at her face.

"If it leaves a bruise, I apologize," he said.

"Apology accepted. It's your own fault, you know."

"What is?"

"Them taking Henker."

"How is it my fault?"

Beide took off her cap and removed a folded piece of paper from its crown. "Your remarks this afternoon about the note you found in Kropold's suit." She passed the note to him, although he recalled it even before he read it: *Thank you Hanging Artist.*

"What about my remarks?" Franz asked.

"We're not the only ones who are processing all of the information, you know," Beide said. "We have to share what we find with the local police."

"Then why do you have the note?"

"It's a copy."

"Again—what have my remarks got to do with Henker's arrest?"

"He hasn't been arrested. He's merely wanted for questioning."

Franz returned the note to her. "It's because I said something about the grammar of the thing, isn't it?" he asked. "Let me guess—they think Henker wrote the note because 'Thank you

Hanging Artist' could be Henker's way of thanking Kropold for being such an excellent agent."

"Agent?" Beide asked.

"Yes," Franz said. "You've certainly considered the possibility. Henker was the mastermind, but his alibis have been fairly airtight—he couldn't have been at any of the crime scenes at the times the murders occurred. Which suggests an associate. A henchman. Leo Kropold."

"Go on," Beide said.

"If, for some reason, it's true that Henker was in league with Kropold, how did they meet? Why did Kropold cooperate? And why did Henker get rid of him?"

"Perhaps his killing spree has come to an end."

Franz showed him the tin collar. "Do you think that's likely?"

Beide smiled and opened her tunic at the neck, revealing a tin collar snug against the flesh of her soft neck. "One can only hope," she said.

"But you think otherwise," Franz said.

"Must we talk here?" Beide asked. "This is hardly the most congenial of places to discuss this."

"There isn't a congenial place in all of Vienna," Franz said as Beide buttoned her tunic. "And we talk here and now, because you have a habit of slipping away."

"Very well."

"Which—again—I don't understand. You came to me, inspector. You begged me to solve these crimes. You were dead certain Henker was the killer…"

"We were very *interested* in Henker," she said. "I don't mean to interrupt and correct you, but it's a fine point."

"Have I proved that Henker *couldn't* be the killer?"

"You haven't proved anything. But you've been experiencing things that neither I nor anyone else in an official capacity could have experienced."

"You want proof?"

"Of course we want proof. I wish you wouldn't be so angry about it."

"I'm not angry!"

"You are; you look ready to explode."

"Because I'm *not a damned detective!*" Franz said, exploding. "But I've gamely gone along, trying to *be* a detective, and all I find is more questions, more confusion, more darkness! And you've been no help at all! You beleaguer me into spending my convalescence here in Vienna chasing around clues that don't mean anything, while you pop in and out of places like a magic lantern slide!"

"This afternoon, I suspected I was getting in your way," Beide said, placing a hand on Franz's arm. Franz noticed again the scent of oranges on her person, the same he had smelled at the hotel, when Beide was his male self. "I decided to step back for a while," Beide continued, "because I know you are not a professional detective, a trained investigator, and I felt that my constant presence was curbing your... well, I realized I should have given you a free hand from the very start. So you could learn whatever you could learn in your own, unique, Franz Kafka fashion. Perhaps I was wrong."

"I want to go home," Franz said. "But I said I'd help you, and I do what I say. What do you need to put an end to these crimes?"

"Solid proof that someone did them."

"Like Henker? Kropold? What would you consider solid proof?"

"The murder weapon."

"Which is a rope of some sort."

"Yes."

"And you think it might be Henker's performance rope, the silken noose."

"Don't you?"

"Logically? No."

"No?"

"Have you ever seen it except when Henker uses it during his performance?"

"I told you—we can't account for it outside this theater. Henker doesn't carry it on his person, and we've searched the theater."

"How well?"

Beide bristled. "We are experts, Herr Kafka. We searched extraordinarily well."

"Come."

Franz led her backstage to a bank of levers just beyond the stage left exit. "Do you have a torch?" he asked.

Beide unclipped her torch from her belt and switched it on.

"Shine it here," Franz said, indicating the levers. "One of these ought to do the trick."

She obliged, and Franz pulled a lever. An amber special shone down from above.

He pulled another. A white light, aimed at the backdrop, blinked on from the other side of the stage.

He pulled another. Nothing.

"The hell with this," he said, and threw every lever and switch on the board.

The theater filled with light.

"This way," he said, leading Beide around the many curtains to the backstage area and up the spiral staircase to the dressing rooms. "Remind me to tell you about my experiences up these stairs," Franz said as they clanged up the steps. "They'll turn your hair bone white."

"Tell me now," Beide said.

"No time," Franz said. He opened the door to Henker's dressing room and turned on the light.

"Nothing," Beide said. "We've been through this room once already, Franz."

"It's not an empty room."

"There's nothing in here except what we see."

"And what do we see?"

"A sink. A table. A mirror. A chair. There are no hiding places, nowhere one could conceal a bread crumb, let alone a length of rope. We've looked."

Franz approached the chair. It was shabby and old, something dragged down from an attic or up from a cellar. The dark wood was thick, the seat smooth, and wide enough for two people sitting together hip to hip. The table was its twin, solid and ancient. It was no more than a table; no drawers on either side.

"Henker arrives at the theater at the beginning of every performance," Franz said, "and sits here until it's time for him to perform. Why?"

"There could be a million answers to that," Beide said. "What are you getting at?"

"How closely did you or your officers inspect the furniture in this room?"

"As closely as we are now: we saw a table, we saw a chair."

Franz knelt in front of the chair and ran his thumbs under the edge of the seat.

"It has to be something fairly simple, given its age," he said.

He pushed the seat, and it came loose.

He and Beide could see, then, that the seat doubled as a lid.

"My god," Beide said. "Not even locked. And there are no hinges to give it away."

"They are within, and all of a piece," Franz said, "for that very reason: concealment. This is craftsmanship from a long-forgotten age, Inspector."

He raised the seat.

They gazed upon a rotting pile of material, slimy with age, reeking of the centuries. The material was coiled in such a way as to suggest what it had once, long ago, been.

A silken rope.

CHAPTER THIRTY-FIVE
WORDS

"THERE'S NO WAY Henker or anyone killed anybody with that mess," Beide said. "And there's also no way he uses it during his act. It'd crumble to pieces."

The seat of the chair had, at one point, originated as a chest lined with velvet, which had also rotted over time, and this accounted for the apparent thickness of the chair and its solidity: its crude construction masked subtle workmanship.

Franz picked up the rope as gently as he could manage.

"It holds together," he said. He weighed it in his hands. "It's extremely fragile, yet it remains in one piece."

"But it won't for long, not if you keep handling it," Beide said.

Franz laid it to rest again on its ancient velvet bedding.

"How old do we think it is?" Beide asked.

"I haven't the slightest idea," Franz said. "But it's very old. A hundred years? Two hundred? I'm no expert. The Henkers, however, seem to specialize in old and rare artifacts. The sister gifted me a set of Borgia wine glasses."

Beide whistled. "Genuine?"

Franz shrugged. "Again—I wouldn't know."

"What did you do to deserve such a gift?"

"Nothing, Inspector."

"There's writing on the lid," Beide said. "Look."

A legend had been carved on the underside of the lid, in simple, blocky letters; the letters themselves bore enough traces of a reddish paint to stand out in relief.

"Shine that torch on it," Franz said, and Beide illuminated the writing.

"It's Latin," Beide said.

"It's not Latin," Franz said. "I know Latin, and this isn't it."

"Is it German?"

Franz cocked his head and squinted at it. "It *resembles* German, but…"

"Can you read it?"

Franz sounded out what he read to the best of his limited ability.

> "*Swer an rehte güete*
> *wendet sîn gemüete,*
> *dem volget sælde und êre.*
>
> "*Er hat den lop erworben,*
> *ist im der lip erstorben,*
> *so lebet doch iemer sin name*
> *er ist lasterlîcher schame*
> *Iemer vil gar erwert,*
> *der noch nâch sînem site vert.*"

"I understand some of it, and yet it sounds so unfamiliar," Beide said.

"It's *Mittelhochdeutsch*," Franz said.

"Oh?"

"I'd stake my life on it."

"And how, may I ask, do you know that?"

"I had been studying the Yiddish language for years before I died," Franz said absently, his curiosity consumed by the impersonal writing before him. "Middle High German is a sort of precursor to the Judeo-German language. I didn't learn enough about it other than that. I had hoped, at one time before my illness really took hold, to study the *Nibelungenlied*, which was written in this language, and..." He trailed off and looked at Beide. "If I'm correct, that makes this piece of furniture at least five hundred years old."

"And at most?"

"Seven or eight hundred years old."

"I see. And when, Franz, did you die?"

Franz got to his feet.

"When did I die?" he asked. "I didn't die. As you can see. Why did you ask a ridiculous question like that?"

"You said you had been studying Yiddish before you died."

"I did?"

"Yes, otherwise I wouldn't have brought it up."

Franz looked around the small room, at the old table, at the rope's crypt. He looked at himself in the mirror.

"I have no idea why I said that," he said, regarding his reflection. "Perhaps because I was so certain my time was up. Up until a few days ago, when I regained my health, while I was still able to speak, my most oft-uttered phrase was, 'When I'm dead and gone.' I suppose I haven't been able to shake that. Yet." He looked at Beide. "We need to tie some things together, Inspector. I'll need your unflagging cooperation."

"You have it. Which things do you wish to tie together?"

"Everything. Do you have your notebook?"

"Of course."

Franz took the torch and shone it again on the writing. "Copy down exactly what you see," he said, "word for word, and the way each line is spaced."

Beide retrieved her black book and pencil from the depths of her cape and knelt at the chair to begin her task.

"I don't know if it's possible," Franz said, watching her work, "but I'd like a translation of that."

"And where am I supposed to get it?" Beide asked.

"One of the universities, I'd assume. A scholar."

"That might not be the world's easiest thing, and even if I could locate one, I don't know how fast we'll get results. Is it important?"

"I don't know," Franz said, helping her up when she'd finished, "but I think we should know as much as we can about anything and everything involving ropes and our friend The Hanging Artist, no matter how many centuries are involved."

"All right, I'll see what I can do. It's now after midnight."

"Is it?"

"Yes, it is now officially Saturday. Time flies when you're trying to solve a mystery, if that's what we're doing. What's next on your agenda?"

"Get out of this place as fast as we can."

"Why?"

"I hate the theater."

CHAPTER THIRTY-SIX
A NOCTURNE

WE SEE THE man stretch his legs in the first class carriage.

He feels marvelous.

He really and truly does.

He looks forward to four hours of sleep as the train rocks and sways.

He puts his hat over his eyes and nods off, planning a commission. He knows so many wonderful writers, all friends, all of his mindset; why should he chase after the wretched Viennese hacks?

No reason at all.

He hears the door of his compartment slide open.

A woman clears her throat in a manner that can't be mistaken for anything other than, "Get your feet off the seat."

He removes his feet from the seat opposite.

Hearing a cracking noise, he lifts his hat and looks.

The nun eating walnuts smiles and nods to him.

The nun with the newspaper sitting opposite her swats her with her newspaper.

He lets his eyelids slide down and sleeps, awakening when he feels the train slow to a halt.

As if a giant hand has fronted the locomotive, barring it from further progress.

He looks out the window at deep purple nothing.

The severe nun is looking at him, her newspaper folded and creased into a tight unyielding rectangle on her lap.

The other nun, covered in walnut shells, stares into space.

"Why have we stopped?" he asks.

"Because of you," the severe nun says.

"I didn't want the train to stop," he says.

"Neither did we," says the nun.

The door to the compartment slides open. Two policemen enter. They are followed by a tired-looking man in a long, gray coat, who in turn is followed by the conductor.

He hears the man in the gray coat say his name. He agrees that it is his name.

The man in the gray coat says to the other men, "This is our man."

WE SEE A young woman, clad only in her woolen nightgown, slide from between the sheets of her narrow bed.

We hear the snoring of the other young woman in the room from her own narrow bed.

The young woman leaves the bed chamber, and creeps down the hallway to the parlor.

We see her glance into another bedroom, and hear one set of snores from a woman in a narrow bed.

The young woman finds it odd that the other bed is not filled with snores. She discovers it is because the bed is not filled by another young woman.

We see the young woman tiptoe into the parlor.

She selects one pocketbook from a row of three beneath the coatrack.

We see her open the pocketbook; it is full of everything except the one thing she wanted.

"Which one of you bitches took it?" we hear her whisper.

We see her wring her hands.

She turns her head sharply, as if remembering something, then hurries to the one bookcase in the parlor.

We see her drag the ottoman to the bookcase, climb upon it, and remove four books from the top shelf.

We see her grope for something, then replace the books and get down off the ottoman.

We see the prize in her hand: a bottle, with an inch of brown liquid at the bottom.

She pulls the cork.

Although it is faint, she starts as thought the cork has made the sound of a cannon, and waits to hear if there is movement in the apartment.

Calm.

She has waited all day for this.

It has been unbearable.

She tilts the bottle to her mouth.

She is careful to not drain the bottle; she must always have the promise of one more swallow.

She corks the bottle, steps on the ottoman, and hides it again behind the books.

She gets down.

Her heart starts beating faster.

A sickening taste floods her mouth.

She gags.

She claws at her throat.

WE SEE THE old man, unaccountably ravenous at this time of night, grope his way down the stairs.

His temper is at its worst: he is hungry when he shouldn't be, and it is night, and he is stiff.

His anger at the night stems from his expectation that it should be evening.

His anger at the stiffness stems from his expectation that everything about him should have remained as useful as it was to him thirty years ago.

He would tell his wife, were she not asleep in bed, that it was her fault for letting him doze off in the parlor after supper.

He would tell his wife—were she not *actually* awake and waiting for him to come to bed, because she knows she snores and doesn't want him to come to bed while she is doing just that, because then he'd awaken her and lecture her—that if she kept a proper fire going in the sitting room even in early summer he wouldn't be so stiff.

We see the old man light a single candle because he doesn't want to waste electricity, secondary to its costliness. It is fine for the whole family—which he defines as his wife and daughters only, his useless son being... well, the less said and all that—during practical hours, but he doesn't require it for his late-night foraging.

God, he's hungry.

He is angry about his heft and heaviness.

His anger at his ever-growing corpulence stems from his wife's inability to feed him properly, requiring him to make these late-night trips to the larder.

He would tell his wife, were she not upstairs listening to him knock about the kitchen like a confused bear, how remiss she is and how stingy she is with food.

He finds the salami his daughter had been saving for a small party she had planned to throw for her friends. He finds a pot of mustard.

We see him open a drawer in the pantry. We see a collection of glittering steel.

He removes his father's prized *hallaf* from the drawer. It glints in lethal glory in the candlelight. The knife is twice as long as the thickness of an animal's neck. Eternally sharp.

We see the old man, long negligent of his religion, use the *hallaf* on the salami in the manner his father had shown him, making a silent apology to the memory of his father for the irreverent application of steel and meat.

He raises the perfectly cut slice of salami to his mouth, and pauses as the cat winds its way around his feet.

He drops the salami.

The cat died years ago.

We see the old man crash to the floor as he's pulled off his feet. He's dragged across the kitchen on his back, then heaved up, feet first, struggling all the while.

He finds his voice at last. He is yelling. He thinks he is calling out names, calling for help, but he can't be understood.

He brandishes his dead father's beloved *hallaf,* eternally sharp and true and, the old man hopes, forgiving of its current use.

We see him slash in the air.

There is an inhuman scream that can't, therefore, be a scream, but it is a cry that no one in the house or anywhere on the planet has ever heard before.

We see the old man slash again.

CHAPTER THIRTY-SEVEN
REQUESTS

BEIDE ASKED FRANZ to slow down.

Not the automobile, because Franz wasn't driving; his mouth.

"Frankly, I'm astonished by your verve, if that's the proper word," Beide said.

"I can't explain it myself," Franz said, quietly bouncing his fist on his knee. "Can't this thing go any faster?"

"Not without sending word to the pedestrians in advance." Nothing from Franz. "That was a humorous remark, Kafka."

"Very droll," Franz said. "As for my 'verve,' as you call it, there's no explanation for it, so just accept it so we can make some progress. I feel marvelous, Inspector, and that's all there is to it. Let's make the most of it, shall we? Now, what do you want me to repeat?" He was sitting forward in his seat, urging the car through the dark, winding Vienna streets.

"Everything," Beide said, "after your request for an automobile. I'm still trying to process that."

"It's faster than a train."

"In certain cases."

"I want to be in Schwechat first thing in the morning, after a few hours' sleep. Assuming I *can* sleep."

"Insomnia?"

"No, work."

"Work?"

"As I requested, I want everything you have on every victim since Ulla whatever her name was."

"Ulla Stach."

"Yes, I want to know who her friends were; friends are very important, I think, particularly with the younger victims. Even, too, the older victims, like that second murder—"

"Walter Furst. But I filled you in on many of the early murders—"

"Yes, yes, but I want to read all of this for myself, talk to people."

"Do you think I was withholding information from you?"

"Not intentionally. You merely had no idea what I'd want to know." He noticed Beide wasn't writing. "Please, inspector. Automobile, and all of your files on the victims."

He also noticed Beide was a man.

"It's gotten so I no longer notice when you switch like that," Franz said. "And, quite honestly, your edges are becoming a blur."

"My edges?"

"Your boundaries."

"Of?"

"Dammit, I don't know what I mean. Now, come on— automobile, files... how soon can I get them?"

"You might already have them."

"One of your conjuring tricks again?"

"Who's to say? And what after the automobile and the files?"

"I want you to put in a telephone call to a land agent in Schwechat."

"Which one?"

"I don't know. Is there more than one? Well, anyway, find one or two or however many and tell them to expect me first thing in the morning. Official business."

Beide smiled.

"Official business, Kafka?"

"You're to make me an honorary member of the whatever-it-is you say you represent."

"The ICPC."

"Yes. It's no use being Monsieur Choucas, because I'm no good at it, and I'm always afraid somebody is going to ask me to play something on their drinking glasses and who opens up to a verrilionist anyway? I can continue to play out my insurance investigator background, but I want to look official and show people I mean business." He paused for breath. "In short, inspector, I want a card."

Beide laughed. "You've had one since Thursday," he said.

"Of course I have," Franz said, reaching for his billfold, "because it's nothing but sleight of hand with you. No wonder you've been dogging Henker all this time, you're birds of a feather..."

"Your coat pocket," Beide said.

Franz felt in his inside coat pocket and produced a card. He caught a glimpse of it from the light of passing streetlamps. White letters on a black background read:

KAFKA
Inspektor

"That's the other side," Beide said.

Franz flipped it over. Black letters on a white background read:

Inspektor
KAFKA

He nodded, and put the card back in his pocket.

"Very well," he said. "Now we're cooking with gas. Where was I?"

"Automobile, files, land agent. Why land agent?"

"I want to confirm some suspicions I have about Kropold."

"Care to share?"

"I think he killed Inge Hirsch."

Beide said, "If that's your instinct, at this point—"

"I know it sounds farfetched, but if I'm right, I'll have a piece of the puzzle."

Beide closed his notebook. "You're trying to get our Hanging Artist off the hook," he said.

"This goes beyond Henker and Kropold and that bank cashier…"

"Hermann Herbort? I'd forgotten about him already."

"I haven't," Franz said. He looked out the window. "Here we are."

The driver let Franz and Beide out, saluting both and stepping out of earshot. The engine purred as it waited for the inspector. Franz and Beide regarded the tall, crooked façade of Frau Alt's rooming house, which sat in the middle of the street like the precarious heap of gingerbreaded boxes it probably was. Here and there a lamp shone in a window. Curtains were drawn. High atop the house a dim light glowed from the windows of the Henker rooms.

"She's waiting for him, of course," Franz said.

Beide followed his gaze to the top of the house. "The sister?"

"Someone has to tell her where he's at. That he most likely won't be home tonight."

"And then again he might be home right now, as we speak."

"You saw the police take him away."

"But we didn't see his interview. He could have exonerated himself in a matter of minutes and been on his merry way an hour ago."

Franz shook his head. "I have to see her again regardless," he said. "There's a long history of tragedy with her, a history of which I was only allowed an accidental glimpse this afternoon." He smirked. "If anything in this case," he said, "can be said to be accidental. Oh, and one more thing."

"You want me to turn back time?"

Franz blinked. "Can you do that?"

"Do please cultivate a sense of humor, Kafka."

"You seem to be able to do everything else, so far, uncanny or not."

"What is the one more thing you want me to do?"

"I want some time alone with Henker."

For the first time, Beide looked wary. "To do what to him?" he asked.

"Talk."

"Talk?"

"You know what talking is?"

"Don't patronize me, Kafka."

Franz stepped closer to Beide.

"Regardless of whether Henker is still in custody or not, I need him alone as soon as I return from Schwechat. I think it's going to crucial, no matter how my investigations turn out. Do you understand me?"

"No."

"Will you do as I ask anyway?"

"I'll do my best."

"Thank you."

"Good to know you've given up on your little book."

"My what?" Franz asked.

"That ridiculous book you bought on how not to be a detective."

"Oh," Franz said. Well, he hadn't been in his room longer than five minutes the entire day. "I forgot all about that thing."

Beide sighed. "I wish you would allow me to join you on your little adventure."

"I must have freedom."

"I'm giving you freedom."

"Yes, well, I need to feel I'm *truly* on my own, inspector. It's how I always felt before, but not since I woke up on Wednesday morning. I'm used to being on my own in this world, and with the exception of the wretched tuberculosis, I think I've managed to survive on my own, foraging ahead, making my own way, not beholden to anyone. Can you understand that?"

"Of course I can. I'm not an unsympathetic person."

"Good. And I need to act quickly. It's not the world's shortest journey from here to Schwechat, so I want to make good time; the sooner you can spare me an automobile, the better. I'm hoping to have my answers—or, failing that, better questions—in time to return here before The Hanging Artist gives his final performance."

"His final performance?"

"Before he moves to Die Feier. Before the Sabbath."

Beide took Franz by the hand and put his other hand on his shoulder.

"Use your time well, inspector," Beide said.

Franz smiled. "I'm learning to do just that," he said. "Better late than never, eh, inspector?"

CHAPTER THIRTY-EIGHT
THE LADIES OF THE ROOMING HOUSE

FRANZ FOUND A woman in his room, drinking.

Which is exactly what he didn't want.

"I hope I haven't ruined your glass harp," Julia Dierkop said, "but…"

"How did you get in here?" he asked, shutting the door. There is no space on Earth smaller than a confining room full of an anxious man, a woman drinking brandy who never drinks brandy, and a bed.

And a highly flustered three-foot-tall insect huddled in the corner giving the room's rightful occupant a stock company helpless shrug.

"It wasn't locked," Julia said. She had one of the Borgia goblets in her hand. A bottle of liquor was perched on the washstand. "I hope you'll forgive my being so bold, monsieur. I just had to see you again."

"Tonight?" Franz asked. "Breakfast is only a few hours away."

"I had to see you privately," she said.

"Oh?" came his incisive retort. "Is that allowed?"

"Allowed, monsieur?"

"I didn't think to ask at the time, but are Frau Alt's morals…

that is, what are the rules of the house regarding men and women who aren't married or related to one another occupying the same room after hours—or any hour, for that matter—"

"I don't know, I've never had the opportunity," Julia said.

"And tonight you thought you'd make an opportunity?"

"You were so kind to me tonight," she said, "and it seemed to me like you truly understood my fears for Herr Henker, and… well… I wanted to thank you, seeing how I was so rudely dragged away by my cousins. They're horrid prudes, you know, they make"—she hiccupped—"my life miserable, excuse me."

"I'm sorry to hear that."

"So am I." She hiccupped again. "Oh, no," she said. "Once these start, I can't get rid of them."

"Tell her to stick her head in a bag," Gregor said.

"Put your arms over your head," Franz suggested.

Julia hiccupped and belched at the same time.

"Pardon me," she said, giggling. "I don't usually drink drinkohol. I mean *alcohol*."

"Well, what do you usually drink, and why didn't you?"

"Tea," she said, "because my cousins are such bitches. This French brandy," she said, showing him the bottle, "is supposed to be very good."

"And is it?"

"I've no complaints so far," she said, slurring left and right. "And I'm sorry, too, that I couldn't wait. I didn't know when you'd be back, and, well…"

She shifted from one foot to another and batted her eyes.

Gregor covered his eyes as best he could with his stick-like legs. "If she vomits, demand a new room," he said.

Franz reached out and took the glass from her hand.

"Easy does it," he said, returning it safely to the ornamental tray. "That's a very old goblet."

She picked up the goblet, apparently unable to take even the broadest hint.

"Really? How old?"

"Oh, I'd say two hundred years, give or take a decade."

"Gosh. I *am* sorry. But I was very careful... and you don't have any other glasses I could use. You didn't have any other *anything*, in fact. Except the water jug. Couldn't very well have filled that up, could I? Drinking brandy from a water jug... I'm a *lady*, monsieur." She made a face and said, "Bleah." Her hand went to her throat, and he realized she was wearing the tin collar.

"Are you going to be sick?" he asked.

She stuck out her tongue and frowned. "Brandy is very burny," she said. "How do you Frenchmen stand it?"

"We export much of it to the Viennese," he said, hoping she'd find it funny, but she just hiccupped. If there was ever a time he wished Gregor could make his presence known to others, now was the time.

He cast a significant look to Gregor, raising his eyebrows and looking at the floor.

"I have no idea what that means," Gregor said.

"Which note is this?" Julia asked, holding the goblet to the light.

"I beg your pardon?" Franz asked.

"Of your glass harp. Is this A? Or middle C?"

"It's anything I wish it to be, depending on how much liquid I put into it," he said, pointing to the floor repeatedly.

"What are you pointing at?" Gregor asked.

"Something wrong with your arm?" Julia asked.

"It gets tingly when it's going to rain," Franz said.

"Rain?" she asked. She squinted one eye at Franz, then the other. "It's not raining."

"It will."

"Is your arm reliable?"

"Well..."

A bolt of lightning and an aggressive crack of thunder tore through the night.

"Right on cue," Gregor said.

Julia, however, had been so startled that she let go of the goblet. It flipped from her hand into the air with a delicate pinging sound.

Franz barely had time to curse.

Gregor kicked the pillow across the bed, and the goblet landed on it with a soft thump. Franz looked at Julia—had she seen the pillow move?

Only if she could see through her hands, which were currently clamped over her eyes.

Rain beat against the window. It was probably already leaking in.

"Terrified of"—she hiccupped—"thunder and lightning."

"Perfectly understandable," Franz said, replacing the goblet, "and probably a million other things."

"Oh, yes."

"Rats, for instance. Mice."

"Horrible."

Franz raised his voice for Gregor's benefit.

"Spiders. Bugs. *Insects of any kind.*"

Gregor said, "Gotcha," and shoved himself under the bed.

"The very worst," Julia said, swaying, eyes closed.

"Don't close your eyes," Franz said. "It will only worsen your giddiness."

Julia opened her eyes.

Just in time to see Gregor, now a reasonable two inches long, scramble from underneath the bed.

"How's this?" Gregor asked in a tiny voice.

The occupants of the rooming house heard the first blood-curdling scream of the night.

"How is it you can manifest yourself as a normal-sized insect but not when you're the size of an ottoman?" Franz asked after Julia had fled from the room, leaving the door wide open.

"It's what you wanted," Gregor answered, back to his normal unsettling size.

Franz let that pass.

"I take it you're no longer angry with me?" Gregor asked.

"I wasn't angry in the first place, I... never mind, I haven't got time," Franz said, picking up the tray of priceless goblets as gingerly as if he were hoisting a case of nitroglycerin.

"Where are you going with those?"

"Upstairs. And you're not coming with me."

"So you *are* still angry with me."

"Gregor, shut up. And stick around; I'm going to need you tonight. There's work to be done."

Franz walked slowly to the door, mindful of his burden.

"What sort of work?"

"Can't talk," Franz said. "Must concentrate."

He hadn't set both feet on the landing when he was confronted by the towering Frau Alt adorned in yards of rose-colored nightwear.

"What was that scream, monsieur?" she asked.

"It was a scream, madame."

"I know it was a scream, monsieur. But whose?"

"Not mine."

Frau Alt barely suppressed her exasperation. "It came from your room," she said.

"Your hearing is excellent, madame. Now, if you'll excuse me..."

"There was a woman in your room, monsieur."

"Pure speculation, madame. It might have been the howling of the wind. Now, if you don't mind..."

"Which of our female guests was it, monsieur?"

"It was I, madame. When I become affrighted by the sight of vermin, I become a countertenor. Now, if you could let me pass..."

"Vermin, monsieur?" Frau Alt's indignation soared past her nightcap. "In *my* rooming house? Impossible! This edifice is highly regarded as the cleanest of its kind in the whole of—"

The occupants of the rooming house were treated to the second blood-curdling scream of the night.

"ENJOYING YOURSELF, ARE you?" Franz asked Gregor as he met him outside the doors to the Henker suite.

"It's useful, no?" Gregor asked. "I could do without the running, however."

"What's she doing? Has she fainted?"

Gregor peered down the staircase.

"Her husband's there," he said, "wielding a sledgehammer. She's telling him to get the bleach... and the carbolic... and the pesticide... Look, hurry up with what you're doing, I'm done for if they have all *that* stuff in the house."

Franz shifted the tray of goblets. They became heavier the longer he held them.

"Knock on this door," he said. "I daren't put these down."

"Why?"

"Just knock!"

Gregor knocked.

"Hansel?" asked Mathilde from within.

"It's Monsieur Choucas, Mademoiselle," Franz said. "I apologize for the late hour, but I must see you."

"One moment, monsieur."

Franz whispered to Gregor, "I'm expecting a great many files tonight from Inspector Beide. When they arrive... don't eat them."

"May I read them?"

"If you must."

"Yes, sir." Gregor scampered down the stairs.

Franz waited for Mathilde to open the door.

And waited.

And waited.

One moment became fifty.

At last, the door was opened, and Franz entered, the delicate, antique collection of glass humming ever so slightly in his arms.

MATHILDE HENKER SAT, unmoving, in the chair nearest the door. The knuckles of both gnarled hands, each clutching a cane with such force as to threaten cracking, flared white. Outside, the raging storm continued to do its raging while Franz continued to stand in the cold room with the Borgia glassware in his hands. His arms ached. He had been with her for nearly five minutes.

"I knew you weren't French," Mathilde said.

"Thank you for having the grace to not expose me," Franz said.

"How would I have benefited from that?" she said. "The question is, why you are telling me now?"

"May I put these down? They're very heavy."

She waved him to the dining room. He carried the glasses into the dark room and waited for a lightning strike to illuminate the table.

"You didn't answer my question, Herr Kafka," she called after him. She heard the ornamental tray land on the table with a slight tinkling sound. He returned to the parlor.

"Because your brother has been detained," he said.

She showed no surprise at this.

"Detained?" she asked. "By whom?"

"The Viennese police, from what I can gather. The men did not introduce themselves, only commanded him to go with them."

"Which he did, of course."

"Without so much as turning a hair."

She smirked. "Of course not," she said. "He knows he's safe."

"Safe? From what?"

She fixed the sternest of stares on him. "First tell me what you want of us."

"I want nothing."

"You ingratiated yourself to us. Why?"

"May I sit?"

"No."

Franz clasped his hands behind his back. "Very well," he said, "but let me remind you that I did no such thing. I took a room—closet, really—in this house only yesterday; Thursday, if you wish to be precise, because it's now a few hours into Saturday. I had not approached you or your brother. It was you who sent me the Borgia glasses, which led to my meeting your brother, which led to his invitation to accompany him to the theater tonight, which led to my presence when he was taken away. I didn't engineer any of that."

"But you have an interest in him. What is it?"

"I am a writer, Fraulein."

"So you said. I won't say something so fatuous as 'I've never heard of you,' because I know the world is full of writers of whom I haven't heard. Regardless, I'll have to take you at your word."

"Then to be completely forthcoming with you, I offer this further honesty: I am a pensioned investigator of the Worker's Accident Insurance Institute who, at one time or another, wrote some things that were published. That makes me a writer."

"And what does being a writer have to do with my brother?"

"He has been causing a sensation," Franz said, knowing full well he was about to launch into a fabrication despite wanting to be entirely honest and open with the woman. "A sensation who is also a mystery. What better subject for the writer who, finding himself in middle age and without any success in fiction, so desperately wants to make a name for himself among his fellow scribblers?"

Mathilde let a succession of growling rolls of thunder fill the time between Franz's speech and her response. Her face, as much as it could, softened.

"Please be seated," she said, and was taken aback when

Franz sat next to her on the sofa. She was unaccustomed to any man except her brother being in such close proximity, but she did not rebuke him. She looked into Franz's unwavering, intense gaze and sensed a fellow wounded soul. It was the eyes, she said to herself, the eyes that told the truth of a person.

"You want his biography," she said.

"You've already supplied many enticing details," he said. "But I know there's so much more to learn, and if I could only be assured of exclusive access…"

"…Your fortune would be made?" she asked. "You are brazen, sir. And foolish. Had you continued to masquerade as a French player of wine glasses, I might have gone along with you, just for the sake of your company and… never mind. But now that I know your true goal, well… I don't care how honest you are, I'd be ignorant to be complicit in your exploitation of my brother. Particularly when you will no doubt make much of the murders that have been associated with him these past few months. You'd have no problem obtaining a publisher with sensational literature like that. Well, Hans had nothing to do with any of those people. You, like the police, will come upon a dead end if you insist on following that tack."

"As they are now, as we speak. Presumably."

"Hans has nothing to fear. They'll release him, as they always do, no matter how cunning they think their questions. He can't be tripped up."

"I believe you, Fraulein, but the police—"

"Are unimaginative. From beginning to end, first murder to last, Hans knew none of those people, from Ulla Stach to Leo Kropold."

Franz sat back against the hard cushions. Rain pelted the windows in waves.

"The last reported murder was Inge Hersch's," he said. "How did you learn of Leo Kropold's death?"

"The newspapers, obviously," Mathilde said, reaching for her canes. "I read several each day. One can't live on a steady diet of Goethe. They help pass the time. Of course, one has to read about all of the horrors in the world and the great cruelties people commit against each other when one relies on newspapers."

"But Kropold's death hasn't been in the news," Franz said. "Not yet, at least."

"I'm sure you're mistaken."

"I'm not. And even if it were, it would have been described as a suicide."

"Then why are the police questioning Hans about his death?"

"The question is, Fraulein, how you knew his name and why you assumed he was murdered?"

"Dear me, Herr Kafka, your questions! Are you working for the police?"

But Franz's reply was interrupted by the third scream of the night.

CHAPTER THIRTY-NINE
THREE PRIVATE ROOMS

A SMALL, WINDOWLESS room. A single lamp suspended from the ceiling. One table. Two chairs. One gloved gentleman. One ungloved and perturbed, the third of his profession, so far, to share the room with the gloved gentleman.

"Then why is your name on this note?" Nagel asked.

"It isn't," Henker said.

"It says 'Hanging Artist' clear as day."

"Which isn't my name."

"It's the name you use when you perform."

"It isn't."

"Don't try to be tricky with me."

"I'm not. I'm helping you to see, to understanding. 'The Hanging Artist' is just something it says on the bills out front and in the newspapers. It never says—nor has it ever said— 'Hans Henker, The Hanging Artist.' It's a pure theatrical construct, a leftover from my first engagement, created by a person I've never met."

"You refer to yourself as The Hanging Artist during your act."

"You were asking about this note the late Herr Kropold allegedly wrote and left behind," Henker said, and Nagel marveled again at the man's smooth and easy manner, "not about my act. I've already told you I have no idea why this man would have referred to a Hanging Artist in writing."

"Well, who the hell else—?" Nagel began.

Henker held up a gloved hand. "Yes, yes, all right," he said, "I know what you're getting at, and if it helps you any, I will go along with your assumption that the Hanging Artist to which he referred is me, however—again—the only time I met the man was when he shared the stage with me for approximately four minutes in front of a few hundred people on Thursday night."

The door to the room opened. Henker could not see who it was.

Nagel walked to the door and listened, for some time, before thanking the unseen visitor.

The door to the room closed.

Nagel returned to The Hanging Artist.

"Where were you between ten and eleven o'clock tonight?" Nagel asked.

"Ten and eleven o'clock tonight hasn't happened yet," Henker said. "It's only two o'clock in the morning."

Nagel was too tired to bandy any more words with the infuriatingly composed gloved gentleman.

"Please tell me where you were four hours ago," he said, "up until the time you were brought here."

"I was at the theater," Henker said.

"I'VE TOLD YOU a hundred times now, I was at the theater!"

A small, windowless room. A single lamp suspended from the ceiling. One table. Two chairs. One handsome gentleman. One less handsome and perturbed, the second of his profession to share the room with the handsome gentleman.

"You exaggerate," Habitzel said. "I've asked you many times, certainly, but not a hundred. But then I should remember you are an actor, Herr Lowy, and therefore have a tendency towards exaggeration."

Few things angered Yitzchak more than being called an actor. Even though he was.

"I'm not the one doing the exaggeration," he said. "Your lot has been exaggerating the realm of logic by keeping me here. I was nowhere near Werdehausen when he was killed."

"That we know of," Habitzel said.

"What is that supposed to mean?"

"Nothing."

"You're holding me on suspicion of a murder I could not have committed. Why?"

"There are many witnesses—"

"I know, I know, who saw me at the Aktorhalle earlier in the evening, so you've said. But none of them saw me return."

"Then you *did* return!"

"I did not."

"You just admitted—"

"I said none of the men who saw me earlier saw me again."

"You didn't say 'again,' you said 'saw me return.' In other words, you're saying you *did* return, but—to your knowledge— no one saw you when you did."

"I wasn't saying that at all."

"Then why did you say you returned?"

Yitzchak experienced a wave of exasperation so profound that he felt he had suddenly become a character in one of Franz's maddening tales. How could he combat such illogic? It made up its own rules, or followed none to begin with.

"I went to dinner," he said. "I went to a tobacconist. I went to the Aktorhalle. I went to the theater, the Traumhalle. I went to the station. I boarded the train for Prague. I was on the train until your men extracted me from it. Those are the facts."

"We are not interested in facts," Habitzel said. "We are interested in the truth."

"Then tell me the truth," Yitzchak said. "Tell me the only reason I'm sitting here is because a handful of men happened to mention that I had a rather heated exchange with certain members of the club, one of whom happened to be Herr Werdehausen."

"It isn't the only reason," Habitzer said.

"What is the other?"

"There are two further reasons."

"Yes?"

"It has been suggested that you had a very good reason for removing Herr Werdehausen from this world."

Yitzchak laughed. "What, that we were rivals?" he asked. "We weren't rivals at all. I have my own audience. I am a progressive artist. Christian was a two-bit stock player... There was no genuine rivalry. Others may have said we were rivals, but that is what one does in the theater—imagine rivalries between two popular yet otherwise dissimilar celebrities. There's nothing to it."

"The people we spoke to seemed to think otherwise."

"Well, they're sheep. What's the other reason?"

"You've yet to tell us the name of the person with whom you dined and later conversed after the performance at the Traumhalle."

Yitzchak's mouth nearly got the better of him—he nearly blurted Kafka's name—but his sense of loyalty prevented him. Franz had given him leave to announce his existence and location to close friends and family in Prague, but did that leave extend to anyone else? The police, for instance? Would his involvement in the hanging murders be compromised if his name was uttered?

"You have some three hundred witnesses to my appearance at the theater," he said instead. "Ask any one of them, they'll tell you. After I was onstage, I returned to my seat and remained there until the conclusion of the performance."

"After which you could have nipped around to the Aktorhalle, murdered Werdehausen, and made it to the station in time to be on the 12:05 to Prague."

"Is that right?"

"It's possible."

Yitzchak admitted to himself that it was indeed possible, but there was no way he would admit as much to Habitzer.

"The name of your post-theater companion, Herr Lowy," Habitzer said.

"Ignaz Seipel," Yitzchak said.

"The Chancellor?"

Yitzchak nodded.

"I call him Iggy," he said. "He's very fond of the acrobats."

A LARGE, WINDOWLESS room. Two chandeliers suspended from the ceiling; one enormous round table; eleven chairs, each containing a person.

"It's similar, yet different," one said.

"That's all?" asked another.

"And then, of course, there's the surname."

"And relationship."

"Yes."

"And there's evidence," a third one said.

"Inexplicable evidence," said the first.

"It's been preserved?" asked a fourth.

"Yes."

"And the man?"

"Sleeping."

"Guarded?"

"Until we decide otherwise."

"Will he cooperate?"

"He is rather a recalcitrant individual."

"Is that a yes or no?"

"Neither. It remains to be seen, depending on our decision."

There was silence in the room.

Ten people turned to the eleventh.

"And what," the first one said, "is your recommendation, Inspector Beide?"

CHAPTER FORTY
A MURDEROUS INTERRUPTION

"You people work fast," the officer said, twirling the card in his hand, white side, then black side, then white side, and so on. "I suppose you won't give me a straight answer if I ask the ICPC's interest in this?"

Franz plucked the card from the officer's hand. "What's your name, officer?" he asked.

"Bamborger."

"Bamborger *what?*"

"Just Bamborger."

Franz raised an eyebrow in what he hoped was an imperious manner.

"Oh," Bamborger said. "Bamborger, *sir.*"

"Thank you."

"Should I salute?"

"No."

Two tired-looking men in white coats transferred the woman's corpse onto a litter and covered it with a sheet. Julia Dierkop and two of her cousins huddled in the corner of the apartment, Julia speaking to an officer who was writing down everything she said. The other two women sat together on the sofa, their hands folded in their laps, watching their sister's removal with all the dispassion they could muster.

"Now then, Bamborger," Franz said, surveying the suite's parlor with a cold, controlling gaze, "what do we have here? And don't say 'a dead body,' because I can see that. I'm asking the nature of the case. Suicide? Murder?"

"Difficult to say, sir."

"Why?"

"Because I don't know the answer to that."

Franz remained standing in the doorway, hoping his presence would not be noticed by Julia. "I'm not asking you to solve anything," he said. "I want to know what's known. The facts. You have the facts, don't you?"

"Yes, sir."

"Well? Out with them!"

Bamborger nodded to Julia. "The lady there says she came back to this apartment and went straight to her bedroom, which she shares with... um, I think it's the lady on the right."

"The right as one sits on the sofa, or the right as we're looking at them?" When it became clear Bamborger was struggling to figure it out, Franz barreled on. "All right, we'll skip that for the moment," he said. "What then?"

"She changed into her, um, *nocturnal attire*, sir, and felt the need to, um, *pass water*, sir..."

"Speak plainly, for God's sake," Franz said. "We'll get through this so much faster if you do."

Bamborger brightened at the suggestion. "Very good, Inspector," he said. "As the bathroom on this floor is at the end of the hallway, she would have to leave the apartment to visit it, and she couldn't find her slippers. She went to the second bedroom to borrow..."

"Why didn't she borrow her roommate's slippers?" Franz asked.

"She said her feet are too small."

"Go on."

"She went into the other bedroom and noticed one of the beds was unoccupied, that of the deceased."

"And?"

"She found a pair of slippers that fit, left the apartment, and went to the toilet."

"Skip to her return from the toilet."

"When she returned to the apartment, she noticed the deceased sprawled on the floor."

"She hadn't noticed before?"

"Apparently not, sir."

"But when she noticed this time…"

"She screamed."

"And what is the name of the deceased?"

"Lisy Dierkop, sir. Of the famous Dierkop Sisters."

The Dierkop Sisters were anything but famous, but Bamborger had possibly been bullied into believing so by the surviving members of the four-woman-trio.

An elderly, unkempt man carrying a shabby medical bag nodded to the white-coated men and joined Franz and Bamborger at the door.

"One side, gentlemen," he said, and the white-coated men carried the litter with the covered Lisy Dierkop out of the apartment. None of the women so much as sniffled.

"What's the good word, doctor?" Bamborger asked, yawning.

"Murder," the doctor said. He was practically all beard and spectacles.

"How was she killed?" Franz asked.

The beard and spectacles glanced at him, then at Bamborger. "Who's this?" he asked.

Bamborger mouthed "ICPC," and the old doctor nodded.

"Poisoned," he said. "Prussic acid. She reeked of it. Stuff smells like bitter almonds. Skin turns red. Had all the signs. Not a fun way to go."

"How did she…?" Franz began, but he was interrupted by the officer who had been speaking to Julia, who now joined them, showing them a brandy bottle with perhaps a half-inch of liquor remaining.

"Drank this," the officer said.

"How did she not notice the smell of the acid?" Franz asked.

"Because there is no odor," the doctor said. "It smells like brandy. Cheap brandy, too."

Franz stopped himself from asking one of the stupidest questions in the universe; unfortunately, Bamborger asked it anyway.

"Could she have only swallowed the poisoned part of the brandy, unpoisoned part behind?"

The doctor and the officer, disgusted, turned away from him.

"It couldn't have been suicide, either," Franz said, "if there's no evidence of poison in the brandy and we are certain this is all she drank—unless she took the poison in some other form immediately before she drank the brandy."

Bamborger was awed by the suggestion. His partner made a hasty note in his notebook. The doctor, however, shrugged. "I'll cut her open, see what's sloshing around inside," he said, a little too loudly. The Dierkop sisters could be observed to stir in the background, while Julia choked a sob. The police hurried the doctor down the hall as Franz went in to Julia.

She wound up in his arms. The sofa-bound Dierkop Sisters gasped.

"Monsieur, this is beyond hell," Julia said, and Franz disengaged from her in as gentlemanly a manner as he could. She cast a glance at the women. "These are my cousins, Flora and Katharina," she said.

"We had no idea she drank," Flora said in a defensive, schoolmarmish clip.

"We certainly wouldn't have allowed such a thing," Katharina said in the same tone, an octave lower. She was evidently the mezzo of the quartet.

"We never thought to look in the bookcase," Flora said.

"Those aren't even our books," Katharina said.

"They came with the room."

"This is a furnished apartment."

"Lisy never smelled of alcohol."

"And never showed any signs of inebriation."

"I can't help but think that this is all a mistake."

"It certainly is an imposition."

The sisters had somehow gone back to talking to each other, forgetting Franz and Julia.

"We can't cancel our booking," Flora said.

"Heavens no. Nor should we," Katharina said.

"We need a second soprano."

"Without question. You'll have to sing lead until we find one."

"I don't know the melodies."

"Incredible!"

"Don't look at me like that. You've always been just as wrapped up in your harmonies as I."

"Well, fortunately we won't have to revise our billing."

"Yes. Perhaps in future we can shorten it to 'The Three Dierkops' and have done with it."

"Why not just 'The Dierkops'? That way it won't matter if we have three or four or more on the stage."

"Never more than four, the money's stretched out enough as it is."

"A non-Dierkop should, by rights, receive a smaller percentage."

"Yes. Hand me that pad and pencil, I want to work this out..."

Julia led Franz out of the apartment and into the hallway, shutting the door on her cousins. With the departure of Lisy, the white-coated men, the doctor, and the officers, the house had begun ringing with the slamming of doors as the residents satisfied their curiosity and returned to their beds.

"I feel absolutely dreadful about this," Julia said. She had been shocked into sobriety, and Franz pitied her.

"It's a tragedy," he said, unable to think of anything more original to say.

"And to think," Julia said, "only an hour ago I was complaining about her."

"You were?"

"Well, not Lisy specifically. Them, in general." She cocked her head at the closed door.

"How do you mean?"

"Before you arrived. When I was drinking the brandy I'd brought to your room. I had been miserable about the way they treat me, the grueling rehearsals, the prudishness. Oh, they were kind enough, monsieur, I suppose, but..."

"Where'd you get the brandy?"

"Beg pardon?"

"The brandy you brought to my room."

Julia blushed. "I bought it," she said. "Some time ago. For my own use, if ever the occasion warranted."

"Your cousin, then, must not have known you had it."

"No, otherwise it would have been gone by now. Poor Lisy. We really had no idea she was a souse, monsieur. I'll never stop blaming myself."

"Why should you blame yourself in the first place?"

Her eyes misted over. "Because," she said, "of my shameful thoughts. Oh, it's too much to consider, monsieur. To think that at the very same time I was drinking brandy and thinking those selfish things poor Lisy was in here drinking her own poisoned brandy, as if I somehow willed her to die."

"I'm sure you did no such thing," Franz said. "The coincidence is just your fancy, and for all you know she could have perished before you ever lifted the glass to your lips. The correlation is superficial. Don't torture yourself with this foolish talk."

She thanked him, although he knew not for what, and he bid her good-night. As the door closed behind her, he shook his head at the notions people will sometimes entertain.

Of course, there was a certain irony (if it indeed *was* irony) that Julia had been drinking from a goblet once owned by a member of a family historically known for poisoning. The

Borgias, if their spirits lingered in the ether, would have been pleased, albeit frustrated that the victim had been nowhere near the actual goblet. Still, poison was poison, and perhaps their otherworldly influence wished to favor a long-suffering woman by bumping off—

Franz sharply drew in his breath, provoking the first coughing fit he'd experienced in days.

He tried to stifle the coughing so as not to disturb the house any further, but the suppression only aggravated the fit. He clutched the newel post of the stairs to the upper floor and fought to steady himself.

Once under control—with tiny stars swimming before his eyes—he climbed the stairs to the Henker suite. He knocked, but no answer came, so he tried the door, hoping Mathilde Henker hadn't locked the door after he'd abruptly left her to investigate the last scream nearly two hours earlier, but his hope wasn't met. No light came from behind the doors. All was quiet.

He had not had enough time with Mathilde, although he couldn't say exactly what more time might have yielded. And now, with the ridiculous notion of Julia's rattling around in his brain and clanging like the Borgia goblets would have done had he only played them, Franz couldn't fathom what he wanted to discover from her in the first place. Did he want to share his new theory with her, regardless of how foolish it sounded? Did he want to tell her that her priceless Borgia glasses might have poisoned an innocent woman?

Franz coughed, took his handkerchief from his pocket and, out of habit, spat into it.

No blood.

He went down the stairs to the landing and saw Gregor sitting outside his room.

"I have good news and bad news," Gregor said.

"What's the good news?" Franz asked, clearing his throat.

"The files arrived."

"That's fine, although God only knows when I'm going to get the chance to read through all of them."

"No worries, I've nearly gone through the lot," Gregor said.

"You have?"

"If you only knew the mounds of paperwork I had to work through in my days as a salesman," Gregor said. "Of course, you *do* know, I suppose."

"What's the bad news?"

"I still have some more good news."

"Yes?"

"The automobile you requested has been delivered. It's waiting outside."

"Well, I didn't think it'd be waiting in the dining room, Gregor. Anything else?"

"It stopped raining."

"Splendid."

"And now the bad news," Gregor said.

"Here it comes," Franz said.

Gregor pointed to the steamer trunk outside the door, a trunk that looked very familiar to—

"I've been kicked out?" Franz asked.

"That woman was muttering something about artists as her bull of a husband lugged your things out of the room."

"But it's four in the morning!"

"It's actually twenty minutes to five. If you want the exact time…"

"No, I don't want the exact time," Franz said. "Frau Alt could have at least had the common decency to have faced me with the news; after all, I paid good money…"

"You don't want to go in there anyway," Gregor said. "She practically gassed the place with Black Flag. You'd suffocate. Oddly enough, I don't mind the stuff. So much for insect repellant, eh?"

"Is that the only bad news? It seems there should be more."

"I'll let you see the automobile for yourself."

Franz looked at the trunk and the pile of his things. He'd a good mind to leave it all sitting there. What, after all, did he really need? He was starting over in life, wasn't he?

It was the first time the thought occurred to him, and it made him break into a cold sweat.

It hadn't been much of a new life since Wednesday, had it? While he admitted it had certainly been a great deal different from his 'old' life, had it been promising? Rejuvenating? Encouraging? Had it filled him with the beauty and promise of life, or with a renewed fascination for the world and humanity?

Not really.

It had been littered with death.

Populated with people who not only kept secrets, but actually appeared to personify them, embody them, and act as if those secrets were the only things ruling their lives.

It had been populated with people who were one thing, then another, or both at the same time. It had been impossible to know the truth of them.

It had been mostly illogical, and what little logic he had encountered led to conclusions too terrible to face.

It had been filled with glimpses of human misery. It had been filled with intimations of lust, greed, envy, revenge, and desperation.

It had shown him a dark void where monstrous, unseen beings swarmed around him, watched him, and closed in on him.

It had given him Gregor.

It had baffled him.

In short, this new life was much the same as his old life, differing only in that the privately held beliefs he held about humanity had now become flesh and word and deed.

But he suspected he was not going to be given much of a choice between the two.

He sighed.

"Help me with this," he said to Gregor, and the two of them

struggled down two flights of stairs with the trunk between them.

Once outside Frau Alt's, the gradually vanishing moonlight and the promise of dawn illuminated an odd-looking machine on wheels stationed at the curb. Franz dropped his end of the trunk, which caused Gregor, who had been ill-advisedly maneuvering backwards, to lose his grip and fall. He teetered on his great round shell, every leg waving in the air.

"*That's* Beide's idea of an automobile?" Franz asked.

"Help," said Gregor.

It was certainly a machine with four wheels: a Daimler Tourer, which must have cut quite a sporty figure on the streets of Vienna fifteen years prior. What was left of its sky blue paint did nothing to offset the great patches of rust that speckled the machine like a teenager's complexion. The tires were thin and brown with wear. The seats of the two-seater were swollen with mildew. The canopy top had been patched so often it resembled a quilt stitched together by a madwoman.

"It's fifteen kilometers to Schwechat," Franz said. "We won't make it down the block."

"It's a beautiful car," Gregor said, rocking back and forth in an effort to right himself. "Built to last. Worm gears, shaft drive... they don't make them like that anymore. Help me up, will you?"

"Where's the driver?" Franz asked as he assisted Gregor.

"What driver?"

"That thing didn't arrive by itself, did it? Where's my driver?"

"I don't know. Did you ask for one?"

"I asked Beide to send me an automobile. I didn't think I had to spell out anything further."

"Well, you got what you asked for," Gregor said. "Let's get your trunk strapped to the back and get on our way."

As Gregor helped him with the trunk, Franz said, "I've some bad news of my own."

"Oh?"

"Yes."

"What?"

"I've never driven an automobile."

CHAPTER FORTY-ONE
AN EXCHANGE AT DAWN

"WELL, I'M GLAD to hear the Dierkop woman was poisoned."

"Hans. Don't say that."

"Because had it been the other way... I couldn't have accounted for it."

"Had anyone asked you, that is. And nobody would."

"Still. It's a relief. Comfortable?"

Mathilde, surrounded by pillows of every size and thickness and tucked into her bed with the blankets up to her chin, smiled.

"As always," she said. "Safe and sound. There's no one who can do this like you."

"Good. Sleep all day if you like. I'll be quiet."

"Don't go just yet."

Henker sat at the foot of her bed.

"What is it?" he asked.

"There's been another, hasn't there?" she asked.

He looked down at his gloved hands and rubbed them together.

"You know there has," he said. "This time it's someone famous."

"Whom?"

"An actor. Christian Werdehausen."

She lay back on the pillows. "They'll not let this one rest," she said.

"They've not let any of them rest," Henker said. "But I know what you mean. The profile on this one will definitely be... higher." He pounded his fist into his hand. "Which isn't to say that one death is more important than another, more deserving of attention than another. It's sickening, when you think of it, how one person's injustice is given shorter shrift than another's simply because of... I don't know... obscurity? Lack of achievement? Social standing? Wealth or notoriety?"

"What are you saying, Hans?"

"I hardly know what I'm saying anymore," he said. The bed creaked under his added weight. "I've been saying all of this hasn't affected me, but..."

"It happens every night, now," she said. He nodded.

"When will it stop?" she asked.

"Sleep, Tillie. You know I don't know the answer to that."

"I told you there needed to be more."

"There have."

"But more than this."

"When I start at Die Feier, I'll be asking for three volunteers per performance. Now get some rest."

"But will that be enough?"

"I don't know," he barked.

Mathilde's hand flew to her mouth. "I'm sorry, Hansel," she said, "I'm so very... I don't mean to press, but..."

He patted the bed. "I'm sorry, too."

"I'm looking forward to the Hotel Das Gottesanbeterin," she said, as brightly as she could. "Such luxury."

She noted the hint of a sad smile on her brother's face in the pale morning light. "Yes," he said, "if nothing else, we've had the money to make it all just a little bit more bearable, Tillie."

"How soon do we take possession of our new 'home,' such as it is?"

"Monday."

"That quickly!"

"I'll be spending every ounce of today packing everything we have."

"Can't we just... leave all of it here, forget about everything, let these things be someone else's burden?"

"No," he said. He rose and drew the curtains. "Now, I want you to get your rest," he said. "And, Tillie..."

"Yes?"

"It struck me, tonight, that perhaps our stay in Vienna... ought to be curtailed as soon as possible."

"But your contract at Die Feier! The money, the opportunities..."

"Yes, yes, I'm well aware of all that," he said, returning to her bed. She could barely see him now. "I'm thinking that the world is a big place, and the time will come when my act will have overstayed its welcome, and no one will be interested in seeing The Hanging Artist, particularly when... Well, you know..."

"I understand," she said. Pain pulsed at the base of her spine, and she asked him to reposition her. He did so with all the delicacy and care he could muster, as always.

"Travel is difficult for you, I know," he said, "but we'll have to face it."

"Where to next?"

"North to Prague, perhaps... or maybe it's better to clear out of this area altogether. How's your Italian? Or French? Or English?"

"I can learn anything quickly enough," she said.

"And there's always America," he said.

"All those people," she said.

"And if anyone loves sensation, it's the Americans. We could be set for years."

"Do you really think it'll be years, Hans?"

"I hope not. But it's best to be prepared, to have a plan."

"Hansel…"

"Yes?"

"Do you… have we reached a point where…"

"What is it, dearest?"

"You know what I'm trying to ask, don't you?"

"You're exhausted, Tillie. This night has been a trial for you."

"But, Hansel… have you reconciled your feelings… when it comes to me…?"

He hushed her.

"You are to have no more worries," he said. "You must believe me."

"Oh, I do, Hansel."

"I'll never be able to forgive myself, and I'm consigned to that. Any hatred I feel is towards myself."

"You mustn't."

"It can't be helped. From my first thought in the morning to my final thought at night, and possibly even while I dream, although I can't remember the last time I actually dreamed anything except silent darkness.

"But it's self-hate that fuels my hope, Tillie. I think it actually gives me power; I think it's been giving me unheard-of strength. My own strength. It's certainly given me hope, hope that there will come a time when I will call for my final volunteer.

"Until then, we must bear it as best we can, as we have with all that life has already thrown at us.

"So sleep without worry, Tillie. I love you."

On his way out the door, she called to him. "Hans?"

"Yes?"

"My canes. Put them a little closer to the bedside, will you?"

CHAPTER FORTY-TWO
ON THE ROAD TO SCHWECHAT

"For the love of God, be careful! That last one nearly jarred all the teeth out of my skull!"

"Let the record show that I never said I was a *good* driver," Gregor said.

"Regardless," Franz said, "try not to *aim* at every hole and ditch."

The battered Daimler wheezed its way through Landstrasse as fast as Gregor could urge it. The insect had estimated the journey southeast to Schwechat would take them no more than an hour, but he was beginning to revise his estimate. Daylight would definitely overtake them long before that, and keep going. Perched as he was on the box of files provided by Beide and the ICPC, he could barely reach the accelerator and brake.

"I should be wearing a hat," Gregor said.

"If it will help you drive better, you can have mine," Franz said.

"Beggars can't be choosers," Gregor said. "I'm thinking ahead to when these roads begin to fill up with traffic. Folks are in for a shock when they see me at the wheel of this thing. I'm sure you don't want any attention drawn to us."

"I thought you couldn't be seen?" Franz asked.

"I've told you several times now that I started out by saying that I wasn't *sure* if you would be the only person who could see me," the giant insect said. "It's better to be safe than sorry."

"Plenty of people have been in your presence, who haven't remarked on the phenomenon," Franz said. "And I don't think you're the sort of thing that goes unremarked."

"Well, we'll see. Hold on."

They rattled across a wooden bridge. Franz felt every board.

"Do you know any shortcuts?" he asked.

"Yes, but it would require us to travel over farmland, and I don't think you or I *or* this automobile is equipped for that. No, Landstrasse to Erdberg to Simmering to Schwechat is the fastest, safest, and best-paved route I know."

"Very well."

"And while we're on the subject—and knowing that it's probably neither my place nor the best time to ask, which would've been right before we left—is this journey completely necessary?"

Franz stopped himself before saying *I'm not certain*. He was certain in that his theory, if it were to be borne out, could be verified in Schwechat. Beide had left him an envelope containing two things: the name of the land agent in Schwechat he had telephoned—a man by the name of Gauss—and a brief note that Yitzchak was being questioned about the murder of Christian Werdehausen, who had perished the night before in the same manner as all of the previous victims, with the exception of Leo Kropold's, whose death he was now sure was either a mockery or a homage.

The news of Yitzchak's detainment had nearly caused Franz to postpone the trip to Schwechat, but he reasoned that there wasn't anything he could do to help his friend other than to pursue his line of investigation and, with luck, present a solution to Beide that would explain all that had occurred over the past two months, no matter how incredible it would sound.

And Franz knew it would sound incredible, if his suspicions

were correct. Incredible and improbable.

Not *impossible*. He had learned over the last few days that nothing was impossible.

And yet if the answer to the riddle of The Hanging Artist and the strange, horrific murders that had taken place was what he feared, the improbable would become, after all, probable.

They continued to rattle down a lonely road that cut through a sparse forest. They had yet to reach Erdberg, and the sun was on the horizon, a ribbon of pale orange.

"You were telling me about Ulla Stach," Franz said, "before our spines were nearly snapped in half."

"Where had I left off?" Gregor asked.

"You told me about her family, and I don't think the answer lies with them," Franz said. "And, quite frankly, I'd rather not have to face a still-grieving mother. You started saying something about a law firm."

"Oh, yes," Gregor said. "Ulla Stach had only been employed as a secretary at a law firm for five days before her death. Not just as any secretary, mind you, but as the private secretary of the head of the law firm, a gentleman by the name of Werner Gauss."

"Wait a minute—isn't Gauss the land agent we're going to see?"

"The land agent is Georg Gauss. Werner is his cousin. Any significance in that?"

"It'll have to be taken into account. Anything further on Ulla Stach?"

"Only that the files noted her family had been very proud of her new employment. A few girls had interviewed for the position, but Ulla was chosen."

"Was that surprising?"

"From the way everyone seemed to talk about it, yes, but no reason for the surprise is noted."

"These other girls—friends of Ulla's?"

"Yes, all three. Do you want their names?"

"I might. God, if I have to track down three women… I haven't the time. What about Walter Furst?"

"No sex stuff, if that's what you want to know."

"Not even a hint of it, a suggestion?"

"Nope."

"Then what was the disposition of his estate?"

"All of his money went to his wife."

"What of his business?"

"Reverted to his partner in the event of his death. So, as he died, the partner acquired full control of the business."

"The partner's name?"

"Josef Kramski."

"Bachelor? Married man?"

"Married."

"Please tell me he resides in Schwechat, too."

"He does indeed."

"I think we'll visit him, too… but not directly."

"How do you mean?"

"I mean that I think I shouldn't attempt to be up front with these people. I think the way to piece things together accurately is to avoid coming right out and asking the two questions that matter the most right now."

"What are the two questions?"

"I'll come to that shortly," Franz said. "Now, what about Emmanuel Buchner?"

"The custodian."

"Yes."

"There's nothing much about him. Bit of a dimwit. Not married. Lived in a boiler room."

Franz frowned.

"That's all?"

"A married sister who hadn't seen him in two years."

"Why not?"

"The files didn't say. There was a note that she didn't show too much remorse at the news of his death, however."

"Any reason why?"

"None given. And yet she practically lived within shouting distance of the school at which Buchner was employed."

"Was the sister older or younger than Buchner?"

"Older, by five years. Buchner was thirty-two, so do the math."

"Any children?"

"Buchner? Or the sister?"

"The sister, obviously."

"Three daughters."

"Ages of the daughters?"

"I'll have to look. They'd have to be young, though. What, exactly, are you looking for, Franz?"

"Eyes on the road, please!"

Gregor swerved to miss a milestone.

"I'm trying to discern," Franz said, trying to relax, "why any of these people would be better off dead."

"Better off dead?"

"Well, perhaps that's not the best way to put it," Franz said. "And really, who's to say anyone is 'better off' dead?"

"I used to know a few people."

"Let me put it another way," Franz said, doing his best to sort out his scrambled thoughts and fight off fatigue at the same time. "I want to find out if there is any reason someone would have found life better with Ulla, Walter, and Emmanuel... and all of the other victims ... out of the way. Permanently."

The Daimler chose that moment to slow down of its own accord.

"What's happening?" Franz asked.

"Either this thing is coming to a halt," Gregor said, "or the scenery is taking its own sweet time to pass."

As it turned out, they were going uphill. Gregor smashed the accelerator over and over again.

"Don't do that," Franz said. "That can't be good for the engine."

"Says the guy who doesn't know how to drive."

"I'll push," Franz said. Gregor held him back.

"You weight ninety pounds soaking wet," Gregor said. "It'd be like someone trying to move a hippopotamus with a playing card. *I'll* push."

"But who's going to drive?" Franz asked, the cold sweat returning.

"You are," Gregor said, sliding off the box and landing in the road. "Hurry up," he said.

Franz slid over to take the wheel. "I can't drive this thing!"

"Keep your right foot on that thing there," Gregor said, pointing, "and let the automobile do the rest. All you're really doing is steering the thing, not driving it."

"Get back in here!"

"You're doing fine. Just keep the thing on the road, that's not so hard."

He heard Gregor grunt as he shoved the automobile up the incline.

Franz clung to the steering wheel as if it were a life preserver and prayed all the prayers he knew.

And some he didn't.

CHAPTER FORTY-THREE
HISTORIES

"A GREAT LOSS," said Werner Gauss. "Everything about her was excellent."

The young woman in the chair opposite Franz cleared her throat, but otherwise kept writing in her notebook.

"Fraulein Ascher's cartoonish way of butting in," Gauss said, "is meant to imply that I should edit my remarks to leave no impression that I am referring to the late Miss Stach's physical appearance." He looked at Fraulein Ascher. "Every word, Fraulein Ascher. Even those. And I'll thank you not to interrupt."

Franz did not particularly like the lawyer, but he did not particularly dislike him, either. The man was a self-righteous pillar of society with an overriding desire to let everyone know his scruples and morals were pristine. They might have been; they might not have been. His private secretary's none-too-subtle interruption suggested she either knew otherwise or was concerned about the impression her employer was making on the visitor. Franz directed his next question to her.

"Actually, Fraulein Ascher," he said, "I understand you were Fraulein Stach's friend. Do you agree that everything about her was excellent?"

Gauss scowled at the young woman, but nodded to her that she could answer.

"We were classmates at the institute, Herr Inspector," she said, then turned to Gauss. "Am I to write down my remarks, too?"

"Everything," Gauss said. "I've made it a habit of ensuring that a record be made of every conversation that goes on in this office," he said to Franz. "You understand, I'm sure."

"But you weren't exactly friends, then?" Franz asked the private secretary.

"We were friendly," Fraulein Ascher said, writing as she spoke.

"Were you happy for her?"

"In which regard, sir?"

"When she became your predecessor in this position."

"Ah. Of course. It is a great honor to work for Herr Gauss."

Franz felt this last bit was said for her employer's benefit, and the man duly puffed out his vest.

"Fraulein Ascher, of course," Gauss said, "was my second choice. Which is not to say that she wasn't better than Fraulein Stach."

"Then how did you choose between the two?" Franz asked.

"Fraulein Stach could type seventy words per minute," Gauss replied. "Fraulein Ascher could type sixty-seven."

"I can now type seventy-two words per minute," Fraulein Ascher said.

Both seemed very pleased with this fact. Franz tried another approach.

"Then you didn't really socialize with Ulla?" he asked the secretary.

"It wasn't from lack of trying," she said. "We girls were always asking her to join us for this and that."

"Fraulein Stach was most circumspect," Gauss said to Franz, with a wink.

"But she didn't join you?" Franz asked.

"Not once."

"Perhaps she didn't enjoy the social whirl most commonly afforded the young," Franz said. "Dining with friends, the dance hall, the cinema, the theater… "

"In truth," Fraulein Ascher said, "she consented to go out with us the one time, and I assume it was only because the evening was to be in her honor."

"Her honor?"

"She had taken this position earlier in the week, and the rest of us thought it would be nice to treat her to an evening out by way of celebration. Dinner, then the variety hall."

"But in the end, she decided not to join you."

"No, she didn't."

"The lot of you went anyway?"

"Yes, and it's just as well she didn't join us, the food was awful and there was a horrible act at the variety hall, a man who hanged himself. It was perfectly dreadful."

"It caused a bit of a sensation for a bit," Gauss added. "Tasteless trick, I understand."

"You think Fraulein Stach would not have enjoyed this— um—professional suicide?" Franz asked.

"Certainly not," Fraulein Ascher said.

"And you found it dreadful, too. You said so yourself, just now."

"After he hanged himself, of course. Disgusting."

"But before he hanged himself?"

"Well, we all thought it was silly, that he was a comedian or something. He asked for a volunteer, I went up."

"Did you?"

"I just said I did."

"A simple 'yes' or 'no' will do, Fraulein," Gauss said. He looked to Franz for approval.

"We're not in court, Herr Gauss," Franz said.

"Why are you interested in that wretched man?" asked Fraulein Ascher. She had ceased writing in her notebook.

"I'm not," Franz said. "I was just remarking on your fascinating experience at the theater the night Ulla Stach died."

"How do you know it was that night?" she asked.

"Was it?"

She hesitated. "It was, in fact."

"Thank you."

"IT WAS A falling out, that's all," said Liesl Franke, up to her arms in soapsuds and dishes. Her three daughters sat about the kitchen slowly doing various chores, all of them trying very hard not to look at Franz. "I don't remember what caused it. These things happen in families. Is it very important?"

"One never knows," Franz said. "It might have affected him in some acute manner. Internally, I mean."

"You mean like his heart?" Liesl asked.

"His conscience," Franz said.

"Manny never had the brains to have much of a conscience," she said.

The eldest girl looked up, then down.

"Was he a drinker?" Franz asked. "Perhaps he said something rash that caused the rift. While he was in his cups."

"Never touched a drop in his life. That I knew of."

"Was there reason to doubt?"

Liesl shrugged, and beckoned the eldest girl to the sink to begin drying the dishes.

"People do lots of queer things and keep them secret," Liesl said, turning to Franz and drying her red hands on her apron. "Even when they're your own flesh and blood."

"Yes, that's so," Franz said.

A dish clattered in the sink.

"Careful," the mother said to the daughter.

The daughter gave the mother a dark look, and was careful.

"May I congratulate you on your well-behaved children?" Franz asked. "My own are devils."

"You've children, sir?"

"Three," Franz said. "The same number as you. Unless there are others around I've yet to meet?"

"This is the lot," the woman said. "They can be devils at times, too."

"Perhaps mine are just too young to be very mindful just yet."

"How old are they?"

"The eldest is six, the twins are four. All boys."

The woman nodded in satisfaction. "That's boys for you. Girls are a bit different." She nodded to each as she dashed off their ages. "Ten, twelve, and fifteen. Of course, they get older, different problems come up."

Another look from the eldest, who had been washing the same dish for well over a minute.

"You still call him Manny," Franz said, startling the mother. "You retained some affection for him, then, even after whatever caused him to stop seeing you and your family?"

"I hadn't noticed," she said. "He was over here regularly, every Sunday for dinner, and of course birthday parties and Christmas. Once a year he'd join us for a bit of fun at the variety hall."

"And, of course, all of that stopped two years ago."

"Yes."

"The parties, the trip to the theater…"

"Oh, our lives went on as before," she said. "We just didn't include him, is all."

"So you'll be going to the theater again this year?" Franz said. "That's delightful. A family outing…"

"We've already been," the eldest girl said.

"Nobody asked you," the mother said.

"It's all right," Franz said.

"Lovely time," the middle girl said.

"Great fright at the end," the youngest girl said, smiling. "Man went and hanged himself!"

The middle girl nodded. "Great treat, that."

"A man hanged himself?" Franz asked.

Liesl Franke gave him her first smile of the morning. "Magician," she said. "Tacky, really. The girls had a great laugh because I went up there when he asked for somebody to search him. Stupid, really."

The younger girls giggled.

"Manny would've loved it," the mother said.

"Do you miss your uncle?" Franz asked the youngest.

The eldest girl ran from the room.

The mother had stopped smiling.

"Moody, that one," she said to Franz. "Something you've got to look forward to, the older your children get. Of course, you have boys. Boys are always different."

"You say there's insurance involved, Herr Kafka?" Frau Kramski asked.

"An old policy," Franz said. The woman sparkled in jewelry and fairly floated in her expensive dress. Franz wondered if he should make up an exorbitant figure to see how far he could push her. He chose to wait.

"And Josef's the beneficiary?"

"Indeed."

"Poor dear Walter," she said. "Such a good, kind, generous man." Franz felt the thickness of the insincerity. She switched to a shrewder manner. "I'm surprised you didn't arrange to meet with my husband at his office."

"This was the address we had," Franz said. "And as it's Saturday…"

"Oh, he works the half-day, same as everyone else," she said. "That's Josef. What's good enough for the workers is good enough for him."

Franz surveyed the opulent room.

"Do his workers live as well as this?" he asked.

She laughed. "I should hope not," she said. "Would you like me to telephone him? I'm sure he could be here in twenty minutes, fifteen if he hurries."

"I wouldn't dream of inconveniencing him."

"I'm sure it's no inconvenience. Not when it comes to money. I mean, money from dear sweet generous Walter. Although it surprises me that the insurance money won't go to Edith."

"Edith?"

"His wife."

"Ah." Franz had to think about that one. "Well, as I said, this is an old insurance policy," he said, "which he probably took out before he was married. Either that or it was supplemental to one he made out to his wife."

"Don't you know?"

"Perhaps hers was with another company."

"I see," said Frau Kramski. "Well, I always knew Josef would come up in the world. This is his year, no? What with the business and now this money... how much did you say it was?"

"I'm glad to know your husband is finally fortunate. Was he not so before?"

She picked at her teeth with a lacquered nail. "He'd have been more fortunate had he possessed a little more gumption, Herr Kafka," she said. "He's always been one to wait for things."

"And you believe the opposite."

"I've always believed in ambition."

"And you wanted your husband to be ambitious."

"I think any woman wants that of her husband."

"I wonder if mine wants that of me?" Franz said.

"I'm sure she does," Frau Kramski said.

"I'm loath to admit it, Frau Kramski, but I'm a bit of a stick-in-the-mud."

"I don't believe it."

"It's true," Franz said. "I've never been much of a go-getter, as the boys at the office say. I've always been content to find a situation and remain comfortable. I'm certainly not one for parties, or making connections. I can't stand the cinema, because it gives me a headache. And opera is three hours of screeching I could do without. And as for the theater..."

"I adore it," she said. "So much fun, although there isn't much locally. The variety changes every fortnight."

"Does your husband join you for that?" Franz asked, sitting forward.

"Heavens, no," she said. "He says it embarrasses him. I don't know what he means by that. Possibly because I love getting involved. If there's a sing-along, I give it all I've got, first note to last. If there's someone who says he can identify objects while wearing a blindfold, I'm the first to offer up a bracelet. Not too long ago I helped a man hang himself."

"A suicide?" Franz asked. Frau Krasmski laughed a laugh as big as her sitting room.

"Of course not!" she said. "Well, in a way, yes, I suppose it was. But it was all a trick, you see. The man was all right in the end, although you wouldn't know it from the way the act ended."

"How did you help him?"

"Oh, he wanted a volunteer to come up and check the rope for something or other. You know, just someone from the audience who could come up and say there was 'nothing up his sleeve,' or whatever those magicians say."

"And was there anything up his sleeve?" Franz asked.

"Only his arm," said the woman.

"THIS IS SAD news," Georg Gauss said. "How awful for Leo. He has a great-uncle in Bern; perhaps that's why he said he was from there, although he wasn't. Never even been there, from what I know. My goodness, the boy had never been anywhere at all."

"Never?" Franz asked.

Georg Gauss was everything his lawyer cousin wasn't: quiet and modest. He had taken the news of Leo Kropold's death with a measure of introspection.

"He made one very short trip to Vienna late last year," Gauss said. "Shortly after his father's death. Perhaps it was Leo's way of… breaking out, I guess you'd call it. I can give you his great-uncle's address, if you think it proper. I think it's unkindly to let poor Leo sit on ice any longer than necessary—unless you want *me* to identify the body?"

"Would you?" Franz said.

"Of course, of course," the little man said, nodding. "I can make the trip."

"You are very kind," Franz said.

"Not at all," Gauss said. "I always felt sorry for the boy. Here I am calling him a boy when he was a man, wasn't he? His father always treated him as a boy. As a hired boy, in fact. They had that farm, and that's all life meant for Leo's father, you know. I say he treated Leo like a hired boy—that was my impression. They'd come into town every so often for things they needed, or a delivery of feed or whatever it was, and he's have Leo there with the wagon, hauling and loading, barking orders at him…"

"In this day and age?" asked Franz. "There are trucks now, and—"

"That was old Kropold," Gauss said. "The century never turned for him. He did everything the way his father had done, and he kept his son under his outmoded thumb all those years."

"Why Vienna?"

"Why Vienna what?"

"Why did Leo go to Vienna last year? Why there and not anywhere else?"

"It's a city, sir," Gauss said. "Less than an hour away, but as unlike that remote, lonely farm as a stone is to an apple. He'd never seen it. He'd never seen anything."

"How long was he in Vienna?"

"Only a few days."

"Did he stay with anyone? A friend?"

"He hadn't any friends. I don't know who he stayed with. Possibly he put up at a hotel or a boarding house or something like that. I don't know that he knew anything about how to travel, what to do and what to avoid."

"He came back, though."

Gauss nodded. "Yes, he came back," he said. "We went the winter without him emerging at all, except to see Doctor Eustace."

"Was he ill?"

"You'd have to ask Doctor Eustace. But I don't think so. Leo came to see Doctor Eustace once a year, of course, just to be looked over... No, he didn't, at that! Doctor Eustace used to drive out to the farm. Leo's father believed a medical man should make house calls and earn his fee. Maybe Leo came to see Doctor Eustace of his own accord, save him a trip, make up for all the hassle his father put him through those years with the drive out there..."

"And that was the last time you saw him in town?"

Gauss scratched his chin. "The last time *I* saw him," he said. "But for a little while there were others who said they'd seen him at the inn, at the tavern, at the variety hall, even the cinema... it all must have been overwhelming for the boy. There I go again, 'boy.' I don't know what was the reason, although I can guess."

"What's your guess?"

"He'd been to the city, seen things. Seen there was much more to life than getting up before dawn and going to bed at sundown. More to life than haying and plowing and everything else—more to life than chores. When his father died, he dared to step away from his father's land, even though it had become his. And my guess is Leo liked living the faster-paced life. I understand he particularly liked the variety hall, went there nearly every night for a while."

"And then he sold the farm," Franz said.

Gauss got up from his desk and went to a cabinet, where he opened a drawer, leafed through some documents, selected one, and showed it to Franz.

"Said he'd take anything he could get for it," Gauss said. "I told him it was valuable land, asked him didn't he want to keep it for his children?"

"He had children?" Franz asked.

"No, but he was young enough that he could've found himself a woman and gotten on to the children side of things."

"What did he say to your suggestion, Herr Gauss?"

"Nothing, at first. He laughed. A good long laugh. Then he said he was pretty sure he'd never have children."

Franz looked at the signature on the document. It wasn't a signature at all, but the name *LEOPOLD DIETER KROPOLD* in the same block letters as Leo had used in his journal and on the note he had left behind.

"And the farm?" Franz asked, handing the paper back to Gauss.

"Fastest sale I ever handled," Gauss said, refiling the document in the cabinet. "There's been a few companies have wanted that land for years, even before the war. Factories, you know. Sold it to the highest bidder."

"Much money?"

Gauss's eyes went wide. "Let's just say that Leo Kropold was suddenly a very wealthy man."

"And then he disappeared."

Gauss sat behind his desk. "Yes," he said. "A month ago."

"He left no forwarding address? Not to you? Or his bank? Friends?"

"No bank, no friends. Old Kropold kept his money on his property; I expect Leo just assumed that's what you did—get your money in cash and keep it where you can get at it."

Gauss wiped his eyes. "Look at that," he said, regarding his wet hand. "Now why in the world should I be upset about that boy?"

"You're a kind man," Franz said. "You saw a young man bear the brunt of a hard-headed father for all those years, and now that you learn that the young man has come to a cruel and senseless end..."

Franz found that he couldn't complete the thought.

He coughed, a hard cough that tore his throat as it blasted forth.

He waited. There would be at least four more until he'd have to stand up.

But the other four never came.

He swallowed, begged Gauss's pardon, and took a deep breath.

GREGOR WAS STILL underneath the exhausted Daimler when Franz came out of the land agent's office, an array of spanners of various sizes within reach.

"Herr Kafka," said a voice.

Franz saw Beide standing beside a sleek black limousine, a door open.

"I'm sorry to curtail your investigations," Beide said, "but I must get you back to Vienna."

"What's happened now?" Franz asked.

"There's been another incident."

"When?"

"Last night."

"Another murder?"

"Nearly."

Franz felt hot and tired. The night storms had cleared to a hot, humid day. His legs felt like lead, and he found he couldn't muster the strength to get into the automobile.

"What do you mean, 'nearly'?" he asked.

"The man survived," Beide said. "I think you need to meet him."

"But I know who's been doing the killings," Franz whispered.

"Who, Franz?"

"We have," Franz said.

"Catch him!" Beide yelled, and Franz felt arms around him.

CHAPTER FORTY-FOUR
AN ATTEMPTED SOLUTION

INSPECTOR BEIDE SAID, "Here he is."

Franz opened his eyes. Beide sat across from him in the fold-down seat of the limousine.

"Who are you talking to?" Franz asked.

"Myself," Beide said.

The automobile was speeding across the countryside that Franz and Gregor had inched across only hours ago.

The uniformed driver rapped his knuckles on the separating glass, and Beide reached for the speaking tube.

"Yes?" he asked into the instrument, then held it to his ear.

Franz couldn't hear what the driver was saying.

Beide listened and then spoke into it: "No, we'll retrieve it in due time, if it's worth it."

He replaced the speaking tube and smiled at Franz.

"Blacked out there for a moment," Beide said.

"Haven't slept," Franz said.

"So I understand. Your dedication to this case has been an example to us all."

"It's just that things kept happening..."

"Funny how things do that, isn't it? Now tell me what you meant when you said 'we' have been doing these murders?"

Franz sat pushed himself up on his elbows to sit upright. "I said that?" he asked.

"You did."

Franz blinked and tried to clear his head. "I suppose I did," he said. "But I meant 'we' as human beings, collectively, not 'we' as in you and me, specifically. But perhaps we can be implicated, too. I don't know, yet. Perhaps I'll never know."

"It's certainly the most original deduction I've ever heard. I'm hoping you plan on explaining it to me."

"I'll try," Franz said. "Is there any water, or something stronger?"

Beide produced a flask and passed it to Franz. Franz opened, sniffed whisky, and took a grateful pull from the flask.

"Leo Kropold murdered Inge Hersch," he said.

"But that doesn't follow…"

"Please, Inspector, let me finish. If you keep interrupting everything I'm about to say, it'll be midnight before you'll have a full explanation.

"In a way, we should be grateful to Leo Kropold. If he hadn't killed himself, we'd have been sorely pressed for a key to this riddle. Had he allowed himself to go on living, his existence might have gone unnoticed until his death. It's hard to say. But it doesn't matter, because I think he knew what we were after, and because he knew, he decided he was the only way we'd notice the truth… by noticing his death. I'm going to try to tell you the story of Leo Kropold as best as I can from what I've been able to piece together."

"All right," Beide said. "I'm listening."

"Leo Kropold was a sheltered, hardworking man his entire life: farm life, compounded by an antisocial, reactionary father. When his father died last summer, Leo struck out to see a bit of the world. He got as far as Vienna. Fifteen kilometers mightn't seem like all that far to you and me, but to Leo Kropold, it was another world.

"I think he completely embodied the 'hick in the city' cliché, the story they like to retread so often on the stage and in books and in the cinema. I think he did the whole wine, women, and song routine. Which is how he met Immerplatz Inge.

"No doubt it was his first sexual encounter, and perhaps he just assumed that such things came at a price. He had a little ready money on him, a small legacy from his father. I don't know how he found Inge Hersch, if he was directed to her by a procurer who frequented one of the taverns Leo must have sampled, or if she approached him... your characterization of her as a professional woman who no longer had to walk the streets suggests the former. Anyway, Leo probably confused his encounter with Inge as the beginning of a courtship, and I've no doubt she quickly disabused him of the notion.

"Leo returns to the farm, having seen and certainly done much. I would say he goes back to farm life for, oh, a few months, until he notices some changes about himself, and discovered he's sick.

"He sees his physician rather than wait for the doctor's visit, because his symptoms are strange and frightening. And I've no doubt the doctor gave him a grave diagnosis, and tried to spell out the prognosis for Leo as gently as he could.

"And Leo is beside himself.

"He takes the bichloride of mercury, takes other ameliorative measures, but it's no way to live. And all for a little love, eh? He decides he's not going to go quietly, tucked away on the farm. He goes out, distracts himself as best he can with food, drink... Any amusement will do, even the second-rate acts at the local variety hall.

"Except one act isn't second-rate, not to Leo. The man who hangs himself. The man who talks about people being the best judges of themselves, and so on. You know Henker's spiel.

"It has a profound effect on Leo, and he returns. He might even have decided to take notes on Henker's act so he can refer to it in the lonely hours of his sickness on that dark, desolate farm.

"Soon, Leo notices something else: people are being murdered, and they show signs of being hanged. Coincidence? Hardly, with an unknown performer doing essentially the same thing to himself night after night, and surviving.

"I think, at the start, Leo behaved the same way we have, Inspector—he tried to solve the murders. But after a while he began to pay closer attention to the *volunteers*.

"Now, before I explain what I mean by that, let me talk a little about Leo's wants and needs. I won't pretend to be an expert on them, because I didn't know the man, and even knowing the man I wouldn't necessarily have known; however, I have a basic idea as to where his mind may have turned.

"How did he contract syphilis? Physiologically, from Inge Hersch. Morally, himself. There wasn't anything he could or would do about himself... After all, he had to live with himself. But he could do something about Inge Hersch. He could kill her. Not just for what she'd done to him, but to prevent her from doing the same to others."

"And you think he got Henker involved?" Beide asked. "Made a deal with him, offered him money or something?"

Franz shook his head. "No," he said, "I don't think Leo Kropold had the mind of a murderer. I don't think he knew what to do with himself when the decision to kill Inge Hersch appeared in his head. I think it scared him, to be quite honest.

"I think he also began to notice that the phantom murderer's victims had never been to the theater."

"How would he know that? Newspaper accounts never mentioned whether or not the victims had been to see The Hanging Artist."

Franz nodded. "I know," he said. "But I think perhaps he began to look very closely at the volunteers, as I've said."

"But none of the volunteers were murdered."

"Correct. But each of the victims knew someone who had volunteered."

"How did you discover that?"

"Robert Prinsky was the first to give me the idea. Do you remember him?"

"Yes. The little mousy bank official."

"Yes. He was at the Traumhalle the night Hermann Herbort was murdered. It was the first time, I think, that one of the volunteers and one of the victims had actually been at the same performance at the same time."

"And you think Prinsky killed Herbort?"

"I know he did."

"Why?"

"Because Prinsky thought his life would be much easier if Hermann Herbort were out of the way."

"How do you know that?"

"Prinsky is in love with Hannah Bickel."

"I don't recall him ever saying as much."

"He didn't. But he had her photograph on his desk. Framed, no less. And when I pretended to mistake her for his wife, he went right along with me. Didn't even blink. Had I not known otherwise, I would have believed that he was married to Hannah."

"And yet Hannah, from what I can remember, seemed dismissive about Prinsky."

"She was. And Prinsky knew that. And it *ate* at him. Because there he was, day after day—the handsome, popular Hermann Herbort. It was a constant knife to the heart.

"With all that going on inside Prinsky, he goes to the stage when The Hanging Artist picks him out. That night, Hermann Herbort dies."

"But how did he do it? The man has alibis a mile long."

"I'm coming to that. I have a theory, but listen. It's more than Prinsky."

"Oh," Beide said, "you're talking about the timings of the murders and Henker's brief contact with the volunteers? Is that the case you're trying to make?"

"Like I said—Prinsky volunteers, Herbort dies. Kropold

volunteers, Inge Hersch dies."

"Because Kropold wanted her dead."

"This coincidence can be traced all the way back to the first case, Ulla Stach."

"How?"

"Ulla Stach was one of four girls who had applied for the position of private secretary at a prestigious law firm. She got the job, the others girls did not. Those girls went to the theater, saw Henker's act, one of them volunteered. That night, Ulla dies."

"Which of the girls volunteered?"

"The girl who's now got the job."

"Why would she want Ulla Stach out of the way?"

"Because this other girl—Fraulein Ascher—was the second choice. Suppose the first choice died? The second choice would obviously be hired as her replacement."

"She couldn't know that for sure."

"Regardless, she thought it."

"And Walter Furst?"

"His business partner's wife was Henker's volunteer."

"And why would she want Furst out of the way?"

"She was ambitious. She wanted money, status… and her husband wasn't doing much to realize her ambitions. But if Furst, his business partner, was dead, her husband would get full control of the company, and there'd be more money…"

"Did she confess as much?"

"Not in those words. But it was very clear to me that she felt she was stuck in a rut, and the only solution to her problem would be if Furst was out of the way so her ineffective husband could just slide into a new, wealthier life without having to do anything at all… which suited him, I gather."

"And Emmanuel Buchner?"

"I'm a bit hazy on that," Franz said, "but I think he molested his niece."

"What?"

"I'm not positive, but while I was observing his sister's daughters, especially the eldest—"

"That quite a leap in inference, Franz. So you're saying the girl wanted him dead, and when she was at the theater—"

"Not the girl. Her mother. Emmanuel's sister. She was the volunteer. Here was a man who, I understand, wasn't the brightest star in the sky, but he had a loving, warm, and trusted connection to his family; he was always at their house. Then, one day, two years ago—completely cut off. Now what happened to cause that rift?"

"Wouldn't the woman say?"

"No. Which leads me to believe that she discovered something unforgivable, either by direct observation or by questioning the girl. Perhaps she discovered the girl's own confused, troubled confession. Again, I can't prove it, but—"

"But you just knew."

"Yes. And I'm positive that if we keep digging, if we go back and read the files again on all of the victims, we'll be able to find some link, direct or indirect, to someone they knew who, for one reason or another, wanted them out of the way."

"You're forgetting Christian Werdehausen," Beide said.

Franz hesitated before answering.

"Yes," he said.

"That's all you care to say about that?"

"I suppose you're going to scold me for Yitzchak Lowy."

"I recall cautioning you about bringing in friends and family," Beide said.

"I didn't. That is to say, I didn't consciously bring in Yitzchak. He said I'd sent him a radiogram, and, well…"

"You got him involved. And he got onstage with Henker. And now another person is dead. If we follow your explanation of things, Herr Lowy is culpable for Werdehausen's death."

"Lowy isn't capable of murder, Inspector."

"Perhaps."

"In fact, none of these people we've been discussing could be described as capable of murder."

"With the exception of Leo Kropold."

"Yes, well, that's another story altogether."

The limousine tossed them about as it went over a railway crossing. Beide grabbed the speaking tube and gave the driver a short, pointed lecture on speed versus caution.

They had reached the city, and Franz looked at the streets teeming with people. He wondered about their characters, their darker impulses; how many went through their lives with pure hearts, how many were charred and warped at the core?

"Is Lowy in much trouble?" he asked.

"He's the prime suspect," Beide said, "despite there being no way to prove he was anywhere near Werdehausen at the time of the murder. And the larger question remains as to how he could be connected to all of the previous murders. That's always been the problem, Kafka—each prime suspect exonerates the previous prime suspect."

"Is it completely necessary to pin these crimes on one person?"

"Let me ask you: twenty-five murders committed by twenty-five different people who all use the same method. Does that make sense to you?"

"The answer I have doesn't make sense to me, either, but it reduces the list of killers from twenty-five to one."

"And who is that one golden suspect?"

"The one person you've been trying to prove committed these crimes all along, even though no one has been able to directly tie him to any of the crimes," Franz said. "The Hanging Artist."

CHAPTER FORTY-FIVE
AVATARS OF EVIL

BEIDE LET OUT a low whistle.

"What are you suggesting??" Beide asked. "That Henker somehow knew about the murderous desires of each volunteer and acted upon it? How would he know? Are you suggesting telepathy? Or that he psychically intuited these hatreds from each of his volunteers? Even if you could get me to believe that, what about all of the nights when he performed and a murder *didn't* occur?"

"That's simple," Franz said. "Not everybody carries hate in their heart."

"Oh, Herr Kafka. You'll have to do better than that."

"I think I can," Franz said. "If not exactly 'better,' at least it's something that offers an answer for everything, and when I've told you, you may do with it as you please."

"What do you mean by that?"

"I mean I don't think this is a matter for the police," Franz said, clearing his throat. "Not for the Vienna police, not for you... There's nothing anyone, really, who can do about it."

Beide watched the streets for the next crossing and spoke to the driver via the speaking tube. "Drive around until I tell you to go on to our destination," he said. He looked at Franz. "I have a feeling what you are about to tell me might take a while to explain."

Franz shrugged. "Not at all," he said. "There's only one way all those people could have been killed in the same manner despite living in such far-flung places; places it would be impossible for any human being to reach in so little time while being observed.

"The killer isn't The Hanging Artist, Inspector. The killer is The Hanging Artist's *rope*."

"The rope."

"Yes."

"Acting on its own."

"On behalf of the volunteers."

"It carries out its own sentencing and punishment."

"On its own."

"Aided by a malignant, supernatural agency we can't begin to fathom."

"So it would seem."

"I see. And where is this malignant, supernatural agency?"

"At the theater."

"Right this moment?"

"I don't know. But certainly every time The Hanging Artist performs."

"And what brings you to this certainty?"

Franz told him about his traumatic experience the evening before while backstage at the Traumhalle. He tried to convey the way he'd felt and why he'd felt that way, when trapped in pitch darkness; he could only describe sensations. He could do no more than tell his story, had no way to rationalize the experience or assign any implication. What these unseen entities were, what they wanted, or where they came from and why were answers he couldn't even begin to hazard.

Beide listened to Franz. Listened, very carefully, to everything Franz said.

Beide listened and, when Franz was finished, spoke.

"It would be customary, at this point," Beide said, "to say one or more things to you, many of them entirely justifiable, starting with 'You're insane,' and ending somewhere along the lines of 'It just isn't possible in this world,' but I'm not going to do that for a variety of reasons. I'm going to behave like a perfectly normal inspector working out a theory or two with a perfectly sane colleague or special consultant, both of which I've come to consider you. How does that sound to you?"

"Very fair."

"Good. First question: how long have you suspected this?"

"Not long at all. It's been an accumulation of suggestions and happenings."

"Such as?"

"Well, as much as I dislike maligning the lady, my first suspect was Henker's sister."

"Mathilde Henker?"

"Unless he has another sister of which I'm unaware, yes."

"The woman can barely move. And when she does, she needs two canes. She can walk across one room in perhaps fifteen minutes, if she can muster the wind. And you thought she was traveling all over Austria to hang people?"

"We only think she's an invalid because that's the only way we see her. We've never seen her in private. For all we know, she may be as spry as a teenager who's taken the highest honors in gymnastics."

"And what was your theory as to how she knew where to go and whom to hang?"

"I had the idea that Henker communicated with her via radio or some such electrical arrangement. The gramophone, for instance. He would say something in code, it would be picked up by the gramophone, the receiving end of which was concealed in their suite of rooms at the boarding house, and she could be on her way, unobserved, unfollowed—"

"And you decided that couldn't be the case because that

explanation is miraculously *more* ludicrous than saying the rope is the killer."

"Ludicrous?"

"I'm sorry, I'm editorializing, and I told you I wasn't going to do that."

"Apology accepted."

"At any rate, you've since rejected this explanation. Perhaps it's because Mathilde Henker is a bona fide disabled person?"

"Her work as a nurse during the war led me to believe—"

"Her what?"

"She told me she was a nurse during the war, and because she was in the wrong place at the wrong time, her injuries resulted in her current condition—"

"My dear fellow," Beide said, "the only link between Mathilde Henker, the war, and a nurse is that Hans Henker paid a nurse to attend her until he could return to care for her."

"Come again?"

"Henker has been his sister's sole caregiver since the death of their parents, nearly twenty years ago. He's been devoted to her, and when it came time for his military service, he spent no more than three weeks away from her while he tried to straighten out his military obligation by hiring a replacement."

"She told me that he served with distinction as an engineer."

"Whoever he paid to serve in his staid served with distinction, Franz. Henker has been servile to his sister since adolescence."

Franz let that sink in a moment, then said, "I can understand why she would lie to me about that."

"You can?"

"I think she found in me a sympathetic ear while I was under the guise of 'Monsieur Choucas,'" Franz said. "While she can't mask her infirmities, she can always amend their cause and duration. I think, if anything, she is embarrassed more by her brother's lack of participation in that wretched war than any horrors that have been visited on her own body."

"The rope, Franz. Mathilde Henker aside, what then made

you come to the incredible realization that the rope was doing the killings?"

"Henker's gloves."

"He has psoriasis."

"He told you that, too?" Franz asked. "Well, perhaps he does, but I think he wears those gloves to protect himself."

"From the rope?"

Franz nodded. "Oh, yes. I think Henker is all too aware of the rope's power, that it has a lethal life of its own, and the only way he can control it and—dare I say—*feed* it is to ensure others touch it, not he."

"You're saying the rope senses the dark intentions of whomever holds it?"

"I am."

"Then the whole act... the speeches, the gramophone records, the gallows, Henker's nightly deaths..."

"As show folk say, 'It's all an act.' Because if you found yourself in the thrall of some avatar of evil that had its own, otherworldly blood lust, how would you get it into the hands of as many people as you could?"

"Ask for volunteers."

"Exactly."

"And it allows Henker to live?"

"It allows Henker to endure the punishment for his sentence again and again."

"And why is he being punished?"

"Why do you think?"

Beide thought a moment. "Henker wanted someone out of the way."

"Yes."

"But we've found no history of unusual deaths surrounding him *or* his sister. His parents contracted dengue fever and died from it; there are no cases of anyone even remotely associated with the Henkers that involve hanged corpses and missing weapons."

"That's because the person Henker wanted out of the way is, miraculously, still alive."

"Who?" Beide asked. "Wait; don't tell me. Mathilde."

"I'm almost sure of it."

Beide had become pale during the conversation, and with an exhalation drained the remaining whisky from the flask.

"I hate to ask what correlate caused you to believe the rope is our culprit," Beide said.

Franz gave the details of the murder of Lisy Dierkop, and the off-hand comment that was made about the Borgia goblets in connection to the supposedly poisonless poisoning.

Beide reddened. "Oh, come on. Now you're going to tell me all Henker does is go around collecting things that have retained some unearthly power to kill? How can that be? The Henkers just happen to be magnets for all the ancient evils of the world?"

"Well, you and I have seen Henker's centuries-old table and chair, inspector. We've seen the concealed compartment containing the rotted rope…"

"And that's another thing," Beide said. "The rope in the old chair is clearly dysfunctional. The rope Henker uses in his act is definitely solid, and strong, and—I hate to say it—looks beautiful. Are there two ropes?"

"I don't think so," Franz said. "I think it reconstitutes itself by virtue of Henker's performance and goes on its way once it has hanged Henker and that curtain comes down. What happens in the fifteen minutes or so after the curtain comes down and the lights go out? We don't know. Whatever occurs—and we may never know—both Henker and the rope are back where they're supposed to be, both in their original state."

Beide took an envelope from within the hidden pockets of his cape and handed it to Franz. "Now's as good a time as any to give you this," he said.

Franz laughed. "Is this the infamous 'third envelope' that I chucked from the train days ago?"

"No," said Beide. "It's the translation of the writing we found inside the chair."

Franz opened the envelope, removed a sheet of paper, and read:

"Whoever to true goodness
Turns his mind
He will meet with fortune and honor.

"He won such fame that
Although his body died
His name lives on.
Of sinful shame
He will forever be free
Who follows his example."

Franz returned the paper to the envelope. "Henker uses a variation of these words during his act," he said. "When you take everything into consideration, Inspector, it's a horrifying proposition."

"And Leo Kropold?" Beide asked.

"...had figured out only that in order to have his bidding done he would merely have to get his hands on the rope," Franz said. "I don't know if he knew the deeper history of what Henker had discovered, but he had become sure that the rope was the agent of destruction, so he returned to the theater, again and again, performance after performance, in the hopes that he would someday be chosen to volunteer. When that night finally came, he only cared about handling the rope—he didn't care to go through the other meaningless motions of searching Henker, because he knew Inge Hersch's death was imminent."

"And that's why he wrote 'Thank You Hanging Artist' on his last note?"

"Yes, he was thanking Henker for the vengeance of the rope. And also, with his suicide, he left enough clues about himself and his purpose to point someone in the right direction—the direction of seeing The Hanging Artist's act for what it is, what it means. Because I think enough humanity remained in Kropold to know that whatever dark forces were behind the rope had to be stopped. If possible."

"*Is* it possible?" Beide asked.

"I don't think so," Franz said. "Certainly not on a purely rational level. Other than the marks the rope leaves on the necks of the victims—and we'll never be able to seize the actual rope to do any comparisons—we've no practical way of connecting the rope to the crimes, and therefore no way of implicating Henker."

Beide grabbed the speaking tube and gave an order to the driver. The car swerved on the boulevard and sped to its new destination.

"What you've just told me could solve a long string of mysteries," Beide said. "And we've kept our guest waiting a little too long."

"What guest? The man you wanted me to meet?"

"I hope you'll forgive my bringing him here," Beide said, "but I felt certain you'd need to see him and hear his incredible story. And it saves time."

"Saves time?"

"Our guest is from Prague, two hours away."

"Prague?"

"Yes. Your home."

"Prague is a big city, inspector. Just because this person is from Prague doesn't mean I know him."

"When you meet him, Franz, I want you to remember one thing, based on the theories we've discussed this afternoon."

"Yes?"

"You, too, touched that rope."

CHAPTER FORTY-SIX
THE MAN FROM PRAGUE

FRANZ WAS ALONE in the small room with the man from Prague, who was not happy.

"So this is what you do, you play tricks on me?" the old man said. He was twice the size of Franz and, even at his age, looked to be four times as hearty. "For you I have to be dragged here, to be made to wait? You should be ashamed of yourself, but no, you don't know from shame, do you? Do you?"

Franz lowered himself into the chair opposite the man.

"Hello, Father," he said.

"Don't you sit down in my presence," his father said. "Get up until I tell you to sit."

Franz stood.

"So this is you, this is you walking around healthy as a carrot, this is you not bothering to tell your mother you are not at that place with the white walls?"

"I can't really understand it myself, Father. Only the other day..."

"Or a word to your sisters, who love you, God knows why? Shame! You spit on them. Me, I don't matter, spit on me all you like, I know you've washed your hands of me, and so be it, but your sisters! Your mother! Ungrateful, is what I'm looking at. Ungrateful dressed in a cheap suit."

"What happened, Father?"

"As if you don't know."

"I don't. I haven't been told."

"So I'm to tell you? They don't believe me, is that it? They think my telling you will make a difference? Is that it?"

"I want to know what happened, Father."

"Because why?"

"Because I might have an answer."

The red-faced old man wiped the spit from his mouth.

"Last night," he said, "I was in the kitchen. Never mind what I was doing in the kitchen, I was there and that's all there is to it. Suddenly something goes around me feet and I'm caught and it pulls. I'm dragged across the floor like a cow going to slaughter. And then I'm up in the air, hanging by my ankles, I'm trussed up like beef, I'm yelling and nobody's coming, I don't know why, everybody comes when I yell, even the neighbors, but then, no, and I can't free myself."

"Who did this to you?"

"I didn't see anyone. But there was someone there, I knew it, I felt it."

Franz swallowed hard, suppressing a cough.

"How did you get free?" Franz asked.

The old man smiled a grim smile. "I had the *hallaf*," he said, "and I hacked my way free."

"Grandfather's butcher knife?"

"The same. And then I fell to the floor, bumped my head something terrible, but look! No bandages! Hard head, not like you—you, you would crack like an egg. And this thing"— he nodded to a steel box on the table—"was all that was left behind. I wanted to throw it out, but your mother, she told me the police would want to see it."

Franz eyed the box.

"What is it?" Franz asked.

"Filth," his father said, "garbage. A turd."

Franz raised the lid of the box.

The object inside, no more than two inches in length, did indeed resemble a turd, but Franz saw it as what it was—the decaying remains of a silken rope. He slammed the lid.

"This is some trick on me you arranged?" his father demanded. "This is why you're here, you charlatan, you faker? You sponge? As if my sufferance of you for a son hasn't been indignity enough, you go and do this? For why? For to teach me some lesson? For to make more of a mockery of me? Where do you think you're going? *Come back here right now with that, you cretin!*"

FRANZ HANDED THE box to Beide.

"Judenstrafe," he said.

"Beg pardon?" Beide asked.

"Judenstrafe," Franz said, and dropped onto a chair. He could still hear his father screaming behind the closed door down the hall. "It's why he wasn't killed outright."

"I don't understand."

"Judenstrafe," Franz said, absently caressing his own neck as he spoke, "was the so-called 'Jewish punishment' during the Middle Ages. It was done to Jewish thieves, mostly; inverted hanging by the legs, either as a torture or execution method."

"And how do you know this?"

"I've already told you about my deep studies into my faith," Franz said. "The Judenstrafe was part of my learning. That bit of rope is of the same appearance as the rope we discovered in Henker's dressing room. It came after my father, inspector. It tried to kill him."

"But why differently than the others?"

"I suspect none of the previous victims have been Jewish. And my father—even though he has long since abandoned our religion and mocks anything we consider holy—is a Jew.

His father, my grandfather, was a kosher butcher. And that awful man"—he gestured to the apoplectic harangue going on down the hall—"uses his father's sacred knives to prepare his midnight snacks."

"Well, it saved his life."

"Yes," Franz said. "No thanks to me."

Beide put a reassuring hand on Franz's shoulder.

"What do we do now, Franz?" Beide asked.

"About my father?"

"About Henker."

Franz got to his feet, swayed, and burst into a barrage of coughing that knocked him back onto the chair. Beide handed him a handkerchief. Franz coughed up what he could, but began making sounds like steam being forced back into a teakettle. Alarmed, Beide thumped Franz on his back, but Franz pushed him away. He raised his arms above his head, and indicated that Beide should help him to stand. Once standing, Franz forced air into his lungs until he became calm. He gave a final cough into the handkerchief.

Franz showed Beide the handkerchief's new bright red spots.

Franz smiled. "I'll put an end to this," he said. "Let Henker go on tonight as usual."

CHAPTER FORTY-SEVEN
TILLIE

"Hansel was born first," Mathilde Henker said, "and he was the perfect child."

She and Franz were sitting together on the sofa in the stripped parlor of her rooming house suite, surrounded by crates. A single lamp was perched atop one of the crates; most of its yellow light was cast upon Mathilde.

"The doctor had no little difficulty delivering me," she continued. "Perhaps I didn't wish to be born. Who knows? Do you know what a nuchal cord is, Herr Kafka?"

"When a child is born with the cord wrapped around its neck," Franz said. She nodded.

"I understand it isn't an uncommon occurrence at all," she said. "In my case, however, I was being slowly strangulated, and what saved me..."

She raised her fists to her cheeks.

"...were my own two hands." She dropped her hands to her lap and gazed at them. "My father would joke that perhaps Hansel had tried to kill me. That was no joke to Hans. My father learned not to joke about that as Hans grew older.

"Having survived birth, I grew up as best I could... Not because of any unkindnesses done to me by anyone, but...

Well, my life was one illness after another; always some new condition I developed, yet another disease waiting its turn to cripple me.

"Hans took care of me. Always. He put my needs ahead of his, my comfort far above his own. I daresay he could have married several times, he could have had a family of his own by now, but no—he had to see to me. He never brought it up. He would never turn on me in resentment."

"Had you ever encouraged him to... leave you?" Franz asked.

She looked at him. "Always," she said. "He took it as an insult. He thought it was my way of saying he was doing a terrible job, that he was more hindrance than help."

"Was he?"

"No," she said softly. "He was perfect."

She gathered her canes and went on.

"He filled our house with beautiful things," she said, "things of value, things with history. Our father had left us very well off indeed, but it wasn't as if Hans just bought things for the mere reason of having them. He searched. He chose. He was critical. He said it wouldn't do for us to have 'just anything.' He wanted the rare, the special.

"And then he found the table and chair. I thought it crude and ugly—and it is, you've seen it. He told me it could very well date back to Arthurian times! I remember asking him why we should give a damn about old British legends. He was a bit put off by that. It sat in our parlor for I don't know how long until one night when he was fooling it, trying to polish it up a bit in a vain attempt at making it presentable, he found that the seat was a chest, and that's the first sight we got of the rope."

She looked away, off into the deep growing shadows of the room.

"He said those words," she said, recalling the scene, "and he held that filthy, rotten rope in his hands. And in the next moment, something oily and foul was writhing its way across my lap, over my chest, and to my throat."

"How did it not kill you?" Franz asked.

Once again, Mathilde raised her fists to her cheeks. "Just as I had done in my mother's womb," she said. "Only that time, I had these in each hand." She picked up the canes and held them to her cheeks. "The snakewood. Carved specially for me by my father. One of the strongest, hardest woods on Earth. The rope crushed my hands, but it couldn't crush the canes as it tried to get to my neck."

She put the canes down and rubbed her swollen, misshapen knuckles.

"It never attacked me again, and later we discovered why, when Hans had done some research on the chair, its legend, the rope within. It never attacked me again because Hans never touched it with his bare hands again."

"And he told me, later, that it was at that moment—when I was struggling against the rope—that his hatred for me, his resentment towards me that he had endured and held in for all those years, had disappeared, like a candle flame being blown out. Seeing that unholy thing wrap itself around me terrified him no end, and he knew he didn't wish me to die."

There were tears in her eyes.

"Why the performances, Fraulein? Why has he taken to the stage to loose this avatar of evil upon the world?"

"Because it is his punishment," she said. "He dies at every performance. He dies an inhumane, violent death, and is then resurrected to live that death again and again. His volunteers, the people who approach him with either noble or corrupt hearts, feed the dark forces that have allowed that wretched instrument to survive the centuries. My brother has chosen to survive for my sake, Herr Kafka. If he doesn't appease these malignant, unseen jurors, if he decides to turn the rope's justice on himself... Well, who will take care of me?"

Franz wanted to turn on the electric lights, but he couldn't bring himself to see the wretched woman in more than shadow at the moment. He wanted to put a comforting hand on hers, but he felt that doing so would make her withdraw in revulsion, sensing false pity in him.

"Now that you know these things," Mathilde said, looking into Franz's eyes, "you must..."

"Find a way to stop him?" Franz asked.

"My brother is not a monster," she said. "He is the unfortunate slave to this monstrous thing. Perhaps the darkness of his own heart is what led him to find the rope in the first place—or led the rope to him, I don't truly know—but he, himself, is not an evil man."

"But he's allowing these people to be murdered," Franz said.

"And one day," she said, "he will have to answer for it... to a power higher and greater than the evil forces he now faces."

"It has ruined him," she said, staring off into the darkness. "It has ruined him as a human. His hatred is now only for himself. Even if there were a way to end this nightmare, Franz, it would only end for others. Not for Hans. He is ruined for good. There's nothing we can do."

"It went after my father," Franz said, "because of me, because of the hatred I've nursed for him... my entire life, I suppose. So I know what it's like to be ruined."

"You said it didn't kill your father," she said.

"It didn't," Franz said. He stood. "If there was any true justice in this world, it should have killed *me*."

He went to the door.

"Goodbye, Tillie."

CHAPTER FORTY-EIGHT
A HANGING ARTIST

HANS HENKER SAT in his empty dressing room, eyes closed, and began the process of escorting every trace of himself away from his mind.

He couldn't do it.

He couldn't raise the gray wall that would separate Hans Henker from The Hanging Artist.

It took time, and it took dedication. He was finding neither.

The show had begun.

He turned to his words.

He knew his words, and would probably know his words until his dying day, perhaps even longer. He knew his words but said them anyway, because they were of The Hanging Artist. There would never be any variation to his words, because variation indicated contemplation—a fiddling about, making things better or worse—and Hans did not require variation or improvement. What he needed were the words, and...

Why had none of them come for him tonight?

Why had no one stopped him, prevented him from going on?

Hundreds of people out there. And hundreds more come Monday.

Twice daily.

Three at a time, on the stage, with him, touching, thinking themselves great sports for volunteering, reveling in a few minutes of fame...

No. Out. Away, down, in, shut, locked.

Good evening, my friends, my dear new friends.

THE HANGING ARTIST leaves his dressing room and closes the door behind him.

He walks down the spiral staircase, one hand on the railing.

He hears the audience laugh, but he hears the strain in their laughter, because they are waiting, waiting for The Hanging Artist. They've been waiting all week, all day, all night. Any other reaction is automatic: surprise, appreciation, laughter.

He does not step aside as a clutch of barely-clothed dancers rush to get to the stage. They flow around him, southbound geese parting and rejoining around an unexpected weathervane.

He waits where he always waits, next to the harp case, which may or may not contain a harp.

He knows the dancers are doing their brightest routine. The music is wicked, the stamping insistent, defiant.

He hears the applause for their efforts, plentiful but meaningless.

The dancers swarm backstage, all tearing off their beaded headdresses at the same time, file up the stairs, their shoes making sounds like cannonball raindrops falling into tin pails.

The Hanging Artist hears his music.

It is the music of sunshine and romance.

The violin has never sounded sweeter, the muted trumpet more coy.

A young man in a cap and shirtsleeves, his powerful arms prepared to haul up the curtain, nods to The Hanging Artist, who smiles, but does not return the nod.

The curtain and the olio rise.

The orchestra stops. The conductor nods to the musicians. They douse their lights.

The Hanging Artist walks onstage. He stops center stage and gives the audience a moment to take in his smart linen suit the color of fresh caramel, his pomaded hair, his spring green necktie, his polished fudge-brown shoes, his butter-colored calfskin gloves.

He assumes a casual but authoritative stance: legs together but feet turn slightly outward, one foot an inch forward of the other, the left hand in the pocket, the right hand, unconcerned, at his side.

He speaks.

"Good evening, my friends, my dear new friends—and, I hope, new friends who have become old friends who have returned. You are welcome, and I thank you. Thank you for finding me."

He turns to his right and crosses to the gramophone perched on its delicate table. He winds the machine until the spring has no more give. He pushes the turntable brake, and the record spins. He lifts the reproducer and lowers it onto the spinning disc; the needle slides into the groove.

He crosses back to center as the elegant, spry music— "Gigolette," performed by Marek Weber & His Famous Orchestra—flows from the gramophone's flowered horn, sounding as if smothered beneath a wet woolen blanket.

He smiles.

"I propose to hang myself," The Hanging Artist says.

He waits for the reaction to abate. It is much the same as it always is: the low, rolling expressions of alarm and disbelief, one or two nervous laughs.

He continues.

"Because justice must be done. And who am I, you might ask, to judge myself and pass sentence? Who am I to take my own life? Why, I am myself, and who else would know better than I for what sins I must answer?

"The sins of living, my friends. The sins that live in my thoughts, my desires, my regrets, my hurts, my slights, my envies. Are these sins or are they demons? They are both.

"But are all of our internal demons just that—internal? Perhaps they are real: external, and gnawing at us. Perhaps those demons are your friends, your neighbors, your lovers, your spouses, your children...

"The list, my friends, goes on and on.

"And so, the rope, fashioned into a noose and slipped around the neck. The noose that cuts off air, cuts off consciousness, cuts off your relationship to this place of suffering and offers— what? Peace? Perhaps. An escape? Definitely.

"Am I taking my own life? No. Do I do this to encourage you to take yours, to pass your own harsh judgments on yourselves? I would never do that. I would never encourage anyone to do something that I myself have not done.

"Lastly, who am I to ask you to sit there and watch me do it?

"I am The Hanging Artist, my friends.

"It is expected of me."

He sketches a military bow to his audience and returns to the gramophone, as "Gigolette" is over. He replaces the record with another, winds the gramophone, and drops the needle on the new record. Everyone recognizes the tune: "Ausgerechnet Bananen," although most of Europe has been singing the nonsensical American song in its English iteration: "Yes! We Have No Bananas!" The audience loves this record, loves this popular band—Efim Schachmeister Dance Band—and toes start tapping.

While the audience adjusts and is soothed by the music, The Hanging Artist walks upstage to the chair. He takes up the rope coiled on the seat and returns to the audience.

He shows them the rope, spooling it out as he speaks, until the noose is revealed.

"This," The Hanging Artist says, "is the artist's instrument, the finest there is, delicate silken strands braided together into a larger and stronger form. And why shouldn't this rope be made of excellent silk and not ordinary Manila hemp, or jute, or common straw? One could argue that the sinner deserves nothing more than the roughest fibers, that the demons must be routed by the coarsest means possible.

"But this is the theater!"

He raises the noose so all can see.

"Does the sight of this strike fear in your heart? Terror? Be calm. Be sensible. Be joyous! There is no need to fear anything—for, as you know, whoever turns his mind to true goodness will be met with fortune and honor, and forever be free of sinful shame! Observe."

He gently shakes the rope, and the noose becomes undone.

The audience responds in awe, because they think it's impossible to undo a hangman's knot so quickly. The Hanging Artist nods, holds up a hand.

"Please, it is no miracle. I'm just showing you there is nothing to fear. This is just a rope. And to prove it to you—to prove *myself* to you—I will need a volunteer, someone to come up here, with me, to inspect this fine silken rope and my own person, to demonstrate that, after all, there is no trick. Now—who will do it?"

A hundred hands, two hundred, three hundred.

One arm rises from the front row, slowly but with confidence. Its owner signals as if hailing a taxi: index and forefinger.

The Hanging Artist points to the front row, the calm, confident arm and its owner.

"You, miss," he says, "the young lady in the lovely pale green frock. Please."

The Hanging Artist returns to the gramophone, just in time to lift the needle from the record as its last calamitous sounds play out. When he turns, he will have a new friend. He selects the next record, but a fresh needle in the reproducer, cranks the machine, and plays the new selection: "Tutankhamen." Exotic, lively, mysterious.

The Hanging Artist returns to center stage to meet the young lady.

Franz Kafka stands before him, looking like Death.

Kafka holds out his hands to The Hanging Artist. "Please," he says.

Hans Henker stands still.

Kafka takes a step towards him, arms outstretched, palms up.

"Please," Kafka says. "You're my only hope for salvation."

Hans Henker takes a step backwards.

The audience murmurs.

Kafka takes another step towards him.

"Please, Hanging Artist," Kafka says, "show me what it is to pay for my sins."

The music ends.

The needle is trapped in the dead space on the record between the grooves and the label.

Hans Henker can feel them watching, waiting, pressing down on him.

He throws the rope over his shoulder.

He removes his gloves, revealing his beautiful, delicate, smooth hands.

He throws his gloves to the stage, takes up the rope, holds it above his head.

He turns to the audience, triumphant.

"And now," he says, "we begin... the end."

He looks at Franz.

"The gramophone," he says.

Franz crosses to the gramophone, removes "Tutankhamen," and places the final record on the turntable. The music is delightful. There's not a member of the audience doesn't recognize the tune. Is that Eric Borchard's jazz band? It is.

The Hanging Artist speaks the loudest he's ever spoken.

"What, after all, *is* a trick?" The Hanging Artist says. "By definition, a trick is a cunning or skillful act or scheme intended to deceive or outwit someone.

"But I have no intention of deceiving or outwitting you. I am here to do what I proposed to do. I intend to pass judgment on myself and live.

"Do I deserve to live?

"I leave that to…"

The rope coils itself around The Hanging Artist in one swift, sickening movement, dropping the noose around The Hanging Artist's neck.

He clutches the noose.

The rope flings itself across the stage, dragging The Hanging Artist along, and then, to the astonishment of all, flies to the top of the gallows and anchors itself to the beam.

The Hanging Artist kicks and struggles, but it's almost as if he is struggling with the rope to pull himself down, harder, further, aiding gravity all that he can.

The song shouts from the gramophone:

"Ev'rybody shimmies now.
Ev'rybody's learning how.
Brother Bill, Sister Kate
Shiver like jelly on a plate.
Shimmy dancing can't be beat,
Moves ev'rything except your feet.
Feeble folks, mighty old,
Shake the shimmy and they shake it bold.
Oh! Honey, won't you show me how?
'Cause ev'rybody shimmies now!"

There is a long cracking sound from The Hanging Artist, as if dried wood wrapped in wet blankets was being torn asunder.

The Hanging Artist's face becomes the color of a dark cloud obscuring the moon.

His eyes start from their sockets.

He becomes still.

The music ends.

The rope disappears.

The lifeless body of The Hanging Artist plummets to the stage.

Many in the audience rise from their seats in horror. They find their voices, inflamed with terror. They push to the aisles, to the exits. They look to the stage, they look away from the stage.

Franz Kafka hears a great shrieking from the darkness offstage, from all sides, from above. He can barely distinguish it from the shrieking of the audience.

He crosses to the gramophone and takes the needle off the record.

He smashes the record against the machine and waits for the curtain to come down.

It doesn't.

He is alone onstage with the body of The Hanging Artist.

CHAPTER FORTY-NINE
THE INSPECTOR

"How we're going to explain this to the reading public completely escapes me," Inspector Beide said to Franz. "I don't suppose I can just fob them off on Leo Kropold, can I?"

"It would be a disservice to him," Franz said. His voice had hoarsened considerably, and his throat felt raw and hot. "Don't have the memory of that poor man be that of a homicidal maniac. He didn't deserve what he got, and we shouldn't compound it with the crimes of another."

"Particularly when that other is... Well, whatever it is. Was. Is?"

"Is, I fear." Franz coughed and choked at the same time.

"I'm very sorry, Franz," Beide said. "May I get you anything?"

Franz held up a hand until the spasms subsided. When they did, he drew a grateful breath.

"A taxi," he said.

"Where are you going?"

"The train station."

"And then where?"

"Has my father gone back to Prague?"

"I had someone drive him back immediately. He was still hollering."

Franz nodded and allowed Beide to help him from the empty lobby of the Traumhalle to the curb, where Beide blew a whistle.

"The rope?" Franz asked.

Beide gave him a troubled look. "No sign of it."

"But the chair?"

"Still in the dress room. Empty."

"I don't know if burning it will do any good..."

"...but what the hell, right?" Beide asked, and smiled.

"Send along my things to the station," Franz said. "I'm not sure where they are. I last saw them piled onto the Daimler back in Schwechat."

"We'll take care of it," Beide said, and blew the whistle again.

"Tillie?" Franz asked.

"Don't try to speak so much," Beide said.

"I'm not. Tillie?"

"I don't know what will become of her."

"Look into it," Franz said as a taxi pulled to the curb. Beide opened the door for him.

"If she needs care, we'll find a way to see that she gets it," Beide said.

"No 'if,'" Franz said. "She needs it. Don't abandon her." He sighed. "It's bad enough that I have to abandon her." Beide helped him into the taxi.

"You have my word," Beide said.

Franz groped in his pockets.

"My card," Franz said. "I won't be needing it anymore."

"Card?"

"Inspektor Kafka."

"If you ever find it, keep it. You might need it again. We might need you again."

Franz smiled weakly.

"Oh, and thank you," Beide said.

"I did the best I could," Franz said.

"I wasn't referring to the case."

"Then what?"

"For finally seeing me as me."

"I don't understand."

Beide shut the door and leaned into the window.

"For seeing me completely," they said, "and not categorically."

They looked past Franz to the corner of the cab.

"Look after him," they said.

"You can count on me, Inspector," said Gregor.

The taxi sped away from Beide, the theater, and people of Vienna.

Franz did not look back.

CHAPTER FIFTY
A NOCTURNE

WE SEE TWO figures standing beneath a lamp on the train platform. In the distance, a pinpoint of light and a lonely whistle heralds the midnight train to the sanatorium.

The tall, thin figure says, "Beide saw you."

The short, round, insectoid figure says, "And I saw Beide."

"Even spoke to you."

"And I answered."

"Beide never acknowledged your presence before."

"That's a cross I have to bear."

"Then that means you're real, Gregor."

"Or it means Beide is imaginary, Franz."

"You can't both be imaginary."

"Why not?"

"I'd prefer it if you were both real."

"Then so be it."

The train draws nearer. We can hear the bell.

"Be well," the short figure says to the tall figure.

"Thank you," the tall figure says.

"And if you can't be well, then just... *be*."

"I'll try."

"Now if you'll excuse me, I have a date with a trash heap

behind the Jaegerhaus. It was schnitzel night."

We see the tall, thin figure, alone, get swallowed up by the steam from the locomotive.

CHAPTER FIFTY-ONE
THE JOURNEY

FRANZ KAFKA SAT in the hot compartment and watched the lights of the city give way to the darkness of the woods.

He reached up and opened the window, savoring the breeze.

If he let it, the motion of the train would lull him to sleep.

But he wouldn't let it.

He stood and leaned his arms on the open top half of the window and let the wind ruffle his hair.

Something delicate landed on his face.

He sat down and peeled the object from his face.

An envelope with his name on it.

He smiled and wished Beide was there.

"Odd way to get your mail delivered," said a woman's voice. "But then again, there's everything odd about you."

Franz saw a black-haired young woman sitting opposite him.

She smiled at him, and her deep black eyes welcomed him back to warmth.

"Dora," he said.

He no longer had any desire to question anything.

Dora was there, with him, and that was final.

"Go on," she said. "Open it."

Franz tore open the envelope.

Inside was a scrap of paper carefully clipped from either a newspaper or journal. It read:

> In deepest sorrow we announce that our son, Doctor of Law Franz Kafka, died on June 3, at the age of 41, in the Kierling Sanatorium near Vienna. The burial will take place on Wednesday afternoon, June 11, at 3:45, at the Jewish Cemetery in Straschnitz. Prague, June 10, 1924. Hermann and Julia Kafka, the parents, in name of the bereaved family. We request that there be no visits of condolence.

"Got my age wrong," Franz said. "Won't be forty-one until next month."

"What is it?" Dora asked.

He smiled at her.

"The future," he said. "What's today?"

"It became the 7th about twenty minutes ago."

"Good."

"Where are we going and what are we doing, Franzel?"

Franz crumpled the envelope and its contents into a ball and threw it out the window.

"As I've got a few more days until it's official," he said, "let's just go wherever and do whatever together."

"Until what's official?" Dora asked.

Franz coughed.

"My new life."

THE END

ACKNOWLEDGEMENTS

I WISH TO thank the two evil imps who visited me one winter morning, the first who gave me the idea and said, "This is the stupidest idea you've ever had," and the second who said, "Write it anyway." Imps aside, I thank my mother and father, who were the first to hear the idea and didn't have me committed. My thanks, too, to the Sanibel Public Library on Sanibel Island, Florida, which had exactly what I was looking for exactly when I needed it, and most of all to David at Abaddon for his unflagging enthusiasm, championing, and so much more. Lastly, unending thanks to Franz Kafka, who has been inspiring (if that's the word for it) me ever since I first read *The Hunger Artist* when I was 15. I've been haunted ever since.

ABOUT JON STEINHAGEN

Jon Steinhagen lives in what is known (somewhat affectionately) as The Chicagoland Area, near the historic Brookfield Zoo. His writing career began in theatre, first as a composer and lyricist for several musicals (particularly *Inferno Beach, The Teapot Scandals, The Next Thing*, and *The Arresting Dilemma of Mr. K*, a musical adaptation of Kafka's *The Trial*), then as resident playwright at Chicago Dramatists (his notable plays include *The Analytical Engine, ACES, Successors, Devil's Day Off*, and *Blizzard '67*). As a screenwriter, he has written *Party Favors*, and is developing two television series, *Willing Spirit* and *New Kid*. Somewhere along the way he began writing stories, too, and many are collected in *The Big Book of Sounds* (Black Lawrence Press). He has received numerous Joseph Jefferson Awards for his work in Chicago theatre as either author, actor, or musical director, and can be found on twitter as @JonSteinhagen (inventive fellow, this Jon Steinhagen), where he can be found blathering on about his ridiculous ideas for movies, his collection of vinyl records, and his desire for cookies to be delivered every time he does something he should have done weeks ago.

FIND US ONLINE!

www.rebellionpublishing.com

/rebellionpub /rebellionpublishing /rebellionpub

SIGN UP TO OUR NEWSLETTER!

rebellionpublishing.com/sign-up

YOUR REVIEWS MATTER!

Enjoy this book? Got something to say?

Leave a review on Amazon, GoodReads or with your
favourite bookseller and let the world know!